COLLECTING
EVIDENCE

BY
RITA HERRON

DID ... PURCHASE THIS BOOK WITHOUT A COVER?
If you ... ... ported
unsol ... ... plisher

All the c... ... ... nation of
the autho... ... al have ... ... in th... ...me name
or names... ... ... by no... individ... known or
unknown ... ... , and ... ... incident ... ... authori...

First published in Great Britain 2010
Harlequin Mills & Boon Limited,
Eton House, 18-24 Paradise Road, Richmond, Surrey TW9 1SR

© Rita B. Herron 2009

ISBN: 978 0 263 88262 9

46-1010

Harlequin Mills & Boon policy is to use papers that are natural, renewable and recyclable products and made from wood grown in sustainable forests. The logging and manufacturing processes conform to the legal environmental regulations of the country of origin.

Printed and bound in Spain
by Litografia Rosés S.A., Barcelona

Award-winning author **Rita Herron** wrote her first book when she was twelve, but didn't think real people grew up to be writers. Now she writes so she doesn't have to get a *real* job. A former kindergarten teacher and workshop leader, she traded storytelling to kids for romance, and writes romantic comedies and romantic suspense. She lives in Georgia with her own romance hero and three kids. She loves to hear from readers, so please write her at P.O. Box 921225, Norcross, GA 30092-1225, or visit her website at www.ritaherron.com.

To Jamie, a brave and courageous young girl—
may all your dreams come true!

Prologue

Special Agent Dylan Acevedo pressed the blade of the knife against Frank Turnbull's fleshy neck.

"Go ahead, kill me," Turnbull muttered.

Dylan jabbed the blade into his skin, a smile curving his mouth as a drop of blood seeped to the surface. He should just do it.

The man deserved to die.

The images of the women the serial killer had brutally murdered—all young Native Americans in their twenties—flashed into Dylan's head in sickening clarity. Their delicate throats slashed, bodies left exposed in the rugged terrain of the desert, blood dripping as if to lure the wild animals to feed on their remains.

Young lives lost for no reason except to fulfill the sick cravings of a demented mind.

Dylan glanced down at the knife in his hand. The knife that had belonged to Turnbull. The same kind he'd used to cut the women's throats.

It was only fitting he die by the same instrument.

With his throat sliced open by a Ute ceremonial knife made from white quartz and Western Cedar, the kind of knife used to cut the umbilical cord of a newborn or to harvest herbs for sacred ceremonies.

Another important component of Turnbull's MO was his calling card—he'd left a piece of thunderwood by each victim. Another dig to the Ute people who had a religious aversion to handling thunderwood—a piece of bark from a tree struck by lighting. The Utes believed that thunder beings would strike down any Ute Indian who touched it.

Turnbull's swollen eye twitched with menace and a dare. A challenge to Dylan to feel the thrill of the kill, Turnbull seemed to say silently.

Dylan clenched his jaw. He wanted to see fear in Turnbull's eyes. Wanted to hear him scream as his victims had. Hear him beg for his life.

Instead Turnbull laughed, a hideous deep growl that punctured the night like a wild animal just before it tore into a smaller one's carcass.

"You're just like me," Turnbull mumbled. "I can see the evil in your eyes."

Dylan's fingers tightened on the knife handle. At that moment he did crave the kill. But his need was driven by revenge and justice, not depraved indifference.

"Dylan, don't…."

His brother Miguel's voice rumbled from behind him. Miguel, who was a saint compared to him. He'd been an altar boy while Dylan had been the troublemaker.

They hadn't always gotten along, but as adults they'd forged a bond and developed a healthy respect for one another's differences. Miguel was a forensic scientist, and they often worked together on cases, relying on each other's expertise.

Miguel's footfalls echoed on the ground as he approached. "Come on, Dylan. We've got him. Let's take him in and make him pay for what he did. Make him face the families of the victims."

Dylan's hand trembled as his gaze once again locked with the monster. Then he saw the fear in the man's eyes. Turnbull wanted him to kill him.

Because he didn't want to face the families.

Miguel was right. Having to look into the pain-filled eyes of the parents of the women he'd hurt would be his worst punishment.

His hand slipped, caught the skin just enough to cause a flesh wound, then he gestured for Miguel to cuff the bastard.

HOURS LATER, after their debriefing and a press conference to announce they'd finally arrested the ruthless Ute killer, Dylan walked into the Vegas bar. All he wanted was to purge his rage, and drown out the images of the girls he hadn't been able to save.

Just like he hadn't saved his fifteen-year-old sister, Teresa, when she'd been gunned down in a gang-related drive-by.

Suddenly, the most exotic creature he'd ever seen approached him. Long black hair that hung down to her waist swayed seductively as she walked, her dark chocolate eyes raking over him appreciatively.

She was Ute, fit the profile of the victims he'd fought so hard to obtain justice for. Could have become number eleven on Turnbull's kill card. Yet here she was, alive and smiling at him.

"Agent Acevedo," she said in a purrlike voice with

the faint accent of her heritage. "I saw you on the news. Thank you for arresting that killer."

He shrugged. "I only wish we'd caught him sooner."

Wise, sympathetic eyes met his, along with a sultriness that made his body go rock hard and achy.

He was mesmerized by her beauty, wanted her naked and in his bed, soothing the heat and rage in his soul.

When she finished her shift, they talked for hours. Her name was Aspen Meadows. She was working as a cocktail waitress while earning a teaching degree.

Finally he escorted her to her apartment. Before he closed the door, she was in his arms and he was tearing off her clothes. He took her on the floor, against the wall, on the bed and in the shower.

A week of lovemaking couldn't assuage the pain or guilt in his chest. He didn't deserve her. Didn't deserve to be loved or soothed when he'd failed so many.

But he stole the hours and days anyway, desperate for a slice of heaven to ease the hell he lived with daily.

He knew it wouldn't last, *couldn't* last, though. A phone call the following Friday night reminded him too well.

Another murder. An undercover assignment.

He had to go.

He kissed her goodbye and left while she was sleeping. He wouldn't see her again. He couldn't.

His work put anyone he cared about in danger.

And he had enough dead girls haunting him to last him forever.

Chapter One

A year later

Aspen Meadows had been missing for nine weeks now. Nine weeks of wondering if she was dead or alive.

Nine weeks of wondering if he could have done something to save her.

Dylan stared at Aspen's cousin, Emma Richardson, fearing the worst. He'd left Aspen last year to keep her safe, yet now she might be dead.

Possibly murdered by the same hit man who'd killed his fellow agent, Julie Granger. The FBI's theory— Aspen had witnessed Boyd Perkins and Sherman Watts disposing of Julie's body.

The case that had brought them to the Southern Ute reservation.

Emma pressed a hand to her head as if to clear her vision. "Aspen is alive."

His chest tightened as hope speared him. He didn't often trust a psychic, but Emma's visions had proven right before, and his brother, Miguel, who'd obviously fallen for the woman, believed her wholeheartedly.

And he trusted his twin brother more than anyone in the world.

Still, he had to swallow to make his voice work. He'd prayed for this news ever since he'd heard Aspen's car had been found crashed into a tree near the San Juan River.

But something about the tortured look on Emma's face disturbed him. "Are you sure she's alive?"

Emma nodded, although she swayed, her face pale, her eyes gaunt. Miguel rushed to help her to the sofa. She leaned her head back and closed her eyes with a shudder.

"What did you see?" Sweat beaded on the nape of Dylan's neck. He was terrified that Aspen had died and that he'd lost her forever.

Just as he'd lost almost every woman he'd ever cared about. His little sister, Teresa. Then his friend Julie.

Miguel rubbed Emma's arms, his voice low and worried, "Emma?"

"I...don't know. The vision... I just know she's alive, but she's scared." She opened her eyes and looked up at Dylan, cold terror streaking her expression. "And she's in danger."

Dylan paced across the room, his heart pounding as Aspen's son, Jack, cried out. The sound shattered the air as if he'd heard Emma and understood that his mother might be in trouble. Emma started to rise to go to the baby, but Dylan waved her off. She looked as if she might faint if she tried to stand.

He strode over to the bassinet and picked up the squirming baby. Jack flailed his tiny fists, his face red, his nose scrunched as he continued to bellow.

"Shh, little man," Dylan said, jiggling him on his shoulder as he paced the room. The poor little fellow must miss his mother terribly. In the first few weeks of his life, he'd been in a car accident with Aspen, abandoned and left with Emma.

He patted the baby's back, cradling him closer. The scent of baby powder and formula suffused him.

If Aspen was alive, why hadn't she come back for her son?

The Aspen he'd known loved children more than anything. During their short affair—the best sex of his whole damn life—she'd told him her plans to return to the Ute reservation and teach.

Baby Jack kicked and screamed louder, a shrill sound that added to the tension thickening the room, his dark skin beet-red, contrasting to his thick black hair. He had Aspen's high-sculpted cheekbones, her hair, her heritage. It made Dylan long to see her again, to reconnect and hold her. To see if they could pick up where they'd left off and possibly have more than just a week of mind-boggling sex.

But she had a son now.

Everything had changed.

He rocked Jack back and forth, lowering his voice again to calm him. "Shh, it's all right. We'll find your mommy. I promise, little man."

Jack quieted to a soft whimper and Dylan turned him to his back, cradled him in his arms and gazed into his eyes. Eyes so blue that for a moment he felt as if he was looking in the mirror.

Suddenly a wave of emotion washed over him, sending his mind into a tailspin. He studied Jack's features more closely while he mentally calculated the baby's age, and the time lapse since he'd last seen Aspen. A little over a year ago, they'd met and fallen into bed. A week later he'd left and hadn't heard from her again.

Aspen had been missing now for nine weeks.

Jack was fifteen weeks old.

Dear God, could Jack possibly be his son?

The baby suddenly cooed up at him, his chubby cheeks puffing up as he gripped one of Dylan's fingers in his tiny fist.

Dylan's chest swelled. "Is it true, Jack? Are you my little *mijo?*"

And if he was, why in the hell hadn't Aspen told him?

THE NIGHTMARES TAUNTED HER.

Every night they came like dark shadowy demons with claws reaching for her and trying to drown her in the madness.

If only she could remember her name, what had happened to her, how she had wound up near death and here in this women's shelter in Mexican Hat.

But the past was like an empty vacuum sucking at her, imprisoning her in the darkness. Only at night in her dreams, memories plucked at the deepest recesses of her mind, trying to break through the barrier her subconscious had erected.

Terrifying memories that she wasn't sure she wanted to recall.

She forced herself to look into the mirror, to probe her mind for bits of her past. She knew she was Ute— her high cheekbones, long black hair and brown eyes screamed Native American heritage.

But those eyes were haunted by something she'd seen, something that lay on the fringes of her conscience.

Her head throbbed, tension knotting her stomach. She rolled her shoulders to stretch out her achy muscles, but exhaustion was wearing on her. In the weeks since she'd come to the shelter, she'd recovered from her physical injuries, the hypothermia and bruises, but she still hadn't regained her strength.

The other women and children had gathered after dinner for a support group session in the common room. Sometimes she gathered the children into a circle on the floor for storytime, but tonight one of the mothers was teaching them how to string Indian beads to make necklaces.

Grateful to have some time alone, she gave in to fatigue and crawled onto her cot by the far wall. Dusk was setting, the hot sun melting in the sky, gray streaks of night darkening the room. She closed her eyes, pulled the thin sheet over her legs and turned on her side. But a hollow emptiness settled inside her. She had felt it the moment she'd awakened in the shelter, freezing and delirious. She'd known then that she'd lost something. Something precious.

A loved one maybe.

Tears trickled down her cheek, but she angrily wiped them away. Remembering what had happened could help her return home. But what if she was right?

What if she'd blocked out the memory because someone she loved had died and she couldn't bear it?

Finally, exhaustion claimed her, but the nightmares returned to dog her, dragging her under a rushing wave of darkness, smothering and terrifying.

Someone was chasing her across the unforgiving land, toward the deep pockets and boulders. She tried to run but her legs felt heavy, her body weighted, and she skidded on the embankment, rocks tumbling downward and pinging off the canyon below. She tumbled and rolled, the sharp edges of the stones jabbing her skin and scraping her flesh raw.

Then his hands were on her, fingernails piercing as they bit into her shoulders. She fought back, swinging her hands up to deflect his blow, but he hit her so hard her head snapped back and stars danced in front of her eyes. Another blow followed, slamming into her skull and pain knifed behind her eyes, her breath gushing out as she tasted blood. She tried desperately to focus, to crawl away, but he yanked her by the ankles and dragged her across the rugged ground, the stones and bristly shrubs tearing at her hands and knees and face as she struggled to grasp something to hold on to.

God help her—he was going to kill her....

Somewhere close by, the river roared, water slashing over jagged rocks, icy cold water that would viciously suck her under and carry her away from everyone she loved.

No, she had to fight.

But the hands were on her again, this time around her throat, punishing fingers digging into her skin, gripping, squeezing, pressing into her larynx, cutting off her oxygen. She gulped and tried to fight back, swung her arms and kicked at him, but her body felt like putty, limp and helpless, as the world swirled into darkness.

Her heart pounding with terror, she jerked awake, disoriented and trembling. She'd only been dreaming; it had been the nightmares again....

She was safe.

But as she exhaled and her breathing steadied, a deadly stillness engulfed the pitch-dark room, the kind of eerie quiet before a storm that sent a frisson of alarm through her.

Then a breath broke the quiet.

A wheezing, whispery low sound. Someone was in the room.

Praying it was one of the sisters coming to check on her, she clenched the sheets and glanced across the space. The tall silhouette of a man stood in front of the open window in the shadows, the scent of sweat and cigarette smoke rolling off of him in sickening waves.

Pure panic ripped through her. Was it the man who'd tried to kill her in her dreams? One of the male abusers the women in the shelter were running from?

His hand moved to his waistband and the shiny glint of metal caught her eye.

She froze, body humming with adrenaline-spiked fear. A knife was tucked into the leather pouch attached to his belt.

She had to run.

Slowly she slid off the bed to escape and yelled for help, but he moved at lightning speed and trapped her. His big hands covered her mouth to silence her screams. She bit his hand, then clawed at him and cried out, fighting with all her might to throw his weight off of her.

Suddenly hall lights flickered on and footsteps clattered toward the doorway, doors banging open. The man's gaze shot sideways and he cursed, then lurched up, ran to the window and jumped out.

The sisters and three other women poured into the room, baseball bats in their hands, ready to attack.

The light flew on, throwing the room into a bright glare that nearly blinded her. Sister Margaret rushed to her, pulled her into her arms and soothed her. "He's gone now. You're safe, child."

It took her precious seconds to stop trembling, then anger ballooned inside her. She was tired of running, of hiding, of not knowing. They'd all assumed that whoever had hurt her had been a violent boyfriend or husband she'd been running from.

But she couldn't go on living like this. She had to know the truth. If her attacker was a boyfriend or husband, he'd found her. And she refused to be a coward.

Somewhere she had a life she'd left behind. And she wanted it back. Wanted the man who'd hurt her to pay.

And the person she'd lost—she had to face that truth, too.

"We should call the police," she whispered. "Send them my picture, Sister. I want to find out who I am and who's trying to kill me."

ONCE THE IDEA that Jack might possibly be his son entered Dylan's mind, he couldn't let it go. The baby shifted against him, finally falling back asleep, but Dylan didn't want to put him down. If the child was his, he wanted to know.

Dammit, he deserved to know.

Memories of his father taking him camping and fishing rolled back, and he saw himself doing the same thing with his own son one day.

When he'd first heard Aspen's baby had been found in her abandoned car, he'd assumed she'd moved on with her life, that she'd forgotten him, and had become involved with another man, someone on the reservation.

Because they'd been careful. And he'd trusted Aspen, trusted that she would have told him if she'd gotten pregnant with his baby.

But looking at Jack's big blue eyes now, he didn't know what to believe.

He settled into the rocking chair while Miguel made Emma herbal tea. Color returned to her cheeks as she sipped the hot brew, although distress still lined her face and her hand trembled slightly as she set the teacup back onto the saucer.

"Emma," he said quietly. "I have to ask you something, and I want you to be honest."

Her gaze met his, and she nodded, although she fidgeted with the afghan Miguel had draped around her shoulders. "I told you all I saw."

"It's not that," he said gruffly.

Her eyes softened as she watched the baby, indicating how much she loved her nephew.

"Emma, who is Jack's father?"

Emma bit down on her bottom lip and glanced away.

"The truth," he said, knowing if Aspen had confided in anyone it would have been her cousin. When Emma was a teenager, her mother's abusive boyfriend had set fire to the house, killing himself and Emma's mother. Emma had moved in with Aspen and her mother, Rose. After that, the girls had been more like sisters than cousins.

"I don't know," she said in a low voice. "Aspen never told me."

He arched a brow, a muscle ticking in his jaw. "Are you sure? You're not keeping some secret?"

Miguel squared his shoulders and draped a protective arm around Emma. "If she says she doesn't know, she doesn't."

"It's important," Dylan said, his throat thick. "Was she dating someone?"

Emma frowned. "Kurt Lightfoot, a builder from the reservation, was interested in her. They went out a few times. But… I'm not sure he fathered the baby." She hesitated. "He certainly hasn't claimed paternal rights."

"Where are you going with this?" Miguel asked. "Are you thinking that Jack's father might have been the one who attacked Aspen? That it wasn't like we suspected, that Boyd Perkins and Sherman Watts tried to kill her because she saw them dump Julie's body?"

Dylan hissed between clenched teeth. "I'm just considering every angle. And knowing Jack's father is important."

"Why is it so important to you?" Emma asked with odd twitch of her lips that made him wonder if she had a sixth sense about this, too.

He traced a finger over Jack's cheek, then decided that Emma might confide more if he came clean. "Because I might be the father."

Surprise flickered in Miguel's eyes, although Emma gave him a sympathetic look. "I honestly don't know," she said gently. "Aspen simply said that the baby's father wasn't in the picture. I assumed that he didn't want to be and didn't push her on the subject. It seemed to upset her too much."

Dylan's jaw snapped tight with the effort not to defend himself. He would have wanted to be in the picture. And if he discovered Jack was his, Aspen wouldn't get rid of him, either. Above all things, Dylan valued family and believed in a father's duty to take care of his children.

"You and Aspen?" Miguel asked.

Dylan gave a clipped nod. "The timing is right. We met in Vegas when I'd just come off that serial-killer case." God, the images of the dead Ute girls Frank Turnbull had killed still haunted him.

"Aunt Rose had just died then," Emma said quietly.

Dylan nodded. "I guess we both needed someone."

And he needed Aspen now and so did her baby… Possibly *their* baby.

Dammit, where was she?

Emma said she was in danger. Had Perkins or Watts found her?

Another possibility, one they hadn't considered, nagged at him.

If he wasn't the father, who was? Jack had been in that car when Aspen had crashed. He could have died, too.

If another man had fathered the little boy, had he tried to kill Aspen to keep his paternity a secret?

Chapter Two

Dylan's cell phone cut into the tense silence in the room, jarring Jack from sleep. He whimpered, and Dylan reluctantly handed him to Emma and connected the call.

"Acevedo speaking."

"Dylan, it's Tom Ryan. Listen, we just caught a break."

Dylan's pulse pounded. "What?"

"I'm at the Bureau now, and we received a fax from a women's shelter in Mexican Hat. It looks like we've found Aspen Meadows."

The blood roared through Dylan's veins. Trembling with relief, he muttered a silent prayer of thanks and crossed himself. "Is she all right?"

"She's alive. According to the sister I spoke with, she was brought in with injuries and has been healing there."

Fear gripped him again. "What kind of injuries?"

"I'm not sure. We didn't go into it. But I thought you might want to go to Mexican Hat and talk to her."

"Thanks. I will." In a brief moment of emotion, he'd confided in Tom that he had been involved with Aspen, that finding her was personal.

"I need to call Emma and tell her that we found her cousin."

"I'm with Emma and Miguel right now," Dylan said. "I'll let her know, then I'm on my way to Mexican Hat."

He disconnected the call, and turned to see Emma and his brother waiting with anticipation.

"They found Aspen?" Emma asked.

He nodded. "She's at a women's shelter in Mexican Hat."

"Thank God." Emma sagged in relief, although a second later, her nose wrinkled in confusion as she rocked Jack. "But if she's alive, why hasn't she called any of us? Why didn't she come back for Jack? She loved this baby more than anything in the world."

Dylan gritted his teeth. "I don't know. Only Aspen can tell us that. I'm going to bring her home."

"You want me to go with you?" Miguel asked.

Dylan shook his head and glanced at the baby. "No. Take a DNA swab from Jack and send it to the lab. And stick close to Jack and Emma. If Aspen is still in danger, her son might be, too."

Miguel agreed and Dylan rushed to the door, then outside to his sedan, worry knotting his stomach. Had Aspen been injured so badly she couldn't contact Emma? Had she been trying to protect her son by not returning?

He started the engine and raced away from Emma's house on the outskirts of Kenner City, anxious for answers.

If Jack was his son, he wanted to know why in the hell she hadn't trusted him with the truth. Not that he'd tried to contact her....

The little boy's baby blue eyes flashed into his head, and he grimaced. Jack had to be his—he knew it in his gut.

But as that possibility sank in, guilt assailed him.

If he'd been with Aspen and the baby, he could have protected them.

"ACCORDING TO THE FBI AGENT who phoned, your name is Aspen Meadows," Sister Margaret said.

Aspen clenched her hands together, weighing the name on her tongue. "Aspen…" Yes, that sounded right. Familiar.

Yet a sense of dread filled her as she waited for more information. "What else did he tell you?"

Sister Margaret stroked her arms to soothe her. "Just that your car was found crashed near the San Juan River, and that you've been missing for nine weeks. He's sending an agent here to talk to you and take you back to your family."

"Family?" Aspen jerked her head up, tears blurring her eyes. "I have family?"

Sister Margaret nodded with a smile. "I'm sure they've been worried sick about you. But don't fret now, child. You're finally going home."

Aspen bit down on her lower lip, more questions assailing her. If she had family, why didn't she remember them? And if she'd been running from an abusive boyfriend or husband, why hadn't she turned to her family for help?

A half-dozen scenarios raced through her head, fear gripping her. Maybe her family hadn't been loving at all. Maybe someone in that family had abused her.

Something about the scenario felt all too real…a distant memory plucking at her subconscious? Or had her contact with the women in the shelter stirred her imagination?

Since she'd arrived, she'd heard horror stories of wife and child beaters, fathers who'd sexually molested their daughters, of stalkers and possessive men who threatened and intimidated the very people they professed to care about, men who treated their women like property.

Had she left her family to protect them from the man after her?

Twice she'd seen a tall Ute man lurking outside, lingering near the fence surrounding the shelter. A Ute man who'd watched her and the other women with intense gray eyes that chilled her to the bone….

Was he the man who'd sneaked into her room and attacked her? Had she known him before?

And if he wanted her dead, would this FBI agent be able to protect her?

DYLAN'S EMOTIONS pinged between hopeful anticipation and trepidation over what he might find when he saw Aspen. He couldn't imagine the woman he knew deserting her child or not contacting her cousin to assure her she was safe.

Which meant her injuries must have been serious.

That or she was too scared to call home. And if that was the case, what had changed her mind?

The landscape swept by him with its pieces of flatland mingled with red-and-gray rocks, some twisted into convoluted shapes that as children, he and Miguel had played a guessing game to name when their family had driven through Colorado and Utah on family vacations. His mother had stopped to photograph the children playing outside their Navajo Indian houses. They'd camped along the San Juan and Colorado Rivers, visited Goosenecks State Park with its view of the steep cliffs and terraces, parked along the overhang and watched rafters take the long boat trip to Lake Powell.

God, they'd had so much fun during those trips. Muley Point had offered another view south over the twisting entrenched canyon to the desert beyond, and Monument Valley and the Valley of the Gods had been other favorite stops.

Baby Jack's face flashed into his mind and he wondered if he'd ever get to take his son camping along the ridges. If he'd be able to drive through the eerie formations of the Valley of the Gods and watch Jack's reaction when he first saw the sixty-foot-wide sombrero-shape rock that had inspired Mexican Hat's name.

He scrubbed his hand over the back of his neck— jeez, he was already thinking like Jack was his. Hoping he was….

If so, he had to find a way to make sure he stayed in the boy's life. Nothing Aspen could say would deter him.

U.S. 163 led him straight into town, and he let his GPS guide him down a side road to the shelter, a nondescript adobe building surrounded by a ten-foot iron gate. Inside, a massive cross stood in front of the steel door as if to guard its residents and stave off evil.

Dust and a wave of heat engulfed him as he climbed from his sedan, the gray night sky casting the center in dark shadows. He glanced around the outside but saw nothing amiss, so rang the buzzer at the gate entrance.

A second later, a woman's voice echoed through the speaker. "Yes?"

He produced his badge, then identified himself.

"Special Agent Ryan spoke with you about the photo you faxed to the Bureau, about the woman you have staying here. Aspen Meadows."

"Yes, just a minute." A buzz sounded, and the gate swung open, a nun appearing in the doorway to the building. She checked his identification before letting him enter, then led him to a small office to the right.

"I need to see her," he said without preamble.

Her eyes seemed to be assessing him. "First, we need to talk. My name is Sister Margaret."

He gave a clipped nod, noting the modest furnishings, a battered wooden desk and desk chair, two wooden Windsor chairs and a ratty plaid sofa that had seen better days. She gestured for him to take a seat, so he claimed one of the Windsor chairs, and she settled onto the sofa. But the pinched look on her face and the way she fidgeted with her habit spoke volumes about her mental state.

His gut churned with anxiety. "Is something wrong, Sister? Is Aspen all right?"

She pursed her lips and sighed, a sound that disturbed him even more.

"Did you personally know Aspen?" Sister Margaret asked.

He was accustomed to asking the questions. But this woman was as protective as a mother hen, so he knew he had to answer. "Yes. A while back. I've been investigating her disappearance for weeks. Her cousin is worried sick about her."

"Yes, about that…"

Dylan leaned forward, bracing his elbows on his knees. "Just cut to it, Sister. Is Aspen all right?"

"Yes, and no," the sister said. "When she first came to us, she was suffering from hypothermia, and multiple bruises and lacerations covered her body and face. Along with that, she had a couple of broken ribs, a fractured wrist, concussion and it appeared as if someone had tried to strangle her." She shuddered, and Dylan's mind raced with the visual image she'd painted.

"Can you tell me what happened to her?" Sister Margaret asked. "Who hurt her?"

Sweat beaded on Dylan's neck, and he took a deep breath, struggling to control his anger. "We don't have all the pieces of the puzzle yet. We believe she may have witnessed a murder. Either that or she saw the killer dumping a woman's body. When the killer realized Aspen had witnessed his criminal actions, he came after her. We found her car crashed along the San Juan River. Her son was inside."

"Oh, my." A horror stricken look passed over Sister Margaret's face. "Aspen has a son?"

"Yes, a baby boy named Jack. He's fifteen weeks old now." *And he might be mine.*

Sister Margaret pressed a hand to her pale face. "We thought she might be running from an abusive boyfriend or husband, but she never mentioned a child, so we had no idea. If we had, we would have reported her missing right away."

Dylan arched a brow, confusion clogging his head. "I don't understand. Didn't Aspen tell you what happened?"

"That's the reason I wanted to talk to you," Sister Margaret said softly. "Aspen was unconscious when she was brought in. And when she regained consciousness… well, she didn't remember anything."

Dylan's chest pounded. "You mean, she didn't remember the car crash or attack?"

Sister Margaret shook her head sadly. "I mean, she didn't remember *anything*. Not about what happened to her, not even her name or that she has family."

Dylan sat back in the chair, trying to absorb the missing piece the woman had just revealed. Amnesia would explain why Aspen hadn't contacted Emma or returned home for Jack.

Or called him for help.

"What did the doctor say about the amnesia?"

Sister Margaret looked shaken. "That the head injury could have caused her memory loss, but that the trauma could have been a factor, as well."

"Basically, she blocked out the events because they were too painful," Dylan said.

"Yes."

"Will she regain her memory?" Dylan asked.

The sister shrugged, her hands twisting together in her habit. "Probably. But that may take time. And Dr. Bennigan advised us not to push her, that doing so might traumatize her even more."

Dylan stewed over that revelation, bracing himself to meet an Aspen who had no idea who he was. "So what prompted you to finally report her appearance to the police?" Dylan finally asked.

The sister shifted nervously. "Someone broke into the center earlier, into the room where Aspen was sleeping and attacked her. She told us to call the police."

Dylan fisted his hands by his sides. Dammit, had Perkins and Watts tracked down Aspen and broken into the shelter to finish the job?

ASPEN SAT ON THE FLOOR with the children surrounding her, her voice low as she recanted the legend of the Sky People. "Manitou is the Great Spirit—he lived all alone in the sky. But he was lonely so he made a big hole in the sky and built the mountains, then sent snow and rain down to make the world more beautiful."

"Did he make the animals, too?" a curly red-haired four-year-old asked.

"Yes," Aspen said with a smile. "He made all the animals and the birds. But soon, like children and grown-ups do sometimes, the animals began to fight. So Manitou decided he needed a king to rule them all."

"Was it a lion?" a little boy asked.

"A dinosaur?" another suggested.

Aspen shook her head. "No, a grizzly bear." She reached up her arms and held them wide. "Now give me a big bear hug and say night-night."

The kids giggled and hugged her, and as they parted, she looked up to see Sister Margaret standing with a man in the doorway.

Her breath lodged in her chest in a painful surge. He was broad-shouldered and tall, so masculine with his wide jaw and chiseled features that her stomach fluttered with nerves. Thick black hair brushed his ears and forehead, long black lashes framing the bluest eyes she'd ever seen, eyes like the sky on a clear Colorado day.

Yet he looked dangerous and imposing, anger radiating off him in waves. And those startling eyes were intense, haunted, seemed to be trying to see deep into her soul, and made a chill skitter up her arms.

So did the scar that slashed his chin.

Although even that scar didn't detract from his good looks.

One of the mothers herded the children to the back rooms for bed, and Aspen stood slowly, her ankle still slightly weak from her tumble with her attacker.

Sister Margaret offered her a tentative smile and gestured for the man to follow.

"This is Special Agent Dylan Avecedo. He came to take you home, Aspen."

Fear slithered through Aspen as she met his gaze. Then he extended his hand and she placed hers inside his large palm, and a warm feeling of awareness shot through her. Something about those eyes seemed… familiar.

Had she met this man before?

But how would she have known a federal agent? Did he have the answers to her missing past?

And if he did, was she ready to hear the truth?

Chapter Three

God, Aspen was even more beautiful that he'd remembered. Seeing her sitting on the floor with those kids triggered childhood memories of his mother doing the same with him and his siblings.

And served as a reminder that Aspen had intended to help children before her life had been interrupted by a murder.

Her long dark hair hung in a thick braid over her shoulder, her chocolate colored eyes huge and so sultry that once again he lost himself in the beautiful depths.

They were also pensive, pained by her loss.

Damn, he could almost feel the turmoil inside her, the need to replace her missing past with the truth. Yet she instinctively knew the truth wouldn't be pretty, and she was frightened.

"Detective?" Her voice was pleading, searching his for answers. Answers that he didn't have.

He studied her for any sign of recognition, for any glimmer that she would welcome him back in her life. That she knew that he could be trusted to stay by her side.

But he saw no indication that she knew who he

was…or that she'd ever melted beneath his hands and mouth like a wanton lover.

Instead she looked at him as if he was a perfect stranger.

That hurt. He wanted her to know him, to recall what they'd had together, to want his touch as much as he craved hers.

Her face flushed slightly as he clung to her hand, and the trembling in her petite body and flushed expression in her eyes offered him a seed of hope. Even if she didn't remember him, there was something there, a simmering, immediate attraction, just as the first time they'd touched and fallen into bed.

She was serving cocktails in that casino in Vegas, wearing a short little black skirt with a cropped T-shirt that hugged her breasts and exposed the smooth brown flesh of her flat stomach. Her voice had purred like a kitten, her movements fluid and seductive, her body so tempting that he had had to caress her bare skin.

That body he knew so well. One he'd tasted and explored and memorized.

One he'd wanted so often over the past few months that he'd fantasized about having her again and again.

Somewhere in the building, a baby cried out, and he thought of Jack. Along with relief that she was physically okay and the instantaneous heat that ripped through him at the sight of her, anger churned through his gut.

Dammit, if Jack was his, why hadn't she told him?

Finally, she retreated and pulled away, wiping her palm on the side of her skirt. "Sister Margaret said you know where my family is."

A slight tremor laced her voice, and he tried to place himself in her shoes, to understand what it must be like to be lost and alone with no memory of what had happened, but obviously aware she was in danger.

"Yes, your cousin Emma is waiting at the Ute reservation. That's where you live. She's been searching for you ever since you disappeared."

A frown creased the delicate skin above her huge almond-shaped eyes. "How could I forget my own cousin?"

The doctor's advice trilled in his head like a warning bell, and Dylan forced an understanding smile. "You suffered a head injury," he said, hating the distress lining her face. "Sister Margaret said in time you may remember everything."

She shivered and wrapped her arms around her waist.

"Sister Margaret also said a man broke into your room. Did you get a look at your attacker?"

She shook her head. "No, it was too dark. All I saw was his shadow. Then he attacked me, and I fought back and screamed." Her voice broke, her breathing rattling out as if she was reliving that horrible event. "Then the sisters and other women ran in, and he jumped out the window and got away."

A fresh bruise darkened her cheek, and he gritted his teeth to keep from touching it and pulling her into his arms to comfort her. She looked so small and fragile and...vulnerable. "What else do you remember?"

She chewed her bottom lip. "He had a knife in a leather pouch attached to his belt."

Dylan's blood ran cold. "How tall was he?"

She hesitated, rubbing her head in thought. "I don't know. It was just a shadow."

"Did you notice a distinctive smell?"

"Cigarettes," she whispered. "And sweat."

Watts used to smoke but had supposedly given up the habit. But perhaps the man had picked it back up. "Did he say anything?"

She shook her head. "No, he just grabbed me and shoved his hand over my mouth. Then I…I think I bit his hand."

Her feistiness might have saved her life. Twice now. "I'd like to look around that room and see if I find any evidence."

Sister Margaret nodded, and he went to the sedan to retrieve his crime kit. He flipped on a flashlight, waving it across the room in an arc as he searched the corners, the bed and floor.

With a grunt, he knelt and with his gloved hand, retrieved a loose hair that had fallen on the floor. It might belong to one of the other women or children, but he'd check it out. The hair was longer than Boyd Perkins's or Sherman Watts's—but still, it might be a lead if there was a third perp.

Continuing the search, he paused at the window, then used a pair of tweezers to pluck a small piece of fabric that had caught on a nail on the windowsill, and bagged it along with the hair to send for analysis.

Maybe forensics would turn up something to help them nail the bastard and make sure the charges stuck when they finally tracked him down.

Stewing over the circumstances, he carried the evidence bags to the car while Aspen said goodbye to the other women. Outside, he phoned Miguel to explain the situation.

"Amnesia?" Miguel asked.

"Yes. She didn't recognize me. I'm hoping that seeing Emma and Jack will jog her memory."

"I'll warn Emma about the doctor's diagnosis," Miguel said. "And tell her not to push, to give Aspen time."

Five minutes later, Aspen returned carrying a small paper bag holding the meager possessions she'd accumulated since staying at the shelter.

Sister Margaret gave him a concerned look as she escorted them to the gate. "Take care of her, Agent Avecedo."

He squeezed her hand with a nod. "Don't worry. I won't leave her alone until we find out who hurt her." He paused and lowered his voice. "And, Sister, I'm going to need the medical report from when Aspen was brought in. When we find out who did this, it will help with prosecution."

If he let the son of a bitch live that long.

"I'll speak to the doctor, but we'll need a release from Aspen."

"I'll talk to her about it," Dylan said.

Sister Margaret agreed, then thanked him, and he walked Aspen to the car. She settled into the passenger side and buckled her seat belt, the tension thickening as he drove away from the shelter.

"Sister Margaret said that you were injured when you arrived at the center. That you thought that someone, an abusive boyfriend, was after you."

She shrugged. "It seemed like a likely story, Agent Acevedo."

"Call me Dylan."

She gave him an odd look, then nodded.

"Did the abusive boyfriend idea come from a memory?" he asked.

She fidgeted, looking back at the center as if she wanted to return to the safe haven she'd found within that iron fence. "Not really. Just a feeling that I was running from someone." Her voice warbled. "And then there are the nightmares."

"Nightmares?"

She nodded, her brown eyes huge in her face. "Nightmares of fighting some man, of running, of hearing the river and being cold…"

She angled her head to study his face. "Can you fill in any of the missing pieces?"

"Some, but not all. We found your car smashed into a tree by the San Juan River." He paused, debating over whether to tell her that her son had been left in her car. "There was evidence of a struggle. Blood in the car. We didn't know if you'd survived or if you might have drowned in the river."

She made a low sound in her throat. "My cousin… She was worried?"

He nodded and gently placed his hand over hers in an attempt to calm her, although heat radiated through him. He wanted more, wanted to hold her and assure her everything would be all right.

Wanted to shake her for not telling him that they had a son together.

"Yes, Aspen, her name is Emma, and she's anxious for you to come home."

Relief filled her eyes, and she relaxed slightly. As much as he wanted to press her, he forced himself to rein in his emotions and let her absorb what he'd told her.

"You look exhausted," he said. "Why don't you try

to rest during the drive? I know Emma will want to talk
when we arrive."

She gave him a wary look, but nodded. A second
later, she curled up against the door and fell asleep, but
even in sleep, her body seemed wound tight and braced
for battle as if she expected her attacker to reappear any
minute and end her life as he'd tried to do before.

THE NIGHTMARES RETURNED AGAIN.

Aspen struggled to wake herself, determined not to
let them suck her into the darkness, but the heavy pull
of fear yanked her back to the day she'd been running.

Running, but from whom?

If she could only see the man's face…

She crawled along the steep rocks, fighting to steady
herself as the river raged below, the snow-capped ridges
reminding her that the water would be dangerous and
freezing. That although she was an excellent swimmer,
there was no way she could survive the icy temperatures
or strong current.

Then the hands were upon her, clenching, hitting,
choking her, dragging her into the murky depths of death.

She screamed, snippets of her life flashing in front
of her. The Ute reservation, the casino, the Trading Post,
the children gathering for a Ute celebration. The Bear
Dance in the spring and the Sun Dance at Mesa Verde.

Her mother teaching her the ways of the people. The
childhood stories of the Sky People, the legend of the
Sleeping Ute Mountain, and the ghost stories her
mother insisted she pass on about the sacrifices of their
ancestors.

Then she was drowning, the icy water sucking her

down to the bottom, the rocks beating against her skin, the whisper of death calling her name.

She jerked awake, shaking and disoriented. Suddenly she felt the agent's hand on hers again. "More nightmares, Aspen?"

She lifted her head, pushed a strand of hair that had escaped her braid from her eyes and tried to steady her labored breathing. "Yes." She glanced down at his hand, aching to cling to him for protection, but she hardly knew the man. Still, he made her feel safe as if he wouldn't leave her to the terrifying memories that hacked at her sanity, tapping at the fringes of her conscience yet evading her.

While she'd slept, the weather had changed. Dark ominous clouds hovered above the ridges, the mountain runoff filling the potholes and shoulder with rising water. A chill filled the car, the temperatures dropping as they neared the canyon.

The road was virtually deserted, the landscape colored with shadows, prairie grass and scattered rocks. In the distance, the sound of a coyote rent the air, the slap of the windshield wipers battling the light rain eerie in the silence.

Occasionally they passed a pueblo style house, the elements having beaten its beauty to a muddy brownish orange. The story she'd told the children earlier reminded her that this area was dangerous territory for the reemergence of the grizzly bear.

And the ghost town that had once been a miner's haven made her anxious to return to civilization.

A gust of wind that sounded like a freight train sent tumbleweed swirling across the road, then suddenly bright headlights appeared behind them, racing up on their tail.

Aspen tensed as Dylan swerved, the car bounced over a rut in the road and hit a wet patch. The car behind them rammed into their tail, sending the sedan fishtailing across the dark highway, skimming rocks and spewing gravel and dirt.

Dylan cursed in Spanish and steered into the skid in an attempt to regain control.

But the car raced up behind them, rammed them again, then swerved to their right and a gunshot pierced the side of the car.

Aspen screamed, and Dylan shoved her head down. "Stay low!"

Dylan sped up, weaving left then right, as if he intended to outsmart their attacker at his own game of cat and mouse. The sedan sent the other car sliding off the road toward the creek, which looked as if it was about to flood from the mountain runoff.

Aspen covered her head with her hands, leaning down so her forehead touched her knees. But a second later, the other car's tires squealed and the vehicle slammed into them again. Another shot shattered the window on the passenger side, sending glass raining down on top of her.

She cried out again, and Dylan shouted another obscenity, losing control as the sedan careened off the road, bounced over shrubs and rocks and hit a tall rock formation. Metal screeched and gears ground together as they spun toward the ridge out of control. The car flipped on its side, rolled and landed upside down in the creek bed. The air bag exploded, knocking the wind out of her and trapping her in the seat.

Aspen thought she might have passed out for a moment, and when she recovered, her breath huffed out in tiny pants as water began to seep through the window.

"Are you okay?" Dylan shouted.

They were both hanging upside down, the seat belt cutting into her neck. She glanced sideways and noticed blood dotting his hands, and felt it trickling down her arm where glass had pelted them.

"Aspen?"

"Yes, I'm okay," she rasped. "But water's coming in."

"I know. Hang on to the seat belt and side of the car while I cut you out."

She sucked in a sharp breath and braced herself with one hand on the roof of the car and another on the door. Dylan retrieved a knife from his pocket and sawed at her air bag, puncturing it. It deflated with a whoosh, then he sawed at her seat belt. The icy water gurgled and spewed through the window, dripping onto the roof and soaking her.

"Hurry!" she whispered hoarsely as déjà vu struck her. She'd been in another crash and had almost drowned....

Her dreams of running, of being cold—they weren't just nightmares. They had been very real.

"Almost got it," Dylan said between clenched teeth.

The belt finally snapped, and she slid downward, her head hitting the roof. "Try to climb out," he said. "I need to cut my belt."

Terror seized her. She didn't want to go out there alone.

"Go, Aspen!"

His sharp voice jerked her from the fear gripping her, and she maneuvered sideways, then kicked the rest of the glass free with her feet. Water gushed inside the vehicle, and she held her breath, grabbed the seat and shoved her weight through the window. The freezing water swallowed her, and numbness claimed her, but her foot connected with rock, and she used it as a springboard to propel her. Teeth chattering, she waded to the embankment.

Dragging in huge gulping breaths, her limbs shaking, she searched the creek and finally saw Dylan wading toward her in the waist-deep cold water.

He crawled from the creek, carrying the crime-scene kit in one hand. Another gunshot blasted the rock beside her, and Dylan grabbed her hand. "Come on, let's go!"

Her legs felt like Jell-O as he yanked her to her feet and dragged her across the embankment. She stumbled over rocks, and her ankle twisted but she plunged on, ducking low to dodge another bullet.

She couldn't die now, not when she'd just found out her name, and that she had family waiting for her.

Chapter Four

Dylan stuffed the evidence box beneath a boulder, then buried Aspen in the crook of his arm to protect her from the gunshots as they raced in an upward climb into the mountains. The terrain was rocky and pitted with shrubs and brush, the jagged ridges posing their own danger.

It was also a good place to hide.

Another shot pinged off a stone jutting out from the ridge, and they ducked, dodging it as he pushed her behind a boulder. The dark sky and mixture of rain and snow added to the dangers, making their footing slippery. A second later, he steered her toward another indentation carved into the red stone, pushing her to climb higher as they dodged more bullets.

Dylan crouched beside her, removed his gun and braced it to fire. "Stay down," he whispered. "I'm going after the bastard."

She grabbed his arm. "No. Don't leave me alone."

The cold terror in her voice and eyes made his chest clench, and he hated the shooter for putting it there. All the more reason to catch the SOB.

He brushed his hand against her bruised cheek. "I'll be back."

Slowly rising behind the boulder, he searched the ridges and cliffs, then spotted movement to the right. He fired, a shot pinging over the shadow, and rocks skittered down the ridge as the man scrambled to escape.

Dylan gestured for Aspen to stay put, then lurched forward in chase. He fired again and saw the shadow moving at lightning speed around a boulder, then disappear. Dylan wanted to pursue him, but a low cry escaped Aspen and a faraway look glazed her eyes as if she was reliving the trauma that had caused her amnesia.

Her arm was bleeding, too, and cuts from the shattered window marred her hands.

The sound of a car engine sliced the night, and Dylan breathed a sigh of relief, then stooped down and gathered Aspen in his arms. She trembled against him, wet and shivering, and he hugged her to his chest, whispering low words of assurance.

Thank God they had survived.

But he'd find the man who'd tried to kill him and put that terror in Aspen's eyes and make him suffer.

ASPEN CLUNG TO THE AGENT, memories of another crash and running for her life bombarding her. She survived, she reminded herself, and she would survive now.

At least this time she wasn't alone.

"It's all right, Aspen," Dylan said. "He's gone now and you're safe."

She forced a calming breath, then looked up at him. "But he'll be back. And how can I fight him if I don't even know who he is?"

"Sister Margaret said you would get your memory back," he assured her. "You need time. Just trust me for now."

She folded her arms. "It's just so frustrating and scary. I feel as if I'm living in the dark."

He stroked her back, soothing her. "I won't stop until the danger to you is over and the man responsible for the shooting and for your memory loss is in jail, or dead."

She took solace in his strength, relaxed slightly and pulled herself together.

He wiped the blood dotting her arm. "We need to take you to the E.R."

"No. I'm all right," she said. "It's just a few scratches." She pressed a finger to his forehead. "But you might need stitches."

He shrugged off her concern and slowly extracted himself from her arms. "I'm fine. But I need to call for help."

She nodded, then he removed his cell phone and made a call, thankful it still worked.

"Tom, it's Dylan. Listen, I was driving Aspen back to the reservation and someone ambushed us. My car is upside down in the creek and we need an extraction. Also, I want forensics to go over the car for paint samples and bullets." He gave him their location, disconnected the call, then turned to her and took her arm.

"Come on, let's head back down to the car. I need to retrieve the evidence box to send to forensics."

Aspen took his hand as he helped her down the slippery rocks, grateful the precipitation had stopped, although the wind rustled the brush and ruffled her damp hair. Her hands and feet were numb already, the chill inside her mounting. He paused to grab the crime scene kit with the evidence bags he'd stowed inside and hoisted it in one hand while keeping the other firmly on her arm to steady her.

By the time they reached the bottom, the sound of a helicopter echoed from above, its blinking lights sweeping the terrain and promising a recovery.

The helicopter touched down in the flatter part of the canyon and two men climbed out, the pilot and another big guy, an Indian, who frowned as he stalked toward them.

Dylan stepped forward. "Ryan didn't say he was sending you, Bia. But I'm glad he did." He gestured toward Aspen. "This is Aspen Meadows. Aspen, Special Agent Ethan Bia. He's an expert tracker with the Bureau."

The Indian nodded and glanced at Aspen. "Nice to meet you, Miss Meadows."

"Please, call me Aspen."

"Sure." He angled his head toward Dylan. "Ryan didn't know what we'd find, if the shooter was still hiding around here and you might be holed up in the mountains."

"I ran him off," Dylan said. "But we need to collect the bullet casings and take paint samples from my car. When we find this SOB, I want to make sure we have forensics to back up an arrest."

Ethan nodded. "Absolutely. I'll look for the bullet casings while the pilot flies you two back. Ryan's sending a team and a tow truck for the car. I'll wait on them and make sure CSI processes it."

"Thanks." Dylan shook his head, and curved an arm around Aspen, coaxing her toward the chopper. "Come on, let's get you warmed up and to the E.R."

Aspen had never ridden in a helicopter but she was

too cold and tired to argue, so she crawled in beside Dylan, accepted the blanket he offered and burrowed beneath it while the blades of the chopper whirled and they lifted off.

Her gaze fell to Dylan's car where it lay upside down in the rising creek, and she flinched. They could have died and they might not have been found for days or weeks.

The realization that that was the shooter's plan sent another shudder through her. She had to remember what had happened nine weeks ago.

Her life depended on it.

THE NEXT FEW HOURS were hectic and strained as the helicopter transported them to the emergency room in Durango, and doctors examined and treated them for scrapes and cuts. Dylan earned four stitches to his forehead, but thankfully Aspen didn't need stitches. Still, she was bruised and battered and had suffered minor lacerations on her hands and legs.

He phoned Miguel, explained the circumstances and suggested he take Aspen home to rest before she saw Jack. Miguel promised to leave a key to Aspen's house hidden in the mouth of the horse sculpture in her front yard.

Fatigue lined her face as he secured a vehicle, dropped the evidence he'd collected earlier at the Kenner County Crime Unit in Kenner City, and drove toward the reservation. It was early morning, the gray dawn sky filled with the shadows of another impending storm. Neither of them had slept for over twenty-four hours, and he desperately needed a shower and food.

"Where are we going?" Aspen asked.

Her labored breath as she pressed a hand to her

chest indicated her ribs were bruised from the impact of the air bag. If she felt like him, every bone in her body ached.

"To your house for some sleep. Then we'll reconnect with your family. Your cousin dropped off some groceries earlier if you're hungry."

"But, Dylan—"

"Don't argue, Aspen," he said, cutting her off. "You've had a lot to deal with in the past twenty-four hours and need some rest before you face your family."

And so did he. Because he wanted to be prepared when she saw Jack for the first time. "The doctor warned that you need to take it easy and not push things for your own health."

Wariness dimmed her features, but exhaustion and trauma outweighed any protest as her eyes slid closed. He clenched his jaw, hating the bruises on her battered skin and the fact that she'd forgotten everyone she loved. That fact alone confirmed the extent of physical and mental trauma she'd suffered.

And as much as he wanted to question her about Jack's paternity, he had to refrain.

Earn her trust. Give her time to heal. To reconnect with her family and home and let her memories return on their own.

Or he could drive the truth deeper into her psyche.

Which meant it would be even more difficult to find out who had attacked her.

And he had to do that to protect her.

If Boyd Perkins and Sherman Watts had tried to kill her, she'd have to testify so they could put the men behind bars.

Of course, they had to find the bastards first.

And if someone else was involved…well, he'd find that out and uncover their motive. If Jack wasn't his son and another man was in the picture…

No, he couldn't go there yet.

But he needed to brace himself for that possibility. Couldn't allow himself to get too close to her or the baby until he knew the truth.

Did she think he wasn't father material? Couldn't she contemplate a future with him?

Agitated, mind racing with questions, he drove onto the reservation toward Aspen's. He wasn't surprised at the small pueblo style house with its adobe colors and Native American look. During their one glorious week in Vegas together, she'd talked about life on the reservation, her love of her culture, and her desire to teach the children and instill in them the importance of their heritage.

Aspen was deep in sleep, so he parked in the stone drive, climbed out and grabbed the key, his instincts on full alert as he scanned the property.

Satisfied no one was hiding in the shadows of the trees, he left Aspen in the car while he went to search the inside. Darkness bathed the interior as he entered, and he paused to listen for sounds of an intruder.

First thing tomorrow, he'd install a security system in Aspen's home. One that went straight to him if anyone set off the alarm.

Slowly, he crept inside the dark entryway, flipped on a light, then scanned the foyer. Native American artwork decorated the adobe colored walls, collections of hand-made baskets, beaded jewelry, pottery and other artifacts and books filled the built-in shelves. A picture of a native Ute on horseback was centered over a soft brown leather couch opposite a woodstove in the den, which opened to the kitchen.

He moved to the left and found a master suite and bath, decorated in earth tones with accents of red, yellow and orange, and more Ute art. He searched the closet, beneath the bed, then moved to the guest bedroom on the opposite side of the kitchen.

His lungs tightened at the sight of the nursery. A primitive wooden crib sat in the midst of the freshly painted baby blue room, which held an assortment of stuffed animals, children's books and infant toys.

Hissing a breath of relief that no intruder was inside, he stowed his gun inside his jacket, then went outside to the car and lifted Aspen from the seat. She moaned softly in her sleep, and snuggled against him as he carried her to the front stoop.

She was wrapped in the blanket, wearing the scrubs the nurse had given her at the E.R. when they'd removed her damp clothes, so he carried her to her bedroom, pulled down the covers and laid her on the crisp clean sheets. For a brief second her eyes flickered open, and she looked at him with glazed eyes.

He inhaled her sweet fragrance, the softness of her skin, and ached to crawl in bed beside her. To rekindle the heat between them.

"You're home now," he said gently, then pulled the quilt over her and brushed back her hair.

She tugged at his hand, and a hollow feeling of need gripped him.

"Where are you going?' she whispered in a sleep-laced voice that triggered images of the two of them in bed together, of her voice purring his name after a night of lovemaking.

"I know it sounds silly," she whispered, "but I don't want to be alone."

God, he didn't want that, either. He wanted to make love to her.

Instead, he brushed the pad of his thumb across her cheek. "I'll sleep on the couch," he said, his voice thick and hoarse. "If you need me just call."

She nodded, closed her eyes again and curled into her bed. He ached to drop a kiss on her cheek, then her mouth, but remembered the doctor's warning and forced himself to leave the room.

Still, his body hummed with arousal and a fierce hunger that could only be sated by Aspen.

A woman who saw him as a perfect stranger.

Chapter Five

Dylan was exhausted but on edge, too wired to sleep.

It was the first time he'd been in Aspen's home and he felt uncomfortable and intrigued at the same time. Her furnishings were exactly as he'd expected, reminiscent of her culture, yet the sight of the nursery made his chest ache.

How would she react when she saw the empty baby bed? When she saw Jack? Would she remember her son?

He yanked off his shirt and walked around the den/kitchen combination, wishing he was here under other circumstances. That Aspen had invited him into her home because she wanted to see him again.

He studied the Ute items in the room and was once again reminded of the road trips his family used to take when he was younger.

Once they'd stopped to observe a young Ute woman with a horde of children surrounding her as she taught them to weave baskets. His mother had photographed her, and he'd thought about that photograph when he'd first seen Aspen.

The Uncompahgre beaded horse bag on Aspen's wall was made from tanned mule deer hide. Thousands of glass trade beads and tobacco balls were stitched into the sides and rim. The bags were used to hold pipes, carvings and religious totems and were opened only for private ceremonies.

An Uncompahgre Ute Shaved Beaver Hide Painting hung above the fireplace, and ceremonial pipes of salmon alabaster and black pipestone sat on the mantle. Several ceremonial rattles made from buffalo rawhide that were used to call spirits in Ute ceremonies decorated a pine sofa table.

Some Ute still used peyote in healing rituals. He wondered if Aspen did, or if she would use a traditional doctor with their son.

Her *son—you don't know yet that Jack is yours.*

Still, his gaze was drawn to the photographs, and he walked over to study the scattering of pictures. The first photo showed Aspen cradling a newborn to her chest. Dylan touched the frame, memorizing the picture. The baby's eyes were squished closed, his lips pursed, his fists on his chest.

The next one had been taken a couple of weeks later. A smiling Jack was propped against a Mexican blanket. The scant few pictures chronicled his young life up until the time Aspen had disappeared.

Jack had only been four weeks old at the time.

Aspen had missed almost three months of her son's life because of the attack.

And if Jack was his, he had missed those months, as well.

Dammit, he would find out who'd stolen those weeks from her and make sure she and Jack were never separated again.

HOURS LATER, Aspen woke from an exhausted sleep to the delicious aroma of coffee. Still groggy, she rolled over in bed and looked at her surroundings. A fog still hovered over her memories, but the room, the art, the scent of lavender seemed familiar and evoked a warm fuzzy feeling as if she was finally safe.

Then the events of the night before crashed back, shattering her peace. Her limbs throbbed as she swung her legs over the side of the bed. A sharp pain splintered her midriff from her bruised ribs, and she breathed deeply to stem the pain, gripping the edge until her legs steadied enough to support her.

She was still wearing the scrubs the nurse had given her in the E.R., and desperately wanted a shower.

Footsteps in the den sounded, and she hesitated, the fear that had clawed at her the last few weeks returning. Who was in the house?

That agent—Dylan? Or someone else?

A tremor rattled the windowpane, and she stood and walked to the edge of the door and glanced into the den. Dylan Acevedo was sitting at the table, drinking coffee and looking at an opened folder.

Relief surged through her, and she hurried into the bathroom. The warm water felt heavenly on her achy body and helped to wash away the scent of the river and soothe her aching limbs. After toweling off, she let her hair hang loose to dry, and dug through the closet, noting the long flowing Indian skirts and beaded blouses. She chose a bright blue skirt, pale yellow blouse and a pair of leather sandals and dressed, then walked into the den.

Dylan glanced up, his dark blue eyes raking over her and sending a tingle through her.

But his mouth was set in a firm straight line, and the sultry look she thought she'd seen suddenly died, an iciness replacing it.

"I can't believe I slept so long." She accepted the mug of coffee he offered, surprised when he automatically dumped a packet of sweetener in it as if he knew how she liked it.

She started to question him about that, but he cleared his throat. "Your cousin Emma has already called. I told her we'd let her know when you woke up. She's anxious to see you."

Nerves fluttered in Aspen's stomach. "What if I don't recognize her?"

His dark look softened. "Don't worry. She knows about your amnesia."

A helpless feeling engulfed her. "But how could I forget my own family?"

He took her elbows in his hands, then guided her to the table. "You will remember. Just give yourself time to heal. Now why don't I make you something to eat and then we'll call Emma?"

She nodded and sipped her coffee as he made himself at home and whipped up two omelets. Odd that Dylan seemed comfortable in the kitchen—and in his skin.

When he placed the plates on the table, he set the hot sauce on the table. She immediately reached for it, something niggling at the back of her mind. How did he know she liked hot sauce on her eggs?

"Any more nightmares?" he asked as he sprinkled salt and pepper on his food.

She pressed a hand over her forehead, struggling with the tiny snippets of life that flashed in front of her. Another man cooking for her, feeding her in bed...

His big body taking up all the space in the room just as Dylan's was now.

"Aspen, are you all right? You're not eating."

She blinked to clear her head and cut into her omelet. "I think I was too exhausted to have nightmares. Either that or I felt...safe for the first time in weeks."

His breath rushed out and their gazes locked, the moment stretching between them before he finally broke the strained silence. "I'm glad you felt safe."

She frowned. Her comment seemed ridiculous—how could she feel safe when they'd been attacked and nearly died the night before?

Because Dylan was watching over her, protecting her, guarding her house. Deep down, she sensed he wouldn't let anyone hurt her.

He was an excellent agent, took his job seriously.

But there was more. He'd promised to protect her. And somehow, she knew that he kept his promises.

Still, nerves pulled at her sanity. And a voice whispered inside her head that she couldn't grow dependent on the agent. That she needed to keep her distance.

That hollow ache clutched her insides again. She'd never be whole again until she found out the truth.

Time for her to meet her cousin.

THE FACT THAT ASPEN FELT SAFE with him helped to dissipate his anger over the awkward situation.

A knock sounded at the door and he gestured to her that he'd get it. He checked the window and saw Miguel's vehicle, then heard the rumble of his brother talking to Emma through the door. His jaw tightened as he opened it and saw Jack cradled in Emma's arms.

"Come on in, Aspen is waiting."

When he glanced back at Aspen, she was standing in front of the mantle, studying the baby pictures, tears shimmering in her eyes.

Emma's expression lit with excitement, although nerves also shimmered in the depths of her eyes as Aspen turned to face her.

Miguel closed the door, and Dylan angled himself to watch the reunion, feeling touched, but out of place as if he was an outsider, an intruder in this family.

A family that should be his.

"Oh, Aspen…" Emma's voice choked as she walked over to her. "I've been out of my mind with worry."

Aspen raked her dark brown eyes over Emma and Jack. "Emma?"

"Yes, it's me. I'm so relieved to have you home." Emma gestured toward Jack, a loving expression softening the anxious lines on her face. "We've both missed you."

As if he understood, Jack whimpered, scrunching up his nose and Emma rocked him back and forth.

"My baby…" Aspen whispered.

Emma nodded. "Jack. They found him in your car after the accident."

Aspen paled, and Dylan hurried over and coaxed her to the sofa. "Take a deep breath," Dylan murmured.

She did as he said, then turned tortured eyes to him. "I abandoned my little boy?" Shock made her voice sound screechy. "I can't believe I'd do that. What kind of mother am I?"

"You were—are—a wonderful mother," Emma said firmly.

Dylan stroked her back. "You didn't leave him of your own accord."

"Then you know what happened to me?"

Dylan, Emma and Miguel exchanged a frustrated look, each questioning just how much to confess. "We know that someone ran you off the road and attacked you," Dylan said. "That was evident from the injuries you sustained and were treated for at the shelter."

"I knew I was missing something," she said in a heartbreakingly agonized voice. "Every time I hugged one of the kids at the center I knew it."

"You love Jack," Emma said gently. "You would never have left him willingly."

"Who did this to me?" Aspen asked, her tormented gaze lingering on her son.

"We're not sure," Dylan said. "Miguel and I are both on the team investigating your disappearance."

Aspen nodded weakly, then pressed her hands to her thighs as if to dry the dampness from them, then reached up toward Emma. "Can I hold him? Can I hold my baby?"

"Of course you can, Aspen," Emma said softly. She moved closer then settled down beside Aspen and jiggled Jack to quiet him.

Aspen's chin trembled and a tear slid down her cheek as she took the squirming baby into her arms. "You are mine, aren't you, Jack?" Aspen whispered. "My God, I've missed you." She hugged him to her and Jack immediately quieted, a little chirp coming from his mouth as he gazed up at his mother. Aspen brushed a hand across his thick, dark hair, then lowered a kiss to his cheek.

"I'm home now, son." She nuzzled his cheek with her own and Jack cooed, reached out his tiny fist and pulled a strand of her hair. Aspen laughed softly, then kissed his cheek. "I'm so sorry I left you, Jack. You must have been so scared…" She lifted him to her chest and hugged him tightly. "I promise I'll never leave you again."

A tenderness warmed Dylan's insides, as well as protective urges that nearly overpowered him.

But once again Aspen looked at him as if he was a stranger and a pang ripped through his heart. He was already coming to think of Jack—and Aspen—as his.

Which he couldn't allow himself to do.

There might have been another man in her life since they'd parted a year ago, another man who'd fathered her child.

But if there was, why hadn't he stepped up to take care of her and Jack?

And if there was, was he responsible for the attack on Aspen at the shelter, or had that been Perkins or Watts?

ASPEN'S HEART MELTED as she hugged her son to her. She finally felt whole again, as if she'd found the most important part of her missing life.

Yet frustration filled her as she studied her son's features and searched her memory banks for some semblance of details about his birth.

And the person who'd taken her away from him.

Dylan frowned, then asked Miguel to step outside, leaving her alone with Emma and the baby. Jack nestled against her shoulder, poked his thumb in his mouth and made sucking sounds.

"Are you really all right?" Emma asked.

"I will be," Aspen said, trying to sound convincing although questions swirled in her head.

Emma placed a comforting hand on her shoulder. "You know, I saw you," she said in a strained voice.

"What do you mean? Were you there at the accident?"

"No, not exactly." A shyness crept into Emma's blue eyes. "I forget that you have amnesia. I have psychic visions, Aspen. I saw you running from a man. I was terrified for you."

Aspen glanced down at Jack, who'd fallen asleep on her shoulder.

"Come on," Emma said, taking her elbow.

"Where are we going?"

"To put Jack back in his own bed."

Aspen followed her to the second bedroom, and a smile crept over her face at the sight of the nursery. For a brief moment, she saw an image of herself painting the room, of Emma helping her set up the changing table, of baby Jack watching the mobile twirl as it played a lullaby.

Another memory followed, this one of her and Emma playing together as children. Of Emma crying because a man had hurt her mother.

The memories blipped in and out of focus so quickly that she thought she might have imagined them. But they were so real, she knew they were truths pushing their way through the darkness that had consumed her the last few weeks. Those brief snippets gave her hope that she'd remember everything.

But the image of Emma crying disturbed her. Her father…no her mother's boyfriend had been abusive just as some of the women's husbands had been at the shelter.

She gently placed Jack inside the crib, then glanced at her left hand. She hadn't been wearing a ring on her finger when she'd been carried to the shelter. And there was no imprint indicating she'd ever had one.

She turned to Emma, debating over whether to ask, but she needed answers. The sisters had thought an abusive man might be after her. What if it was Jack's father?

"Emma, can I ask you something?"

"Of course, Aspen. Whatever you need."

Aspen tucked a yellow baby blanket over her son. "Who is Jack's father?"

Emma sighed softly and motioned for her to go to the den. After they settled on the sofa, Emma took her hand. "You didn't tell me, Aspen. All you said was that he wasn't in the picture."

"What about another friend? Is there someone else who I'd have told?"

"You're friends with Naomi Rainwater, another teacher on the reservation, but you told me that no one knew, and you intended to keep it that way."

Aspen frowned and glanced at the baby pictures on the mantle. Why wouldn't she have wanted anyone to know Jack's father?

Was he dangerous? Had she been running from him?

DYLAN ACEVEDO thought he would trap him. Thought he would keep the Indian girl and her kid safe by hovering over them.

But he was wrong.

Acevedo and the other pigs had treated him like dirt way too long. Had hunted him like a dog and would keep on hunting.

But he was the hunter now. He was watching their movements. Knew exactly where they were and what they were doing.

Because he was smarter than them all.

And the girl...killing her would serve his cause *and* torture Acevedo.

Pure pleasure bubbled in his chest as he flicked the cigarette butt to the ground outside Aspen's house and watched the embers spark to life on the brittle scrub grass, then slowly fade as the fire turned the blades a parched brown. He'd quit the cigarettes once, but his craving had returned.

No one knew he was here now or the reason why.

But they would soon.

Because the girl absolutely had to die.

A smile curved his lips.

In fact, he was looking forward to it.

Chapter Six

Dylan left Miguel to guard Aspen and Emma while he headed to the crime lab in Kenner City. But first he drove to Durango to his apartment to pack a bag to carry to Aspen's. He fully intended to stay with her until he was certain she was safe.

His mail had piled up, but he bypassed it and showered first, then packed his clothes and toiletries and stowed them in the rental car. His apartment seemed bare, quiet, empty. Lonely. As if no one lived there, not homey like Aspen's comfortable pueblo style house.

There was no baby here. No woman to love. No one to come home to or to care if he lived or died.

His chest ached, but he clamped a mental stronghold on his thoughts. He'd grown up in a loving home, but he'd gotten into some trouble as a teenager with a gang, but finally turned himself around. He'd told himself his job didn't fit with a wife and kid. That his work would put them in danger.

Although he'd stayed away, Aspen was still in danger.

And if he'd been around this last year, she might be safe now.

A brown manila envelope jutting out of the stack of mail caught his eye and he thumbed through the other pieces, then picked up the envelope with a frown. It was from Julie Grainger.

Ben Parrish and Tom Ryan had received packages from her with different medals inside. Ben had received the medal of St. Joan of Arc, the patron saint of captives, and seemed upset by the sight of it, Tom received a St. Christopher medal, the patron saint of travelers. Dylan wondered what his held and what the significance of each one meant.

Why had she sent each of them a gift? Had she known she was in trouble, that she might die?

Anxious to see if the contents led to a clue to the case, he ripped open the envelope and found a religious medal of Raphael the Archangel, the patron saint against nightmares.

He smiled at her choice.

Julie had known how much his sister's death and the Turnbull case had destroyed his nights. She'd tried to convince him to forgive himself, that he couldn't save them all, but dammit, he felt responsible.

His thumb brushed something else, and he dug deeper and found a photograph inside. An old black and white of a young Vincent Del Gardo and Belinda MacBride Douglas, Callie MacBride's mother.

What did the photo mean? That Del Gardo and Callie's mother had known each other years ago? That they'd been friends?

Or lovers?

Did Callie know they shared a past?

Hell, Del Gardo was a crime boss and their main

suspect in Julie Grainger's murder. They also believed that Boyd Perkins had killed Del Gardo, which had brought Del Gardo's rival crime organization, the Wayne family, into the limelight of the investigation, complicating matters more.

Dylan would take the medal and photo to the crime lab, show them to Callie and see what she said. Maybe it was a missing clue of some kind.

He hurried to the annex building housing the Kenner County Crime Unit, took the elevator to the third floor and decided to check with ballistics before he talked to Callie.

Jerry Griswold, the crime lab's firearms expert, was examining a bullet as he entered and had several more shell casings spread on the table.

"Are those from the shooter who fired at my car last night?"

Jerry nodded and gestured toward the screen indicating the National Integrated Ballistics Information Network. "Bia did good. Looks like the bullet casings came from a .38. I checked NIBIN but didn't find a match. If I had the weapon, I could compare and verify if it belongs to the shooter."

Dylan rubbed his chin, then caught himself as his fingers brushed his scar. Boyd Perkins had a nine millimeter. Of course, he could have a whole cache of weapons, for all they knew. "I'll do my best to find it," Dylan said.

He thanked Jerry, then headed to the other part of the lab. Callie, the head of forensics, glanced up from her microscope. "Hey, Acevedo."

"Hi, Callie. Have you had a chance to process the evidence from the Sisters of Mercy Women's Shelter in Mexican Hat?"

She called to Ava Wright, another forensics specialist, who appeared from a neighboring cube. "What's up, Callie?" She glanced at Dylan. "Hi, Acevedo."

He murmured hello. "Did you get the results on that hair I collected from the women's shelter?"

Ava nodded. "It belongs to a Native American male. That's about all I can tell you right now. Bring me a suspect and I can match it."

A Native American? "What about Sherman Watts?"

She shook her head. "Sorry, not a match."

He frowned, his mind spinning. "Did you get anything on the piece of fabric?"

"A denim shirt, cotton blend, inexpensive. The brand is one you'd find at the trading post or a dozen different stores, including online." She drummed her fingers on the table. "So far nothing distinctive about any of it, but I'll keep checking."

"How about the paint samples from my car?"

"We're still working on those."

He pulled the envelope from inside his jacket. "Callie, I stopped by my apartment and found this waiting. Julie must have mailed it to me before she died."

A wary expression made her lips thin. "What's inside?"

He hesitated, not wanting to upset her. After all, the man with her mother in the photo was a big-time criminal. But they had to know what the picture meant and if it was significant.

First though, he showed her the medal, and Callie examined it with gloved hands. "Why did she send Raphael the Archangel to you?" Callie asked.

"He's the patron saint against nightmares." Dylan scrubbed a hand over the back of his neck. "And during the Turnbull case, God knows I had my share of nightmares."

"We all had bad dreams about that one." Callie offered him a sympathetic look, then gestured to the medal. "I'll dust it for prints."

Dylan nodded. "There's something else."

Callie's brow pinched. "What?"

"Look inside."

She hesitated warily, but removed the photograph, her mouth twisting as she studied it. "It's my mother and Vincent Del Gardo."

He nodded, watching as the wheels spun in her head.

Finally a low sound of discomfort escaped her. "Oh, my God." Her gaze rose to meet his, shock settling in the depths of her eyes. "It looks like they knew each other. Like…"

Her sentence trailed off, and Dylan understood the dark place her train of thought had carried her. Del Gardo had his arm around her mother in the photo, and they were both smiling.

As if they had a personal relationship.

Before they could speculate further, Bree and Patrick Martinez entered the room. Patrick was the sheriff of Kenner City and Sabrina a Ute police detective. They'd struck up a romance while investigating Julie's murder and Aspen's disappearance.

"We heard you found Aspen," Bree said. "I'm glad she's alive."

Dylan explained about her amnesia and Bree sighed. "I'll try to stop by and see her. That poor girl and her baby have been through so much."

Patrick grinned and placed his arms around Sabrina's

waist, pulling her up against him. "Speaking of babies. We're going to have one of our own."

"That's wonderful," Callie said. "How far along are you?"

Bree placed a hand over her belly. "Three months."

Dylan congratulated them, although a seed of envy stirred within him.

He hadn't thought much about being a father before, but now that he suspected Jack might be his son, he couldn't think of anything else.

His last encounter with Frank Turnbull flashed back, though, and he grimaced, doubt seeping into places in his mind he didn't like to visit.

Like—maybe he didn't deserve to be a father.

Maybe that was the reason Aspen hadn't contacted him....

She'd met him, *been* with him right after he'd arrested Turnbull. He'd been pent up, so full of rage that he'd admitted that he'd almost killed the man in cold blood.

That he had wanted to inflict pain on Turnbull, make the man suffer before he died.

Hell, he'd tried to pour all that anger and emotion into making love to her, into passion, but there were moments he feared it had bled through.

That he'd frightened her.

"Well, we have rounds to make," Patrick said with a sheepish grin. "Keep us posted on any new evidence. If Perkins and Watts are hiding out on Ute land or in Kenner City, we'll find them. It's only a matter of time."

"Yeah, let's just make that arrest before someone else dies," Dylan growled.

Murmurs of agreement rippled through the room, then they said goodbye.

When Callie turned back, Dylan saw the turmoil on her face as she glanced back at the picture.

But his mind was already straying to the unanswered questions regarding Aspen. He could continue living in a fantasy world, imagining that Jack was his son, or he could find out the truth. And the truth might lead to the unsub after Aspen.

Her safety was all that mattered.

"How about the DNA sample from Jack Meadows?"

Callie and Ava exchanged curious looks. "You think the baby's father might have attacked Aspen?"

He shrugged. "Just covering all the bases. If Watts or Perkins weren't at the shelter, then someone else is after Aspen, too."

"We haven't finished running the DNA," Callie said. "You know paternity tests take time, Dylan."

Frustration knotted his neck. "What if you had a sample to compare it to? Could you at least tell if it was a match?"

"That would help," Ava said. "Do you have one?"

Dylan hesitated, not sure if he wanted to divulge his personal reasons for wanting the test rushed. But he wanted answers. He *needed* answers. And who knew how long it would take for Aspen to remember.

He cleared his throat. "Yeah, mine."

ASPEN FELT ANTSY, as if she was crawling out of her skin. For some reason, having Dylan around had given her a safety net, and although she was comfortable with Emma, the tension of struggling to recall details of her past was draining her. She kept imagining a faceless man attacking her, chasing her, trying to kill her.

Kept wondering who that face belonged to.

Miguel had moved to the porch with his computer and made himself scarce, obviously to give her and Emma privacy. She wondered about her cousin's relationship to Miguel and wanted to ask. Frustration filled her. This was yet another lost part of the past that everyone knew but her.

"You really don't remember anything that happened or how you wound up in that shelter?" Emma asked as they put together a light supper of pasta and salad.

Aspen shook her head, feeling inept, as if she was failing her son. "Not really. But when that car ran us off the road last night, I experienced déjà vu. And I've had nightmares for weeks…."

"I'm so sorry about all this," Emma said quietly. "It must be terribly frustrating."

"It is," Aspen admitted, wringing her hands together. "I don't even remember giving birth. How could a woman possibly forget one of the most important days of her life?"

Emma smiled with compassion. "Maybe you didn't want to remember the labor pain."

Aspen laughed softly. "Were you with me when I was in labor?"

Emma nodded. "Yes. The midwife on the reservation delivered Jack."

Aspen returned to the counter and tossed the salad. "Tell me the truth, Emma. What do you think happened? Why would someone want to hurt me?"

Emma hesitated, her words and tone measured. "How much did Dylan tell you?"

Aspen frowned. "Not much. Just that they thought I might have witnessed a crime."

"That's true," Emma said cautiously.

Aspen seemed to sense she knew much more. "Tell me," Aspen said, almost pleading. "I hate being in the dark like this. Everyone looks at me like I'm a freak."

"You're not a freak," Emma said gently. "But the doctor warned that we should let you remember on your own, not to push you."

Irritation gnawed at Aspen. "It's driving me crazy not knowing." She touched Emma's arm. "Please. I'm not as fragile as everyone thinks. I need to know the truth."

Emma studied her for a moment, then seemed to accept what she'd said and gestured to the kitchen table. "Then sit down, and I'll tell you what I know."

"Thank you." Aspen claimed a kitchen chair while Emma took the one opposite her.

Emma folded her hands on the table. "Dylan and Miguel are brothers. Twins actually. Dylan works for the FBI. Miguel is a forensic specialist for the Kenner County Crime Unit." She hesitated and inhaled a deep breath as if to fortify herself, and Aspen realized that her disappearance had deeply upset her cousin. But before she voiced her concerns and an apology, Emma continued.

"One of their friends, a federal agent named Julie Grainger, was murdered during the process of an ongoing investigation into Vincent Del Gardo, a major crime boss. The FBI believe that a hit man named Boyd Perkins killed Del Gardo and Julie." She paused as if weighing her words and Aspen encouraged her to continue.

"They found evidence that you might have witnessed a hit man, Boyd Perkins, who worked with a man named

Sherman Watts, a local Ute man, dumping Julie's body. Apparently they saw you and chased you, causing you to crash. We thought you'd drowned in the river, but somehow you must have escaped."

Aspen massaged her temple, the horrific images of fighting the river current sending a shudder through her. "That makes sense. I've had dreams about nearly drowning and being chased."

Emma closed her hand over Aspen's. "I'm so sorry, honey."

Aspen squeezed Emma's fingers. "So how did you and Miguel get involved?"

A faraway look settled in Emma's eyes, one that indicated that Emma did see things more deeply than others. "When they found your car, Jack was inside. They brought him to me to keep until we found out what happened to you." Emma traced a finger along the hand woven placement. "Because of my visions, they had me visit the place where your car crashed. I sensed that you were alive, but I couldn't see anything specific to help."

Aspen's chest clenched at the frustration in her cousin's words. "I'm sorry. That must have been difficult for you, Emma."

Aspen swallowed. Moisture gathered in Emma's eyes. "Yes, it was. I was so afraid you were dead…."

"No, I'm all right. And thank you for taking care of Jack for me."

"I love him, Aspen. You two are the only family I have."

Aspen hugged her, the two of them bonding, memories of other times when she and Emma had shared problems surfacing. Aspen traced a finger over Emma's hair, pushing it back behind her ear. "So tell me about you and Miguel."

Emma dabbed at her eyes, then glanced toward the porch. "Miguel was working the case with Dylan. At first he didn't believe me, but then I led him to the gutter where we found a Native American leather necklace in the snow. That's how they connected Perkins to Watts and to you."

Aspen's mind raced. "So I was just in the wrong place at the wrong time?"

"I'm afraid so," Emma said. "Then…"

"Then what?"

Fear darkened Emma's eyes. "One night I had a vision and went back to the river, hoping to remember more. But Sherman Watts was there and tried to kill me."

Aspen clasped her hand. "Oh, my God."

Emma shivered. "I was terrified, but Miguel showed up and saved me."

"And he's been hanging around ever since," Aspen said with a smile.

Emma blushed and ducked her head. "Yes, we've grown close."

"I'm glad you found someone," Aspen said sincerely. "He certainly seems protective of you."

Emma blushed again. "Yes, well… Apparently the Feds think that Watts and Perkins are hiding out on the reservation somewhere. They're afraid he'll come back for me and for you." She glanced up at Aspen with terror streaking her face. "Apparently they did come after you."

The breath in Aspen's lungs tightened.

"But don't worry," Emma said. "Miguel will protect me, and I know that Dylan will stay with you until the men are arrested."

Aspen shifted, threading her fingers together. The thought of Dylan protecting her made her uneasy. He seemed angry, intense…and darkly sexy.

She was attracted to him in a way that she sensed she hadn't been attracted to another man before.

The sound of an engine jerked her from her thoughts, and Emma went to the door while Aspen glanced out the window. Speaking of the devil, the sexy agent was back. She could practically see the chords of muscle playing on his chest beneath that gun holster. Could feel the power radiating off of him.

Dylan met Miguel on the steps, both speaking in hushed tones that made her wonder what he'd learned at the crime lab.

A second later, a big black truck parked in the drive and a tall Indian climbed out, his sun-streaked ponytail accentuating a lean angular face. He was tanned and lanky, his body coiled with tension. "Who's that?" Aspen asked.

"Kurt Lightfoot," Emma said. "He works for the Weeminuche Construction Authority. He's very adamant about enforcing the code that all projects are performed on a merit shop basis with maximum use of Native American laborers and craftsmen."

"Do I know him?" Aspen asked.

Emma's face twisted. "Yes. You've gone out a few times."

Aspen's head throbbed with all the revelations. How well did she know Kurt? And how did she feel about him?

Dylan's stance turned protective, and he blocked the doorway, his arms crossed, his muscular legs spread wide. She imagined him interrogating Kurt and felt a margin of relief that he was present, that she didn't have to face this other man alone.

The tunnel of darkness into which she'd fallen seemed endless and growing deeper and more frightening every second. If she'd dated Kurt, why would she be afraid of him?

A tense heartbeat passed, then the three men stepped inside, Miguel and Dylan on each side of Kurt, like armed guards—or cobras ready to strike. "There's someone here to see you," Dylan said, although distrust and something even darker laced his voice.

Anger?

A smile broadened Kurt's angular face and he strode over and pulled her into his arms, then spoke in the ancient language of their ancestors. "Thank the gods, I'm glad you're home."

She studied him, trying to place him in her lost past. "What are you doing here?"

He cupped her face in his hands and kissed her briefly.

She forced herself not to react, waiting for some kind of response to shift inside her, for a pleasant memory to surface, for her to want this man.

But no sparks flew, no tingle of attraction or passion stirred as it had when Dylan Acevedo had first looked into her eyes at that shelter.

He pulled away slightly, examining her with narrowed eyes. "I came to see you and Jack," he said. "I've missed you both so much."

Distrust flooded her along with another disturbing thought. Could Kurt possibly be Jack's father?

And if so, why did she feel no attraction to him, only the need to put distance between them?

DYLAN BARELY BIT BACK A CURSE.

This big Indian in the suede-fringed jacket was the man Aspen had been dating? And he had just kissed her as if he owned her.

Pure rage ripped through him like an out-of-control brush fire, eating him alive. He fisted his hands and started to yank the man away from her, but Miguel caught his arm and gave him a warning look that reminded him of when they were teenagers after Teresa had died, and Dylan had been quick-tempered, spoiling for a fight.

Dammit. His brother was right. He was acting like a crazed, jealous husband, when he had no claims on Aspen.

But what if he wanted to have claims on her?

And what if Jack was his?

To fill the awkward silence, Emma rallied to explain about Lightfoot's work for the WCA, making his anger mount. Dammit, the guy sounded like a stand-up man.

But not everyone was as honorable as they appeared on the surface. Plus, the hair he'd collected at the shelter when Aspen had been attacked belonged to a Native American. What if Lightfoot had tracked down Aspen and broken into her room?

He'd have to get a warrant to compare his DNA.

And until he found the answers he needed, he'd stick by Aspen 24/7.

Aspen took a step back, and massaged her temple as if fighting a headache. "Jack fell asleep. I don't want to disturb him."

Lightfoot shoved his hands in the pockets of his faded jeans. "Of course. How are you feeling?"

"Actually I'm tired." Aspen's gaze flitted to Emma, then to him as if pleading for a way out.

"We had an accident on the way back last night," Dylan said, jumping in to circumvent a long stay by the other man. "The doctor gave her a clean bill of health, but she didn't get much rest."

Aspen nodded and rubbed at her head again. "Maybe we could visit another time, Kurt. I need to lie down for a while."

"I don't mind staying," Lightfoot offered with a shrug. "I can sleep on the couch and be here if Jack wakes up."

"That won't be necessary," Dylan cut in. "I'm Aspen's bodyguard until the threat to her is over and the men who attacked her are in jail."

Anger glinted in Lightfoot's eyes a second before he masked it. "Good. Nice to know the FBI is doing their job instead of ignoring us Utes."

Anger shot through Dylan at Lightfoot's implication, but again, Miguel held him in check with a forceful look.

Aspen excused herself and went to her room, and Lightfoot shifted uncomfortably, glancing at the nursery as if he wanted to go in. As if he had a right.

But Emma took him by the arm and diplomatically led him to the door. "Why don't you come back once she's had time to rest and adjust."

Dylan waited until she walked him outside, then went to Aspen's door, knocked and pushed it open a fraction. "He's gone. Are you all right?"

"Yes." Jack stirred and Aspen rushed to the nursery then returned, cradling him as if she'd never let him go again while Emma finished preparing dinner and set it on the table.

The meal was strained, and Aspen appeared fatigued, so Emma and Miguel said good-night afterward. Dylan insisted on cleaning up while Aspen fed Jack, then he watched as she read him a story, sang a Ute lullaby to him and rocked him to sleep.

His chest grew hollow with the fear that this family wasn't his to have, an ache so deep inside him that he didn't know what he'd do if he had to walk away from her and her son.

Yet what if she didn't want him in her life when the investigation ended? What if there was another man, either Lightfoot or someone else, who had stolen her heart while he'd stayed away?

Jack fell asleep and she tucked the baby into the crib, then yawned, and Dylan encouraged her to go to bed.

But, dammit, he wanted to join her. If he touched her, held her, kissed her, would she remember what they'd shared?

Of course, he did none of that. He was working a case, and staying alert meant keeping his emotional distance.

And protecting his heart.

But after forty-eight hours with no sleep, exhaustion finally claimed him, and he stretched out on her sofa and fell asleep, dreaming about the night he and Aspen had met.

But sometime around 4:00 a.m., he jerked awake, his senses on full alert, his heart pounding.

Had he heard something outside?

A scream?

Aspen or Jack crying out?

He grabbed his gun off the coffee table, rose and checked Aspen's room, but she seemed to be resting. He tiptoed to the nursery, but when he peeked inside, Jack was sound asleep.

Nerves cramping his chest, he went back to the den, eased back the window curtain and looked outside. Darkness bathed the property, the stillness almost alarming in its own right. In the distance a motor rumbled, and a prairie dog wailed its call.

Dylan had to check outside.

Senses honed, he inched to the front door, unlocked it and slowly cracked the door open, the chain still intact. His gaze shot sideways, searching, scanning, his fingers gripping his weapon, ready to fire.

A stray cat trotted across the dirt, and dust swirled in a cloud from the road in the distance as if a car had just roared away. He glanced down at the porch and an icy chill rippled through his blood.

Frank Turnbull's calling card—a piece of thunderwood lay at his feet.

No…it couldn't be possible. Turnbull was supposed to be in jail….

Chapter Seven

She was drowning.

The raging, icy current dragged her under, slamming her already battered body against the rocks. Pain shot through her limbs and head, and she battled for a breath but the water slapped her face and she choked.

She opened her eyes, saw the bottom of the river, felt the murky floor sucking at her feet, mud seeping into her shoes, the darkness swirling above her. Her head throbbed, her lungs aching as if they were going to explode....

What had happened?

A faint memory stirred. The car crash. Then the men chasing her...clubbing her in the head...then the black emptiness.

And now the icy river, her burial spot.

Her lungs squeezed, desperate for oxygen, and she was fading, her energy waning. She wasn't going to make it.

Terror crawled through her.

No...she didn't want to die.

She was a good swimmer—she had to make her arms

and legs work. Push away the numbness, forget the pain. One stroke, then another.

She had to survive. Someone was waiting on her. Someone important.

Determination raged through her, and she fought the waves, using her feet for momentum to push off the bottom and propel herself upward. Suddenly she was moving, swimming again. Her lungs begged for air, and her teeth chattered, but she ignored the burning ache and pushed harder.

One stroke, two, three, kick, kick, kick… She imagined the night sky above, the stars, a sliver of moonlight… Warmth.

So beautiful. She would see it again. She would feel warm and safe. Then she'd go home. Home to…home to something…

Finally she broke the surface, gasping for air. Light and cold air swirled around her, disorienting her as to which way to swim. She struggled to orient herself. The current tugged at her again, and she let it carry her forward.

Finally, through the shadows she spotted trees in the distance and kicked harder, aiming for the shore. Another stroke. Another. She could do it. She would make it to the edge and climb out.

Someone was waiting on her. Someone important. Someone who loved her and needed her to survive.

And then she was there, the riverbank only inches away. She reached for the edge, lost her footing and slipped under again. But sheer determination spiked her adrenaline and she kicked to the surface. Her arms shook as she clawed at a tree branch and used it to drag herself to the bank. Coughing and spitting out water, she collapsed in a fit of exhaustion, shivering and shaking, too numb to move.

A second later, fear shot through her again.

But this time she was in the bed, and a man was lurching toward her. A knife glinted in the darkness.

She screamed, and kicked at him as he approached. She'd survived once, she could do it again.

His angular face filled the darkness, his breath hissing across her cheek as he grabbed her. A sliver of moonlight caught his profile. He had high cheekbones. Long hair.

He was an Indian.

But who was he? And why did he want her dead?

DYLAN HAD JUST BAGGED the piece of thunderwood when Aspen's scream shattered the silence. He slammed the front door shut, grabbed his gun and raced to her bedroom, sweat beading on his neck.

What if Turnbull had escaped? What if he'd gotten in to Aspen's room?

Darkness bathed the room, so he flipped on the light, quickly searching for the intruder. But he didn't see one.

A quick glance at the window confirmed it was closed.

Aspen was sitting up in bed, trembling as she rocked herself back and forth.

He inhaled a steadying breath, stowed his gun in the waistband of his slacks, then walked over to the bed. "Aspen…"

She jerked her head toward him, her terror-glazed eyes wrenching his heart.

"What happened?" he asked gruffly. "Are you all right?"

For a moment, she simply stared at him as if she hadn't

understood what he'd said. Hating to see her in agony, he inched closer to the bed, wanting to console her.

"You're safe now," he said as he slowly lowered himself to the mattress beside her. "I won't let anyone hurt you again." He stroked her arms gently, aching to hold her. "Was someone here in the room?"

Her face seemed to crumple but she shook her head no, her teeth chattering. "I was running from a man, then he hit me over the head and threw me in the river. Then I was drowning," she whispered. "Drowning in the icy water. It was so cold…and I couldn't breathe."

"It was a dream, a memory of your attack," he said. "But you're safe in your house now."

She shoved a tangled strand of hair from her damp cheek. "I fought, had to swim, to escape. And then I was in the room at the shelter and that man was there. He had a knife and he came after me."

In light of the piece of thunderwood on her doorstep, her reference to a knife sent alarm down his spine. "Could you describe the knife?"

She frowned, her eyes narrowing as if in thought.

"Could it have been a Ute ceremonial knife? Was it made of white quartz and cedar wood?"

"I don't know. I didn't get a look at it," she said in a hoarse voice.

He tilted up her chin, forcing her to look at him. "What else do you remember, Aspen?"

"He was an Indian," she said. "I think I might have seen him before. Maybe hanging around the shelter."

Hope sprouted inside him. If she'd seen him, at least he'd know who to go after. "Was it the same man who threw you in the river?"

She clenched the sheet between her fingers. "No… I'm not sure."

Maybe he should show her some photos, see if they jogged her memory. But the doctor had warned him not to push. "Do you remember any more details, the color of his hair, his height?"

Her eyes were glazed as she stared up at him. "He had long hair, high cheekbones—I think he might have been Kurt Lightfoot."

He clenched his jaw. Maybe his theory about Lightfoot being Jack's father was on target. Maybe he hadn't wanted to claim the child and he'd tracked down Aspen at the shelter to silence her.

Then he'd shown up at Aspen's to test her to see if her amnesia was real.

Which meant he had to be nervous.

Dylan gave her arm a reassuring squeeze. "All right. I'll get a warrant for a DNA sample from him and run a background check. We can compare the DNA to the hair I found at the shelter."

He started to get up, but she grabbed his hand, clinging to him, and heat bolted through him. She was vulnerable now, not asking for a repeat of their Vegas week.

Although he couldn't erase the erotic images from his mind.

But if Jack is yours, she didn't tell you.

His anger returned, sharp and intense, and he steeled himself against feeling anything else. He had a job to do and he'd damn well do it.

"But what if I'm wrong?" Aspen said. "I don't want to accuse an innocent man of something he didn't do."

He frowned, wondering if she might have had feelings for the man. "Trust me to see just how innocent Lightfoot is."

Her big dark eyes studied him, probing, looking lost.

She finally nodded, and his breath whooshed out in relief. "I'm going to call and get a security system installed today. I want you and Jack to stay at Emma's while I go back to the crime lab."

"All right."

He stepped outside and phoned the warden at the Colorado State Penitentiary. Sweat beaded on his neck as he waited to be patched through to his office.

It seemed like an eternity before the man answered in a thick Hispanic accent. "Warden Fernandez."

"Warden, this is Special Agent Dylan Acevedo."

A long sigh echoed over the line. "You were on my list to call today."

That didn't sound good. "Really. About Frank Turnbull? Has he escaped?"

Another tense pause. "We're not certain. We think he may be dead."

Dead? God, he hoped to hell the man was.

"What do you mean, you *think* he may be?"

"Yesterday he was on a bus with three other prisoners we were transferring to the ADX in Florence."

The ADX, the Alcatraz of the Rockies, where the prisoners deemed most dangerous and in need of tightest control were locked away. The home of the notorious Terry Nichols, Eric Robert Rudolph, Timothy McVeigh and Richard Reid, the shoe bomber.

The air in Dylan's lungs stilled. "And?"

"And the bus had an accident, caught on fire and exploded. There were six people on board—the driver, two guards and three prisoners. We found six bodies. So we're assuming Turnbull died in the accident, but the ME is studying the remains. That's going to take time, though. Wasn't much left but charred skin and bones. He's requested dental and medical records to verify the IDs."

"Tell him to rush it," Dylan said.

"You don't have to remind me. These were all lifers who needed maximum security."

Dylan pulled a hand down his chin. Two others as mean as Turnbull. Not good.

"We're investigating the accident to make sure it wasn't an attempted prison escape or sabotage from an outsider."

Damn, that would create panic.

"How did you find out?" Fernandez asked. "We've tried to keep it quiet so as not to frighten locals."

People needed to be warned. "I'm on the Ute Reservation, investigating the murder of one of our agents and working protective custody of a Ute woman. Early this morning, I found a piece of thunderwood on her doorstep."

"Turnbull's calling card," Fernandez muttered.

"Exactly." And Aspen fit the profile. Plus, Turnbull had vowed to get revenge on Dylan at his trial.

"Could be a copycat. Someone who knows you worked the case trying to yank your chain."

"I know. But we need to verify that Turnbull didn't escape," Dylan said, trying to focus. "If he has, he's been planning it and may have had help from the outside. I want to look at all his prison correspondence. Because if he's out, he'll start his crime spree all over again."

And he had to stop him before any more women died.

ASPEN MANAGED TO GRAB A SHOWER, dress and make coffee before Jack woke up, although her muscles and limbs were still sore. The sound of her son cooing brought a smile to her lips, and she hurried to the nursery and stood over him, soaking in his features.

This was her child. Her little boy with the thick jet-black hair, brown skin and high cheekbones. He definitely had her Ute blood.

Except for those startling deep blue eyes…

He waved his hands and kicked his feet, and she picked him up and hugged him to her chest, savoring the sweet scent of baby powder and softness. "Good morning, little one. You're in a good mood today."

"Maybe because he's happy to have his mother home," Dylan said behind her.

Her chest squeezed. "Poor little guy must have thought I'd abandoned him."

"He seems resilient," Dylan said.

She carried Jack to the changing table and unsnapped the legs of his sleeper, laughing as he tried to put his toes in his mouth. "You silly boy, you. You can't eat your feet."

Dylan walked over and watched him for a moment, an odd look on his face. But a knock sounded at the door and he quickly left to answer it.

She finished the diaper change and snapped his jimmies, then carried him to the kitchen and retrieved a bottle while Dylan let two men from the security company he'd called inside to install the security system.

While they worked on the installation, she placed Jack in his baby seat, then made breakfast, pancakes with the fresh blueberries Emma had stored in the refrigerator.

Jack cooed and shook a toy rattle between his pudgy

fingers while they ate, intrigued by Dylan when he turned to talk to him. But tension stretched between them, a silence filled with the questions she couldn't answer.

"Thank you for breakfast," Dylan said as he finished the stack of hotcakes and carried his plate to the sink. He rinsed it and placed it in the dishwasher, then started to clean up the pan.

"I'll take care of that," Aspen said, a warmth enveloping her. It felt oddly comforting to share breakfast with the man. Comforting and sexy...

And vaguely familiar, as if they'd done it before.

"Then I'm going to give Jack a bath before we go to Emma's."

Dylan nodded. "I phoned Miguel and told him you were coming."

"Thanks."

The workers finished with the security system, and Dylan explained how to set the alarm and deactivate it. "You need to leave it on at all times, even when you're home."

She nodded, picked up Jack and took him to her bathroom to bathe him. But anxiety plucked at her nerves. She didn't want to live in fear for the rest of her life.

She just hoped that Dylan found the person after her soon so life could return to normal. Maybe then her memories would surface, and she'd remember who Jack's father was and why he wasn't in her son's life.

AFTER THE SECURITY TEAM LEFT, Dylan drove Aspen and Jack to Emma's. Unlike, Aspen's house with its

Native American look and feel, Emma's was a small ranch, the furnishings eclectic and more modern.

Aspen carried Jack inside and Dylan followed. Emma had set up a crib in the second bedroom along with baby paraphernalia, and eagerly welcomed her cousin and son inside. From the loving expression on Emma's face, she'd grown quite attached to Jack during their time together.

Aspen smiled gratefully as they settled in to visit, although her features were still strained.

Dylan gestured to the door. "Miguel, can I talk to you outside for a minute?"

Miguel nodded, his eyes narrowing as they moved to the front porch. "What's up?"

Dylan explained about the piece of thunderwood and his conversation with the warden.

"Good God," Miguel muttered. "You think Turnbull may have escaped?"

Dylan shrugged. "I don't know, but we have to consider the possibility."

Miguel grunted. "Jeez. This just keeps getting worse. Now we're not only hunting Perkins and Watts but possibly an escaped felon."

Dylan grimaced. "Yeah, and not just a felon, a man who likes to carve up Ute women."

Miguel's face paled. "I was on my way into the crime lab today for work. But I hate to leave Emma and Aspen alone."

"We can't," Dylan said. "If you need to go in, call the locals to dispatch a unit out here until I get back."

"Where are you going?" Miguel asked.

"Last night Aspen remembered that the man who attacked her at the shelter was Indian. The crime lab has a hair I found at the shelter. I want to get a warrant for a DNA sample from Kurt Lightfoot to see if it belongs to him."

"Did they compare it to Watts's?"

Dylan nodded. "No match. And the hair could have been there before. Or the man who came in could be one of the abusers another woman at the shelter was running from. But if it's Lightfoot's, then I can bring him in for questioning."

"I'll call Bree," Miguel said. "Ask her to watch Emma and Aspen. It sounds like the lab needs me now."

Dylan nodded. "Thanks, man. And if you don't mind, check with the state ME and see if he's ID'ed the bodies from the prison bus. We need to know if one of them is Turnbull's."

HE STUDIED THE PHOTO of Aspen Meadows, his hands twitching to finish her off. She should have died in that river, but she was stronger than anyone thought. Had fought her way out of the raging current and wound up being rescued.

Those stark features, her high cheekbones, long black hair, big brown eyes—the Ute woman had seen too much with those eyes.

The paper said she had amnesia. But her memory could return at any minute.

Then she'd squeal on him and he'd rot in prison.

No, he wouldn't get caught.

Rage shot through his blood, and he tensed and drew

an X over the picture. Frustrated, he crumpled the paper in his hands and threw it against the wall.

Yes, Aspen Meadows had to die. The sooner the better. And he'd make sure the end was painful....

Chapter Eight

On the way to the Kenner County Crime Lab, Dylan phoned Tom Ryan and asked him to assemble the other agents and crime scene specialists for a meeting in the conference room.

Ben Parrish and Tom Ryan were the first to join him and Miguel, then Callie, Ava, Jerry Griswold and Bart Flemming appeared.

"Griffin Vaughn, his son, Luke, and new wife, Sophie, have come to Kenner City," Ben said.

"Interesting," Tom commented.

Everyone looked exhausted and frustrated as if they'd worked too many hours for too many weeks now with no hope of seeing the end in sight.

But he and Tom and Ben had been friends with Julie and had vowed to avenge her death.

And Aspen's safety was personal. *Very* personal.

Tom grabbed a cup of coffee and rapped his knuckles on the table to get everyone's attention. "Let's have an update. Any leads on where Sherman Watts and Boyd Perkins are hiding out?"

Ben shook his head. "No spottings. They could be

anywhere." He paused with a hand gesture. "Or long gone by now."

Dylan grimaced. "I doubt that. With Aspen alive, they'll want to tie up loose ends. The fingerprint we found at the Griffin estate points to the fact that Perkins shot Del Gardo and that he's a hired gun with the Wayne crime family." Dylan gestured toward Jerry. "Griswold identified the bullet casings from my vehicle as coming from a .38. Could have been from Watts's gun." He glanced at Ava. "How about the paint samples from the car that ran me off the road?"

Ava consulted her notes. "They match the samples we found on Aspen's car, the ones that belong to Watts's vehicle."

Dammit. "So they are after her," he said, and everyone exchanged frustrated looks. So far Watts and Perkins had been as invisible as Ute ghosts.

"There's another complication," he continued, then gestured to the whiteboard where they were keeping lists of all the clues, evidence and suspects. "The hair I found in the room at the Sisters of Mercy Women's Shelter where Aspen was attacked belonged to an Indian, but not Watts. So we're also looking for another suspect."

"Why would someone else want to harm Aspen?" Ben asked.

Dylan added Kurt Lightfoot's name to the board. "We're not sure yet. But a Ute man named Kurt Lightfoot has shown interest in Aspen and her son." He hesitated then continued, forcing his emotions at bay as he glanced at Callie. "Do we have an ID on the baby's father?"

Callie shook her head. "Hopefully soon."

Dylan tugged at his shirt collar. "Apparently Lightfoot and Aspen dated for a while. I'm not sure how, or if the relationship ended but we need to check him out." He directed his attention to Bart, their computer analyst. "Lightfoot works for the Weeminuche Construction Authority. Dig up everything you can find on him."

"Will do," Bart said with a nod.

"And, Ryan," Dylan said. "I need a warrant for Lightfoot's DNA."

"You'll have it before you leave today," Tom said. "And, Bart, make that background check on the man a priority. I may need it for the warrant."

Bart stood. "I'll get on it now."

"Wait," Dylan said before he could exit the room. "There's something else."

Concerned looks floated around the room, then Dylan explained. "Frank Turnbull, the Ute Slicer, was being transported from the Colorado State Pen to the ADX Florence when his bus crashed and burned. Six charred bodies were found in the van. It appears Turnbull may have died, but the ME's analyzing the remains now to confirm. Until we have confirmation, we have to work under the assumption that he might have escaped."

"And you're basing that on what?" Ava asked.

Sweat trickled down the back of Dylan's neck. "On the piece of thunderwood someone left on Aspen Meadow's doorstep."

Startled gasps and low curses met his announcement. "Jesus, people will panic if this news leaks out," Ava said.

"Maybe we should issue a warning so the Ute women will be careful," Callie suggested.

Tom gave a brisk shake of his head. "Not until we know more."

"I'm going to push the ME," Miguel said. "See if we can get answers on that ID ASAP."

Callie gestured to speak. "I'll drive up there and offer my help. Won't hurt to have a set of our eyes on the investigation there."

"Thanks, Callie." Dylan felt marginally better knowing she'd be breathing down their necks. "I requested all of Turnbull's prison correspondence for analysis. I'm going to look at his visitors, letters, phone calls, e-mails, along with any inmates who might have befriended him," Dylan said. "If this so-called accident was the result of an attempted prison break, we need to find out."

"You think someone on the outside might have helped him escape?" Ben asked.

"It's possible. Let's face it. Turnbull didn't get away with ten murders before we stopped him because he's dumb. He's cunning, manipulative, well organized, a methodical cold-blooded killer. We all know the kind of violence he's capable of." He paused, wiping at his brow as he tried to banish the images of the dead girls from his mind. "And we all also know that some women get off on writing prisoners. If he has a fan club, I want to know about it."

"Good point," Tom said.

"And if Turnbull is dead?" Ben asked.

Dylan was sweating again. "Then we may have a copycat on our hands." He hesitated. "And Aspen fits the profile. With all the hype about her disappearance, and me working the case, he might come after her."

"All the more reason to smoke out anyone else who's after her," Ben mumbled.

Tom met his gaze, his brow pinching. "I agree. Dylan, I've been thinking about what you said. That Perkins and Watts won't stop until they kill Aspen."

A cold knot of anxiety clawed at Dylan's insides as tension thrummed through the room. "And?"

Tom's gaze turned to stone, and Dylan knew he wasn't going to like whatever Tom suggested.

"This mess has gone on way too long. We're all tired of chasing our asses and coming up with nothing." He planted his hands on the conference table and gave Dylan a dead-serious look. "I think we should consider setting a trap for the men. Flesh them out."

Dylan gritted his teeth. "How do you suggest we do that?"

Tom shrugged as if the answer was inevitable. "We use Aspen as bait."

ASPEN FED JACK HIS BOTTLE while Emma prepared lunch, a well of sadness engulfing her as she thought of the weeks she'd lost with her little boy. "The word *Ute* comes from the Spanish name for our tribe, Yuta," she said softly as Jack gazed up at her. "Most Utes speak English, but I'll try to teach you a few of the words of our Native language."

Jack splayed one little hand on the edge of the bottle and sucked vigorously. Apparently her son had a good appetite and seemed to be healthy despite the situation.

"The word *maiku* is a friendly greeting, and *tog'oiak'* means thank you." She stroked his thick black hair. "A long time ago our people lived in wickiups. They were small round houses shaped like a cone and made of a willow frame covered with brush. But times have changed and now we live in houses on a reservation." She laughed as he squirmed against her, grateful she hadn't forgotten her heritage. "A long time ago we traveled the rivers by building rafts. And we still like to hunt and fish. When you get big enough, I'll take you to see the Bear Dance and the Sun Dance at Mesa Verde, and as you grow up, I'll teach you more about the Ute ceremonies and how to use roots and plants for healing."

Bree smiled at her from the kitchen where she was slicing fruit for a fruit salad. But the gun at the detective's waist reminded her of the real reason Bree had stopped by.

"You're a wonderful mother, Aspen," Bree said.

Suddenly an image of her and Emma drifted into Aspen's consciousness. The two of them as little girls playing with their dolls on the reservation. Then another, she and Emma skipping after her mother to the trading post. Her mother buying penny candy for them as a treat. Emma being quiet, shy, almost withdrawn at times. Emma finally confiding that sometimes she saw things she didn't want to see.

Like her mother's boyfriend hitting her.

And then her grandmother's ghost…

She glanced up as Emma placed salads and herbal tea on the table. "Emma?"

Her face must have revealed her concern because Emma rushed to the table and sat down. "What is it?"

"A memory…I think."

"Of the man who attacked you?" Emma asked, and Bree paused at the kitchen counter to study her.

Aspen shook her head. "No. Of you and me when we were young. What happened to your mother?"

Emma's face paled, and she knotted her hands on the table.

Jack was dozing so she eased him into the baby seat, then reached out and squeezed Emma's hand. "I'm sorry. I didn't mean to bring up a painful subject."

Emma sighed. "No, it's all right. It was a long time ago." She took a deep breath. "My mother's boyfriend abused her. One night they got in a terrible fight, and he set the house on fire. Both of them died."

"That's right. I had a memory about a fire," Aspen said.

"That's when I came to live with you and Aunt Rose."

Rose…her mother's name. An image of her face flashed back, bittersweet and painful because it felt as it was so long ago. As if it was another thing lost. Maybe forever.

"And my mother? She's dead?"

Emma's gaze met hers, tears glittering in her eyes. "Yes, Rose died last year of cancer. Right before you went to Las Vegas to finish school."

"And my father?"

"He was never in the picture. I think that's why you were so determined that you could handle raising Jack alone."

The rumble of a motor startled them all, and Bree held up a warning hand, indicating for them to wait, then removed her weapon from her holster and went to the window.

"Is it Miguel or Dylan?"

"Neither," Bree said. "Kurt Lightfoot."

Aspen tensed. Emma had said that she and Kurt had dated. And she had wondered if he had been the man she'd seen at the shelter, the one who'd attacked her.

"Should we let him in?" Emma asked.

Bree shrugged. "I've known Kurt for a while. I don't think he's dangerous, if that's what you're worried about."

She opened the door, and Kurt's voice echoed from the porch. "I came to talk to Aspen. I figured if she wasn't at home, she might be with Emma."

"She is," Bree said, then gestured for him to come in.

Kurt shifted awkwardly as his gaze met hers. He was a handsome man, she supposed. Tall and muscular, and from what she'd been told, he was doing good things for the reservation by working for the WCA. But his gaze bore into hers as if she'd betrayed him by forgetting him.

And the dream of the Indian man attacking her haunted her….

"Can we talk in private?" he asked.

Aspen glanced at Emma, then Bree, and Emma gestured to Jack who'd stirred from sleep and was cooing at her. "Bree and I will take Jack out on the porch for a minute. If that's all right with you, Aspen?"

Aspen reluctantly nodded. If Kurt was dangerous, he certainly wouldn't try to hurt her with the detective and Emma present.

She dropped a kiss on her son's forehead, hating to let him go. She'd missed so much already. But Emma gently cradled him in her arms and whispered to him as she carried him outside, and Aspen took comfort in knowing that he was only a few feet away.

She'd never lose him again.

Kurt waited until Bree joined Emma before he claimed the chair beside her. "How are you feeling?"

"I'm doing all right, just frustrated that I can't re-member my life." She twined her fingers together, nerves knotting her stomach.

"I'm sorry. I didn't come to push you," Kurt said in a deep voice. "I just wanted you to know that I'm here if you need me." He reached out and squeezed her hand, and a ripple of unease tripped through her.

"I care about you, Aspen. You may not remember it, but we were…are good friends." His lips curled into a smile. "In fact, we've been more than that."

Her gaze shot to his, probing, searching for the truth. "What are you saying?"

"That we talked about a future together, about mar-riage," he said quietly. "About me moving in and taking care of you and little Jack."

Confusion clouded her head as she struggled to recall that conversation and the relationship Kurt implied they'd had. Had she considered marrying Kurt? Had she been in love with him?

And if she had, why did she feel more drawn to Dylan Acevedo, the federal agent who was protecting her and Jack than Kurt?

"What about Jack's birth father?" Aspen asked. "Did I tell you who he was?" He stroked his thumb over her hand.

"No," Kurt said, glancing down at her fingers, which were curled into a knot. "But that doesn't matter to me, Aspen. I'll love Jack and raise him as my own."

She chewed over his words. "Did I say anything about Jack's father?"

A frown marred Kurt's face, causing wrinkles to crease across his forehead. "You said you didn't tell him about the pregnancy because you were frightened of him," Kurt said. "And that he'd never know about your son."

The front door squeaked open, and Aspen glanced up to see Dylan standing in the door, a thunderous expression slashing his chiseled face.

IT TOOK EVERY OUNCE of Dylan's restraint not to lunge forward and rip Lightfoot's hands off of Aspen. Aspen had told Lightfoot she was afraid of the baby's father. Had she been afraid of him?

Or another man?

He folded his arms. "What are you doing here, Lightfoot?"

The Indian didn't budge, but Aspen slipped her hands down to her lap, twisting them together.

"I came to see Aspen and Jack," Lightfoot said with a scowl.

"About what?"

"I care about her," he said matter-of-factly. "I figured that she needed her friends now."

"She does need her friends," Dylan cut in sharply, "but I'm not sure you're one of them."

Lightfoot took a step closer as if he had no intention of backing down. "What makes you say that?"

Dylan held up the warrant. "The fact that we found a hair belonging to a male Native American in the room where Aspen was attacked at the women's shelter where she was recuperating."

A sarcastic expression curled Lightfoot's mouth. "In case you haven't noticed, I'm not the only male Indian in this part of the country."

Dylan shrugged. "Still, I'll need a DNA sample."

His tone challenged him to decline. "For elimination purposes, of course."

Lightfoot threw up his hands in warning as Dylan stalked toward him. "Wait a minute, you have no right."

Dylan smiled. The hell he didn't. "This warrant says I do."

"How did you obtain a warrant?" Lightfoot asked. "I've done nothing wrong, nothing suspicious."

The fact that he was all over Aspen was enough to make Dylan hate his guts. "The judge saw differently. Now about that sample?"

A muscle ticked in Lightfoot's jaw, then he growled. "You don't need to take a sample."

"Why not?" Dylan asked.

"Because I was there," Lightfoot admitted. "In Mexican Hat."

Chapter Nine

"You broke into the room at the shelter?" Aspen asked.

Kurt reached for her but Aspen backed away from his touch. "It's not what you think."

"It sounds to me like you attacked her," Dylan suggested.

"No," Kurt said harshly. "You've got it all wrong."

"But you grabbed me," Aspen said. "I didn't make that up."

"I didn't attack you," Kurt argued. "I only wanted to talk to you, to make sure you were all right, but you panicked and started screaming. Then everyone ran in and I figured I had to get out of there before a dozen women pounced on me."

Aspen frowned, struggling to make sense of his explanation and debating over what to believe. She'd been terrified, having nightmares, and then she'd seen a man sneaking into her room.

Could she have mistaken his intent?

"We're not buying that story," Dylan said. "If you wanted to talk to her, you would have gone to the door like a normal person. Besides, how did you find her when the police hadn't located her yet?"

"I can explain." Kurt shifted nervously, one hand running over the length of that leather pouch. The one holding the knife Aspen had seen.

Dylan studied the man's body language, his senses on alert in case Lightfoot decided to attack. Kurt pressed his hand over the pouch.

"Don't even think about it," Dylan warned.

Kurt's gaze shot up. "Think about what?"

"About using the knife." Dylan gestured for him to remove the weapon and hand it over. Kurt muttered an obscenity, but gave him the knife.

Then he turned to Aspen. "Let me explain. Please."

Dylan pointed to the kitchen chair. "Sit down. And put your hands on the table in front of you where I can see them."

Kurt did as Dylan instructed, but gave Aspen a desperate look. "Please listen to me. I would never hurt you, Aspen."

Aspen frowned. "Then explain why you broke in my room and scared me to death."

"I'm sorry I frightened you." Kurt glanced at Dylan with wary eyes. "Aspen and I had been seeing each other for the last few months, ever since she moved back from Vegas to the reservation. But she confided that she was afraid of Jack's father, that he wasn't Ute, and that if he discovered he had a son, he might try to take Jack away from her."

The scar on Dylan's chin twitched with a frown. "So you aren't the baby's father?"

Kurt shook his head. "I offered to be, though." He glanced at Aspen with a soulful look. "I wish you remembered. I wanted to marry you and promised to raise the baby as my own."

Aspen massaged her temple. Kurt's words vaguely rang true and stirred distant memories of a conversation, yet the details didn't quite break the surface. Had she been afraid of Jack's father physically? Afraid he'd try to take her son off the reservation?

"Did Aspen say the man was physical with her?" Dylan asked.

Kurt shrugged. "Not in so many words. But he wasn't Ute, and Aspen wanted to raise her son in the Ute way. So, when she went missing, I was afraid that the baby's father might have gone after her."

Dylan drummed his fingers on the table. "But if he wanted the baby, why leave him in the car?"

A shudder coursed through Aspen as she thought about her little boy in that car for God knew how long, cold and hungry and alone.

Kurt ran a hand over his forehead, sweating. "I don't know. Maybe he was married or a politician or something and didn't want anyone to know he was Jack's father."

Aspen twisted her hands in her lap. Something about that scenario seemed wrong. She might not remember much about her past, but she didn't think she would have gotten involved with a married man.

Her gaze met Dylan's and once again she lost herself in those blue eyes. Blue eyes like Jack's…

But that was impossible. She must be imagining things.

She'd only met Dylan at the shelter after the attack. And there were other blue-eyed men. She must have known someone in Las Vegas when she was working there. Another student maybe. Or a patron from the bar or casino.

"Anyway," Kurt gave Aspen another pleading look before turning to address Dylan. "She told me that if Jack's father came looking for her, she'd go to a women's shelter and disappear. That she'd adopt a new identity and start over somewhere else. That's when I decided to start looking at the shelters around the area. I thought if she was alive, that she might seek help from one."

"But I would never have left Jack," Aspen said.

"I didn't think you would," Kurt said. "That's why I figured you were hurt. Or that you might be coming back to get him. And when I found you at the Sisters of Mercy, I assumed you were making arrangements for a new life, and that you'd somehow get Jack and then take off."

Aspen tried to follow his logic. It made sense, but somehow still felt out of place.

"That doesn't explain why you didn't go up to the door and talk to the sisters," Dylan pointed out.

"Are you kidding?" Kurt asked. "Those women don't trust any man. They would never have let me near Aspen." He turned to her, his brown eyes darkening. "I swear, Aspen. I saw you a few times out in the courtyard, but you looked at me as if you didn't know me. That's when I knew something was really wrong. I only slipped into your room that night to talk to you, to see if I could help. To tell you that if you wanted to go somewhere else, that I'd take you and Jack."

"If that's true," Dylan said, "then you won't mind giving me your DNA." He laid a warrant on the table. "And then I'll need to search your house."

A flicker of anxiety registered on Kurt's face but he quickly masked it. "What are you looking for?"

"A gun," Dylan said. "And anything else that might prove you're lying."

"I don't own a gun," Kurt said gruffly.

Dylan cut him off, then ordered him to open wide while he swabbed the inside of his mouth.

DYLAN LEFT ASPEN, Jack and Emma with Bree again while he followed Lightfoot to his house to enforce the search warrant. Mentally, he sorted through the man's story, searching for the truth.

He wanted Lightfoot to be bad. Wanted to have a reason to get him away from Aspen.

But the man seemed to sincerely care for her. The fact that he'd offered to parent a child that he hadn't fathered was admirable.

Not that Dylan wouldn't do the same. He would.

But something else bothered him about Lightfoot. He said all the right things—maybe too right?

Or maybe you don't like him because he wants Aspen.

He wanted her, too.

Only wanting her had nothing to do with Jack. It had to do with the heavenly way she'd felt in his arms, in his bed. Her lips against his. Her body welcoming him inside hers. Her sultry voice whispering his name in the throes of passion.

"You're not going to find a weapon," Lightfoot said. "I'm a man of peace, not violence."

Dylan glared at him then proceeded inside the man's house, a simple wooden ranch that he assumed had been built by the WCA. The deer-hide rug, artwork and orange and yellow muted tones showed definite Native American influences.

It seemed Lightfoot and Aspen had a lot in common. Had she been in love with Lightfoot before the crash?

Worry gnawed at his gut. What if she hadn't told him about Jack because she didn't want him in her son's life? Lightfoot wasn't violent, claimed not to own a gun, worked for the WCA, whereas he was none of those things.

But he couldn't imagine Aspen leaving his bed in Vegas and jumping in bed with someone else so quickly. *Although she slept with you the first night you met.*

But that was different. A hot, intense sexual chemistry had drawn them to each other immediately. And during that next week, the fire had only grown hotter.

He'd also learned more about her, found the woman beneath the exotic looks to be fascinating. Kind. Sincere. Intelligent.

And mesmerizing.

Lightfoot made a disgusted sound as Dylan rifled through his desk, but Dylan ignored him and searched the living area, closet, kitchen cabinets and pantry, then the bathroom before finally moving into the man's bedroom. A giant oak bed dominated the room with more Indian artwork. He grimaced as he checked beneath the mattress. Had Aspen ever been in this bed with Lightfoot? Moaned his name the way she'd moaned his when he'd made love to her?

Clenching his hands into fists and then unclenching them to regain control, he forced himself back to the job. He examined Lightfoot's dresser drawers, well aware Lightfoot watched with his arms folded angrily. The closet came next, and he pawed through the man's suede jacket, buffalo-skin coat, jeans and the top shelf.

Dammit. No weapon. Nothing suspicious.

He stalked to the other bedroom and searched it, as well, and again came up empty. Nothing to incriminate Lightfoot at all.

"Satisfied?" Lightfoot asked through clenched teeth.

Dylan offered him a stone-cold expression. "Just because it's not here doesn't mean you haven't had a gun and dumped it."

"You're looking at the wrong person," Lightfoot snarled. "I told you I would never hurt Aspen, and I meant it."

"You'd better not hurt her," Dylan said. "Because if you do, you'll answer to me personally."

Dylan headed to the door. He would keep digging. If Lightfoot had any ghosts in his closet, Dylan would expose every last one of them.

By the time he arrived back at Emma's, Miguel was there and Bree was gone. She'd received a call to check out some trouble on another part of the reservation. He hoped to hell it was a lead on Watts and Perkins. He wanted them in jail so Aspen would be safe from their evil clutches.

Aspen and Emma were playing with Jack on a pallet on the floor, and the baby laughed and cooed as Aspen told him a story about a game they played as children.

Miguel met him at the door, his look when he gazed at Emma one of a man in serious lust.

Dylan wondered if his own expression when he looked at Aspen was just as transparent.

"What did you find?" Miguel asked.

"Nothing." Dylan ran a hand over the scar on his chin.

"I heard Ryan suggest setting a trap by using Aspen as bait," Miguel said in a low voice. "Maybe you should consider it."

Rage seared Dylan, quick and raw. "Absolutely not."

Miguel shrugged. "It might be the only way to smoke out Perkins and Watts."

He narrowed his eyes at his brother, unable to believe what he'd suggested. "Would you use Emma as a trap?"

Miguel's face paled as he looked back at Emma. "No, I guess not. But I didn't realize you were in love with Aspen."

Dylan's chest clenched. He was attracted to her, wanted her back in his arms and in his bed. Hell, he wanted to take care of her and Jack whether Jack was his son or not. But he wasn't in love with Aspen.

Was he?

ASPEN HEARD THE PROTECTIVE tone in Dylan's voice when he'd refused to use her as a trap, and something warm, mellow and sweet bubbled inside her. And what had Miguel said—something about Dylan being in love with her?

Had she heard him correctly?

No…he must have been talking about loving Emma. While they were gone, more memories of Emma had returned, and she was glad that her cousin had found someone special to care for her.

She was also tired of being in the dark, living in fear while everyone tiptoed around her as if she'd lost her mind, not just her memories.

Dylan and Miguel had instantly hushed as soon as she approached them, driving home her point.

"What did you find at Kurt's?" she asked.

"Nothing." Dylan's intense eyes skated over her with a dark look that sent a tingle down her spine. "But he could have dumped a gun if he had one."

"You really don't trust him?" Aspen asked.

Dylan shrugged. "I'm not sure. I know I don't want you alone with him."

Aspen shivered, his possessive tone arousing a deep need in her to be held and protected by this man.

But instead of reaching for him, she hugged her arms around her waist. "I can't go on like this. Everyone keeping secrets from me, afraid to talk, afraid I'll break." She injected conviction into her voice. "I'm *not* going to break. I want to remember what happened. I don't like suspecting my friends or people on the reservation. And I hate not knowing who to trust."

Dylan studied her for a long moment, indecision in his eyes. "All right," he finally said. "But I've told you all we know for now."

"You haven't shown me pictures of the men you think I saw disposing of that woman's body."

"Do you think you're ready for that?" Dylan asked.

She nodded, summoning every ounce of courage she possessed. "Yes. Maybe seeing their faces will trigger my memory. Then I want you to take me to the scene of my accident."

A troubled expression darkened his eyes as if he was mentally debating what to do, but also a seed of hope surfaced when he gave a clipped nod. They'd reached an impasse and needed her help. She'd prove she was strong enough to handle it.

Because she and Jack couldn't live in fear forever.

THE WOMAN'S BIG BROWN EYES widened in horror as she realized his intent.

"Please don't kill me," she screeched. "I haven't done anything to you."

"I told you I need a place to hide out." He glanced around the modest little wooden bungalo. Not fancy but it would do. Just like the last place on the rez where he'd hidden.

But he had to keep moving. He couldn't get caught.

"You can stay here as long as you want," she whispered shakily as she tried to back toward the door. "I won't tell the police, I promise."

"Sorry, too late for that," he muttered.

He had to kill her. He couldn't leave any witnesses behind.

She tried to run, to escape, but he grabbed her by her long dark hair and jerked her back to him with a vicious yank. She screamed and flailed her puny arms, but he was stronger, and he slapped her across the face, then yanked out his knife and slashed her throat.

Blood spewed from her flesh and dripped down her pale neck, soaking her blouse in seconds.

Smiling, he dragged her limp body outside, weaving through the trees and brush, then tied rocks to her limbs and dumped her into the river.

Wiping sweat from his brow, he hiked back to the small cabin, went inside and scavenged through her refrigerator. A pizza, a six-pack of cold beer… His mouth watered. Damn, he'd hit the jackpot.

He'd kick back, get some rest, grab a shower and set up camp to watch for the right moment to kill Aspen Meadows.

Chapter Ten

"Are you sure you want to look at those photographs?" Dylan asked.

"Yes," Aspen said. "The sooner I recover my memories, the sooner we can put this mess behind us and move on with our lives."

Then he could leave the reservation and Aspen....

That thought sent his gut into a churning motion, but he had a job to do and he had to focus. Finding the person or persons after Aspen was the only way to keep her safe.

And he couldn't live with her death on his conscience.

Not like his little sister. He rubbed his thumb over his pocket where he kept Teresa's photo. God, she'd been so young and trusting, so full of life, her future looming ahead of her.

All lost in a second.

Hardening himself, he headed to the door. "Let me get the files from the car."

Wind slashed his cheeks as he stepped outside, his gaze immediately scanning the property to see if anyone was nearby. The night sounds of the reservation, of animals in the distance, surrounded him, the silence eerie as if danger lay nearby.

Hoping Aspen was truly strong enough to handle the photographs, he retrieved the files then carried them inside.

Emma was feeding Jack peaches, and Dylan couldn't help but grin as the sticky orange goop dribbled off his chin. But his smile died when Aspen gestured for him to spread the pictures on the coffee table.

The last thing he wanted to do was to hurt or traumatize Aspen more. But she seemed determined to push herself and face this gruesome task.

Which hopefully was a sign she was healing.

Miguel's cell phone rang, and he stepped outside to answer it.

Dylan removed the picture of Boyd Perkins, and Aspen's fingers trembled as she reached out and traced his bald head.

"Perkins is a hired gun," Dylan said.

She swallowed. "His eyes are ice-cold and mean."

"Goes with the territory. He works for a crime family." Dylan shifted. "There are two major crime families in the area, the Del Gardos and the Wayne family," Dylan explained. "We believe that Perkins was hired by Frank 'the Gun' Wayne's nephew, Nicky Wayne, who has taken over his uncle's organization. He ordered the hit on Vincent Del Gardo, the father of his rival Mob team. We also think that Perkins was supposed to locate fifty million dollars that it's been rumored Del Gardo hid from the government. Perkins used Sherman Watts—" he paused and added Watts's picture to the table "—to help him hide out on the reservation. Watts has a sheet for petty crimes, but up until we made the connection between him and Perkins, the police didn't think he was dangerous."

Aspen narrowed her eyes. "He does seem familiar."

"Watts lives on the reservation, so you might have seen him before that night."

Aspen's gaze drifted from Perkins to Watts, who had scraggly black hair that hung down beneath a black flat-brimmed hat.

"Watts is pretty much a loser. He loves booze and women." Dylan paused. "And Perkins probably offered to pay him to help him hide out."

Dylan removed a photo of Julie, his breath tightening. "This is Julie Grainger, the agent Perkins killed."

Aspen glanced up at him with a curious expression. She must have heard the pain in his voice because sympathy softened her eyes. "Her death was personal to you. You were in love with her?"

Dylan frowned and shook his head, studying her for any sign that she'd recognized the men or him. But only a sliver of fear glinted in her eyes. "No, nothing like that. We were friends, we worked together. She… was one of the good guys and didn't deserve to die so young."

She shivered, and he stroked her arm. "You don't have to do this, Aspen."

"No, I want to. I *need* to," she said emphatically. "Please take me to the crash site now." She jutted up her chin, making his heart ache for her.

He had wonderful, erotic memories of the two of them in bed. He wanted to make more of those memories, wanted to kiss her and alleviate the fear in her eyes.

But she was struggling to find her way back from the

dark. And if taking her to see the place where her ordeal had begun might help her, he'd do it.

Then and only then could she tell him the truth about Jack and what had happened to her.

His cell phone vibrated on his belt, and he grabbed it and checked the number. Bree. Hell, maybe she'd found Watts or Perkins.

He hastily punched the connect button. "Acevedo."

"Dylan, it's Bree. Listen, I went to check out that trouble on the reservation and think I may have found out where Perkins and Watts have been holding up."

"Where?"

"It's a small ranch that belongs to the Running Deer family. They were on vacation for a couple of weeks and just returned to find the place a mess, food and dishes piled up, dirt tracked in, beds slept in."

"Any sign of Watts or Perkins?"

"Looks like they left in a hurry. But there were cigarette butts and booze bottles so we should get some forensics. CSI's on its way, and I've called Sheriff Martinez to issue an APB in case they're still close by."

"Good," Dylan said. "Maybe we'll get lucky and catch them this time." He paused and glanced at Aspen. "Call me and let me know if you do. I want to be there for the questioning."

Miguel had stepped outside but strode back in, his expression strained.

Dylan disconnected the call, his pulse racing.

Miguel had bad news.

ASPEN THUMBED HER FINGERS through the tangled strands of her hair. "Did they find them?"

Miguel looked confused, so Dylan explained about

Bree's call. "She thinks they may be close so she and Patrick are searching the rez near the Running Deer house."

"I hope to hell they find them," Miguel muttered.

Emma returned from the bedroom where she'd put Jack down for a nap. "What's going on?"

Miguel relayed the latest on Perkins and Watts. "Dylan, I just talked to the ME," Miguel said. "Maybe we should step outside."

"No," Aspen said. "Emma and I are a part of this. We deserve to know everything that's going on."

Dylan gave a reluctant nod, and Miguel shifted, looking uncomfortable. "It's about a past case. Frank Turnbull, the serial killer who killed all those Ute girls last year." He gestured toward Dylan. "Dylan tracked him down and arrested him. He's been in jail for murder for the past few months."

Aspen frowned, something about the case nagging at her. The Ute women had had their throats slashed. "What happened?"

"He was being transferred to APX Florence, and his bus crashed and burned," Dylan interjected, then turned to Miguel. "Do they have a positive ID?"

Miguel sighed. "The ME said they found a partial bridge plate that belonged to Turnbull. Matched it to Turnbull's dental records. But they're still working on the bones."

Dylan shifted on the balls of his feet. "That's good but not conclusive. After I drive Aspen to the crash site, I'm going to study his prison correspondence. We can't let down our guard until we verify that he's dead." And if he was, a copycat had surfaced. Maybe Turnbull had a fan who'd decided to imitate him.

Or what if he'd had an accomplice? Some serial killers worked in pairs. They'd considered that theory before but hadn't found any evidence to support it.

He glanced at Emma. "Do you mind watching Jack while I drive Aspen?"

"Of course not," Emma said softly. "I'll be glad to take care of him anytime you need."

Dylan placed a hand at Aspen's waist. "Are you ready?"

Aspen inhaled, determined to push forward. "Yes, let's go."

He ushered her to the car, scanning the property as they climbed in and drove off the reservation. Aspen sat in silence, her hands knotted, her gaze focused on the rugged terrain, steep slopes, ridges and brush. The scenery felt as familiar as her name had, and her love of the land returned, welcoming her home. Although it was May, in the distance, snow still capped the mountaintops, and a cool wind rattled the windowpanes, causing goose bumps to scatter along her arms.

The moon struggled to break through dark storm clouds that hovered above like winter ghosts taunting her with the threat of bad weather, the eerie sounds of the isolated area near the river echoing in the night.

Dylan bumped over rocky, dirt-packed ground and steered the vehicle toward an isolated area near the river, tucked in the shadows of the trees and foliage standing guard over the water rushing below.

He pointed toward a large tree across the way, its gnarled branches sweeping down as if to enfold them within its spidery dark hold.

She suddenly felt Dylan's hand slide over hers, the warmth of his body enveloping her as if he held her in his arms, as if he would keep the danger at bay.

"Aspen?"

"I'm ready," she said, mustering her courage and reaching for the door.

He opened his side and exited, then met her in front of the car. Her body trembled but she forced her feet forward until she stood in front of the tree. Even in the dark, she saw paint marks embedded in the bark that had been damaged from the impact of her car.

"This is where your car was found," Dylan said in a quiet but gravely voice.

An image of her red sedan flashed back then terror consumed her as snippets of that night returned. But other memories rushed to the forefront.

She was nine months pregnant, walking along the river when she'd spotted two men in the distance. One with scraggly black hair and a black hat, the other bald. They were dragging something.

Dear God, a body.

Her voice caught on a scream, and the men turned, searching through the trees looking for the source of the sound. A pain shot through her stomach, and she clutched her belly, a contraction hitting her full force. She leaned against a tree trunk and breathed through the squeezing torture, hiding behind the foliage. She had to get of there, get away.

If they'd killed someone, they'd probably kill her, too.

And her baby—she had to protect her child.

The pain slowly subsided, and she took off running, weaving through the brush and branches, checking over her shoulder to make sure they weren't behind her. By the time she staggered to her car, she was shaking and panting. She clutched the door handle, ripped it open and collapsed inside as another contraction seized her.

She leaned against the steering wheel, struggling to breathe through it, her thoughts racing. She should call the police, have them check for the body. Tell them what she'd seen.

But her vision blurred, and the events lost focus. What if it hadn't been a body? Maybe the men had shot a deer or elk...

And if she called the police, what if the men tracked her down and hurt her baby?

No...they'd be safer if she stayed quiet. Another pain caught her in its clutches, and she glanced at her watch. Only two minutes since the last contraction.

She had to make it to the midwife to help her deliver the baby....

"Aspen, are you all right?" A gentle hand stroked her back, soothing her.

She nodded, perspiration beading on her neck. "Yes, I remember seeing two men dragging a body. But I was scared...and having contractions." She heaved for a breath. "So I ran. I had to protect the baby."

"Of course you did," he said quietly. "Then what happened? Did the men see you?"

She clutched at him for support. "I wasn't sure. But later, after Jack was born, I heard about that agent's body being found. I knew then that I'd witnessed a crime..." Tears laced her voice. "I'm sorry, Dylan. I should have come forward sooner."

"You had a child to protect," he said with more under-standing than she deserved.

He massaged her shoulders. "What happened after that?"

She closed her eyes, allowing the memories to come now. They were flooding her mind, rushing at her like a dam had broken.

She'd driven back to the scene, hoping to trigger details about the men to tell the police. But the men appeared out of nowhere as if they'd been watching for her.

She ran again, and quickly strapped Jack into the car seat. She had to get to the police.

Frantically, she cranked the engine, pressed the gas and tore down the graveled road. But a moment later, a dark car raced up on her tail and chased her off the road. Jack was screaming in the back, and she tried to soothe him with her voice, but fear clogged her throat, and she cried out as the car slammed into her and sent her flying into the tree. Tires had squealed, glass shat-tering, metal crunching, but the sound of Jack's distress wrenched her heart.

Dear God, her baby couldn't die…

With that choking thought, she'd fought her way past the air bag and ripped off her seat belt, desperate to reach him and make sure he was safe.

But rough, big hands dragged her from the car, yank-ing her by the hair. A fist slammed into her head and the ground clawed at her arms and legs. She screamed and kicked but another blow to her head made her legs buckle and the world spin into darkness.

By the time she fought through the nausea and the pull of unconsciousness, she was falling, falling, falling…

Through the dark space and into the icy water, her body slammed against the jagged rocks, the cold enveloping her until she was numb and knew she was going to die.

"Aspen?"

She didn't realize she was standing on the precipice of the ridge with the river raging below until Dylan suddenly jerked her back.

She was shaking and crying, the terror all too real as if she'd just been submerged into the frigid river again.

"Shh, baby, I'm here," Dylan whispered. "You're safe."

A warmth engulfed her as Dylan pulled her into his arms, and she burrowed against him, taking solace in his embrace and voice.

"Aspen, honey, are you all right?"

She nodded against him, and he literally felt her grappling for a breath, and sensed the terror in her trembling body.

"It's over now," he murmured into her hair. "I won't let them hurt you again."

"I was so scared for Jack," she whispered hoarsely. "They talked about killing him, but then decided he'd probably die in the cold anyway."

Dylan muttered a curse. Damn bastards would pay for leaving an innocent little baby alone to face the brutal winter elements.

"Jack's safe now, too," he whispered. "I promise they'll never harm either one of you again."

She turned teary eyes up to him, her lip quivering. "Why do you care so much? Why are you here protecting me and Jack?"

It's my job, he wanted to say. But she'd said she wanted the truth, not to be left in the dark. And, dammit, she was in his arms and he wanted to make her remember the time they'd spent together.

That her safety meant much more to him than any damn case.

He tucked a strand of her hair behind her ear, soaking up her features like a starving man. "Because I do care," he said quietly.

Her eyes searched his and for a moment, he thought he saw a flicker of recognition dawn in her eyes as if she remembered him. Her breath caught, her heart beating against his, and his body hardened, aching with the need to touch her, to strip her and join his body with hers.

To remind them both that she had survived.

Unable to resist, he lowered his mouth and pressed his lips to hers. Tentative at first. Testing. Tasting. Begging for her to recall what they'd shared. To invite him to explore her.

To take her the way he once had.

She moaned and threaded her fingers in his hair, all the invitation he needed to deepen the kiss. She opened her mouth, playing her own tongue along his, sending heat spiraling through him in erotic, torturous waves.

His hands slid lower, stroking her shoulders, her back, the soft column of her spine until he pulled her deeper into his embrace, her heat against his own, his thighs cradling her when her legs threatened to give way.

She moaned, the sultry sound indicating she liked the feel of his kiss, and that she wanted more. She clung to him, her hands needy and frenzied as she traced them over his chest and his arms.

Heat seared him, hunger bolting through his body at lightning speed.

Just like it had the first time he'd met her.

But suddenly a shot pinged through the air, whizzing next to his head. Aspen screamed, and he shoved her to the ground behind a large rock, shielding her with his body as he removed his gun and searched for the shooter in the dark.

HE CROUCHED ON HIS KNEES, then crawled along the rocky embankment, his gun trained on Acevedo. He had to take the man out. Or at least impair him until he could get to the woman.

She was the one he wanted now.

But he'd be more than happy to kill the agent, too.

First, though, he had to make the woman suffer....

Chapter Eleven

Dylan cursed, scanning the woods as he grabbed Aspen's hand and led her through the trees toward the car.

Another shot grazed by her head, and she screamed as he jerked sideways to dodge the bullet. It hit the side of the car, and Dylan dragged her behind the rear bumper for cover.

Crouching down, he coaxed her to the passenger side and opened the door. "Get in and stay down."

She crawled into the car, burying her head beneath her arms. He shut the door, then circled back, searching for the shooter. A shadow of a man appeared in the distance, and he contemplated chasing him down.

He was tired of being the target.

But Aspen was in the car and he had to protect her. If this was Perkins and Watts, they might have divided up, might be watching, hoping to separate them so they could get to her.

Another shot hit the dirt beside him, and he inched around the back bumper to the driver's side, staying crouched and hiding behind the door as he opened it. Then he slid inside, turned the key and backed down the graveled drive, flooring the gas as another bullet spun toward them.

As he flew onto the highway, he reached over and stroked Aspen's hair, hating the way her body trembled. They had to find Watts and Perkins. She didn't deserve to live in fear, to have to look over her shoulder.

He grabbed his cell phone and called Sheriff Martinez. "Patrick, it's Dylan Acevedo. A shooter just fired at us from the site where we found Aspen's car."

Patrick hissed. "I'll send some units to the area immediately."

"Thanks. I'll stop by the crime lab and dig out the bullet in the car and leave it for ballistics," Dylan said.

He disconnected the call, but kept glancing over his shoulder as he raced away, relaxing only slightly when he didn't spot anyone behind them.

Finally he told Aspen he thought they were safe, and she crawled into the seat and strapped on her seat belt. "We have to do something," she said in a shaky voice. "I can't keep running."

"We're doing everything we can," Dylan said, although frustration hardened his voice.

"Are you?" Aspen asked.

He frowned at her. "What's that supposed to mean?"

"I heard you talking to Miguel. You said that one of the agents suggested you use me as bait to trap Watts and Perkins."

Emotions pummeled him. "Absolutely not."

She brushed a strand of hair from her cheek. "Why not? I witnessed those men dump the woman's body. I remember them coming after me. I want to testify against them."

"I said no."

Aspen's eyes widened. "I don't understand. They're after me anyway, so why not take the proactive route and set them up?"

"Because they could kill you," Dylan said through clenched teeth.

"But you'll be there to protect me," Aspen argued.

"And what if I can't?" His tone turned razor sharp, the adrenaline from their earlier attack firing his temper. "What if I fail? I couldn't live with that…."

An odd look flickered in her eyes and she suddenly touched her lips. Was she remembering the kiss, the kiss that he'd wanted and had almost taken too far?

The kiss that had distracted him so that the shooter had gotten close enough to nearly kill them.

ASPEN TOUCHED HER LIPS, something about their conversation striking a familiar chord of recognition as if they'd had this discussion before.

His voice had cracked, almost as if protecting her was something more than a case to him, something *personal*.

But that was impossible…wasn't it?

Except that that kiss had stirred feelings inside her. Feelings of hunger and desire and need.

Feelings that disturbed her because they ran deeper than they should for someone she'd just met. Feelings that felt familiar.

"Dylan?"

His jaw was clenched, his hands wrapped around the steering wheel in a white-knuckled grip. "I'm sorry," he muttered. "I can't take that chance."

"But it makes sense, and it may be the only way—"

"No. I care about you, dammit."

Her breath caught in her chest. He'd said that before. "What?"

He growled in his throat and ran a hand through his hair, then steered the car off the road and pulled behind a boulder as if to hide them in case someone was following. Then he turned to her, his blue eyes glittering with emotions she couldn't define.

His breathing sounded choppy in the ensuing silence. Then he clenched and unclenched his fists as if in a silent debate. "God, I'm not supposed to do this."

Aspen touched his arm, automatically feeling his strength seep into her, his heat warming her insides and sparking a fire low in her belly. "You're not supposed to do what?"

"I'm not supposed to push you. The doctor said to let you remember on your own."

"But I'm starting to," she whispered. "And I told you before I don't want to be left in the dark."

His gaze probed her. "But you didn't remember me when I kissed you, did you?"

"We knew each other before," she said in a low voice, then pressed her fingers to her mouth. "It's true, isn't it? That's why it felt so…familiar."

He gave a clipped nod, then reached for her arms and gently held her. "Yes, we knew each other. We met last year in Vegas right after I arrested the Ute serial killer."

"That's why I recognized the name Turnbull."

"Probably, although the case was major news. But we talked about it that first night." He sighed, looking tired and defeated. "I was upset. All those women had died, and for weeks I'd been looking at gruesome photos of

Turnbull's murder victims, then I walked into that bar, and saw you and…"

"And what?" Aspen asked.

"And you were so damn beautiful that I watched you all night, then walked you to your apartment and stayed."

A fleeting memory tickled her conscience. Her in Dylan's arms, kissing, touching…stripping and falling into bed. "The first night?"

"Yes," he said, his voice cracking slightly. "We spent the week together, Aspen. A week in bed, making love to each other."

His words evoked erotic memories that aroused her and made her tingly inside. The first time she'd touched him at the shelter, she'd felt an electric chemistry between them. But she'd chalked her reaction up to fear.

Had thought she was drawn to him because he promised protection when she was grappling to plow her way back to the world she'd lost.

Another thought struck her. She'd wondered about Jack's bright blue eyes…

"I probably shouldn't have told you," he murmured in a tortured voice.

"No, I'm glad you did." Aspen gripped his hand. "Tell me what happened next."

Dylan's look turned pained, but he cradled her hand between his. "I was called away on an undercover assignment, so we parted. You told me your plans to return to the reservation to teach, and you obviously followed through."

Disappointment ballooned in her chest. "You're saying that we had a fling? A meaningless affair?"

Tension stretched between them then he finally

sighed heavily. "I thought my job would get in the way," he finally said. "That you'd be safer without me in your life. Then Julie was murdered and you went missing, and I had to come here to find out who killed Julie." His voice cracked. "And I had to find you, to know if you were all right."

The pain and worry in his voice sounded far too real for her to believe that he hadn't cared. Still, she didn't know how to react. Because the truth was that he'd walked away without contacting her until the case had brought him back into her life again.

And had she just let him leave? Had he meant more to her than a one-week affair?

She struggled to tamp down the hurt eating at her and glanced at the road, suddenly anxious to set the trap, and catch the men after her.

She couldn't become too needy. Couldn't fall for a man who could walk away from her the way he had. She had a child to think of. Her irresponsible days were over, had ended with Jack's birth.

Another memory surfaced—this one of her mother. When Aspen's father had deserted her before she was born, her mother had guarded her personal life. She hadn't paraded a sea of men into their house because she hadn't wanted Aspen to get too attached. To call a stranger daddy then have him walk out on her.

Aspen had to safeguard her son the same way.

DYLAN KNEW HE'D ADMITTED TOO much, but his emotions were bouncing all over the place.

Dammit, she could have died back there, and it would have been his fault. His hand automatically went to his pocket and he felt the folded edges of Teresa's picture taunting him.

Angry with himself, he started the car, checked the road, grateful not to detect a car hunting them down, then headed in to Kenner City to the crime lab.

"Dylan, please," Aspen said. "Call the other agents and let's set a trap. It may be the only way you can catch Boyd Perkins and Sherman Watts. I won't let Jack grow up living in fear."

"I don't want that, either," he said gruffly. Resigned, he phoned Tom and asked him to meet him at the crime lab.

Tension thrummed between them, questions left unspoken. He felt raw, exposed as if he'd finally confessed that she meant more to him than just a job, and it still hurt to know that she had no memory of the incredible week they'd shared.

That he still wanted her and she might not feel the same way.

A stiff wind battered the car as he crossed into the city and parked at the annex building. Senses alert, he scanned the outside of the building, then guided Aspen inside to the third-floor crime lab.

Tom met them at the door to the conference room, and Ava and Callie stepped inside, along with Bart Flemming. He introduced them to Aspen, then explained about the shooting, and Callie asked Jerry to dig the bullets from the rental car to compare to the others.

"We're glad you're safe," Callie said.

The others murmured agreement, and everyone settled into seats around the conference table.

"I'm still working on processing the evidence Bree and Patrick sent over from the Running Deer house,"

Ava said. "I identified Perkins's and Watts's prints inside, which confirms they were there."

"So they still are on the reservation?" Dylan said.

Callie shrugged. "As of a couple of days ago, it looks that way."

Bart piped up. "Well, I have something, too. Not to do with Perkins and Watts, but on Kurt Lightfoot."

Dylan's interest was piqued. "What did you find?"

"He works for the WCA and has done a lot of work for the Ute community, but I dug further into some of the contract jobs and suppliers and found something interesting." He paused. "There may be a link between him and the Wayne family."

"You mean, he's taking money for the WCA to help the reservation?" Aspen asked.

"Maybe."

Dylan chewed over that idea. "In exchange for what?"

Bart raised a hand. "I'm still looking."

"Maybe we should bring him in for questioning," Dylan suggested.

Bart tapped his pencil on the desk. "Give me another day or two and I may have something more definitive."

Dylan nodded and glanced at Aspen, his own need and hunger for Aspen warring with his logic. Setting a trap would definitely be the fastest way to smoke out their perps, but putting Aspen's life in more danger terrified him.

But he didn't have to speak up. Aspen did.

"We visited the crime scene earlier, and I remembered seeing Boyd Perkins and Sherman Watts dumping that woman's body." She paused, a strained look in her eyes. "I should have come forward immediately, but I was afraid," she admitted. "And at first, I wasn't certain what I'd seen. Then when I heard about a woman's body being found on the reservation, I knew I'd witnessed a crime."

Dylan spoke up, determined to cut her some slack. "Aspen was pregnant and went into labor," he said. "But later she decided to come forward, then Watts and Perkins recognized her. That's when they chased her down and she crashed into the tree."

"They tried to strangle me, then threw me in the river," Aspen said in a haunted voice.

"You guys know the rest," Dylan said.

Aspen cleared her throat. "I'm ready to testify. I overheard Miguel and Dylan talking about setting the trap for Perkins and Watts," Aspen said. "And I think it's a good idea. These men belong behind bars."

Dead silence met her declaration. Ryan and Callie shifted, then nervous glances crisscrossed the room between the agents and forensics specialists.

Finally Ben Parrish spoke up. "I think that's a smart move."

"I can contact the press immediately and let them know we have a witness and that Aspen is ready to testify," Ryan said.

Dylan planted a fist on the table. "We'll only agree to do this if I can move Aspen and her son to a safe house."

Murmurs of agreement rumbled through the room, along with excitement that they might finally be taking action.

As if in agreement, everyone stood. "I'll get back to processing the evidence," Ava said.

"And I'll finish that background check on Lightfoot," Flemming added.

Callie cleared her throat. "Dylan. Can I see you in my office for a second?"

Dylan's gaze met Aspen's, an intense heat simmering between them, his heart pounding so loudly at the thought of Aspen being used as bait that her words barely registered.

Then he jerked himself back to work. "Of course." He glanced at Aspen. "I'll be right back."

He followed Callie into her office, shoulders tightening with tension.

Did she have the results of the paternity test?

Was Jack his son, or would he learn that another man had found his way into her bed and given her a child?

Chapter Twelve

Dylan braced himself as he entered Callie's office. "What is it?" he asked without preamble.

She raised a brow with a smirk. "You always are to the point, Acevedo." She indicated a folder on her desk. "The test results you asked for are in."

"Hell, Callie, you enjoy torturing a guy?"

She threw her head back and laughed. "No. But I'm not sure you want to hear this news. I guess that depends on how you feel about Aspen Meadows."

"She's just a case."

"Right."

He steeled himself against an outward reaction, resorting to the training he'd relied on to keep him stable and on task. "It doesn't matter. I just need the truth. Jack's paternity could prove to be a lead…or not."

"It's not," she said slyly.

A seed of hope slivered through him, and he jerked up the file, flipped it open and scanned the lab report.

Jack was his son.

The paternity test proved it beyond a shadow of a doubt.

A slow smile spread on his face as his breath whooshed

out. He stumbled slightly, the exhilaration of knowing he shared a child with Aspen, that he'd known when he'd held him, drumming through his chest.

Emotions he hadn't expected to feel overpowered him. The thrill of knowing that his legacy would live on, that the time he'd spent with Aspen had been so strong that they'd produced a beautiful little boy with their physical bond.

On the heels of that joy, anger followed, the realization that he'd missed the first few months of his son's life.

That Aspen hadn't contacted him to inform him that he had a son.

And that Jack didn't have his name.

Lightfoot's comment that she'd claimed she was afraid of the baby's father taunted him. Why would Aspen have been afraid of him?

He gripped the folder with an iron fist and turned to go to Aspen and confront her.

But Callie planted herself in front of the door. "I know you're upset," she said in a low voice. "But stop and remember the situation, Dylan, and the doctor's warning about pushing Aspen too far."

"This is different," he ground out through the lump in his throat.

"No, it's not," she said gently. "She's still a witness in our protection. And if you upset her, she could run. That would only endanger her more."

Callie's words made nervous sweat explode above his brow, and he dropped into the chair by her desk and lowered his head into his hands. She was right.

But, dammit, he didn't like it.

Still, the last thing he wanted was to see the mother of his son hurt.

Or killed because he'd gone half-cocked, scared her, and sent her running into the night, vulnerable and at the hands of the very men he'd vowed to protect her from.

ASPEN STIFFENED as Dylan entered the conference room. His body language indicated something between them had changed. An air of fury radiated off of him that sent a chill through her.

Dylan rapped his knuckles on the table to get everyone's attention. "Let's work on the details of the trap. First, the press will leak the news that Aspen recovered her memory and is ready to testify." He angled his head toward her. "But you and Jack both remain under protective custody at all times. There will be no personal contact with anyone, not Emma or the other friends you made on the reservation. And when we stop by to pick up Jack, if Lightfoot comes by, we give nothing away."

Aspen nodded, although the thought of breaking off contact with Emma, the one family member she had left disturbed her. She'd felt isolated at the women's shelter in Mexican Hat. Now she'd be totally under Dylan's thumb.

And although she'd sensed different vibes coming from him—sometimes an intense heat that obviously had begun the year before—anger now tightened his jaw and hardened his words.

"Do you understand, Aspen?" he asked. "No contact with anyone. It's just you and me and Jack."

She twined her fingers together. "How long will we be…contained?" She'd almost said *imprisoned*.

His broad shoulders shrugged but his expression

didn't soften. "Until Perkins and Watts are in custody, and I'm certain you're safe."

Her hesitation seemed to irritate him more. "Aspen?"

"Yes," she said, although nerves tinged her voice. Knowing that she and Dylan shared a past, that they'd slept together, made the thought of being totally alone with him for days—or weeks—almost shatter her resolve to set the trap.

But she looked into his eyes and a memory surfaced—Dylan tenderly holding her, caressing her, trailing kisses down her neck and breasts. His hands roaming over her, teasing, exploring, drawing an erotic response from her nerve endings until she begged for more.

Was she always such a wanton lover, or had she only been that way in his arms?

DYLAN COULD BARELY LOOK AT Aspen. He wanted to shake her and make her tell him the truth about Jack.

He wanted to kiss her until she melted in his arms and welcomed him into his son's life.

And into hers.

But how would that work? He still had a dangerous job which would put her and Jack in jeopardy.

His cell phone rang, and he checked the number. Sheriff Martinez. He connected the call. "Acevedo."

"Dylan, you guys need to get over here. Bree and I found a body."

"Perkins or Watts?"

"No, it's a woman's. I've already called the ME."

An uneasy feeling clutched Dylan's chest. "I'll be right there."

He gave him the coordinates, and disconnected the call, then relayed the gist of the conversation to the others. "I'll stop and check it out on the way back to Aspen's to pick up her things for the safe house."

Ava and Callie jumped into motion to retrieve their crime scene kits to go to the scene.

Ben threw up a hand. "I'll set up the safe house in Mesa Verde."

"Thanks." Dylan took Aspen's elbow and guided her to the door. "Let's go."

"What's wrong?" Aspen asked.

"Other than a girl is dead and we're using you as bait for a killer?"

"I'm sorry," Aspen said in a contrite voice. "I just thought there was something else disturbing you."

He gritted his teeth to keep from asking about Jack.

The fact that Martinez had specifically requested him worried him, too.

The wind whipped the car as they climbed in, the windowpanes rattling as they drove across the reservation. Dylan's nerves were on edge as he constantly scanned the deserted roads and hiding spots for another attacker or car following them.

He parked on the ridge by Martinez's police car, and Callie and Ava parked beside him, climbing out with their kits in hand.

He pressed a hand on Aspen's shoulder. "Stay here and keep the doors locked. If anything happens, honk the horn and I'll be here in a second."

"I could go with you," Aspen offered.

Not knowing what he would find or the condition of the woman's body, he shook his head. "No. This is official police work. The fewer people contaminating the scene, the better."

She nodded in understanding, and he climbed out and punched the lock button before heading down the embankment to where Martinez and Bree were waiting. Bree met him at the bottom of the hill.

The scent of the murky water, vegetation and death swirled in the breeze as he approached the river where Martinez stood beside the local medical examiner. Dr. Pruitt, a fortysomething, gray-haired man with a cleft chin, was bent over the body, examining it.

Dylan braced himself to view another dead female body as he stepped closer. Martinez angled his head and moved to the side to give him a better view and Dylan's stomach churned.

Her hair was matted, skin pale white with fish and bug bites, her throat slashed from ear to ear.

"How long has she been dead?" Martinez asked.

"A day at least, but it's hard to tell with the decomp. The temperature of the water helped preserve her but the fish…" He shook his head. "Damn son of a bitch tied her down so she'd sink. But a couple of the knots slipped loose and she floated to the top. Some rafters found her caught between some rocks."

"You questioned them?" Dylan asked.

Bree spoke up. "Yeah, it was a couple of teenagers. They were pretty freaked out. I called their parents and they already took them home."

"Cause of death?" Martinez asked.

The medical examiner lifted the woman's head slightly, and Dylan noted the slash mark on her neck. A slash mark that looked sickeningly familiar.

"She has a bruise on the back of her head and several on her body, but basically, her throat was slashed and she bled out. Forensics may be able to tell us more about the kind of knife the killer used."

The rope tied to the woman's wrist made bile rise to Dylan's throat.

At the end of the rope, he saw the chunk of thunderwood.

Dylan ground his teeth together. Callie muttered something under her breath, and Ava gave a small gasp.

"What do you think?" Martinez asked Dylan.

Dylan's throat thickened with fear. "You know what I think."

"It could be a copycat," Callie suggested.

Dylan met her gaze. "I know. Or Turnbull could have survived that crash and have started all over again."

"But it doesn't quite fit Turnbull's MO," Ava said. "Turnbull left his victims out in the open for us to find as if he was gloating about it. This time the body was tied and dumped in the river so we wouldn't find her."

Dylan stewed over that point. "Maybe he wasn't ready to let us know he'd survived the accident."

"Or Watts and Perkins did it and used the thunderwood to throw us off," Ava suggested.

"Find out who she is," Dylan said. "I'll phone Warden Fernandez to alert him of our suspicions." He'd also see if he'd sent over Turnbull's prison correspondence and take it with him to the safe house. Then he'd review it himself to see if Turnbull had orchestrated an escape or if they were dealing with a copycat.

Because this girl wouldn't be his last victim.

And the fact that he'd found a piece of thunderwood

on Aspen's doorstep meant that the man would be coming for her.

Dylan had to be ready when he did. If he laid one hand on Aspen, he'd forget prison this time.

He'd kill the son of a bitch even if he had to go to prison himself afterwards.

THE TENSION IN THE CAR as they drove back to Emma's made Aspen queasy. She'd returned home again, and now she had to leave her house, her cousin, everything behind. Worse, she had no idea how long she'd be gone.

Only that Dylan was going to be with her around the clock.

Under other circumstances, spending time with the sexy, handsome agent might be pleasant.

His gaze slid over her and her body tingled as she remembered the heated kiss earlier. She amended her thoughts. It wouldn't just be pleasant, it would be downright fun.

They might explore where that kiss could lead and recreate the passionate week he'd claimed they'd spent together when they'd first met.

He parked at Emma's and her heart sputtered with excitement at the thought of seeing her son again. How could she have forgotten him all those weeks? He was so much a part of her that she'd missed him the past few hours.

As soon as they entered, she smelled the scent of homemade stew and spicy jalapeno corn bread, and her stomach growled. Emma greeted her with a hug and Miguel stepped outside with Dylan.

"How did it go?" Emma asked.

Aspen explained that her memory had returned, and about the trap they planned to set for Perkins and Watts.

Emma's eyes widened in horror. "That sounds dangerous."

Aspen shrugged off her concern. "Dylan and Jack and I are moving to a safe house. Other agents will watch my house and if Perkins or Watts appear, they'll catch them. Then the danger will be over and Jack and I will be safe."

Dylan and Miguel came in wearing scowls. "You told Emma about the plan?" Dylan asked.

She nodded.

Miguel moved to stand beside Emma, a protective gleam in his eyes. "Did she tell you that Frank Turnbull may have escaped? That they found a Ute woman killed with the same MO?"

Emma leaned one hand against the table edge with a shudder, and Miguel took her in his arms. "That means you don't go anywhere without me, *Loca Linda.*"

Emma nodded. "Don't worry. I don't intend to."

"I phoned the ME who's been analyzing the bodies from the prison bus crash and told him to put a rush on those bones," Dylan said. "If Turnbull has escaped, we need to put out the word. And if we have a copycat, we need to do the same."

Dylan's gaze met Aspen's. Fear glittered in his eyes for a brief second before he masked it.

Did he have reason to think that Frank Turnbull might come after her?

THE UTE SLICER WAS LEGENDARY. Had earned fame and a reputation that would follow him into eternity.

He'd smiled as he'd watched from the top of the ridge as the Feds and police recovered the woman's body. He hadn't expected them to find her so soon, but hell, maybe this was a good thing.

The cops would be sweating. Sympathizing with the victim. Trying to figure out who he was.

While he was one step ahead of them.

The memory of slicing the woman's throat made his body go hard, and he mentally envisioned the knife piercing the girl's delicate flesh, then the blood gurgling and flowing down his hands.

The whites of her eyes had turned stark with terror when she realized her death was imminent.

Hell, yeah, it had been a rush he hadn't felt in a long damn time.

Let them shake in their shoes and stew for a while now. Try to figure out if Turnbull had survived or if a copycat had surfaced to mimic the man's crimes.

He held the knife up to the moonlight, the sharp blade glinting.

Meanwhile, life for some went on.

But for others, it was time to say a final goodbye.

Chapter Thirteen

"Go pack," Dylan said as soon as they entered Aspen's house. "I want us to get out of here before the evening news airs."

Aspen cradled Jack to her as if he was afraid to release him. "He needs changing before we go."

"I'll take care of it," Dylan said. "Get your things together, then you can pack whatever we'll need for the baby." He hesitated, sensing her distress and reluctance to leave her home when she'd just found her way back. "Unless you've changed your mind." He grabbed her arm. "If you have, it's okay. I'll call off the whole damn plan."

She kissed Jack's forehead, her grip around the baby tightening as if she didn't want to let him go, but resignation lit her eyes and she eased Jack into his arms. "No. Those men have to be caught and put away."

He gently embraced the little boy, Jack's arms and legs kicking playfully. Aspen stroked the baby's cheek, then turned and rushed into her room.

Dylan released the pent up feelings he'd been holding in ever since Callie had given him the results of the paternity tests. Unbidden, moisture pricked his eyes as he pulled the blanket away from his son's face and gazed into his eyes.

His own blue eyes.

"My God, you are amazing," he whispered hoarsely. "You are my little *mijo,* my son, and I will never leave you now."

Jack grabbed his finger and curled his fist around it as if he understood.

Dylan's heart swelled with love. There was no way he could walk away from his baby or Aspen.

He'd die before he let anyone hurt them again.

ASPEN BLINKED BACK TEARS as they left her house. Almost desperately she glanced back, memorizing the details of it as if she might forget where she lived once again.

"We're not going far," Dylan said, giving her hand a squeeze as if he sensed her distress. "We'll still be in Mesa Verde country."

Still among her people. She took some solace in that.

She squeezed his hand in return, grateful to know that he wouldn't leave her until they'd caught the men after her.

But then he would move on.

That realization sent an ache through her, an emptiness that reminded her of how lonely she'd felt the last few weeks when she'd been isolated and scared and had no one to turn to.

Jack gurgled from the back, and she turned sideways to comfort him. "It's okay, sweet one, we're just taking a little trip. An adventure."

Dylan gave her an odd look. "That was what my parents used to call it when we went on vacation."

She relaxed slightly. "Tell me about your family."

A wistful look passed across his face as he steered them toward Cortez. "My family comes from a long line of farmers who grew potatoes and alfalfa in the San Luis Valley. My parents were the first ones to go to college." A proud smile curved his mouth. "Papa is an attorney. He calls himself King Pro Bono. And Mama is an artist and teacher at Adams State College in Alamosa."

"You have other siblings?"

He nodded, although the scar at his chin twitched. "You met Miguel. I also have another brother and sister who are married with kids. And then there was Teresa." His tone lowered a decibel. "She died in a drive-by shooting when she was a teenager."

His story tapped at her memory banks as if he'd shared it before. "I'm sorry. That must have been horrible for your family."

He made a pained noise deep in his throat. "I was standing right there, only a few feet away. It should have been me."

She heard the agony in his voice, the guilt. "Her death inspired you to go into police work?"

He gave a self-deprecating laugh. "In a roundabout way." He sighed and rammed his hand through his hair, spiking the dark strands. "I was enraged, went looking for revenge. My father, Papa, was working the courts, my mother grieving. It was a rough time for all of us."

"And Miguel?"

"He was a damn altar boy. The smart, scientific one where I was the troublemaker."

"I'm sure that's not true."

"Oh, it was," he said with conviction. "Miguel toyed with being a priest. But he got shot defending his girlfriend and had a near-death experience. That changed him, and he decided to go into forensics and study medicine. He claimed that's what saved him. Although my mother always insisted that it wasn't the medical procedures that saved him but the healing soil of El Santuario de Chimayo and prayer."

"I think I'd like your mother," Aspen said softly.

A sultry smile softened his eyes as he turned to look at her. "You would. And I know she'd like you."

Aspen's heart melted at his words. His family sounded loving, honorable, spiritual, and reminded her of her own mother, and the role model she wanted to be for her son.

But what about a father or male figure for Jack to identify with?

She had managed without one. But was it different for a boy? Did he need a man in his life?

ASPEN'S QUESTIONS ABOUT HIS family triggered bittersweet memories. The family trips, the camping, the cookouts, the normal childhood fights between siblings.

The empty hole Teresa's death had created.

The Christmas ornament they still hung on the tree every year in her honor—a graduation cap with her name on it and the date she would have received her high school diploma.

And then there had been the lectures from his family, the rules and consequences, the ones he'd balked at and fought.

The ones his parents had instigated because they loved him so much.

He'd do the same for little Jack.

Hell, he knew he'd make mistakes. But he'd do his

damnedest to raise his son to be the kind of man his own father would be proud of.

They passed ranches and farmland, the open terrain, steep cliffs, ridges and deep canyons that made the majestic La Plata Mountains, the Sleeping Ute Mountain and the sharp-hewn silhouette of Mesa Verde a home for locals and a tourist draw for travelers far and wide.

Jack babbled noisily and Aspen turned to talk to him. "When you get bigger I'll take you to the Ute Mountain Rodeo," she said, and Dylan bit his tongue to keep from correcting her—*We'll take you to the Ute Mountain Rodeo.*

"And we'll visit the Cortez Cultural Arts Center so you can see the Indian dances and artwork of our people," she continued. "The Bear Dance is in June. Legend says it all began when a man went to sleep and had a dream about a bear. In the dream, he thought if he went up into the mountains, the bear would teach him something of great strength. And so he did."

She paused and Jack made a cooing sound as if he enjoyed the sound of her voice and understood the meaning of the story.

"The bear gave him words of wisdom and taught him the bear dance, so he came down and shared it with his people," she continued. "When you get bigger, we'll go to the Mesa Verde National Park to see the celebration. They have a big balloon ride every year and you can watch the colorful balloons float across the sky. Most of the time our Ute people dress in regular clothes, in jeans and dresses, but a long time ago the women wore deerskin dresses and the men wore beachcloths. You'll see some of that at the festivals and dances."

By the time they arrived at the small house in the heart of Cortez, Dylan had learned more about the Ute history from Aspen than he'd ever learned in school. He'd developed a newfound respect for the plight of her people and her devotion to passing on the customs and stories of her ancestors.

The archaeology of the Mesa Verde cities was renowned and had inspired artists for years, the house where they were going to be staying was an adobe cottage that sat on top of a ridge and fit into the sweeping cliffs as if it had been carved naturally from the land.

Except this house had been fitted with a high-tech security system and a view of the mountainside to provide privacy and security for those who needed refuge from the world.

"It's beautiful," Aspen said as she carried Jack inside, and Dylan retrieved their luggage.

"I'm glad you like it." The space suddenly felt very intimate with the three of them inside. She offered him a tentative smile, and Jack cooed up at him from her arms. For a moment, Dylan savored the brief reprieve from the reality they'd left behind and imagined that this was their home.

That he and Aspen and Jack were a real family. That tonight they would put their son to bed.

Then they would fall into their own sanctuary together and make love until dawn.

And for once in his life, there wasn't a hit man or a serial killer lurking to destroy their happiness.

ASPEN'S SKIN PRICKLED with awareness as Dylan watched her settle Jack into the infant seat in the

Mexican tiled kitchen. She'd felt close to him in the car, admired the way he talked about his family and the affectionate tone to his words. He obviously loved them deeply.

What would it be like to be loved like that? To have a family unit who shared hopes and dreams yet still managed to maintain a close bond in the face of turbulent times?

Sadness welled in her chest. She missed her mother and Emma, and wanted her son to have the kind of family Dylan had described.

A family with a mother and a father.

But she had to be careful who she let into their lives.

Jack waved his fist at her and whimpered. He was probably hungry, so she stirred rice cereal into a bowl with the formula she'd heated from his bottle, making it soupy enough for him to swallow. Then she settled down in a chair to feed him.

He gulped down a few bites, spitting out half of it. She laughed. "I know it's not so tasty," she said, "but at least it's not grasshoppers." She scooped up another bite full and pressed the tip of the spoon to his lips, smiling as he sucked in the liquid mush.

"Tourists always ask what we Indians like to eat," she said softly. "Of course, we like modern food and fruits and vegetables. But they want to know about our past." She made a soaring noise with her mouth, swooping toward him with another spoonful as if they were playing a game. He followed the movement with his eyes, opening his mouth wide to slurp the cereal. "Years ago, it's true, that the Utes liked to eat grasshoppers and other insects. The Spanish thought it was disgusting, but they ate eggs and we thought that was gross, too."

Dylan moved up behind her and laughed as Jack puffed up his lips and blew bubbles, making cereal dribble down his chin.

"You'll like fish and meat better, little *mijo,*" Dylan said in a low voice. "Just wait and I'll teach you how to fish."

Aspen froze, her heart sputtering as she turned to look into his eyes. Why would he make a promise like that to her son when they both knew as soon as he caught Perkins and Watts, he'd be out of their lives?

DYLAN REALIZED WHAT HE'D SAID and had to back away. He'd allowed his love for his son and his dreams of fatherhood to destroy his concentration and had almost blurted out the truth to Aspen.

The fact that she didn't remember him or that he'd fathered her baby sent a white-hot rage through him. But the fact that she hadn't told him about their baby drove the pain deeper inside.

Jerking himself away from the table, he turned to retrieve the files they'd confiscated from the prison warden.

"Dylan?" Aspen asked softly.

"Just take care of the baby. I have work to do."

Her look of hurt and confusion added to his guilt, but his own emotions were too raw now for him to even try to explain. The Feds and local police were watching out for Perkins and Watts.

Better bury himself in the job and find out if Turnbull was alive, or if a copycat had surfaced.

He spread the files on the desk in the den, searching

through Turnbull's visitor log. In the past year, he'd had a couple of visitors—a woman named Sally Ann McCobb, and his half brother, Freddy.

Freddy had been present in court. The man had looked so different from the shaggy-headed, tattooed, burly Turnbull that Dylan would never have put them in the same family. But during the trial, he'd learned that Turnbull was half Ute. His mother had married a Ute man and lived on the reservation with him, while Freddy had been born of her first marriage to a man in Utah.

He jotted down both names to follow up on, noting the dates of their visits. Sally Ann McCobb had visited two weeks before Turnbull had been transferred, the half brother only three days.

He'd check them both out.

Next, he scanned the phone calls and found both Sally Ann and Freddy on the list, along with two other women.

There were stacks of letters from other fans to sort through, so he put those aside to look over after Aspen and Jack went to bed.

Then he checked the list of inmates and friends Turnbull had acquired in prison. One name on the list made his blood turn to ice.

Larry Gerome Sawyer—aka the Slaughterer.

He had killed over twelve women in a bloodbath that had rocked the Northern Ute tribe.

Dylan had also worked that case. Like Turnbull, the con hated his guts.

His heart raced as he checked the list of prisoners being transported with Turnbull.

The pendulum of questions began to swing back and forth in his head. Dear God.

Had Turnbull and Sawyer been partners of sorts? Had one or both of them planned the escape and walked away alive?

HE PRIDED HIMSELF on watching the news. He kept up with politics, with the economy, the stock market, but mostly he had a fetish for the crime.

A chuckle rumbled from him as he watched the news anchor.

"Aspen Meadows, the Ute woman who was missing for several weeks, has been found and is safe and alive. Preliminary reports stated that she was suffering from amnesia, but recently her memory has returned. She admitted that she witnessed two men dumping federal agent Julie Grainger's body along the river. The men have been identified as Boyd Perkins, a man believed to be a hit man for a local mob family, and Sherman Watts, a local Ute man who has assisted Perkins in evading the law."

He pressed his hand to his chest and laughed. The damn Feds thought they were setting a trap, but he was smarter than them.

And he'd been lying low. He'd had time to plan.

Their scheme would backfire in their faces.

He looked down at the blood on the girl's neck and imagined Acevedo's face when he found her, her neck slashed, her eyes panicked in terror, her mouth wide-open in a scream.

He had to find a public place to dump her body, some place significant, some place that would mean something to Acevedo.

Some place he couldn't resist leaving Aspen to come to.

He knew the place.

Yes, Acevedo would find her and see her blood in his dreams for the rest of his life.

Then he'd feel vulnerable, guilty, unworthy, imprisoned by the people he couldn't save, as well as the ones he'd put behind bars.

So sweet that he would think the Ute Slicer was back.

Of course he wouldn't know his identity. Wouldn't know if it was Turnbull's knife that had killed the girl or someone who just admired his handiwork.

Not until it was too late and Aspen Meadows was dead.

Chapter Fourteen

Aspen found the kitchen pantry and refrigerator stocked, as well as the nursery. After feeding Jack, she filled the baby bathtub full of warm water, stripped Jack and placed him inside with the rubber duck toy. He chased the little yellow duck as it floated around him as she bathed him, then scrunched up his nose in distaste when she soaped his hair with baby shampoo, then rinsed out the soap. But he seemed infatuated with the bubbles in the water and slapped at them with his hand.

"I'm glad you're taking this so well," she said. "You don't even seem to mind moving around."

While she didn't adjust quite so easily to change. She'd grown up on the reservation and, except for her college days, had never considered living anywhere else. Maybe that was the reason she hadn't kept Jack's father in the picture.

Or maybe he hadn't cared for Jack or her at all.

The water was growing cold, so she wrapped Jack in a bath towel, carried him to the dresser/changing table and laid him down. He kicked and swatted at the towel as she dried him off, then powdered his bottom and diapered him.

"You smell so sweet," she said as she wrestled with a little blue sleeper she found in the drawer. She snuggled him to her, then sat down in the rocking chair and read him a picture book, pointing out the simple objects on the colorful pages and smiling as he tried to grab the book and stuff the corners in his mouth.

A few minutes later, he dozed to sleep, and she rose and tucked him into the crib, covering him with a blanket. "Good night, little one. Sleep good." She kissed her hand, then pressed it to his cheek. "One day we won't be running," she whispered. "One day we'll be home to stay. And you can play with the other children on the reservation and learn to fish on the land. And we'll never have to leave home again."

When she turned to leave the room, Dylan stood at the door watching her, his gaze so intense that she froze. "What?" she whispered.

"You will be safe," he said quietly. "I promise you, Aspen. One day you and Jack won't have to look over your shoulders anymore."

The fact that he claimed they'd made love for a week taunted her. The kiss they'd shared proved the heat was still there, too, the embers of the fire simmering, waiting to be stoked.

She wondered if he was thinking about that week. If he ever regretted them parting.

And if being here alone with her and Jack might tempt him to come back to her bed.

Suddenly his look turned shuttered, as if he'd read her thoughts and had already answered them. And the answer was no.

Then he turned and left the room. She wanted to go

after him. To see if they could rekindle whatever they'd had. But she couldn't.

She had to think of Jack and their future.

She didn't want to be left with a broken heart, or for her son to cry after a man who didn't want him.

DYLAN LEFT THE ROOM before he gave into temptation and kissed Aspen.

And admitted that he was Jack's father.

He wanted her to remember, dammit, and explain why she'd left him out of their lives. Why she'd indicated to Lightfoot that she hadn't considered him father material, and that she hadn't felt anything more for him than lust.

While he'd thought about her every day while he was away.

Damn. He had to focus. He had a stack of letters to Turnbull to check out. It was hard to believe that instead of being terrified of serial killers as one would expect, that some killers drew fans—groupies. That some women actually felt sorry for the bastards and thought their love could save the men's sorry souls.

Foolish, sick, dysfunctional—and a growing problem that still baffled him to no end.

He reviewed the names he'd collected so far. Sally Ann McCobb, the female who'd visited Turnbull in jail. Freddy, the half brother.

And Larry Gerome Sawyer—the Slaughterer.

He had to know if Sawyer had died in the crash.

Wiping his clammy hands on his jeans, he punched the number for the state ME. The man answered on the third ring.

"Hi, Doc, this is Dylan Acevedo with the Bureau."

"Yeah, I've been talking with your brother. I already told him I'd let you guys know when I finished the results."

Impatience gnawed at Dylan. "That means you haven't confirmed that Turnbull is dead yet?"

"The partial dental plate suggests it was him, but I'm conducting more tests to verify since the plate wasn't in the man's mouth."

"How about the other bodies?" Dylan asked. "Who have you identified?"

"For sure, the bus driver, the guards and one of the prisoners."

"Which one?"

"A guy named Barry Burgess—inmates called him Buffalo. Man wore a size seventeen shoe, so his remains were the most obvious. And dental records confirmed the rest."

"How about Larry Gerome Sawyer?"

"I'm working on his body and the one we think is Turnbull's now."

Frustration knotted Dylan's shoulders. "You heard that a woman was killed using Turnbull's MO. We need to act quickly. Let me know as soon as you get the results."

The ME gave a long, labored sigh. "Listen, I haven't slept in over twenty-four hours. I'm working as fast as I can."

Dylan hung up and rubbed the back of his neck, trying to massage away the knots. It was too late to visit Sally Ann McCobb tonight or go to the prison, but he would do both in the morning.

Still, he could do some background work tonight.

He tapped into the federal databases and plugged in

the woman's name. A few minutes later, he had the scoop on Sally Ann.

She was in her thirties, had worked as a hairdresser for years, and recently gone back to school to study psychology. She'd first contacted Turnbull under the guise of research for a paper she was writing.

His interest piqued, he dug deeper. She had no record, no arrests, not even a parking ticket. Although she had been in counseling before she enrolled in the community college.

Counseling for spousal abuse.

The pieces fit with the general profile of prisoner groupies. He copied down her address, anxious to question the woman.

With Larry Gerome Sawyer on his mind, he accessed the files on his trial and crimes. The gruesome, bloody photos of a half-dozen women spilled onto the screen.

His stomach churned as he noted the details of his vicious attacks, stirring memories of the case. Memories he'd tried to banish.

Behind him, Aspen gasped. He stiffened, then turned to see her looking over his shoulder, her wide terrorized eyes glued to the photographs.

Dear God, he hadn't meant for her to see them or to know that another sick man just like Turnbull might be coming after her.

ASPEN STARED AT THE PICTURES of the bloody, naked bodies in front of her in horror.

She'd known Dylan was working but she'd assumed it had something to do with her and the trap they'd set for Perkins and Watts.

Yet he'd told her about the case he'd investigated before they'd met. Violent crime work was his job. Not just his job but his life.

"What are you doing?" she whispered.

He immediately shut down the file and stood. "I'm sorry. I didn't mean for you to see those."

She tried to recover, but she couldn't shake the images from her mind. "How do you do it?"

"Do what?"

"Investigate those crimes. Look at those dead women and not fall apart."

He reached out and stroked her arms. "I do sometimes," he said softly. Gently he lifted his hand and pushed her hair from her cheek. "The night we met. I was on the edge that evening. When I caught up with Turnbull, I wanted to kill him. Not lock him up but make him suffer the way he made those young women suffer." His tone dropped a decibel. "But then I met you and you brought me back to the brink of sanity."

Aspen's heart began to race. His touch felt so tender, but she heard the torment in his voice. "We talked about the case," she whispered.

He nodded. "I talked. You listened. You even thanked me for what I did." He gave a self-deprecating laugh. "I wasn't a hero that night, Aspen. I almost killed Turnbull in cold blood. Almost turned into a monster like him."

Aspen smiled, then reached up and pressed her hand to his cheek. "You could never be like him. He viciously destroyed innocent people's lives. Not just the women's lives he killed but their families and loved ones. You are a hero—you sought justice for them when they couldn't speak for themselves."

He shook his head as if he still didn't believe her, and Aspen's lungs tightened. No wonder she had slept with him the first night she'd met him. He was the sexiest, most honorable man she'd ever met. After working grueling hours to catch a killer and protect lives, he'd needed someone to comfort him.

So he'd turned to her.

How could she have resisted?

How could she resist him now?

She couldn't. She slid her hand into his hair and pulled him toward her, then stood on her tiptoes and pressed her lips to his. He growled low in his throat and yanked her to him as if he'd been waiting on an invitation.

He tasted like coffee and strength and man, a tantalizing flavor that made her crave more. He probed her lips apart with his tongue, then slipped inside to tease her as he deepened the kiss. She moved against him, her body bursting into an erotic song and dance that begged to partner with him.

He slid his arms over her shoulders and back, massaging her as he pulled her into him. His erection pulsed against her abdomen, sending a torrent of sensations through her. His hand found her breast, stroking, teasing, making desire surge through her.

No wonder she had stayed in bed for a week with this man.

She wanted to drag him there now and make love to him all night. To feel the pleasure his fingers and mouth evoked, to sate the burning need deep inside her.

He kneed her legs apart, pressing his hard length into the juncture between her thighs, and she grew moist with want. With a low groan, he dragged his mouth from hers and dipped his head to drop tongue lashes along her neck and throat, then downward until she arched her head backward and purred her delight.

A second later, his fingers traced her nipple through her blouse, and she groaned his name, hoping he'd follow the erotic touch with his mouth.

He didn't disappoint.

He slowly unbuttoned her blouse, parting the sheer fabric until he exposed the lace covering her breasts. His soft murmur of appreciation fueled her passionate response, and she reached for his shirt, anxious to feel bare chest against bare chest.

But he halted her movements by shoving her hands away, tugging her bra down and lowering his mouth to her nipple. He flicked his tongue over the pebbled bud, sending a spasm of need from her chest to her abdomen, then he closed his lips around the turgid peak, and she moaned. He wrapped his arms around her as her legs buckled, and he pulled the tip between his teeth, nipping, then suckling her until she thought she'd die from the pure pleasure of his wet tongue.

"Dylan, let's go to bed," she whispered, clutching him so her legs didn't give way.

Ignoring her, he moved his mouth to her other breast, loving it the same way, and heat shot through her, the yearning so intense that she slid her hand down to cup his sex. He was hard and full and ready.

She wanted him inside her, loving her, reminding her of the week they'd spent together, making her feel alive.

A sound jarred her from her euphoria. Jack. He was crying.

Dylan stiffened, slowly flicking his tongue over her

one more time, then letting go to search her face. His eyes were glazed, his breathing erratic, the stark need in his eyes mirroring the frantic pounding of her heart.

But Jack whimpered again, and she gave him a look of regret. "I guess I'd better check on him."

He gave a clipped nod, and she left the room. Although when she glanced over her shoulder, he was still watching her, his eyes smoldering, and a warm tingling spread through her. Maybe later they could take up where they'd left off.

But as soon as she saw Jack, reality intervened. What in the world was she thinking? She couldn't get involved with Dylan, not when he would leave them both.

Not when she didn't even remember the past and the name of Jack's father.

Or whether he might resurface again and want to be a part of their lives.

His INSTINCTS warned Dylan it was better that Jack had awakened and stopped him from making love to Aspen. But his body betrayed all rational logic and throbbed in protest.

He wanted Aspen just as much as he'd wanted her the very first time he'd seen her.

No. He wanted her more.

He walked to the nursery door and saw her lifting Jack into her arms, and his heart swelled with longing. These two people could be his family.

Jack already was, although Aspen seemed to have no idea.

And until she did and explained why she hadn't told him he had a son, he couldn't take her to his bed.

His cell phone trilled, jarring him from the moment, and he forced himself to back away and answer it. "Acevedo speaking."

"Dylan, it's Martinez. You're not going to like this, but we found another body. A Ute woman, early twenties."

Dylan bowed his head. "Same MO as the Ute Slicer?"

"I'm afraid so."

Dylan cursed and glanced at the nursery door where Aspen stood holding Jack. His heart slammed into his ribs.

If this killer came after her, he'd have to go through him first.

Chapter Fifteen

By the time Aspen rocked Jack back to sleep and returned to the living room, Dylan looked sullen. He was sorting through a stack of letters on the table and didn't even glance up when she stepped up beside him and placed her hand on his shoulder.

She wanted to pick up where they'd left off, but sensed he had withdrawn.

"Dylan?"

He stilled, dropped the envelope on the table and drew in a deep breath. "Go to bed, Aspen."

She felt the tension in his shoulder and rubbed the knot. "Why don't you come, too?"

His breath gushed out, but he didn't move to get up. Instead, he pulled away from her touch. "I have work to do."

Anger and confusion suffused her. "What kind of game are you playing?"

He finally turned and her breath caught at the intense expression in his eyes. Hunger was there, burning raw and bright, but also something akin to fear.

And maybe anger.

Déjà vu struck her. It was the same kind of dangerous look he'd had when she'd first met him. As if he was barely holding on to his ironclad control. As if he wanted to assuage the pain of the victims' faces that haunted him. As if he didn't deserve that reprieve.

"Please, Dylan," she said softly. "You've been working day and night."

His jaw tightened, and he finally stood and faced her, placing his hands on both of her arms. "And I'll keep working until I know that you're completely safe."

"We are safe here tonight," she said, hating to plead, but they both needed comfort.

"Maybe," he said in a deep voice. "But we just set the trap today. I have to stay focused and alert."

Disappointment made Aspen back away. She couldn't remember, but she didn't think she'd ever asked a man—begged a man—to go to bed with her.

She wouldn't do it again.

"Try to get some rest," she said, then she turned and fled to the bedroom before she forgot her promise to her son and convinced Dylan to make love to her anyway.

REFUSING ASPEN'S INVITATION was one of the most difficult things Dylan had ever done. His body hummed with arousal, literally ached from wanting to join her in bed, but the phone call earlier had reminded him that Aspen was in more danger than even she thought.

That a madman, as well as Perkins and Watts, might be after her.

And all because of him.

He spent the next few hours going over the letters

from the women who'd written Turnbull. The man had received hate mail along with letters from holy rollers who claimed they'd pray for his soul, and two other women who had offered conjugal visits. One from a lady in Nevada, another from a woman in New Jersey.

By 5:00 a.m., he called Ryan and asked him to contact someone in those states and check out the two women in case they'd recently been contacted by Turnbull or had helped him escape. He also asked Ryan to come and watch Aspen so he could follow up on the prisoners and Sally Ann McCobb.

Ryan was at the house by six. "I could go to the prison and talk to this woman," Ryan suggested.

Dylan shook his head. "No, I want to do it myself. Turnbull pledged revenge against me." Besides, he needed to put some physical space between him and Aspen.

Jack and Aspen were both still sleeping, so he left and drove to the prison first.

Warden Fernandez didn't appear surprised to see him. "I figured you'd show up sooner or later."

Dylan shook his hand and claimed the wooden chair across from the warden's desk. "I spoke with the state ME last night. It looks like both of your guards received wounds that suggest an attempted prison break. He's identified Burgess's body but is still working on Turnbull's and Sawyer's."

"Two of our most notorious," Fernandez muttered. "Frankly, I was glad they were being transferred. Both were cold-blooded psychopaths."

"Did either of them have any friends in here?"

"Friends?" Fernandez gave a sarcastic grunt. "I'm not sure either man knew what a friend was. Turnbull stabbed Sawyer and was in solitary the last few days before he was transferred."

"So they teamed up? That doesn't make sense."

He shrugged. "They were both tough bastards. Neither one showed any remorse."

And if the two of them had escaped and paired up— God help them all.

"Can I speak to Turnbull's former cell mate?"

"Sure." He punched a button on his intercom and ordered one of the guards to bring the man to a holding room, then gestured for Dylan to follow.

They passed through security, and Dylan stood by the wooden table in the interrogation room while the guard escorted Carl Tanner, a short, bald, robust guy in handcuffs and leg irons into the room.

Tanner was a doctor who'd killed his wife because she'd had an affair. Compared to Turnbull and Sawyer, he was a damn saint.

Although the snarl on his pocked face didn't look saintly.

Dylan produced his badge and introduced himself.

Tanner angled his head to the left. "What do you want?"

"I need to talk to you about Frank Turnbull."

A grin curled the man's lips. "Heard that son of a bitch died."

"That's what I want to discuss. There's a possibility he might not have been killed in the crash. That he could have escaped. Or that a copycat is imitating his crimes." He explained about the two murders following Turnbull's MO.

Tanner whistled. "So. What's it got to do with me?"

"You were his cell mate for a while. Were you two buddies?"

"Hell, no. Turnbull didn't make friends." Tanner yanked open the top buttons of his shirt, revealing a set of deep scars. "He did that with a fork. So, he definitely ain't no friend of mine."

That would work to his favor. "Did he talk to you about escaping?"

Tanner chuckled. "All the damn time. That and getting revenge on the man who put him in here."

"Did he ever mention a partner? Admit that he worked with someone to commit the Ute Slicer murders?"

Tanner shook his head. "Man like him wants control. He wouldn't have a damn partner—he likes to work alone so he can bask in all the glory."

Dylan's frustration mounted. He needed something new, concrete. "How about a name or a contact? Someone who would have helped him try to escape?"

Tanner leaned forward with his beefy arms on the table. "What you gonna do for me if I tell you?"

"What do you want?"

Pain flashed in Tanner's eyes. "To see my kid. I haven't seen him since I've been in. I want to tell him how sorry I am."

Dylan twisted his mouth in thought. "I'll see what I can do."

Tanner worked his mouth side to side. "Some bleached-blond bimbo used to visit him. Name was Sally Ann. He told me he hated the bitch but she'd do anything for him."

Tanner shook his head. "I don't get it. I get hate mail for killing my cheating wife, and he murders girls for fun and women write him love letters."

"You're right, it doesn't make sense," Dylan agreed.

"But a lot of crimes don't." He hesitated. "Can you think of anyone else?"

Tanner shrugged. "His half brother, Freddy. Seems he felt indebted to Turnbull for something but he never said why."

Dylan thanked him and stood. Maybe Freddy had paid off his debt by helping Turnbull escape.

ASPEN STUMBLED INTO THE kitchen to make coffee and was surprised to find Agent Tom Ryan sitting at the table instead of Dylan.

She frowned, grateful she'd thrown on a pair of jeans and sweater instead of wearing her pajamas. "Where's Dylan?"

Tom glanced up from his notes. "He wanted to pursue some leads, so you're stuck with me for a few hours."

She poured herself a cup of coffee and went to look out the window. Situated at the top of the ridge, she had a sweeping view of the land, the snow-capped mountaintops, the shrubs and grass in the canyon that would be turning green as soon as spring resurrected life back to the parched land.

Why had Dylan gone instead of letting one of the other agents pursue the leads?

Because he wanted to get away from you.

She sipped the hot coffee, renewing her vow not to push him again. Obviously whatever they'd shared when they'd first met had meant nothing to him. She was just a case now that he had to finish. A witness to protect.

Not the woman he loved.

"You shouldn't stand in front of the window," Agent Ryan said. "It's too dangerous."

A chill rippled through her at his warning, and she backed away, suddenly angry and claustrophobic. "I hate this," she muttered. "Hate being afraid. Hiding out. Wondering if or when someone might come out of nowhere and strike."

"We have agents watching your house. We'll get them."

She whirled around. "But it's so unfair. He has the control, the power."

"It'll be over soon, Aspen. You just have to hang in there and trust Dylan."

Trust Dylan? That was the ironic thing. She *had* trusted him from the moment he'd picked her up at the shelter.

Jack whimpered from the nursery, and she forced her thoughts about Dylan to the back of her mind. Her baby needed her.

And she would do whatever she had to do to protect him and give him a good life.

Her mother had raised her alone and managed. Somehow, she would do the same.

If only she could stop wishing Dylan would be a part of her life.

DYLAN DROVE TO EAGLE'S LANDING to see Freddy, but the man wasn't home. He found a work address from the database and headed to the garage where Freddy was supposed to work.

A skinny man, probably midforties, wearing grease-stained coveralls and smoking a cigarette loped toward him. "What you want, mister?" He gestured toward Dylan's car. "Need some work done?"

"No." Dylan removed his ID from his pocket and

flashed it. "Name is Special Agent Acevedo. I need to speak to one of your employees, Freddy Lakers."

The man took a drag of his cigarette and blew smoke through his nose. "Freddy ain't showed up at work for going on a week now."

Dylan frowned. "Has he called in? Anyone here heard from him?"

"Nope, not a word." The man puffed on his cigarette again. "But if he does show up, I'm gonna fire his ass."

Dylan gave him his card, told him if he heard from him to call him, then climbed back in his car. He checked Sally Ann's address and turned onto the street, then headed toward Crescent Canyon.

On the drive, his mind raced back to the night before, to the fact that Aspen had wanted him.

And not because she remembered their time in Vegas together.

A smile curved his mouth as a thought struck him. Maybe their time in Vegas hadn't just been a heat-of-the-moment affair. The fact that she wanted him again now meant there might be something deeper between them.

But how could they have a relationship with secrets and lies still between them?

HE KNEW WHERE ASPEN MEADOWS WAS hiding.

He'd followed Acevedo and watched him escort the Ute woman inside that house on the mountain. He thought she was safe.

But none of the Ute women were safe.

Only Aspen could wait a few hours.

First he had to pay a visit to another woman. One he'd fantasized about reuniting with for the past year.

One he wanted to kill.

But first he'd make her suffer.

He stared at the battered old house with hate churning in his gut. Here, his first evil thoughts had been born. Here, he'd fantasized about murder.

Ducking low, he wove between the shrubs and bushes surrounding her small wooden house, memories of her cruel beatings and preaching returning.

The paint on the house had faded and chipped over the years, the windowpanes were dirty, the porch sagging and rotting. He'd heard that his stepfather had long ago run out on her.

Not that he blamed him. The damn bitch would kill any love anyone had for her.

The house was dark inside, the lights off, and a mangy dog lay sprawled in front of the porch steps. He stopped to scratch behind his ears, then the wood floor squeaked as he climbed the rickety steps and let himself inside the house.

He paused to listen. A low humming sound echoed from the back room. He didn't bother to hide himself or keep his footfalls quiet. He wanted to see the look on her face when she saw him.

A minute later, her humming stopped. She'd heard his footsteps. He stood in the den by the ratty plaid sofa and remembered being forced to his knees while she ordered him to pray after one of her famous beatings.

He smelled her before she entered. The lemony scent of floor cleaner and dusting spray that still had the power to nauseate him. Then her rail-thin wrinkled face appeared in the doorway. She'd aged drastically, but those sharp eyes were just as mean.

"My lord," she gasped.

He grinned and reached for the knife at his belt. "Hello, Mama."

Chapter Sixteen

Sally Ann McCobb lived in an apartment outside Crescent Canyon. Dylan noted the weathered siding, the overgrown unkempt bushes and the broken-down car in the parking lot, frowning at the sight of a scruffy little boy riding a battered tricycle on the sidewalk.

Sally Ann lived on the bottom floor, so he knocked on the door. He'd considered calling first, but wanted the element of surprise on his side.

He paced while he waited, and when no one answered knocked again, and finally heard footsteps shuffling toward the door. A minute later, a bleached blonde with red puffy eyes, a swollen lip and a bruise on her left cheek squeaked the door open.

Dylan flashed his ID. "Special Agent Dylan Acevedo."

Her eyes widened perceptively for a brief moment of panic before a resigned look settled over her features. "Yeah?"

"You're Sally Ann McCobb?"

She gave a slight nod. "I ain't done nothing wrong."

Dylan offered her a smile. "No one said you have. I just need to talk to you, that's all, ma'am." The wind whipped through him, swirling dust and a fast-food wrapper around his feet. "Can I come in?"

She hesitated, then seemed to decide she had no choice, and unfastened the chain and allowed him entry. The inside of her place was no more impressive than the outside, with cheap, worn furniture and a battered oak table in the kitchen/den combination.

He immediately scanned the room, searching for a sign that a man had been there. One coffee cup on the table, not two. Although an empty bottle of whiskey lay atop the overflowing trash.

Turnbull liked whiskey.

Sally Ann tugged a faded chenille housecoat around her plump shoulders. She didn't look like Turnbull's type.

"I think you know the reason I'm here," he said.

She twisted her mouth sideways, biting on her lip, then went to the coffeepot and poured herself another cup. "You want some?" she asked.

He nodded, not really wanting it but deciding to stay in her good graces as long as he could. She didn't ask if he wanted sugar or creamer, just handed him the chipped mug and he took a swig, nearly choking on the potent brew.

"You've been writing Frank Turnbull in prison?"

The nervous flicker of her eyes gave her away. "I was doing research for a class I'm taking." She tapped a pack of cigarettes against her palm, pulled one out and lit it. "I talked to several prisoners."

"But you continued writing Turnbull, didn't you? Personal letters? *Love* letters?"

She blew out a plume of smoke. "I guess you already

know that. So why don't you cut to the chase. You're wondering why a woman would write love letters to a prisoner."

He gave a clipped nod. "You know how many women he killed?"

"Yes. But that was before he found Jesus."

And she'd bought that dog and pony show? "Do you know where he is now?"

"Heard he died in a bus crash being transferred to ADX."

His gaze met hers, that flicker of unease giving her away again. "That's what he wants people to believe, isn't it?"

She took another drag on her cigarette, then thumped the ashes into a foam cup on the counter. "That's what happened."

He made a low sound in his throat, deciding to change tactics. "So, Sally Ann, how did you get those bruises?"

"My ex beat me," she said matter-of-factly.

"I thought you were finished with him."

"I am."

"How about Turnbull? If he survived, would you help him?"

"If he survived that crash?" She gave a sarcastic cackle. "Hell, yeah. If I didn't, he'd kill me."

"But you're not his type," Dylan said.

"I know," she said in a pained voice. "That's what he told me. He likes Ute girls."

"Not for sex," Dylan said.

She shook her head. "Not for anything."

He walked over and picked up the bottle of whiskey. "You drink all this yourself, Sally Ann?"

A panicked look shot through her eyes. That look alone was enough to send a cold chill through Dylan. "He was here, wasn't he? And he gave you those bruises?"

Pain darkened her expression. "I loved him," she whispered hoarsely. "I really thought he'd changed. That he'd found the Lord and we could have a life."

Dylan gritted his teeth. "Did he say where he was going?"

"I told you he's dead." Sally Ann gestured toward the door. "But he had a groupie, some guy who wrote him and thought he was a god. Turnbull told me about him during my last visit."

"Did he give you a name?"

"He called himself Ulysses. Said he was going to make Frank's work look like child's play. And that he'd start the game all over again."

Dylan's mind raced. Was Turnbull alive? Or had this man taken on his MO?

"Did Turnbull mention having dental work done lately?"

She stubbed out her cigarette with an annoyed grunt. "Yeah, so?"

"So far, the only concrete evidence that Turnbull might have died in the crash was a partial bridge."

Her face paled.

Dylan's patience snapped. "What? You have to tell me if you know something. We can protect you."

A tense heartbeat passed between them before she replied. "I think that guy Ulysses was a dentist."

Dammit.

His stomach in a cold knot of dread, he grabbed the whiskey bottle with a handkerchief and carried it to his car to drop by the crime lab. If it had Turnbull's prints on it, they'd know for sure that he was alive.

He also had to track down this guy Ulysses. Find out where he lived.

If he was copycatting Turnbull or if they'd teamed up together.

And he had to do it before either one of them found Aspen.

A chill invaded him. If one or both of them had been watching Aspen and him, they knew she wasn't at her home. Could they have followed him to the safe house?

He'd taken every precaution. But still anxiety ripped through him, and as he drove toward the crime lab, he phoned Ryan to warn him to stay alert.

ASPEN HATED that Dylan had left her alone. Tom Ryan was a nice man, tried to be unobtrusive, but having a stranger guarding her drove home the fact that Dylan was only back in her life because of this case.

So did the news clip that aired on TV, a repeat of the earlier broadcast.

"Police have now confirmed that a missing Ute woman, Aspen Meadows, has been found safe and alive. Although preliminary reports stated that she was suffering from amnesia, Miss Meadows's memory has returned.

"The woman witnessed two men dumping the body of Special Agent Julie Grainger on the Ute reservation.

"Those men have been identified as Sherman Watts—" the reporter paused while they flashed Watts's picture on the screen "—and Boyd Perkins—" another pause to show his photograph "—who is believed to be a hit man.

"Police have issued an APB for both men and a man-hunt is underway.

"Meanwhile, Miss Meadows has agreed to testify against the men when they are apprehended. If you have any news about either Perkins or Watts and their whereabouts, please contact the FBI immediately."

Aspen shivered. There was no going back now. She only hoped that the two men took the bait and came after her at her house.

She spread a blanket on the floor and arranged several baby toys around Jack, turning the jack-in-the-box crank handle until the clown popped up. A laugh bubbled from her son's throat, and she pushed the doll down inside and cranked the handle all over again.

Agent Ryan's cell phone trilled, and he glanced at it, then connected the call. "Hey, Acevedo."

She tensed, her nerves on edge as she listened to the one-sided conversation. As soon as Ryan disconnected the call, she asked him what Dylan had said.

"He's following some leads on the Turnbull investigation, then stopping by the lab to check in. He should be back in a couple of hours."

Aspen wanted more details. But Ryan stepped outside with his phone, cutting off her question. She'd have to wait on Dylan. The Turnbull case had obviously gotten under his skin, the reason he'd personally left to do the legwork.

Would the Ute Slicer come after Dylan for revenge?

The idea of something terrible happening to him sent a shudder through her.

Jack grew fussy, and she picked him up and walked him around, talking to him to soothe him. But he was hungry so she fixed another bottle, cradled him in the rocking chair and fed him.

"He has to come back," she whispered as Jack fell asleep. "He just has to."

When Jack dozed off, she laid him in the crib and covered him with a blanket. The door squeaked open and she hurried to the living room, hoping Dylan was back. But Agent Ryan had stepped back inside.

"Is something wrong?" she asked.

"No, I was just checking the perimeter," he said. "And I phoned Agent Parrish to see if Perkins or Watts showed up at your house."

"Have they?"

"No," he said. "But they still might. They're probably waiting until dark."

She nodded, and glanced at the clock. That was hours away. Hours of waiting and pacing and not knowing. Hours of hoping and praying the two men got caught.

Hours of wondering if that psycho Turnbull would come after Dylan.

WORRY NEEDLED DYLAN as he parked at the crime lab and rushed inside. He met Callie at the door of her office and held up the whiskey bottle. "Can you print this and run it right away? I need to know if Turnbull's prints are on it."

Her brow furrowed. "Where did you get it?"

He explained about the prison mail and visitor log.

"Did she admit that he was alive?" Callie asked.

Dylan shook his head. "No, but I read between the lines. I think he paid her a visit and she realized that his talk of redemption was bull."

With gloved hands, Callie took the bottle to her workstation, dusted it for prints then ran them through AFIS.

Dylan watched as she pulled up Turnbull's prints and the computer program worked its magic.

Seconds later, his fears were confirmed.

Turnbull had been at Sally Ann McCobb's house.

Which meant Turnbull was alive.

"Damn," Callie muttered. "How did that SOB walk away from that burning bus?"

"With help," Dylan said cryptically.

"Sally Ann?"

"No. Well, hell, she may have given him some money, but she's not bright enough or devious enough to pull this off." He hesitated, his mind working. "I couldn't locate his half brother, Freddy. I'm going to get an APB issued for him immediately. And Sally Ann McCobb mentioned that Turnbull had a fan. Called himself Ulysses." He snapped his fingers. "I probably have mail from him in that stack at the safe house, the pile I haven't gotten to. I'll analyze when it I get back there. Maybe it will lead us to his real name and address. My guess is that that corpse in the fire either belonged to his half brother or his fan."

Callie nodded and Dylan called the state ME to relay his findings.

"I did ID Sawyer," the ME said. "But there's something odd about the last body. Signs on the corpse indicate that the man suffered from a brain tumor."

"It's not Turnbull," Dylan said, then explained his discovery. "But you need to find out who he is." He told him to get Freddy's dental and medical records and to check DNA. And he needed to find out what this man Ulysses's full name was, if it was, in fact, his real name.

As soon as he hung up, his cell phone trilled. Bree. "Acevedo, you have to get over here. There's another woman's body. And you won't believe who it belongs to."

"Who?"

"Turnbull's mother." Her breathing sounded erratic.

Dylan disconnected, jogged toward his car and drove at a dead race toward the address Bree gave him.

When he climbed out, sweat beaded on his skin and he hurried up to the house.

As soon as he ducked below the crime tape, he met Bree. She was as pale as a ghost.

"It's bad," she said.

The metallic scent of blood and human wastes assaulted him as he entered. Then he saw the blood everywhere. Splattered on the walls and floor, the elderly woman's body sprawled on the kitchen tiles in a river of red where she'd been gutted.

Chapter Seventeen

Sheriff Martinez took Bree by the elbow. "Go outside. Get some air. Agent Acevedo and I have this one covered."

Bree didn't argue. She hurried outside as if she desperately needed fresh air. Dylan remembered her pregnancy and understood Patrick's reaction.

If he'd known Aspen was pregnant, he would have been just as protective.

The crime techs arrived to process the scene, but Dylan studied it, seeing the dark rage Turnbull had had for his mother.

"Who do you think did this?" Patrick asked.

Dylan gave a bitter laugh. "Turnbull. He escaped the crash and he's out here."

Patrick muttered a curse. "Why the overkill?"

"His mother was the source of his rage." Dylan grimaced. "Unfortunately, the past year in the pen has probably fueled his anger. And judging from this bloodbath, the viciousness of his crimes will probably escalate."

"That's all we need," Patrick mumbled.

Dylan grimaced. "Yeah. And if he's going after the people he thinks hurt him, then he's on a personal vendetta."

Which put him at the top of the list.

But he knew Turnbull. He was cunning. He wouldn't just try to kill him.

Just as he had gotten inside Turnbull's head when he'd profiled and interrogated him, Turnbull had gotten into his head. He knew the case had gotten to Dylan.

He'd recognized the vengeance in his eyes when he'd nearly killed the killer.

Cold sweat dotted his body and his heart hammered in his chest.

He'd make him suffer by hurting another woman.

Aspen.

He didn't know how Turnbull had figured out that he cared about her, but he had.

And that was where he'd strike.

The piece of thunderwood he'd left on her doorstep had been a statement.

He had to go back to her now. Trust his fellow agents and the cops to do their jobs.

Nothing else mattered except keeping Aspen and their son safe.

THE SUN HAD FADED behind dark storm clouds, night setting in. Aspen fed Jack and played with him on the pallet until he finally conked out again. She watched him breathing for a few minutes, still unable to believe she'd given birth to such a beautiful and wonderful child.

Finally the sound of a car engine split the tense silence, relief welling inside her as she looked out the window and spotted Dylan climb from the car.

Agent Ryan met him outside, and Aspen ached to

join them, but Tom had given her strict orders not to go outside for fear someone was watching.

She felt like a prisoner.

How long would this confinement last? Would she have to look over her shoulder for the rest of her life? Live in constant fear that someone would try to kill her?

Tears threatened, along with a deep desperation, but she willed herself to be strong and not fall apart.

It seemed like an eternity before Agent Ryan left and Dylan finally came inside. As soon as she saw the solemn expression on his face, she knew something was terribly wrong.

"What happened?" she asked.

Although anger simmered below the surface of his guarded calm, his blue eyes glimmered with emotions she couldn't read. He clenched and unclenched his fists. "Nothing. No hits on your house yet."

He was lying. "There's something else, Dylan. What is it?"

He shrugged. "Is Jack all right?"

"Yes," she said. "Now stop avoiding me. I need to know what's going on."

"You just have to trust me," he said, then walked into the kitchen for a glass of water. But his brow was furrowed and damp, his body language perched for battle, his senses alert as he combed through the house checking windows and locks.

He reminded her of a big cat, like a panther, stalking the place as if in search of prey—or a predator.

"Do you think Perkins or Watts know we're here?" she asked, her heart starting to race.

"No," he said a little too fast.

"You do, don't you?" She grabbed his arm and forced him to look at her. "Did they follow you?"

"No, I told you not to worry. I'll protect you."

Instead of consoling her or pulling her into his arms, he seemed cold, distant.

Impersonal.

"Damn you, Dylan. I don't understand you. You're lying, something is terribly wrong. I'm not an idiot."

"I know that," he said in a clipped tone. "I'm just doing my job."

Hurt and bewilderment speared her along with bitterness. "So I'm just a job to you now?"

His gaze met hers, and for a brief second, something else flickered in his eyes. Hunger. Desire.

Fear.

"Tell me what's going on, Dylan. One minute you're hot and hold and kiss me like you want me, and the next you look at me like I'm a perfect stranger, just some woman you have to protect for your damn job."

He tried to pull away, but she clawed at his arm. "You say we spent a week together, a week in bed, and when you kissed me before and we almost made love, I felt something intense between us. A heat I've never felt before." Her breath feathered out, choppy with her frustration and desperate need. "But now you act as if you don't care about me at all. How can you be so cold?"

A muscle ticked in his jaw, and he reached up and covered her hands as if to pull them away, but his touch was so warm, and she needed it so badly, she whispered his name again.

"Don't you care, Dylan? Don't you care at all?"

Tension stretched between them, her question echoing in the silence.

"Dylan, please," she said, hating the pathetic desperation in her voice. "Please don't shut me out. I need you."

There, she'd said it. Bared her soul and shed her own protective barriers.

"It's not that I don't care," he finally said in a gruff voice.

"Then why pull away from me?"

His mouth tightened as if answering her cost him. "Because I care too damn much."

Her breath caught in her throat along with a painful surge of longing, prompting her to lift one hand to his cheek. God help her, but she wanted him.

"Aspen, don't," he murmured.

But that plea reverberated with suppressed desire. Desire that mirrored the hunger he had to see reflected in her eyes.

He might leave her when the case was over. But she needed him now.

And with death knocking at her door, the moment was all that mattered.

ON SOME SUBCONSCIOUS LEVEL, Dylan knew he was crossing the line, that he should remain alert and not allow his personal feelings to clutter an already complicated and dangerous situation, but he'd lost that game a year ago when he'd first met Aspen.

No, before, when he'd nearly killed Turnbull just because he wanted to see the man die.

Only Aspen had saved him back then. Aspen and her

understanding. Aspen and her sultry looks, her tenderness and passion.

She'd reminded him that the world consisted of something other than ugliness and cruelty, that it could also be beautiful and loving.

Needing that reminder now, to hold on to the fact that she was alive and in his arms instead of in Turnbull's or this copycat's unmerciful hands, he dragged her into his arms and claimed her mouth with his.

Her lips tasted like ripe berries and sunshine and sweetness, causing his chest to clench with a warmth that helped to chase the chill from his body.

The chill that had dogged him ever since he'd found that piece of thunderwood on her doorstep.

The chill that had grown to insurmountable heights at the sight of the man's latest brutalized victim.

His mother.

Don't think about the case. Think about how wonderful it is to finally hold Aspen again. To finally be able to touch her and stroke her bare flesh and meld your body with hers.

She moaned low in her throat, and he delved his tongue inside her mouth, hungry and taking everything she offered.

He deepened the kiss, one hand plunging into her hair while the other one skated over her back, down to her waist, then her hips. He tugged her up against his hard body, his sex jutting against the fly of his slacks and brushing her thigh.

She whispered his name in a low purr as he tore his mouth from her lips and trailed kisses along the long slender column of her neck. His mouth watered for more, his length throbbing to be closer to her. He kneed her legs apart, and fit himself into the cradle of her thighs, then groaned when she arched her hips into him.

Raw need tore through him, and he slid his hand down to cup her breast, kneading the plump mound through her blouse until she begged him to remove her top.

One flick and buttons went flying. He ripped off the garment, her throaty sounds of approval spurring him on. Then her skirt came off, fell to the floor in a puddle, and he paused to drink in the sight of her beauty. Full breasts encased in ivory lace rose and fell with her erratic breathing.

"Dylan?"

"I'm here, baby." Dark fantasies sprang to mind as she reached for his shirt and hastily unfastened the buttons. Her fingers fired his flesh, enflamed him to the point that he thought he might explode with need.

Desperation turned the next few seconds into a frenzy as they yanked at each other's clothes, throwing them onto the floor.

Naked, she was a glorious sight to behold.

Her body was slightly rounder now she'd given birth, a soft lushness to it that, if possible, made him crave her even more.

He thought he'd memorized each inch of her, but as he explored the fine contours of her breasts, her hips and thighs, he knew his memory had failed to imprint her exquisitely soft skin or the exact dark brown of her nipples into his brain.

His senses sprang to life, soaking in her sweet feminine fragrance, his skin erupting with white-hot sensa-

FREE BOOKS OFFER

To get you started, we'll send you
2 FREE books and a FREE gift

- -

There's no catch, everything is **FREE**

Accepting your 2 **FREE** books and **FREE** mystery gift
places you under no obligation to buy anything.

Be part of the Mills & Boon® Book Club™ and receive your favourite
Series books up to 2 months before they are in the shops and delivered
straight to your door. Plus, enjoy a wide range of **EXCLUSIVE** benefits!

  Best new women's fiction – delivered right to
your door with FREE P&P

  Avoid disappointment – get your books up to
2 months before they are in the shops

  No contract – no obligation to buy

We hope that after receiving your free books you'll
want to remain a member. But the choice is yours.
So why not give us a go? You'll be glad you did!

Visit **millsandboon.co.uk** to stay up to date
with offers and to sign-up for our newsletter

2 **FREE** books
and a
FREE gift

IOJIA

Mrs/Miss/Ms/Mr _____ Initials _____

BLOCK CAPITALS PLEASE

Surname _____

Address _____

_____

Postcode _____

Email _____

MILLS & BOON®

NO STAMP NEEDED!

@ MILLS & BOON®
Book Club

FREE BOOK OFFER
FREEPOST NAT 10298
RICHMOND
TW9 1BR

NO STAMP
NECESSARY
IF POSTED IN
THE U.K. OR N.I.

tions as she traced her fingers over his bare chest and arms then lower to his abdomen.

He sucked in a sharp breath when she feathered touches on the insides of his thighs, and images of her on her knees pleasuring him flashed behind his eyes.

She had done it before. Tasted and tortured with him her tongue and lips, and he wanted her touch now.

But he had to taste her first.

Starved for her sweetness, he picked her up and carried her to the bedroom, then spread her on the bed to feast.

She moaned and clawed at his arms as he kissed her breasts, then pulled one hard tip into his mouth and suckled her. She arched her hips as if in silent invitation, but he forced her to wait while he loved her.

Teasing her thighs apart with his hand, he toyed with the soft curls at her center, loving her other breast until she pleaded his name.

"Dylan, please, I need you inside me."

"Soon, baby, soon," he whispered against her belly as he pressed kisses down her stomach to the treasure below.

He licked her folds, spreading her legs and jutting his tongue out to taste her heat. She whimpered, and tried to stop him, but he forced her still and fit his mouth over her core, sucking the heart of her desire until her honeyed juices flowed into his mouth.

She bucked upward, clenching and twisting the sheets between her fingers as she cried out her release.

Need enflamed him, his body aching with the relentless force of a man who needed to pump inside a woman.

And not just any woman.

Aspen.

The woman who'd soothed him a year ago, the

woman who'd reminded him that beauty still thrived in this godforsaken world of killers.

A woman who'd stolen his heart and, he feared, his very soul.

ASPEN CLOSED HER EYES, savoring the brilliant splash of colors sweeping her into euphoria.

The moment Dylan had touched her bare flesh, her inhibitions had fled like rain evaporating on a hot pavement.

Had it always been this way between the two of them? This explosive?

He rose above her, bracing himself on his hands. "Open your eyes, and look at me, Aspen." He nuzzled her neck with his lips and teeth.

"I want you to see me when I'm inside you."

Aspen did as he said, the pure raw passion glazing his eyes, sending spasms of erotic excitement through her.

Slowly he teased her center with his full hard length, back and forth in an exquisite torture that sent her over the edge again. She dug her fingernails into his arms and clung to him as he thrust deeper inside her, stretching and filling her until the memory of him binding himself with her flashed back, sweeping her into the vortex of desire that had robbed her breath a year ago, a hot yearning that had burned through her each time he'd touched her.

The present blended with the past, their dance of lovemaking familiar and overwhelming her.

He lifted her hips with his hands and thrust deeper, angling her so their bodies met so intimately that another orgasm rippled through her.

He hammered harder, faster, his own groan of satisfaction whispering in her ear as his release came, swift and potent.

For a long moment, he held himself inside her, their bodies quivering together as the aftermath of their passion ebbed and flowed.

And as the sensations overrode her earlier fear, another memory surfaced.

The moment she'd realized she was pregnant.

And that her son belonged to Dylan.

The realization rocked her world, and she froze as he turned her over in his arms and held her.

Her breath rushed out as she tried to piece together what had happened between them. She and Dylan had made a baby during their short affair. A beautiful little boy that she'd loved from the moment of conception.

But she hadn't told him he had a son.

And he was going to hate her for it.

DYLAN CRUSHED ASPEN IN HIS embrace, his chest heaving. He had needed her tonight, needed her sweetness, her loving.

Yet he felt her shutting down.

Only this time he refused to let her.

He pulled back slightly to look into her eyes. Dark brown eyes glazed with passion, and a hazy look of arousal that made him want her again.

But she stiffened in his arms and he felt her putting some distance between them just as he had last year when he'd guarded his heart.

"Dylan?" she said softly.

His chest tightened. "Yes?"

"I remembered something else."

"Something about your attack?"

She shook her head, and suddenly the truth dawned on him. "You remembered us being together?"

She nodded, a wariness filling her eyes.

"And what else?" he asked gruffly.

She clamped her teeth over her bottom lip and bit down as if debating on whether to confide in him.

"What?" he asked, his impatience mounting.

She sat up, tugging the sheet up around her, and he gritted his teeth, hating to do anything to encroach on the closeness they'd just shared.

But he had to know the truth.

"Tell me what you remember, Aspen."

She exhaled as if to steady her nerves. "I remember us making love last year. The week we spent together." A faint blush crept up her cheeks. "It was…wonderful."

He nodded.

"But then we parted."

"Yes. I got called away on an assignment."

"And I finished school and went back to the reservation to teach."

"That's right."

She hesitated. "And a few weeks later, I discovered I was pregnant."

His throat tightened as he waited, tension stretching between them. He wanted to prod her, shake her. "Go on."

Her gaze met his, the heat still simmering between them. But lies and secrets stood like a wall they needed to climb.

"Aspen, what else did you remember?"

Tears filled her eyes. "That you're Jack's father."

Chapter Eighteen

Dylan's heart swelled with her words, an overwhelming protective urge slamming into him. He would protect her and Jack with his life.

Yet anger that she'd kept the truth from him made him grit his teeth. "I know. Why didn't you tell me you were pregnant?"

Shock widened her eyes. "What do you mean, you know?"

"For God's sake, Aspen. I put two and two together, and wondered, so I took a DNA sample."

Hurt strained her features. "Why didn't you tell me? Why go behind my back?"

Hell, she was turning the tables on him?

"Why didn't I tell you?" He wanted to shake her. "Why didn't you tell me? Why didn't you contact me when you first realized you were pregnant?"

She pressed her fingers to her temple, massaging her head as if struggling with the memories.

"I did," she whispered. "I tried to contact you a few times, but the Bureau said you couldn't be reached, that you were out of the country."

He closed his eyes on a hiss, and when he opened them, she was watching him. "You should have tried harder."

Tears glittered in her eyes. "Why? You left without telling me where you were going, without asking me to see you again." Pain laced her voice and any bravado she had wilted.

"So why not try when he was born? You could have left messages. If I'd known, I would have come."

She stood, grabbed her robe, put it on and knotted it tightly then walked to the window and looked out.

Anger and fear choked him. He wanted to know the truth, yet what if she said that she hadn't wanted him in their son's life? That he was too dangerous?

ASPEN TREMBLED, hating the anger in Dylan's voice. But how could she blame him? She'd deprived him of knowing his son.

And his question raised her own insecurities and resurrected other memories.

"Why, Aspen?" Dylan asked. "Why didn't you call me when he was born?"

"I didn't want to feel like I'd trapped you."

"It wouldn't have been like that," he said. "Besides, I had a right to know."

"I know that," she whispered. "But I was afraid," she admitted.

"Afraid of what?" He gripped her arms and spun her around, his eyes icy cold. "You were afraid of me? Afraid I would hurt Jack? That I wouldn't be a good father because I told you I almost killed Turnbull?"

The distress in his voice made her heart clench. Then her conversation with Kurt Lightfoot rolled back.

He'd said that she was afraid of Jack's father, but that wasn't true. "I was afraid that you might try to take Jack away from me."

"What?" Hurt tinged his voice.

"I was afraid you'd want custody. That you wouldn't want me to raise Jack on the reservation." Her voice cracked. "And Kurt said that with your government job that you had power and money. That you probably knew people and could convince a judge to give Jack to you."

A sense of betrayal stabbed at him like a knife.

"You listened to Lightfoot instead of coming to me?" he said, his voice thickening. "You told him about our baby and not me. What did you plan to do, marry him and let him raise my son as his own?"

The very thought fueled irrational jealousy.

He had to get out of there. Couldn't look at her and think about her keeping his son from him and allowing Jack to call another man his father.

"No," Aspen whispered.

But he couldn't listen to her now. Couldn't look at her.

Couldn't stay in the room, wearing his feelings on his shoulder and knowing that she'd even contemplated such an idea.

Furious, he yanked on a pair of jeans and stormed from the room. He heard her calling his name, and he shouted for her to leave him alone.

He didn't look back to see her reaction. Instead, he stalked outside, slammed the door, jogged down the porch steps and glanced into the trees shrouding the ridge.

He leaned against a tree and closed his eyes, his chest heaving.

He had to regain his composure.

But suddenly a twig snapped behind him, and he opened his eyes, automatically reaching for his gun.

Dammit, he'd left it inside.

Before he could move to retrieve it, something sharp and hard slammed into his skull, and he collapsed on the ground, the world going black.

ASPEN'S HEART ACHED. She hadn't meant to hurt Dylan but she obviously had.

But she had to be honest with him. She'd wanted him to know about Jack, but she also hadn't wanted to pressure him into marriage or taking responsibility for their son.

She'd wanted him to come to her because he cared for her and wanted to be a part of her life.

Her own mother had faced the same dilemma and had opened herself up to Aspen's father, but he'd walked away without looking back. He'd even accused her mother of lying and trying to use a baby to force him into marriage.

Aspen grabbed jeans and a shirt and dressed, then wrapped her arms around herself. She'd been afraid of the same thing.

Afraid to trust that Dylan might love her.

She had to make him understand that her fears stemmed from her past.

She hurried through the bedroom door into the living room, then to the door. But just as she opened it, she spotted Dylan lying on the ground, facedown, not moving.

Panic sent a bolt of adrenaline through her, and she screamed, and turned to run inside to phone for help. But a big, hard body tackled her from behind, and she pitched forward, then they rolled backward. Her knees hit the steps, her hands clawing for control and digging into gravel and dirt.

Two hands jerked her by the shoulders, and she scrambled to try to escape, but a hard whack on the back of her neck made her reel with pain. Her head spun, the world shifted in a drunken state of nausea, and an icy chill invaded her as the man dragged her up and threw her over his shoulder.

He stalked down the hill, rocks scattering and pinging off the ridge as he wove through the brush to an old van.

She kicked at him and pounded his back with her fists, but he threw her inside and slapped her across the face so hard that her eyes sank back in her head and she passed out.

Sometime later, she aroused from unconsciousness, terror sweeping over her. Her hands and legs were bound with tight-corded ropes, her mouth gagged, and the van was bumping over gravel and dirt.

Who was this man?

And where was he taking her?

DYLAN SLOWLY ROUSED from the black sea where he'd fallen, swimming upward toward the light. He had to paw his way up, had to surface.

Aspen needed him.

He pushed up from the ground, his hands scraping the dry brush as he sat up and tried to regain his senses.

Then he spotted the piece of thunderwood.

Pure panic slammed into him. How long had he been out? Did Turnbull have Aspen or was it a copycat?

Fear made him shoot upward, and he staggered up

the steps, and rushed inside, his gaze scanning the darkened interior.

Pausing to listen, he prayed that she was still alive. Still inside somewhere.

But he inched through the living room to the bedroom and found it empty.

Jack.

God, please don't let him have hurt the baby.

Trembling with terror, he raced to the second bedroom and held his breath as he checked inside. A whimper from the crib made his chest clench, and he flipped on the light and hurried toward the crib.

Jack had stirred and opened his eyes and was looking up at him as if he knew something was wrong.

He quickly checked the baby for injuries, but he appeared to be all right.

Though his mind raced with horrid images of what this man might be doing to Aspen, he shoved the images aside. He had to act fast.

Turnbull had kept his other victims for at least twenty-four hours. But what if this was the copycat?

And if Turnbull had killed his mother so violently and was escalating, what would he do to Aspen?

Cold sweat broke out on his brow.

"I'll be right back, Jack. I have to get help." His heart pounding, he raced to the bedroom and retrieved his gun and phone. Throwing on his shirt, he punched in Tom's phone number. Three rings later and Tom answered.

"Tom, it's Dylan. Either Turnbull or his copycat found us and he has Aspen."

"I'll call the locals and tell them to set up roadblocks and get some choppers in the air."

"We need to figure out where he'd take her. And I need someone to watch Jack."

"I'll call Miguel right now."

Dylan scrubbed his hand over his face, frantic. He had to think. Where would Turnbull take Aspen?

Dear God, please don't let me be too late....

ASPEN'S BODY ACHED from being tossed around in the back of the van as the vehicle careened over the rocky terrain. The interior was pitch-black, the smell of cigarette, sweat and booze an acrid stench that made bile rise to her throat. Was Dylan all right?

Was he alive?

Panic clogged her throat and she tried desperately to choke back the fear.

What if he didn't find her in time?

And what if he was dead and Jack was in that house all alone? No one would even know he was there.

Who would take care of him if she didn't survive?

Emma.

Emma would raise Jack as her own. Emma knew what it was like to lose a mother. She would tell him about Aspen and about how they grew up together on the reservation. She would share the stories that Aspen wanted so badly to pass on to her son.

And even though Emma was only half Ute, she would raise him in the Ute way.

Tears leaked down her eyes, but she was helpless to stop them. She didn't want to leave Jack again—she'd promised him she wouldn't.

She didn't want to die, either. She wanted to watch

Jack grow up. Teach him how to ride a bike. Watch him grow into a man.

And she wanted to tell Dylan that she loved him.

She sobbed with the realization. Why hadn't she realized it before? Why hadn't she confessed her feelings?

Confess how terrified she'd been that he couldn't love her back? That that was the reason she had stopped trying to contact him.

She'd tried to convince herself that having Jack was enough. That she didn't need or want Dylan.

But she'd lied to herself for months.

And now it was too late.

The van suddenly screeched to a halt, and her stomach knotted with a sick fear as the sound of the driver's door opening and slamming rent the night.

Outside the van, footsteps shuffled against rock. Somewhere in the distance, an animal screeched.

Then hard bands of steel snapped around her wrists and dragged her from the van. She kicked again, determined to fight, but he slammed his fist against her cheek and she saw stars.

Then he dragged her across the rocky terrain toward some kind of small building a few feet away.

A church.

She blinked, trying to focus. It was old, weathered, deserted. Overgrown weeds and bushes shrouded the front. The smell of something rotten permeated the air.

And the scent of death floated to her, eerie and numbing as the sight of several graves caught her eye.

Then the shiny blade of a knife shattered the darkness

as he tossed her against one of the cement markers staked in the dirt-packed ground.

DYLAN HAD DROPPED JACK OFF AT Emma's. She was terrified but Miguel had stayed with her to calm her, and he'd promised to call as soon as he found Aspen.

He only hoped he found her alive.

He raced into the crime-lab conference room to confer with the others.

"The ME confirmed that Ulysses Ramstead was the other dead man in the prison bus crash. He must have joined forces to help Turnbull escape, then Turnbull stabbed him in the back and left his body to burn so we would think he was dead. Turnbull left his dental plate to mislead us."

"Where would he take Aspen?" Dylan asked as he paced the room. "I would have thought if he wanted to get revenge on me, he would have just done it right there. That he would have even forced me to watch."

"He does want revenge," Ben said. "But his sickness has to do with killing Ute women."

"That's right," Tom said. "Remember his profile. He hated his mother because she raised him on the reservation. Because she was brutal and a religious zealot."

Dylan fisted his hands, his heart hammering. He had to climb in Turnbull's head. Think like the sadistic sick man he was.

Turnbull hated his mother and he'd killed her. He hated Ute women.

He hated the church.

His mind racing, he hurried to the table and opened up the files on Turnbull, quickly scanning them.

"Send someone to Turnbull's mother's house. Maybe he's going to take her there."

"I'll cover the house," Tom said.

Dylan hesitated, his mind humming with another possibility. "He knows we'll look there, though."

Dylan flipped the page, scanning the psychologist's notes. "This is it. The church." He glanced up at Tom with dread in his belly. "You go to his house, and I'll check out the church. He might take her to the very place his mother forced him to go as a child when she pounded religion into him."

Tom gave a clipped nod. "You might be right."

Both men sprang into action, Tom hurrying to his car and Dylan to his own.

He flipped on his siren, spread the map on the car seat and tore from the crime lab, weaving his way through Kenner City, out of town.

Bright lights nearly blinded him from an oncoming car, and he blew his horn, then sped past, careening around a curve, his hands sweating on the steering wheel and his breathing choppy.

It seemed like days, but was only a matter of minutes until he reached the small dilapidated, deserted church where Turnbull had been baptized.

He spotted a dark van, and his heart thundered. He had to be in time.

Aspen couldn't be dead.

He had to save her and take her home to their son.

Not bothering to slow down, he screeched to a halt, jumped out, his gun at the ready.

The blue lights twirled across the barren land, flickering across the terrifying scene in front of him.

Aspen was on her knees in the dirt by a marker, her hands tied, feet bound, while Turnbull stalked around her, preaching a sermon as he wielded the Ute ceremonial knife.

Chapter Nineteen

Aspen shuddered at the sound of the crazed man humming in the ancient language. He didn't look Ute, but he seemed entranced at the moment, as some kind of demon had possessed his soul.

The scent of death, damp soil and fear invaded her. Her head throbbed where he'd hit her, and her wrists and ankles were raw from trying to free herself from the ropes biting into her skin.

She was going to die.

No, she'd heard the siren. The police were coming.

Dylan would find her and save her before this madman used his knife on her.

He leapt toward her, jamming the pointed blade at her throat, and she flinched as a droplet of blood seeped from her impaled skin.

Then a loud growl broke the silence, the sound almost inhuman, and she looked up and saw Dylan launch himself at Frank Turnbull.

She screamed, fighting to escape her bindings, fear clutching her as her captor swung the knife in a wide arc, then jabbed the point at Dylan.

Dylan shouted an obscenity, and threw his body against Turnbull's and the two men fell to the ground in battle.

It was so dark she couldn't see, but the scent of blood assaulted her, and Dylan's shout of pain rent the air.

Dear God, no. Dylan couldn't die. She needed him.

And so did their son.

RAGE SEARED DYLAN, more painful than the blade that Turnbull drove into his shoulder. Blood oozed from the wound, trickling down his arm, but he ignored the pain, and grabbed Turnbull's hand, then they fought for the weapon.

Turnbull must have been working out in prison, and had gained weight and muscle, but the images of the women he had brutally slain flashed back, fueling Dylan's fury and renewing his strength.

He karate chopped Turnbull's wrist and the knife flew to the ground. Turnbull scrambled to get it, but Dylan tackled him and slammed his fist into the man's nose. Bones crunched and blood spewed, but Turnbull wasn't giving up.

He rammed his head into Dylan's stomach, gripped his arm where he'd stabbed him and pain rocked through Dylan. He grunted and fought back, but Turnbull managed to escape and grabbed the knife out of the dirt.

Aspen screamed as the man ran toward her, and Dylan saw red.

Adrenaline surged through him, and he reached for his gun. He found it on the ground by a cement marker, picked it up and aimed.

The bullet pierced Turnbull in the back, and he

howled, then twisted around with a shocked gleam in his eyes as if he'd never expected Dylan to actually win.

Then Turnbull dove toward him again and Dylan pumped another round into the man. His body bounced backward, and he collapsed on top of a grave.

A sinister smile tilted his lips and his mouth moved. "I knew you were just like me," he said in a croaked whisper.

"I'm nothing like you," Dylan growled.

Turnbull's body jerked, then he took his last breath and his body went still.

Dylan staggered to him, then kicked the knife from his hand. Aspen cried his name, and he turned to see her struggling to free herself from the bindings.

He stumbled across the dirt-packed grave, then fell to his knees.

Moonlight streaked her pale face, and rage shot through him again as he spotted the bruise on her cheek and forehead.

"Are you all right?"

She nodded, tears streaming down her face. "But you're hurt."

"I've had worse," he said. Then he cursed as he looked down at her bound limbs.

A fierce frown pulled at his mouth as he retrieved Turnbull's knife, cut the ropes binding her wrists, then hastily slashed the ones on her ankles.

She fell against him on a sob, and he wrapped his arms around her.

"You're safe now," he whispered hoarsely. Relief ebbed through him as his blood soaked her blouse and they clung together. "I'm sorry I left you. Sorry he got to you—"

She cupped his face between her hands. "Shh. No, it's okay. It's over now."

"Thank God you're alive," he said.

They clung to each other for a long time, but she finally insisted on calling an ambulance. While they waited, she helped him tie his T-shirt around the wound to stop the blood flow.

He leaned against her, his pallor gray and chalky, and fear clutched Aspen. She had to be honest with Dylan.

He had nearly died to save her life.

He might leave again, even if she did confess her feelings, but she had to take that chance. Whether he loved her not, she wanted Jack to know this courageous strong man.

She wanted him to have the father she never had.

"I love you, Dylan," Aspen whispered. "I'm sorry I didn't tell you about Jack."

He gazed into her eyes, a mixture of hurt and hope glimmering in his slow smile.

"I'm just sorry you didn't trust me," he said gruffly. "I would never have tried to separate you from our son."

Her heart fluttered with anticipation, love mushrooming inside her as he fused his mouth with hers.

"And I love you, too," he whispered. "I think I did from the moment I saw you."

Epilogue

Two days later, the team met in the conference room at the Kenner County Crime Unit to review the case.

Tom had located Turnbull's half brother, Freddy, who'd gone into hiding when he found out his half sibling could have escaped.

"We've identified the woman's body we found in the river. She was just an innocent Turnbull killed for fun."

Dylan gritted his teeth. "What about Watts and Perkins?" Dylan asked. "Do we have any leads?"

"They didn't take the bait and come for Aspen," Tom said. "Which makes me think that they've both left the reservation."

"They're probably long gone, in Mexico now," Tom said.

Dylan shifted, although his nerves spiked at the thought that they might return for Aspen. He wouldn't allow them to. Not now.

Not ever.

"We did link Lightfoot to the Wayne family," Ben said. "He admitted he took money to help his people, and that he was afraid they'd call in his marker. He's agreed to go into Witness Protection. I think he's afraid of what they might have asked him to do."

Dylan gave a clipped nod. He was glad to see the man go.

Not that he thought Aspen was in love with Lightfoot. In spite of the pain and stitches in his shoulder, the past two days had been bliss.

"Before everyone leaves," Tom cut in, "Callie and I have an announcement."

Callie grinned and took Tom's hand in hers. "We're engaged."

Congratulations erupted all the way around with hugs and handshaking.

"It looks as if my brother's getting married, too," Dylan said as he clapped Tom on the back. "He called earlier to say he and Emma have eloped to Las Vegas."

They wrapped up the meeting, and Dylan hurried toward his car and drove back to Aspen's. The sight of her pueblo-style house brought a smile to his face and a sense of peace over him.

Aspen had worried that he wouldn't want to live on the reservation and had surprised him by offering to move, but he wanted his son to be raised in his mother's footsteps and to appreciate his culture.

His heart warmed as he parked, walked up to the door and let himself in. She smiled at him and Jack cooed as he rushed over to give them both a kiss.

Aspen was right. This was home. But it had nothing to do with the house.

It was home because the two people he loved most in the world were here.

And soon he would make Aspen his wife, then his son would carry on his name. And no one would ever tear them apart again.

* * * * *

PULLING THE TRIGGER

BY
JULIE MILLER

All the characters in this book have no existence outside the imagination of
the author, and have no relation whatsoever to anyone bearing the same name
or names. They are not even distantly inspired by any individual known or
unknown to the author, and all the incidents are pure invention.

First published in Great Britain 2010
Harlequin Mills & Boon Limited,
Eton House, 18-24 Paradise Road, Richmond, Surrey TW9 1SR

© Harlequin Books S.A. 2009

Special thanks and acknowledgement are given to Julie Miller for her
contribution to the Kenner County Crime Unit mini-series.

ISBN: 978 0 263 88262 9

46-1010

Harlequin Mills & Boon policy is to use papers that are natural, renewable
and recyclable products and made from wood grown in sustainable forests.
The logging and manufacturing processes conform to the legal environmental
regulations of the country of origin.

Printed and bound in Spain
by Litografia Rosés S.A., Barcelona

Julie Miller attributes her passion for writing romance to all those fairy tales she read growing up, and to shyness. Encouragement from her family to write down all those feelings she couldn't express became a love for the written word. She gets continued support from her fellow members of the Prairieland Romance Writers, where she serves as the resident "grammar goddess." This award-winning author and teacher has published several paranormal romances. Inspired by the likes of Agatha Christie and Encyclopedia Brown, Ms. Miller believes the only thing better than a good mystery is a good romance.

Born and raised in Missouri, she now lives in Nebraska with her husband, son and smiling guard dog, Maxie. Write to Julie at P.O. Box 5162, Grand Island, NE 68802-5162.

For my dad. Ace navigator extraordinaire.
The most knowledgeable man I know when it comes
to learning about a place and finding my way.
Yep, there's *double entendre* there.

While Sleeping Ute Mountain and the Four Corners
area of southwestern Colorado are real, full of stark
beauty and dramatic landscapes, I've taken the liberty
of creating some fictional places to serve the needs of
the story. So if you do visit the area—and if you're a
fan of history or geography I strongly encourage you
to do so—you might not find all of the locations
Ethan and Joanna visit on the map. But you will find
friendly people and a beautiful part of the country.

Prologue

"I need you to disappear."

Sherman Watts drained the amber fire of whiskey from his shot glass and licked the dribble from his lips before putting the phone back to his ear and responding to his anonymous contact's hushed command. "What about my money?"

"You've gone through last month's payment already?"

It wasn't this loser's business how he spent his money or how fast he spent it. He'd earned a lot more than this secure cell phone he'd been given so their calls about confidential business couldn't be traced. "I was promised fifty thousand. Your people are ten grand short."

"I can deposit the installment into your account on Monday—under the guise of another government settlement payment. You know I can't authorize the payment any earlier than that. If I pay out the money too fast, it'll throw up a red flag, and someone might start nosing around in our business."

Someone else, you mean. Since the Kenner County Crime Unit and a cadre of FBI agents had come to Kenner City, Colorado, and the nearby Ute reservation where Sherman lived, investigating the murder of a lady agent who'd been messing with some people she ought not to have been messing with, there had been plenty of people nosing around. Funny how the man on the phone wasn't afraid of the hit man Sherman had been hiding on the rez and doing some odd jobs for. Funnier still how the man trying to give him orders could deal with two feuding Las Vegas crime families and keep a cool head, but he had a burr up his butt over the possibility of some accountant questioning why Sherman Watts finally had the money to buy a good bottle of whiskey instead of drinking the rotgut that had curdled his conscience years ago.

Sherman poured himself a second glass to wash down the bologna sandwich he'd eaten for lunch. "I'm perfectly comfortable here in Mesa Ridge." He took a sip and savored the smooth burn down his throat. "Besides, I thought it was my job to be the front man. Nobody knows the rez like I do. I can wander around any corner of it, talk to any man about anything and nobody blinks twice. I run Boyd Perkins's errands and get the information he needs so he can continue his search for that fifty million dollars from the Del Gardo family and take care of whatever private business he needs to. Hell, I'm doing such a good job that I hear the cops think Perkins is down in Mexico." Sherman plunked the glass down on the table in his trailer and sat up straight. Had something happened? This idiot might not be afraid of Boyd Perkins, but *he* was smart enough to know that crossing the ice-cold killer was a damn fool thing to do. He'd seen what Perkins was capable of when he'd disposed of that woman's body for him.

Screwing up and getting on the killer's bad side was not an option. "They think Perkins has left the country, right?"

"They have no clue he's still around."

"So what's the problem? Why do I need to skip town? And why isn't this coming from Perkins himself?"

"I'm doing you a favor, you coot. Giving you a heads-up."

He could tell from the condescending sneer in the man's tone that this wasn't about doing anybody a favor.

This guy was worried about covering his own backside.

"The FBI thinks you're involved in Julie Grainger's murder."

"The feds do?" Accomplice after the fact was definitely involved. He was screwed. Sherman pushed to his feet, stumbling over his chair as he went to the back of his trailer to grab a bag and start packing.

"The feds, the crime unit—they're all one team now. And they think you may know something. They're bringing in some hotshot profiler from D.C. to question you."

"What?"

"One of their own agents is dead. They may not have evidence to charge you with anything, but they're going to explore every possible lead on the case. And right now, that's you."

Screw that. He pulled his gun from his top dresser drawer and tucked it into the back of his jeans. Two boxes of bullets landed in the bottom of his pack. "Who else are they questioning?"

"No one. Like I said, they don't know that Perkins is

still in the neighborhood. But with the way you get around to every bar, whorehouse and the casino, I'm sure they want to ask if you've seen anyone matching his description."

Sherman dropped his bag back onto the bed. These past six months working for the Nicky Wayne crime family out of Vegas had given him the best money ticket of his life. He wasn't going to give it up if the feds just wanted to show him some pictures and ask if he knew a guy. "I can always say no. They've got nothing they can hold me on. You're just worried that I'll mention these phone calls, and then they'll figure out they have a traitor in their midst."

The lengthy pause indicated that Sherman had struck a nerve. "You've got nothing on me. No name. No ID. But can you still say no when the detox kicks in? Can you keep your mouth shut about Perkins? About Grainger's murder? Do you really want to take the fall for our crimes? This is a federal investigator they're bringing in, Watts, not some good ol' boy sheriff who'll give you a sip from his own flask and let you walk away. I hear she's tough. She'll break you."

"She?" He took the news like a punch to the gut.

Hell. It was a woman who had turned him to drink in the first place. Some woman or other always seemed to be standing in the way of what he deserved. His high school sweetheart, Naomi, had married his best friend, Ralph Kuchu, instead of him. Eighteen years later, Naomi had been drunk enough to get herself and Ralph both killed in a car wreck—taking the woman Sherman loved and the money Ralph owed him to their graves.

Women were good for one thing. Sobering him up and poking questions at him wasn't it.

And if she did flash her boobs or nag him enough and get him to reveal what he knew about Julie Grainger's murder or Boyd Perkins's whereabouts, then he'd be a dead man. He was only useful to Perkins and the family he worked for as long as he kept his mouth shut.

"All right. I can hide out for a few days." Sherman carried his bag out to the table and packed the whiskey bottle in with a change of socks and some fishing gear. He grabbed his sleeping bag from the closet and tied it to his pack. "Let Perkins and Mr. Wayne know that I'm out of here."

After disconnecting the call, Sherman opened the trailer door and studied the sky. Clouds were gathering with the promise of spring rain in the next twenty-four hours, give or take. That was good. It'd be hell to sleep in, as the temperature in the mountains was still cold on June nights. But rain also meant he wouldn't leave any tracks. He reached for his black, flat-brimmed hat and pulled it over scraggly hair that was still as black as it had been the day he was born over fifty years ago. With his survival skills, he could last for weeks up in the red rocks and cliffs of the Mesa Verde range.

He could last as long as he had something to drink.

And no woman got in his way.

Chapter One

Special Agent Joanna Rhodes stepped off the puddle jumper flight from Durango into the rain at Kenner City, Colorado.

Though the other two passengers on the same plane made a dash for the shelter of the terminal, Joanna stood on the tarmac, surveying the stark, dramatic landscape of red rock mountains and barren desert spaces of the Four Corners region of the state. Awe-inspiring. Rich in history and mystique. Majestic. She'd read all the descriptors in tourism magazines and advertisements for the nearby casino.

But she couldn't see the beauty. She could barely feel the cool drizzle of rain spitting against her face. An oppressive sense of the world closing in around her, so at odds with the rugged, wide-open spaces, made it difficult to catch her breath.

"Suck it up, girl," Joanna whispered between clenched teeth, her nostrils flaring as she pulled her shoulders back and ordered her lungs to expand. It wasn't the altitude or the faint chill of early spring in the air that had grabbed hold of her. It wasn't the rain, kicking up a familiar, omnipresent dust and washing the scent of ozone down to her level, that made moving from this spot so difficult. It was the memories swirling inside her head, attacking her from every direction, that made this homecoming feel like a walk down a long corridor at a maximum-security prison, ending at a windowless cell with her name on it.

"That's the power of positive thinking," she chided herself with sarcasm, hating that her thoughts had gone off on the morbid metaphor. Fanciful images of any kind didn't fit with the practical, efficient persona she'd worked so hard to cultivate. This wasn't supposed to be a stroll down memory lane for her. "Focus on the work."

She was here to break open a case that the bureau, local law enforcement and the Kenner County Crime Lab had been investigating for five months now. Solve the murder of a federal agent in the area and uncover suspected links to the feuding Wayne and Del Gardo crime families out of Las Vegas. Find a lead on the missing fifty million dollars that the late crime boss, Vincent Del Gardo, had allegedly hid in the Four Corners area.

All she had to do was face down a nightmare from her past to get the answers they needed.

No small task on any front.

This was her assignment. She'd been personally requested by the Durango bureau office because of her ethnic background and ties to the area. Her boss in D.C. had assured her it was a career-making opportunity she'd be foolish to pass up. Besides, a job was a job. And she was damn good at hers.

Blinking the moisture from her long dark eyelashes,

Joanna checked the Glock 9 mm in the holster on her belt, as well as the FBI shield clipped beside it. Then she rebuttoned her pin-striped blazer and shook her ponytail down the center of her back.

"Piece of cake." Armed inside and out, she pulled up the handle on her overnight suitcase and strode toward the terminal.

"Agent Rhodes?" The glass double doors swung open and a tall, lanky man wearing a tuxedo with a cowboy hat and boots jogged out to meet her.

Instinctively, she halted and retreated half a step, her hand hovering near her gun, waiting for the man to identify himself.

"Didn't see you inside and thought I'd missed you. Sorry I'm running late. I had to pick up my wife and son and give away a bride before I could get here." He stopped a few feet away and tipped the brim of his hat before extending his hand in greeting. "I'm Patrick Martinez."

"Joanna Rhodes." Recognizing the name and the general description of dark hair and Irish-blue eyes given her by the bureau chief in Durango, Jerry Ortiz, she reached out to shake hands with the Kenner County sheriff. "You're not late, Sheriff. But I'd like to remind you that I could just as easily have rented a car and driven myself to your office."

He grinned. "Well, that wouldn't say very much for western hospitality, now, would it."

Knowing she was meant to smile at the friendly remark, she curved her mouth into a practiced arc. But when he reached for the handle of her suitcase, Joanna tightened her grip. Long before she'd reached the age of thirty-three, she'd learned to take care of herself in every way that mattered. "I've got it."

With a nod, he turned to walk beside her. "Then let's get you out of the rain and get you briefed on the investigation." Despite her show of independence, his longer stride got him to the doors first, and he pulled one open for her. He glanced up at the late afternoon's overcast sky as she walked through. "We're expecting storms on and off all weekend long. This little sprinkle is just the prelude."

She remembered the all or nothing weather patterns from her childhood. Summers could be beastly hot and dry, yet still be chilly at night. Winters were frigid, especially up in the mountains. And the transitional seasons in between promised torrential rains and flash floods, or blizzards, depending on the temperature. The area was probably going through its spring thaw right now, when massive snowmelts at the higher elevations filled the rivers and streams in the area—the same streambeds that would be bone dry come autumn. But she wasn't here to reminisce or discuss the weather. "How far are we from your office? I understand it shares a building with the crime unit?"

Once they cleared the terminal, the sheriff pointed to the officially marked black Suburban parked at the curb. With a beep from his key chain, he opened the back door behind the passenger seat. "You can toss your bag in here."

"Thank you."

His cowboy-style manners were charming but unnecessary. And once they were both inside the car, he seemed to accept that she was more interested in answers than in making new friends. "We've got a smoothly integrated system here in Kenner County. Budget constraints being what they are, the practicality of housing the area law enforcement units in one location made it a no-brainer. A briefing room, locker rooms, executive offices, plus the interview rooms, lineup room and temporary lockup are located on the first two floors, while most of the crime lab is housed upstairs on the third. We've got a fourth floor for storage." He shifted into Drive and pulled onto the highway leading into town. "We'll be there in ten minutes."

Through the rhythmic swish of the windshield wipers, Joanna watched the landscape change from scrub brush to the metal prefab buildings of a growing industrial park. They passed a neat and tidy residential area nestled in the foothills, filled with square, pueblo-style houses, bungalows and larger Victorian reproduction homes. Finally, Sheriff Martinez turned his car toward the brick and stone buildings that marked the downtown area. Kenner City was a quaint, bustling enterprise of a town, nestled in a bowl between mountain peaks. It boasted striped awnings and pinewood balconies, and flags flew above nearly every storefront and business.

Not one trailer park in sight. No run-down liquor store on the main drag. No tattered teenage girl running the streets, looking for her parents in seedy bars and back alleys, hoping they'd be happy drunk and cooperate with her efforts to get them safely home, instead of mean drunk and belligerent, or just flat passed out from whatever party or paycheck they'd drunk their way through on any given night.

Everything here was charming and well kept and scrupulously clean—a far cry from the Ute reservation where she'd grown up, just a few more miles down the road.

She knew she was expected to say something, to make conversation to pass the drive time. But Joanna had made a career out of watching and assessing before she spoke, learning to listen without saying more than was required. Even before her training, idle chitchat had never come easily for her.

The sheriff didn't seem to have that problem, however. "The hotel where you're booked is just a block from our location, and I figured you'd be doing your interview of the suspect there. If you do want to go somewhere, one of my deputies will be available to drive you. Or we can loan you a vehicle if it's not in use." He slowed as they drove through the heart of downtown, touching his hat to pedestrians hurrying along the wide sidewalks. As they passed the last few businesses, he pointed out a diner-style restaurant with bright lights and lots of windows called the Morning Ray Café. "That's my mom's place. You can get all three meals there. It's good, down-home cookin' that'll fill you up."

The gleam of pride was obvious in his tone and smile. Joanna's mother's idea of a home-cooked meal had involved ripping open packages and zapping them in the microwave—when she remembered to fix any meal at all for her daughter. Joanna had turned herself into a fairly accomplished cook by the time she'd finished the third grade, simply as a matter of survival. But the lack of three square meals a day growing up had been the least of her problems.

The sheriff reached across the seat and tapped her elbow to pull her attention from her thoughts. He pointed to an imposing building with a gray brick and white stone facade on the corner at the end of the street. "There's your hotel. Used to be a mining office, but now it's completely remodeled inside. Want to check in first?"

Alarmed to realize her thoughts kept drifting to the past instead of focusing squarely on her present assignment, Joanna resolutely straightened in her seat. "Let's go directly to your office. I want to familiarize myself with my surroundings before I meet the suspect I'm interrogating."

"You want the home field advantage?" he teased.

"Something like that." They had almost driven out of the far edge of town before Joanna spotted the rambling four-story building with signs that read Kenner City Sheriff and Kenner County Crime Unit. "I read the file from Supervisor Ortiz, but I'd like to get your take on things since you've worked more closely on Agent Grainger's murder. What can you tell me about your suspect, Sherman Watts?"

Good. She got the name out without so much as a stutter of hesitation.

Focus on the job, Joanna. Watts is just a job.

"He's a local troublemaker. Been convicted and jailed on any number of petty crimes—mostly drunk and disorderly, a couple of assaults."

"A-assault?" *That* was a definite hesitation.

But Martinez, fortunately, didn't pick up on the way she stiffened in her seat. He pulled into a slanted parking space in front of the building. "When Watts is drunk, he can get mean."

So some things never changed in Kenner County. "You don't have him in custody?"

"We suspect he's been doing odd jobs for the Nicky Wayne crime family out of Vegas, like helping Wayne's hit man, Boyd Perkins, hide out in the area. However, what we believe and what we can prove are two different things. That's why he's still a free man. But he's definitely a person of interest we've been watching. Could be he had nothing to do with the murder, and he's only funneling information to them—someone sure seems to be."

She'd heard about the information leaks that had dogged the investigation, seeming to give Boyd Perkins—the man reputed to have killed mob boss Vincent Del Gardo, as well as the bureau's chief suspect in Agent Grainger's murder—a heads-up when to go into hiding or carry out another attack. "How do you want me to direct my interrogation? Confirm the source of the security leak? Find out if Perkins is still in the area and pinpoint his location? Or should I concentrate on Watts himself, and tie him to Boyd Perkins and Agent Grainger's murder so you can make an arrest?"

"Anything you can get out of him. I don't make him for premeditated murder—I'd be surprised if he has the backbone for that. But I wouldn't put it past him to hurt someone if he felt threatened."

She didn't need to read the Kenner County Crime Unit—KCCU, according to her mission brief—report to know his assessment of Sherman Watts was on the money. Drunk or sober—if that ever happened—the fifty-eight-year-old Indian was as dangerous and unpredictable as a badger. If he got cornered, he was just as likely to turn and attack as he was to skulk away into some hole. If he felt he was entitled to something, he'd take it—as long as he thought he could get away with it. And damn to anyone who tried to stop him.

"You owe me, bitch."

With her face smashed down into the bed and his heavy weight on top of her, Joanna's screams were muffled. The wool lint from the blankets filtered into her nose and mouth with each gasp, and she could scarcely breathe.

He'd hit her hard enough, too, to make the room spin. But the pain was clear, the humiliation intense. Oh, God, it hurt. Right down to her soul, it hurt.

Son of a bitch. Joanna jerked her mind back to the rain and the sheriff and the present, and forced herself to breathe. So she had a little extra insight into Sherman Watts and how his mind worked. That's what criminal profiling was all about, right? Knowing the truth about the suspect—knowing his secrets—could only help her get this interview done more quickly and efficiently.

Joanna pried her fingers off the armrest to unbuckle her seat belt. She breathed deeply, clearly, in through her nose and out through her mouth, more determined than ever to leave the past in the past so she could help Martinez and his people deal with the present. "Is there any hard evidence to connect Watts to Julie Grainger's murder? Any motive?"

Either unaware of her momentary discomfort, or politely ignoring it, the sheriff continued. "We know that Agent Grainger was on the trail of fifty million dollars that crime boss Vincent Del Gardo hid in the area. If she found it, or had a clue on her that would lead to its location, then that's fifty million reasons why just about anybody would want to kill her. One of our lab teams found a leather necklace that we believe belonged to

Watts at the site where her body was dumped. That puts him at the scene—before or after her death, though, we don't know."

"You think Watts has the fifty mil?"

"No. Someone's still looking for it, or the attacks would have stopped." Martinez muttered a curse, clearly frustrated with the lack of closure on the case. His eyes were clear glacial-blue when they locked on to hers. "Sherman Watts is a survivor. He'll do whatever it takes to stay alive and stay one step ahead of us. There was a time when Watts would pick a fight at one of the local bars, just so he could spend a warm night in jail. Now he's living in a new trailer on the rez and drinking name-brand booze. He claims his money is from an inheritance. I haven't been able to prove otherwise."

"You don't believe him."

He shook his head. "Nicky Wayne and his family have laundered enough money that they could make it look as if Watts's income is from a legitimate source. If they're funding him, Watts may be uncatchable right now."

Letting Watts get away with aiding and abetting, theft, murder—or God knew what—wasn't going to happen. Never again. "I'll get him in a room and get him to talk. I'll find out what he knows."

Martinez nodded, believing the strength of her words. "I've sent a couple of men out to the reservation to bring him in for questioning."

She waved aside the offer of an umbrella, retrieved her bag and followed him inside.

He nodded to the security guard reading a newspaper at the front desk and led Joanna past him to a reception area at the center of a suite of offices. "Anybody home?" Martinez hollered. He removed his hat and knocked it against his leg before brushing away the moisture beading on the shoulders of his black tux jacket. "Elizabeth?"

Joanna frowned, smoothing the damp hair around her face as she surveyed the executive office area and the hallways, elevator and doors branching off in either direction. "I was led to believe this was a fully staffed facility. Where is everyone?"

"Like I said, we had a wedding this afternoon. Our chief forensic scientist, Dr. Calista MacBride, married Tom Ryan. Tom's been with us as an FBI investigator almost from the day I first saw Julie Grainger's body. I guess the two of them went through the academy together—Tom and Julie, that is. I think Tom and Callie were, uh…friends, if you know what I mean, even before the murder brought them back together." He turned toward the locker rooms and staff entrance at the end of the hall. "Elizabeth? You here yet?"

Joanna noted the name plate on the high front counter at the center of the carpeted waiting area. She dismissed the sudden chill of remembrance as the rain trickled down the back of her scalp. This Tom and Callie weren't the only old friends to be reunited by this case. "Elizabeth Reddawn is your receptionist?"

The sheriff set his hat on the counter beside the nameplate. "You know her?"

"Old friend" wasn't exactly the right term. Joanna's parents, Ralph and Naomi, had alienated most of the decent people she knew by the time they'd died in a drunk-driving accident when she was eighteen. And once Joanna had left for college and her career, she'd never looked back. Until now. Yet there were bound to be harder memories to face than this one. She would handle them all. Supervisor Ortiz and her boss back in Washington, D.C., were counting on her. "I grew up on the rez over in Mesa Ridge. Elizabeth worked for the reservation sheriff back then."

"Elmer Watts?"

Probably the man Martinez had replaced when the county and reservation units had merged. Sherman Watts's uncle. Joanna nodded.

Elizabeth had been the only one in that office who'd really listened to Joanna when she'd needed their help. But as a lowly secretary, Elizabeth Reddawn had been as powerless as Joanna had been. And the resulting pity she'd offered had been no help at all.

"Then this will be a reunion of sorts for you."

"I suppose."

Martinez gestured toward the door marked Sheriff. "Let me make a couple of calls to see where my people are." After setting her bag behind the reception counter, he turned back to Joanna. His smile faded and she caught a glimpse of the sharp, protective-of-his-own man in charge Supervisor Ortiz had described. "Don't pass judgment on my team, Agent Rhodes. They can all use a break for one afternoon. This has been one twisted case and we've taken some personal hits that haven't gone down real well. We lost crucial evidence during that blizzard back in March. I've had a witness with amnesia and a crime boss who was killed before he could give me any answers. Our families have been attacked—my people tested in every way imaginable. The lab has gathered plenty of evidence and we've all got our suspicions, but we need to tie the pieces together and make it stick. We need somebody behind bars. Soon."

"Of course, sir." Her acquiescence seemed to appease the protective papa-bear growl of his voice. "I'm here to work—not catch up with former acquaintances."

"In my head, I know you're not the enemy. Still, it feels like a slap in the face for the bureau to bring in a big gun from outside our investigation to get us over this stone wall we've run into." He pulled back the front of his jacket and propped his hands near the gun and badge at his waist. "I guess I can see the bureau's logic in bringing in a Native American to interview Watts. I suppose he's more likely to respond to one of his own."

One of his own? Joanna's skin crawled at the comparison.

But she didn't so much as bat an eyelash. "Possibly."

So not only was she coming into a tightly knit group of co-workers, but Martinez was hinting that there was resentment against her being here. Joanna was used to being the odd man out. As the daughter of Ralph and Naomi Kuchu, she'd grown up not fitting in with normal families who worked hard and paid their bills and protected their children.

Since the day of her parents' funeral, she'd taken that loner persona and turned it into a strength. She was trained to be courteous and professional right down to her painted pinkie toe, but she'd discovered that if she remained dispassionate and in control she was harder to read. And if the bad guy sitting across the interview table from her couldn't get into her head, then he had no advantage over her.

No one had an advantage over her if she didn't let them in.

"I'm not here to mop up any mess or steal any thunder from your people, Sheriff. The bureau just wants vindication for the murder of one of their own." She could handle the isolation, but if Martinez's team resented her enough to actually work against her, then they'd have no chance of success. "Perhaps I should clarify the kind of support I'll need from you."

"Yeah?"

Simple. "All I need is a room, and Watts. If he knows anything, I'll get you the information you need. You're welcome to make any arrests or pursue any leads that might result. I'm just a tool the bureau is providing your investigation. Use me."

Martinez nodded, accepting the arrangement. For now. She could see he still had his suspicions about her motivation for being here. "Ortiz says you're up for a big promotion back in D.C."

No point in lying about that. "If I don't deliver here, they may reconsider."

"This is a test for you, eh?"

More than anyone here or in D.C. would ever know. "Yes."

Any hint of western hospitality disappeared as he leaned in and issued a warning. "I won't have your career ambitions get in the way of my case or jeopardize the safety of my team. Are we clear on that?"

Joanna stood as tall and straight as her dignity and two-inch heels allowed. "Yes, sir. I won't let you down."

He pulled back, relaxing his shoulders if not quite smiling again. "Good. I'll go make those calls and find some people."

"Don't bother, Patrick." A squat woman with a thick black bun on the back of her head waddled into the reception area. She peeled a clear plastic rain slicker off her scarlet blouse and brightly patterned skirt, hanging the coat up beside the reception counter as she talked. "We're on our way back. Since they're only taking the weekend off, I think Callie and Tom are anxious to get their honeymoon started, so the festivities are breaking up." The sixtyish petite woman turned her eyes, dark as night but shining with laughter, up to Joanna. She clapped her hands together. "As I live and breathe. Joanna?"

"Good to see you again, Elizabeth."

"'Good to see…'?" She tutted. "What kind of greeting is that?" Elizabeth Reddawn flung her arms open and squeezed Joanna against her ample bosom. "My goodness, child, how you've grown up."

The woman's enthusiastic welcome seemed to demand some kind of a response before she'd let go. Nonplussed by the effusive human contact she typically avoided, Joanna finally reached around and patted the back of the older woman's shoulders, completing the hug. "It's been fifteen years."

"Has it really?" Elizabeth pulled away, her eyes crinkling with the depth of her smile. She maintained a clasp on Joanna's fingers, alerting her that there was more personal conversation to come, even though she turned away and tilted her head toward the sheriff. "By the way, Patrick? Bree asked if you still wanted to do a movie with her and Charlie tonight because they'd stay in town instead of going home."

"Are you kidding? That new action-hero movie opens tonight. Of course I'm taking my son." He turned to include Joanna in a wink that erased his stern countenance. "Bree would be the wife. She gets to hold the popcorn and keep Charlie and me in line." He nodded to Elizabeth. "You'll keep our guest company for a few minutes?"

"Of course."

"Excuse me."

"So…" Turning her maternal indulgence from the sheriff's retreating back to Joanna, Elizabeth took hold of both hands and quickly inspected her from head to toe. "Joanna Kuchu—Daughter of the Buffalo. You've matured into a woman as beautiful and powerful as your namesake."

As Elizabeth pulled her toward the couch and chairs of the seating area, Joanna gently disengaged her hands. "It's Joanna Rhodes now."

Elizabeth sat and patted the sofa cushion beside her. "You're married?"

"No." Joanna perched on the edge of the couch, curling her fingers into her lap. "I was a Rhodes scholar my senior year at Yale. I liked the name—I liked the honor—so I had it legally changed."

"I see." Her quizzical frown indicated she suspected there were deeper reasons for erasing her past. However, the Elizabeth Reddawn Joanna remembered wouldn't have pried unless invited to do so—even if she was champing at the bit to ask questions. Judging by the way she kept plucking at her wool skirt, the older woman was definitely itching to ask something. But Joanna wasn't offering. "That's wonderful. Congratulations."

"Thanks." Several silent moments passed, leaving Joanna wondering how long Martinez would be on the phone to his wife, and how long she could sit here smiling and pretending that this reunion wasn't awkward as hell for her. "How do you like working for Sheriff Martinez and the crime lab?"

"It's nicer than working at old Elmer's office ever was. And I'm not just talking about the new furniture and state-of-the-art facilities in our lab." Despite Joanna's stiff posture, Elizabeth reached across and squeezed her hand around one of the fists in her lap. "These are good people here. You'll like them."

The other woman's caring touch seeped into Joanna's fingers and shot little tendrils of distracting warmth into her resolve to stay focused solely on work while she was in Kenner City. "I'm only here for a couple of days. I doubt I'll have time to get to know them."

"What about the people in Kenner City and Mesa Ridge you already…? Oh. Of course." Elizabeth politely pulled away, no doubt sensing the protective personal barriers Joanna was pushing back into place. "I don't suppose you have relatives in the area to keep you here."

"No."

"Will you be paying your respects to your mother and daddy?"

"Hadn't planned on it."

"Ethan Bia has been back in town for a few years now, after his stint in the army."

Ethan Bia? A shiver of recognition, of feelings long buried and often regretted, danced along Joanna's spine.

She flashed through the remembered sensations of a young man's eager touch—the patient demands of his mouth on her untutored lips. She blotted out the image of anger she'd seen only once on his tanned, rugged face—the last memory she had of the gentle giant she'd once loved.

"Ethan left Mesa Ridge?" That was almost more surprising than her reaction to the mere mention of his name.

Elizabeth jumped on the question. "For six years. He's a consultant with the crime lab now. Works search and rescue in the area. What about calling him—?"

"I'm not here to socialize."

Joanna hardened herself against the name, as warring memories of strength and warmth, regret and shame, surged inside her.

"*Nüa-rü. The wind.*" *He stroked the long strand of hair off her face and tucked it behind her ear.* "*You're just as elusive to me.*"

"*Ethan…*"

She'd had to leave. Just as surely as Ethan had had to stay. He was tied to the earth and the mountains in a way she'd never been tied to anything or anyone.

A smack across the face. A knife at her breast.

"*You owe me, bitch.*"

Joanna jerked inside her skin. No. No way could she have stayed.

"Honey?" Elizabeth's hand was on hers again.

The locker-room doors swung open, thankfully putting an end to the discomfort of reacquainting herself with the past.

"*Madre de Dios,*" muttered one Latino man, shaking

the rain from his black hair. "It hasn't let up once since noon. It'll be raining buckets by sunset."

"You're telling me."

Joanna pushed to her feet as a second man—same height, same black hair, same features save for the scar that bisected his chin—came up beside him. Both wore suits, although the first one was already pulling off his tie and stuffing it into his pocket as they approached.

The second one pulled a cell phone from his belt beside the gun he wore. "I'd better give Aspen a call at school and tell her I'll pick up Jack from the sitter's. I don't want her on those muddy reservation back roads any more than necessary. I predict a washout in our future. No pun intended."

"Nice one, *hermano*." The first one elbowed his buddy in the arm. "Emma talked about seeing great waters and danger in her dreams last night."

"Maybe she should take up weather forecasting."

"Yeah, and maybe you should call your wife before she forgets what you look like. Again."

"Ouch." Both men laughed as they moved their magnets on the sign-in board behind the reception counter to indicate that they were back in the office and on duty. "Point taken. I'll leave the one-liners to you."

Joanna didn't need Elizabeth mouthing the word "twins" to recognize the resemblance. She didn't particularly need the nudge forward as Elizabeth insisted on introducing them, either. "Miguel? Dylan? I'd like you to meet the daughter of an old friend of mine, Joanna Kuch—" She caught the mistake. "Joanna Rhodes. She'll be working with us for a few days."

Extending her hand in a professional greeting,

Joanna completed the introductions herself. She'd done her homework. "Agent Dylan Acevedo. Supervisor Ortiz told me you'd transferred here because you were friends with the deceased, Agent Grainger."

"Julie and I went through the academy together—along with Tom Ryan and Ben Parrish. We've all been working the case." Dylan—the one with the scar—shook her hand, nodding toward the badge at her waist. "You're FBI?"

"I'm with the D.C. office. Profiling and interrogation specialist. I'm here to interview Sherman Watts."

Dylan's twin shook her hand next. "Good luck with that one. He's a wily SOB. The man's got nine lives when it comes to staying ahead of the law. I'm Miguel Acevedo."

Joanna recognized the name. "You're a crime-scene investigator with the forensic lab."

"That's right." He unbuttoned the collar of his shirt and shucked his jacket, looking like a man who was anxious to get out of his wedding apparel and get back to work. "So you're the big gun Martinez said the bureau was bringing in to crack this case for us."

You don't have to make friends, she reminded herself. *You just have to get the job done.* Her promotion and the ability to walk away from here emotionally unscathed depended on it. "That's my intention. The information in the case file that KCCU prepared for me was very thorough. I'm sure it will be invaluable to the success of my interview."

The locker-room door opened again at the end of the hall. She needn't have worried about the laxness or scarcity of the staff. This wasn't the reservation sheriff's office of fifteen years ago. She was beginning to believe the paperwork she'd read. The KCCU was a diverse, dedicated staff of scientists and area law enforcement. The blond-haired man strolling toward them appeared to be no exception.

He walked straight up to Joanna and the Acevedos and diffused the tension between them by leaning down to kiss Elizabeth's cheek. "Lizzie, you left the reception before that dance you promised me. Broke my heart."

"Oh, Ben." She swatted at his arm. "I'm a married woman."

"All the good ones are taken, hmm?"

Elizabeth blushed at the flirtation from a much younger man.

He grinned as he straightened to introduce himself. "Ben Parrish, FBI."

"Joanna Rhodes, the same."

She noted that his handsome smile didn't quite reach his wary eyes. "Don't let these guys give you any grief. I was the new kid here myself a few months back. Now I've grown on them."

"Like a fungus, Parrish," Miguel teased. "I'd better change and get up to the lab. With Callie taking a couple of days off, I want to make sure we've got everything covered and on schedule for the weekend." His smile seemed genuine enough as he excused himself. "If there's anything you need from the lab, Agent Rhodes, let me know."

"Thank you."

As his brother pushed open the stairwell door and jogged up the stairs, Dylan Acevedo toned his indignation at an outsider's interference down to an I'll-wait-to-pass-judgment-once-I-see-what-kind-of-job-you-can-do status. "Watts and his buddy Perkins have already gone after my wife and Miguel's. One or both of them are responsible for other attacks in the area. I'm guessing Sheriff Martinez already told you we make Boyd Perkins for Julie's murder. There's not a one of us who doesn't want to put him away. If you can help us find the bastard…"

"I'll get what your team needs out of Watts, Agent Acevedo," Joanna reassured him. "And you're welcome to make the arrest."

"What do you get out of this?" Miguel asked.

"Miguel!" Elizabeth chided.

Telling him this was about a promotion wouldn't build any trust. Telling him her personal reasons for accepting this assignment wasn't an option, either. Joanna settled for a truth somewhere in between. "The satisfaction of a job well-done."

"We can all use a little of that," Ben intervened. Joanna nodded, appreciating his support more than she realized. She didn't have to worry about thanking him, though. He turned away to mark himself In on the duty board and nodded for Miguel to follow him into an office opposite the sheriff's. "I want you to tell me more about that medal Julie sent you before she died. There has to be a reason why you, me and Tom all got one."

Once the door closed on their conversation, Joanna became aware of the warmth of Elizabeth Reddawn's hand, still linked through the crook of her elbow. Had the older woman been holding on to her this entire time? Claiming her as a friend? Subtly hanging on in the face of the teasing, doubt and outright resentment from the three men?

As uncomfortable with the show of support as she was unaccustomed to it, Joanna shrugged away from Elizabeth's touch. She busied her fingers, plucking imaginary specks from her blazer and slacks. She was perfectly capable of standing on her own two feet in this investigation without the older woman's help. Joanna just needed a moment to shore up her defenses again, make sure her powers of observation, her strength and intellect, were firmly in place. "Could you show me where the interview rooms are? I'm afraid Sheriff Martinez has been held up on the phone."

"Sure, hon." Elizabeth's frown indicated disappointment at Joanna's abrupt insistence on working rather than resuming their trip down memory lane. But there was also something she supposed was maternal understanding when she patted Joanna's arm. "Come on around this way. There are two rooms, with an observation window in between." Elizabeth led her back toward the security desk and a hallway that ran parallel to this wing of offices. "Can I get you some coffee?"

"Black, thanks. That would be lovely."

"I'll brew a fresh pot and bring it right in."

As Elizabeth bustled away, Joanna paused for a moment to inhale a quieting breath. But she'd switched on the light in the first room before realizing how much Elizabeth Reddawn and the secrets from the reservation they shared had gotten into her head and diverted her focus from the investigation.

"You forgot the case file, Sherlock." Stopping short of thumping herself on the forehead, Joanna retraced her steps. She'd already mapped out her strategy for questioning Watts. Now she needed to choreograph her questions with the placement of chairs and where she would sit or stand during each phase of the interview.

Joanna unzipped her bag and pulled out the thick manila envelope with the case reports and her notes. She'd just acknowledged the security guard in the lobby when the front door opened with a rush of wind and patter of raindrops.

"Elizabeth?" The familiar male voice swept straight through her, mocking any attempt to keep her emotions in check. "You left your purse at the church. What are you carrying in this thing, bricks?"

Joanna stopped in her tracks. Stared.

The man, easily six foot four, froze in the open doorway. His dark eyes narrowed as they locked on to hers. The wind glued his brown suit jacket to his broad shoulders. The rain made his military-short hair glisten like polished onyx.

"Joanna?" The timbre of his voice darkened. The deep pitch of it filled up his chest and rumbled out in a seductive whisper.

"Ethan." Here. In the flesh. Impossibly bigger, broader, harder than the man she remembered. The silent intensity of his dark, nearly black eyes hit her like a sucker punch to the heart.

Ethan Bia.

The man she'd given her virginity and her young girl's heart to.

The man who'd taught her how to survive the mountains—and her family.

The man she'd walked away from fifteen years ago without ever looking back.

Chapter Two

"What are you doing here?" Ethan asked, anchoring his boots to the floor and holding himself still against the impulse leaping through every muscle of his body. Fly across the room and scoop her up in a fierce hug.

But another part of him had grown wiser and more cautious over the years. One, they had an audience in the form of Officer Bates at the security desk. And two, even if they were all alone, he wasn't too keen on getting his ego smacked or his heart crushed again.

He'd seen plenty of death and destruction in his years as an army ranger and his two tours of duty in Afghanistan. He'd dealt with loss in his work as a search-and-rescue team leader. But nothing had ever hit him as hard or left him feeling as powerless as watching Joanna Kuchu's tearstained face when she'd scrambled out of his truck that last warm spring night on the rez.

"There are no good memories for me here. I have the chance to leave and I'm taking it. Goodbye, Ethan."

She was barely eighteen and he was only twenty-one, but he'd known in his bones that they were supposed to last.

But boom. They were done. She was gone.

And he was the man left behind.

"I'm working the Julie Grainger murder investigation," she explained, clutching a thick investigation file against her chest. Her fingers fiddled with the edge of the manila envelope in a subtle revelation of nerves. But they stilled almost as soon as he noticed the unconscious movement.

Always guarded, always with a plan, always thinking two or three steps ahead of everyone else in the room. That part of her personality hadn't changed.

"I knew there was a good chance I'd run into you. We should get this meeting over with so that it doesn't cost either of us more pain than it has to." She pointed over his shoulder. "You're getting wet and so's the rug. Why don't you close the door? I'm sure we can find a private place to talk."

No good memories. Not even him. Them. She'd been through hell those last few months—and the years before hadn't been much better, so he'd never held her need to leave against her. But she'd never even let him try to help. She'd refused his offer to go with her. And his love hadn't been enough for her to stay.

Ethan pushed the door shut behind him. He might not hold her obsessive drive to escape Mesa Ridge and the reservation against her. Didn't mean he had to let her fillet his heart open and char it over the flames of false hope and misguided passion again, either.

"I'm just here to deliver this to a friend," he explained, holding up the purse he carried.

"Elizabeth?" She inclined her head toward the main hallway, exposing a swanlike expanse of neck that beckoned to randy memories from the past. "She's in the break room making coffee. I'll walk you back."

Though this sure as hell wasn't the homecoming he'd once wished for, spending a few impersonal minutes in her company could no longer hurt him. Ethan shortened his stride and fell into step beside her. "Time has treated you well."

"You look good, too." She arched an eyebrow and gave him a glimpse of the hesitant smile he remembered. "Your hair's a lot shorter. And you—" her long, agile fingers gestured in the air "—filled out. Got big. You're taller and broader both, it looks like to me."

More than six years of elite army training and service, plus the rugged outdoorsman life he led, did that to a man. "I guess."

"How's Kyle?"

It made sense that she'd ask about his younger brother. They'd been classmates and good friends. Of course, she and Ethan had been so much more than friends, but she didn't need him to point that out. "He's good. Married. Two kids. Lives in Cortez now."

"Still a man of few words, I see."

"No sense wasting them." Stopping at Elizabeth Reddawn's desk, Ethan set down the purse and unhooked his collar and loosened the black string tie he wore, silently assessing the changes in Joanna's appearance as she turned to face him.

Despite the warmth of her olive complexion and dark brown eyes, there was a brittleness to her ramrod posture and polite words. He idly wondered if a stroke of his fingertip across the nape of her neck could still make her shiver, or if the touch of his lips against hers could break through those invisible barriers she wore like body armor and unleash the warmth and softness and eagerness to explore her own sexuality he remembered.

The black-as-midnight hair she'd pulled back into a sleek ponytail was shorter than the wild horse's tail of a hairdo she'd worn through high school. She'd grown, too. Maybe it was the high heels she was wearing—he'd never seen those on her feet before—but the top of her head was just about even with his chin now. The curve of her lips sported a sheer berry tint that hadn't been there fifteen years ago, and her tailored suit was a far cry from the jeans and tees she'd lived in back then. The beautiful woman standing in front of him looked as polished and businesslike and cold as the gun holstered at her waist.

The curious, coltish tomboy who'd tagged along with him and his younger brother, Kyle, on their adventures around the reservation had vanished. The years apart had erased the young woman with the shy sensuality and big dreams whom he'd patiently coaxed into loving and trusting him. Pity there was no sign of the fire within that had once drawn him like a moth to a flame.

But idle thoughts were as useless as idle words.

"You're FBI?" he asked.

She nodded. "I made it into the program at Quantico after graduating with my master's in psychology. Made it all the way to Washington, D.C., where I'm assigned now as a behavioral scientist and criminal profiler."

"Good." That was what she'd wanted—to move East, to put the entire country between her and the memories of her parents' deaths and the compounding tragedy that followed. She'd longed for urban landscapes and busy, diverse city streets instead of the endless red-rock terrain and isolation of the reservation and the small mountain towns like Mesa Ridge and Kenner City. She'd wanted to carry a gun and take down bad guys and give the victims like herself, who'd been denied a voice, a champion who could save the day. She'd wanted things he couldn't give her. "Congratulations."

"Thanks."

So she'd finally gotten what she wanted. On some noble level, he was happy for her. But deeper down, somewhere between his battered heart and old man's soul, it had always felt like unfinished business between them—as though fate and her stubborn will had seen fit to deny them the wonderful possibilities of loving each other.

Just punishment, Ethan supposed. He hadn't protected her well enough back then—hadn't even sensed how badly she'd needed his protection until it was too late. He'd been more interested in getting in her pants and making her see the world—and their future together—through his eyes.

Yeah. More than anyone he knew, Joanna Kuchu deserved to have her dreams come true. Even if those dreams didn't include him. He was glad that she'd finally found her place in the world.

After moving on for a while, he'd come to realize that he was already where he needed to be. He'd come home from that last hellish deployment to the land whose spirit flowed through him like his own blood. He needed the open space and quiet the way she needed the bustle and technology and new faces around every turn in the big city.

When the silence stretched on long enough for her coffee-dark gaze to drop to the middle of his chest, Ethan knew there was no sense prolonging their would've-could've-should've-been reunion. He smoothed his hand over the top of his cropped hair and down the back of his scalp, taking away a palmful of dampness with it. There was no good way to let this woman go. He just had to do it. "I hope life always gives you what you need, Jo."

Her dark eyes flinched and darted back up to his. "You, too, Ethan. You're kinder than I deserve. I'm…" Those berry lips tightened into a frown that tugged at both his heart and conscience. "I'm—"

"I know." He knew the sentiment by heart. "You're sorry. So am I." Before he could act on the impulse to take her in his arms to trade comforts and remind his body what hers felt like pressed against it, he pointed to the overstuffed bag he'd set on the counter. "Would you make sure Elizabeth gets this?"

"Of course."

Ethan turned, ending the conversation and walking away. He needed the rain on his face to cool his skin along with the desire and regrets simmering just beneath the surface. He needed a long, fast drive into the countryside and a hike up into the mountains to put behind him his feelings for Joanna and the damnable understanding he had for why the two of them could never work.

"Goodbye, Ethan."

Those dream-destroying words grated against his ears. Fifteen years and that woman could still get to him. Must be the guilt. *Keep walking, buddy. You can't change the past.* He pushed open the door.

"Agent Rhodes?" Patrick Martinez's voice echoed

through the reception area behind him. "I finished those calls. My men are en route to pick up the suspect."

Agent *Rhodes?* Ethan glanced over his shoulder and scanned for the second person his sharp eyes wouldn't have missed. Wariness seeped up through the soles of his boots and put him on alert.

"Hey, Ethan." Martinez acknowledged him with a nod as he strode up beside Joanna. "You coming or going?"

Turning, Ethan quickly accounted for every person here. Joanna. Martinez. Bates. *She* had to be Agent Rhodes. What was going on here?

His eyes swept Joanna from head to toe, coming back twice to her bare left hand as she tucked Elizabeth's purse behind the counter. He hadn't even considered the idea that she'd gotten married. That she might find someone else after leaving him.

He hadn't. No one that ever stuck in his heart the way she had, at any rate.

The idea that another man had been able to give her what he couldn't burned through him.

But any questions about new names and old relationships remained unspoken at the sheriff's next words. "If you want to step into my office, I can spare a few minutes now to go over any other questions you might have regarding Sherman Watts."

The current of awareness that flowed from the earth into Ethan's body blazed into a full-blown warning. "What does she have to do with Sherman Watts?"

Joanna's ponytail bobbed against her neck as she gave him a quick shake of her head. *Not a word,* she silently pleaded.

So much for the ice in her eyes.

Martinez didn't know her history with Watts? The FBI was allowing this?

No. He could see it in her face. She hadn't told them.

"Would you excuse us a minute, Patrick?" Ignoring every vow to keep his distance, Ethan clamped his fingers around Joanna's arm and ushered her into the nearest open room he could find. Though her sinewy muscles twisted beneath his grip, he never let go. And she never muttered a sound that might indicate to the sheriff that she was moving against her will.

"You two know each other?" Patrick called after them. "Well, ain't that a surprise."

Ethan ignored the amusement he heard in his friend's tone and pushed Joanna into an empty interview room. He closed the door, releasing her. "What do you think you're doing?"

He blocked the exit with his body as she stormed across the room and came back in a useless attempt to get past him. The file crumpled in her grasp as she tilted her chin to glare in defiance. "You already asked me that. I'm working the Julie Grainger murder. Now move. I have a briefing with the sheriff."

She knew better than to play stupid with him. He rephrased the question. "Why are you messing with Watts?"

"My assignment is to interview him."

"Get someone else."

"Never a man to mince words, are you, Ethan?"

"He raped you."

Her skin blanched beneath her tan. The fire in her eyes went out as her chin dropped and her hazy focus landed on the middle button of his creased white shirt. He felt like a bastard playing the voice of reason here, but someone had to make her see how badly she could be hurt if she went head to head with Sherman Watts again.

The bruises and blood and violation had been bad enough when he'd found her at her trailer that night after her parents' funeral. But the emotional toll had been even more devastating. That night had killed her warmth. Killed her trust. Killed her love for him. He didn't ever want to see her suffer like that again. If she wouldn't protect herself from facing that unrepentant monster, then by damn, he'd do it for her.

Her deep, stuttering breath broke the silence of the room, reminding him to move past his raging emotions and seek out that calming sense of quiet inside himself again. She wasn't a man under his command, and he shouldn't be barking orders to get his point across.

"Joanna—" He reached for her pale cheek, but she knocked his hand away, the same way she had that night.

"Do you think that's something I can forget?" Her gaze briefly touched his before she turned away to dump the file on the table opposite the observation window. Keeping his feet rooted to the spot, Ethan watched her take a moment to smooth a straight strand of hair off her face and pull her shoulders back. By the time she faced him again, that prickly, polite chill was back in place. "This isn't about revenge."

"Bull."

"The statute of limitations ran out on my assault before anything could be proved, so there's no longer a conflict of interest for me to work this case. I've accepted that he'll never pay for what he did to me."

"I haven't."

His stark, growly pronouncement seemed to take her

aback. He watched the muscles travel down her long neck as she swallowed hard before speaking. "The attack wasn't your fault, Ethan."

"I should have been there."

"I told you I needed some time alone that day. You were giving me the space I needed after Mom and Dad's funeral. If I'd known he still had feelings for Mom…"

Her fingers clenched at her side and he got the feeling she was fighting back the urge to reach out to him, as well.

"What happened afterward—Watts's never even being arrested—that wasn't your fault, either."

Didn't make Watts any less of a bullying bastard who'd gotten away with crap his entire life because of who he was related to. Didn't make Ethan feel any more like a man who'd done right by the girl he loved, either. "He can still hurt you. In ways you may not even have imagined yet."

"I've imagined all of them," was her stark answer. "But this is my job."

"Go back to D.C. This is too personal."

Joanna laced her fingers together and tapped her knuckles against her lips, thinking for a moment before she slowly began to pace. She seemed to choose each and every word with laser-beam precision. "I'll concede that I won't lose any sleep if Watts is arrested for a different crime. That's not why I'm here. I didn't volunteer for this assignment, but I didn't argue when it was given to me, either. If I can't face whatever criminal I run up against—even my own rapist—over an interview table, then I'm not tough enough to do this job.

"Make no mistake, there's a reward involved if I prove to myself I can do this. If I break this case—if I can break Watts—I'm guaranteed a promotion in D.C. and I'll never have to come back to this place again." She stopped in front of him, her hands curled into fists as she faced him once more. "I know that sounds cold and calculating, but this is what I do. This is what I *need* to do. I'm the go-to woman who's going to get Watts to talk. He'll tell me who murdered Agent Grainger, and maybe where that fifty million dollars of Vincent Del Gardo's is hidden. Besting him at *my* game will be justice enough for me."

Pulling back his jacket, Ethan propped his hands at his waist, shaking his head at her misguided plan. "I don't want you alone in the same room with him."

"Isn't it fortunate, then, that it's not your decision to make?"

She retrieved her folder, tucked it under her arm and walked up to him as though she thought he would simply move aside. Screw this. Ethan reached out to lightly pinch the upturned point of her chin between his thumb and forefinger. She stiffened for a moment. But when she didn't pull away and the warm coffee of her eyes stayed locked on to his gaze, he traced the line of her jaw, rediscovering the softness of her skin.

"Don't do this, sweetheart."

"Ethan…" She squeezed her eyes shut against the stroke of his hand, pressing her lips into a thin line to block the words and emotions locked up behind them.

"Shh." He rubbed his thumb across the tight frown, urging her muscles to relax. He swept his fingertips lightly across her cheek.

When she turned her face into the caress, something cracked open inside him—his need for a woman to warm his bed, perhaps, or maybe the memories of how this particular woman had once enjoyed his touch. Her timid response took him back in time, when her long legs had caught his eye, and her innocence had captured his soul. Touching Joanna like this made him feel things, want things that weren't his to ask for anymore. He tunneled his fingers beneath the heavy silk of her ponytail and let his broad palm cup the length of her neck. He leaned in, touched his forehead to hers and whispered, "You're not as tough as you act. You weren't fifteen years ago and you aren't now."

Her eyes popped open and looked straight up into his. "Fifteen years can change a person, Ethan." She braced her hand against his chest and gently pushed him away. "I haven't been that teenage girl who had a crush on my best friend's big brother for a long time."

He'd been more than a crush, and she wasn't the only one who'd changed during their time apart. But neither comment seemed to mean much right now. She wasn't here to recapture the relationship that had been, and he wouldn't force her into the relationship that could be. Not when she was so intent on leaving. Again.

As he disentangled his fingers from her hair, he let her nudge him aside. Joanna patted the spot on his chest, then curled her fingers into her palm. It was a kind, but definite, send-off. "I have a new name, a new life. You don't know me anymore."

Ethan stayed in the small room for a moment as the door opened and closed. He listened to the spirit of Mother Earth inside him, listened to his training as a soldier, listened to his conscience—and made a decision. He opened the door and followed her out.

Joanna Kuchu—make that Rhodes now—didn't know him, either, if she thought he was going to let her face off against that bastard Watts on her own a second time.

"GET IT TOGETHER, GIRL," Joanna muttered. The skin at her nape was still tingling with tiny tremors from the warmth of Ethan's hand.

Her heart pounded away at an equally unsettling rate as she left the interview room and forced one foot in front of the other along the KCCU's tiled hallway. She could do this. She *had* to do this. She'd prepared herself to look Sherman Watts in the eye, to see familiar faces and places and deal with the memories they might trigger.

But she hadn't prepared herself for Ethan Bia.

Not really.

She'd forgotten how impossible it was to reason with him—how he could watch her with those dark, nearly black, eyes and get under her skin and into her head and make her think that *she* was the one who was being unreasonable. His inner peace and age-old wisdom—even at twenty-one—had frustrated her as much as it fascinated. His certainty about the world and belief in what was right or wrong had confounded as much as it had comforted her. He'd been a rock in her chaotic young life, a constant she'd never known with her alcoholic parents. He'd also been a mysterious, compelling— completely sexy man.

Maybe that was the part she hadn't prepared herself for.

Stopping to straighten her jacket and tuck her hair back into place, Joanna gave herself a moment to silence the confusion in her head. She'd devoted herself to her career, taught herself that her strongest allies were her own wits and determination. She'd gone through counseling and had prepared herself to accept a man's touch again. It wasn't so much that she was afraid of being with a man at some point in the future, but that she was afraid of needing him.

Ethan Bia, with that deep, rumbly voice and those gentle, work-roughened hands, had undone in fifteen minutes what had taken her fifteen years to firmly fix into place.

He'd gotten her blood boiling with his insistence that she had no business working an investigation that involved Sherman Watts. And then he'd hushed her, touched her—soothed her fears and anger and her constant fight to be strong and independent—and the years between them melted away. She'd wanted nothing more than to burrow against his big chest and feel his sturdy arms around her again. She'd wanted the shelter he offered as much as she'd wanted to welcome his kiss.

Felt a hell of a lot like *need* to her.

"No." The wall beside her reacted to her firm insistence about as well as her turbulent emotions did. "It couldn't work then. It won't work now."

There. Better. Think it through.

She was leaving tomorrow, Sunday at the latest, depending on how well Watts cooperated with her. She was too smart to risk her heart on a relationship that couldn't last. Ethan was a man of the earth; she was a woman of the city. He was a Bia, son of a successful business owner and a tribal elder, a well-respected name on the reservation. She was a Kuchu, reservation trash, daughter of Ralph, a charmer with a big heart whose addictions had cost him his money as soon as he'd earned it, and Naomi, a flirtatious beauty whose drunk driving had gotten them both killed.

Joanna was too fractured inside to believe in anything more than what she could do for herself and control with her own two hands. What she *needed* was to keep moving forward with her life.

A mystic force of nature like Ethan Bia didn't fit into her plans. She stood a better chance of surviving this trip home if he wasn't a part of it.

"So get over it, already." Smoothing her expression and her thoughts into business mode, she found Patrick Martinez pacing a rut into the carpeting of his office.

"Are you kidding me? Hell." He cursed into his cell phone as he peered outside his window into the waning daylight.

Joanna's training buzzed her senses on alert. What was he looking for? "Sheriff Martinez?"

"Yes. Lock it down before this rain gets worse and washes away any trail he might have left behind. No one goes in or out until I get there." He snapped the phone shut and strode from the office. "Elizabeth!"

"I'm right here, Patrick." The Indian woman set down the two mugs of coffee she carried and took a position at her desk, ready to handle whatever the sheriff needed.

"Sorry." He offered the gruff apology in the same breath he started giving orders. "Get Miguel down from the lab and tell him to scrounge up any of his field techs he can call on short notice. I need them over at Watts's place on the rez ASAP."

"Got it." Elizabeth spared Joanna a quick concerned look at the mention of the suspect's name before picking up the phone and punching in the lab's extension, quickly relaying the sheriff's orders.

"Has something happened?" Joanna asked. Nobody—not Ethan, not Elizabeth Reddawn—had to protect her from Sherman Watts anymore.

Martinez grabbed his Stetson, pointing it at Elizabeth before putting it on. "And call my wife. Tell her I'm going to miss that movie."

Elizabeth nodded, reading off an address she'd brought up on her computer screen.

"Trouble?"

Joanna jumped inside her skin at the sound of Ethan's deep voice from right behind her. How could such a big man move without making a noise?

Martinez nodded to him over her shoulder. "Good. I'm gonna need you with me, big guy."

"Sheriff." Joanna ignored her erratic pulse and insisted on an explanation.

"You might as well come, too, Rhodes. Watts isn't at his trailer. The rat must have gotten wind we wanted to talk to him and skipped town. He's cleared out his stuff and gone to ground." His blue eyes shifted back up to Ethan. "I need you to track him for me."

"My gear's in my truck." A hand at the small of her back guided Joanna into step behind the sheriff as they headed for the exit. "You think we had another info leak?" Ethan asked.

"Who knows?" Martinez paused just inside the doorway. "He probably knows that once we bring him in and he starts talking about Julie Grainger's murder, he won't be going back home for twenty years or so. Maybe his survival instincts kicked in."

Joanna took an extra step to move beyond the distracting brush of Ethan's hand. "You don't believe that."

"No. But I like the idea of having a mole on my team even less than I like the idea of Watts's dumb luck keeping him one step ahead of us." The sheriff pulled his hat low on his forehead before pushing open the door. "Makes me think he doesn't want to answer your questions."

Ethan's growly protest didn't matter. The rain hitting her face didn't matter. Joanna hurried out to the Suburban she'd arrived in, purposely choosing the sheriff's ride over Ethan's pickup.

"He'll answer them," she vowed.

Her ability to leave Mesa Ridge once and for all, knowing Sherman Watts and her past no longer had any hold over her, depended on it.

Chapter Three

Ethan knelt at the edge of the road to study the two smears of black rubber marking the bump where Sherman Watts's yard met the asphalt. A quick analysis of the tread pattern in the mud matched the new, all-terrain tires Watts had been sporting on his beat-up black truck the past couple of weeks. Their suspect had been gone for several hours now.

But Ethan's thoughts had drifted back several years.

"So how do you know it's a buck that left these tracks?" Joanna asked, her knees down in the dirt on Ute Mountain, right beside his. "And not a doe or even a mountain sheep or elk?"

"The size of the print tells me it's a deer. The depth of the depression tells me it's a heavier animal—bigger than a doe or fawn." Ethan pushed aside her raven-colored ponytail that the wind had tangled and the pine needles from where they had left their earthy scent when they'd stopped for lunch and a rest. He fought off the urge to bury his face in the fragrant silk, and continued the lesson. He reached around her, bringing her back nearly flush against his chest as he pointed to the

rounder, softer print in the fine gravel beside the deer tracks. "Can you identify that one?"

"Is it a mountain lion?"

"Yeah."

Joanna Kuchu was more than a bright, eager student who took to his lessons about nature the way a parched horse took to water. She was the first girl he'd met who seemed to genuinely enjoy the solitude of a day in the wilderness as much as he did. The adorable ass butting against his thigh as she studied the tracks he'd pointed out had a lot to do with the hormones that seemed to rage out of control every time the two of them were alone together like this.

She turned to face him. "He's tracking the deer, isn't he? That deer is going to be lunch."

Her crestfallen expression demanded some kind of comfort. "Relax, Nüa-rü." *The wind whipped a loose strand of hair across her cheek. Ethan brushed it aside and tucked it behind her ear.* "The deer will be all right."

Her tongue darted out to moisten her lips, and Ethan's twenty-one-year-old body lurched with anticipation at the innocent gesture. "How do you know?" *she asked.*

"The lion's prints are older. He came by here two, three days before the deer."

A smile slowly blossomed across her lips, and Ethan couldn't resist. He dipped his head and pressed his mouth to hers, simply warming hers with the touch of his for a moment, allowing her to either accept or reject his desire for something more.

When her hand settled on his chest and her lips pushed against his, he licked the seam of her mouth, tasting salt and shyness and wonder. With a heavy sigh, her lips parted. Ethan thrust his tongue between them and Frenched her. She laughed against his mouth, played the same teasing trick on him. Soon, she wound her fingers into the long fall of hair at his shoulder and pulled him a little closer, inviting him to deepen the kiss.

It didn't take him long to be ready for more—for all—of her. His jeans were already tight at the prospect of being with her. But they'd just started these kissing lessons a few days ago and he didn't want to rush her. He wanted Joanna to be as ready and eager for him as he was for her. He just had to be patient. His time with Joanna would come one day, sooner or later. He could be a man and wait.

Maybe sensing the carnal turn of his thoughts, Joanna dropped her chin and ended the kiss. Her lips were pink, swollen, yet still smiling. She trailed her fingers down through his hair as she pulled away. "You can tell all that by looking at the prints?"

"I can tell a lot just by taking my time to look and listen to what's important."

Squinting against the steady drumbeat of rain, Ethan looked up into the blank sky. The low canopy of clouds was bringing night on early. The flashes of lightning in the distant squall line indicated it was only going to get worse.

Bad enough to drive an average man indoors. Bad enough that a skilled outdoorsman like Sherman Watts could use it to mask his escape.

But Watts had never had Ethan Bia on his trail.

As an army ranger, he'd recovered casualties under gunfire in the mountains of Afghanistan. As a search-and-rescue team leader, he'd tracked down a deaf boy who'd gotten separated from the rest of his troop on a winter camping trip here in Colorado, and had led countless other lost, injured or stranded hikers to safety. He'd spent half his childhood and teen years hiking the desert hills and arroyos and the peaks of the Ute Mountains that dominated the southern horizon.

Rain or shine, he could damn well find the fugitive witness Joanna was so desperate to face. Watts had gotten away with rape fifteen years ago. Whatever crimes he was guilty of now, he wouldn't get away again.

Ethan glanced up and down the road, tuning out past and present conversations as federal agents, the sheriff's department and crime-scene investigators worked the scene around him. He listened to the sounds of the earth, smelled whatever scents hadn't yet been washed from the air. Somewhere there was a disturbance that could give him an indication of their fugitive's flight path. Birds taking wing. The odor of fresh oil. The hum of new tires on the pavement. He listened to his intuition, sorted through the knowledge in his head. He nodded as a possible scenario for Watts's escape route formed.

Of course, Martinez and the others would expect a few facts to back up what his instincts were already telling him.

The tire tracks led from just outside the trailer's front door all the way to the black marks on the road. Though the rain was already beating the pattern down into the mud and distorting it, the tread marks could still give him some information. He dipped his first two fingers into the pool of water gathering there, until he touched the gravelly muck at the bottom. Only up to his middle knuckles—a sign that Watts had been traveling fast and light to leave such a shallow impression.

"Hey, you. Hold this."

"I beg your—"

"Right here."

Ethan glanced across the yard at the sharp order from Miguel Acevedo. The evidence technician grabbed Joanna and pushed an umbrella into her hands. She stiffened up like a possum caught in the headlights the instant he snagged her wrist. Ethan pushed to his feet, every muscle in him tensed to…rescue her? Sheesh. From what? A good friend who was simply conveying a sense of urgency? There was no slight, no danger there. Still, he didn't exhale the tension until she relaxed against Miguel's grip and let him pull her into position beside him.

"Just like that," Miguel coached, squatting back down to press a ring mold around whatever he'd found on the ground. "I need to preserve this evidence before the rain washes it away."

Joanna stood in place, dutifully holding the umbrella over his work. "It's Agent Rhodes. Or Joanna. I don't answer to 'Hey, you.'"

"Give me the etiquette lesson later and just hold the thing. Please." Miguel pulled a bag of gypsum mix from his kit and started prepping it to cast a mold of the track he'd found in the mud. "Dylan? Patrick? Ben? He's had company."

As Miguel's brother, Ben Parrish and the sheriff gathered around, Ethan decided to head on over to report his findings, as well—and to provide Joanna with some friendly support she hadn't asked for, probably didn't need and certainly wouldn't admit she might want.

"What do you have?" Patrick asked.

Miguel pointed to an odd shoe print inside the plastic ring. "This is too big to be Watts's. And the pattern's unique enough for me to think we've seen this before. I want to compare it to those footprints we took out at Griffin Vaughn's estate during the blizzard we had earlier this year—when we believe Perkins murdered Vincent Del Gardo while he was hiding out there. If they match up, then we can reasonably assume that Perkins is back in the area."

Ben nodded. "And that Watts is working with him."

"These prints don't tell you that." Joanna's shoulders squared off even straighter at the scoffs and shaking heads from the men in the cirle with her.

"I'd bet my next paycheck this belongs to Perkins," Miguel groused. "See the unusual pattern of the sole? It's from a pair of pricey designer hikers. They're not standard-issue oxfords or the cowboy boots most guys around here favor."

"I'm not saying it's *not* Perkins's print," she argued. "I'm saying the two men aren't together. At least, they weren't when they left."

Ethan opened his mouth to explain the task force's theory about Watts working as a front man for Perkins and the mob, but there was no need to speak.

This newer, more mature Joanna was perfectly capable of defending her own point of view. "If Boyd Perkins *was* prowling around here, he never got inside the trailer. He might not even know that Watts has disappeared."

"How do you figure?" Martinez asked.

"There's no mud inside. Whoever belongs to these shoes was here after Watts left." Joanna pointed to the tire marks Ethan had been checking. "Watts left before the rain started and Perkins got here. There are no other footprints. His truck was the only thing heavy enough to leave an impression in the dirt before it turned to mud. This footprint was left after it started raining."

Brava, Joanna. The corner of Ethan's mouth tightened with the hint of a smile. All those months of tagging along with him and his brother, Kyle, and then just the two of them together, analyzing which animal had left what trail, and how to tell which direction their quarry was heading, had stuck with her.

Patrick nodded. "So we can assume the two men were here at different times. It's possible that we're not the only ones Watts is running from. If Perkins got wind Watts was going to talk…"

No one needed to finish that sentence. They'd all seen what Boyd Perkins was capable of. They had a trail of dead bodies and scarred survivors to prove what could happen when the wrong person crossed his path.

Dylan Acevedo seemed to think Joanna's idea had merit, as well. "So do we still concentrate on Watts? Or use this opportunity to bring in Perkins, instead? If we track one, we're tracking both, right?"

"Let's not get ahead of ourselves," his brother, Miguel, pointed out. "I haven't even proved that this is Perkins's shoe print yet."

"Yeah, but you're ninety-nine percent sure. I can tell, *hermano.*"

Patrick Martinez steered the discussion back into focus. "We concentrate on what we *do* know. I want Sherman Watts in my interview room ASAP. Someone tipped him off about Agent Rhodes and the interrogation, and now he's running. We find him, and he'll lead us to Perkins. And I definitely want to catch him before Perkins can kill my most promising witness." His icy blue eyes slid over to Ethan, looking for answers. "How do we do that?"

Ethan simply nodded, accepting the lead on this particular mission. "What do we know for certain on the timeline?"

Ben answered that one. He nodded to the neat, white trailer across the road. "The neighbor said Watts's pickup was parked out front when he left for work this morning. That was eight hours ago."

"Pretty significant head start," Ethan conceded. But not insurmountable.

Dylan offered his two cents. "I checked his bank account. There were no big withdrawals in the past twenty-four hours. In fact, the guy's practically broke. Though he had upwards of ten grand just a couple of months ago."

"The file says Watts never held a job for more than a few months at a time," Joanna commented. "Sounds like a payoff to me. Unless he's hoarding the cash, what's he spending it on?"

Dylan answered. "New trailer. Tricking out his truck. Jack Daniel's. The casino. He's not hoarding anything."

Ben thumbed over his shoulder toward the trailer. "There's no booze in there, and I've never seen Watts without a flask or bottle. A gun that's registered to him is missing, too. Looks like he's planning to be gone for a while. You got an idea how to run this search, Ethan? This guy doesn't want to be found." He rolled his eyes skyward. "And we all know damn well the rain is working against us."

Pulling back the front of his jacket, Ethan propped his hands at his hips. He wasn't dressed or armed the way he suspected he'd need to be for this pursuit, but his brain was already on the hunt. "We'll have to wait until daybreak to track him. This storm will get worse before it gets better."

Patrick swore. "He'll be in the wind by then. We don't even know what direction he headed." He narrowed his eyes, reading Ethan's expression more carefully. "Tell me you've got something, big guy."

Ethan tilted his head toward the blacktop. "He went down the road."

"Wiseass." Patrick shook his head and the others grumbled. "There's a highway intersection a mile from here. Did he head east toward Durango? West into the desert? South to the mountains? Hell, he could be in Denver, catching a flight out of the country already." He pulled his cell phone off his belt and punched in a number. "I'll have Elizabeth check the regional airports."

Joanna's dark eyes narrowed in reprimand. "This is no time to joke, Ethan."

Who was joking?

She must be out of practice, recognizing the difference between dead serious and his dry sense of humor. But the sheriff could read him better. He lowered his phone. "What?"

Ethan pointed to the north. "He went to see his uncle Elmer at the retirement center in Mesa Ridge. Probably to scam money or maybe a credit card off the old man so that he could buy supplies. He might even be buying a new ride so he's harder to trace."

The fine line of a frown formed between Joanna's

sleek, dark brows. "You got all that from looking at a tire track?"

Perhaps she'd forgotten more than she remembered about life on the rez. No doubt she'd made a point of forgetting. But one of the pleasures—and perils—of Ethan's life was that he never could.

Not the land. Not the war. Not her. Not what had once been so perfect between them. Not the way it had ended. Like her, he could move on. But Ethan could never forget.

"I know the people here—their habits," he explained, as if he were once again teaching her some lesson about nature and life. "Watts left a kitchen full of food, his suitcase and a canteen here. Yet he took his backpack, a bedroll and fishing gear. The man's going into the wild. I can't tell you where exactly yet, but he'll need gas to get there, maybe a different vehicle to mask his trail. Food. Whiskey."

Patrick grinned. *"That's* why we pay you the money. Elmer Watts's nursing home is our next stop. Ben? You and Dylan start running down the local outdoorsman shops and convenience stores. See if anyone has seen our buddy Watts today."

"We're on it."

Ethan turned with Patrick as the two federal agents headed toward Dylan's SUV.

"Wait a minute. What do you need me to do? Here. Thanks." Joanna pushed the umbrella into the hands of a uniformed police officer's hands and circled behind Miguel Acevedo, carefully avoiding any contamination of the shoe print as she hurried to catch up and fall into step between them. "I'm coming with you."

Ethan glanced at Patrick over the top of her head and silently asked the sheriff to give them a minute. Seeing the sheriff move on without her seemed to unsettle her almost as much as the touch of Ethan's hand on her arm. She turned to face him, though if it was out of simple courtesy or a subtle way to evade his touch, he couldn't tell. *Patience,* ta'wa-chi, he reminded himself. This woman had always required patience. "You've already lost a couple of time zones today. You haven't eaten dinner or checked into your hotel room yet. Why don't you let us do the searching and bring Watts to you at the station house? Face him fresh tomorrow."

"I'm not on vacation, Ethan. I'm here to work." She scanned the area around them, then leaned in slightly, dropping her voice to a whisper. "You, more than any-body here, should understand how important it is for me to see this assignment all the way through to the end."

Before or after the rape, he'd never known Joanna to back down once she set her mind on something. Some-how, she must have it in her head that as long as she projected strength, she *was* strong. But unlike the sweet young woman he'd once loved, this mature version of Joanna had forgotten that revealing a vulnerability required far more courage and strength than toughing her way through every difficult situation.

"No one's going to think any less of you if you go back to your room and rest."

"I will."

"Joanna—"

"You can't get rid of me, Ethan. Stop trying."

That she might be covering up or denying those fears and vulnerabilities worried Ethan. He'd seen the strongest of men—one of his best friends from his ranger unit—crash and burn mentally and emotionally on the battlefield after a particularly grueling mission. After that last hellish rescue in Afghanistan, he hadn't been far behind. He'd needed the open space and the quiet of the Four Corners area to find his inner peace again. What did Joanna have that gave her peace? This skinny slip of a woman with the barbed tongue and cool demeanor was priming herself for an emotional meltdown.

"I never once wanted to get rid of you, *Nüa-rü.*" The Ute nickname for the wind, which had become an endearment between them fifteen years ago, slipped out. The word felt right.

But a shiver rippled across Joanna's shoulders before she set them firmly into place. Clearly, it didn't feel right to her. "I imagine Elmer Watts has retired as the reservation sheriff by now. If he's in a nursing home, he can't hurt me anymore. I'm not afraid of him."

"I don't imagine you'd admit to being afraid of anything. But he *can* hurt you." Ethan breathed in the moist air and let it cool his frustration. "Elmer has Alzheimer's. His wife had him committed to the home as his behavior became increasingly erratic and violent, and her health declined. He can be mean."

That tiny frown reappeared between the beads of rain dotting her forehead. "I suppose the staff could tell you if Sherman visited today—or if they saw his truck. I wonder what kind of information we can get from a man with Alzheimer's."

"Are you listening to me? You don't want to see him."

"Sherman Watts is *my* man. I'm going."

"I'm just trying to look out for you." Ethan reached

out to brush away the strand of hair that stuck to her damp cheek, but she blocked his wrist and stopped him before he could touch her face.

What happened next convinced him that this tough-talking ice-princess facade didn't go beyond skin deep. As she pushed his hand down, she altered her grip. She wound her fingers around his thumb and squeezed.

It was the subtlest of gestures. But it was a connection. A plea.

"I don't need looking after, Ethan. I need justice."

Chapter Four

"Now, if you was seventeen, girl, I might be able to look at pressing statutory rape charges. But you're eighteen. Legal age." The salty grit of used-up tears rubbed Joanna's eyes like sandpaper as she blinked the wiry, gray-haired man into focus. Sheriff Elmer Watts rested his hip on the corner of his desk and shifted his chaw of tobacco from one pocket of his cheek to the other. "I know you've been through a lot this week, losing your mother and daddy both. It's normal to turn to a man—an older man, especially—for comfort at a time like this."

"Comfort?" Joanna bolted out of her chair. "He raped me!"

"So it got a little rough. Doesn't mean you didn't want it. Some women like it that way."

How could any woman…? Gut-deep emotions swirled inside her skull, making her feel light-headed. The stitched-up cut on her left breast, the bruises where she'd been violated, throbbed in protest. The sickening feeling that, no matter how many showers she took, she'd never feel clean again turned in her stomach. How could any woman possibly want any of that?

"You son of a bitch." Joanna slurred her words around the swelling of her split bottom lip.

The sheriff stood, one hand on his gun, the other holding up a reprimanding finger. *"Don't you go cussing me, girl."*

She ignored both warnings and advanced to look him straight in the eye. *"I went to the hospital. They took a rape kit. Do you have any idea how degrading it feels to be touched and probed after...?"* She swallowed the whimper of shame that caught in her throat. No. She would see this through. *"You can't ignore that kind of evidence."*

"I won't hear anything on that for weeks. Alleged crimes here on the rez aren't a priority for the state lab—"

"Alleged?"

"And we don't have the means to process any evidence here. I'm sorry, but that's how it is."

The instant his fingers closed around her shoulders, Joanna yelped and jumped back beyond his reach. *"Don't touch me!"*

The good ol' boy friendliness of his tone vanished. *"You need to get it together, girl, if you want me to take your accusations seriously."*

"Get it together? You aren't going to do anything? Aren't you even going to write any of this down?"

"You're right." He walked around her to open his office door. *"Elizabeth? Will you take this girl's statement?"*

Elizabeth Reddawn stood right outside, no doubt already responding to Joanna's startled cry. The older woman wrapped her arm around Joanna's waist and gently turned her toward the doorway. *"You come on into my office and sit with me, honey."*

The reality of her situation finally registered. Whatever hopefulness had been left inside her after the attack shriveled and died. Joanna paused at the doorway and glanced over her shoulder at the uniformed man. "What about Sherman Watts?"

"I'll look into it. I'll talk to my nephew, I promise."

Elmer Watts wasn't talking now.

Not about anything useful, at any rate.

"When's my wife coming?" Elmer grumbled. "The party starts at seven. She's always running late."

Joanna shifted back and forth behind the wall of men and residential staff in the cramped room. Though she suspected that the width of Ethan's shoulders blocking her view of the retired, white-haired sheriff was no accident, she'd already gotten a glimpse of Elmer Watts. He was a frail, miserable shadow of the man who'd put family before justice fifteen years ago, and had allowed her rapist to escape any kind of prosecution. It was hard not to feel some measure of pity for his infirmities and the blankness behind his sunken eyes. It was harder still not to resent that he could spark any emotion beyond the anger and resentment she'd carried for so many years.

She'd like to blame her edgy mood on her frustration with Elmer's inability to stay focused on Patrick Martinez's questions. She could feel Sherman Watts slipping further and further from their grasp. But she was afraid that the knot in her stomach was due to the fact that, like Elmer, her memories kept slipping back to the past.

"You aren't going to do anything?"

He hadn't given her the answers she needed to hear back then, either.

"Joanie?" Elmer called out. "You'd better get a move on it, woman, or I'll go to the party without you."

The beefy orderly who'd helped Elmer out of bed knelt down beside the septuagenarian's chair. "These men are looking for Sherman, not your wife. She's gone, Elmer. She passed away last year."

"Sherman's gone, too," he insisted. "Ungrateful boy. Where's my wife?"

Patrick pulled his hat up in front of his face and whispered to Ethan, "How the hell is anything that comes out of his mouth going to be reliable?"

"We know that Sherman stopped by before lunch," Ethan reminded him. The orderly who was assisting them had seen Watts's black pickup earlier in the day. He had no idea what Sherman and his uncle had talked about, but a search of Elmer's things showed that his wallet was now missing. Ethan encouraged Patrick to keep asking questions. "Try talking to him sheriff to sheriff."

With a weary sigh that lifted his shoulders, Patrick turned his attention back to Elmer's gaunt features. "I need your help, Sheriff Watts. We're looking for a suspect."

"Put it out on the wire," Elmer answered. "I've only got two cars to patrol this whole reservation. Can't keep up with my own trouble. You'll have to ask the county cops to help."

"I *am* a county cop. We're looking for your nephew, Sherman."

Elmer glanced from man to man to man in the room without answering. He angled his head to peer between Ethan and Patrick. "Who's there? Sneakin' in behind you."

Now he could think and act like a cop?

"He was here earlier." Patrick ignored the old man's

alarm at spotting Joanna and pulled a mug shot photo from his jacket pocket. "Do you remember talking to this man?"

Elmer took hold of the photo. "My wife is coming to the party." He looked over at the orderly and frowned. "Why isn't Joanie here? You need to unlock the doors and let her in."

It was the orderly's turn to shrug as he pushed to his feet and apologized to Patrick. "I'm sorry, sir. He doesn't have a lot of good days anymore. Beyond seeing Sherm's truck leave about noon, I don't know that there's much anyone here can tell you."

Patrick plunked his hat back on his head. "We tried."

Joanna wasn't giving up so easily. She nudged her way between the two men. "Excuse me, Mr....Laughing Horse?" She paused to read the orderly's name tag. "Does Mr. Watts remember incidents and people from his past?"

"Sometimes. It's pretty typical in Alzheimer's patients for more distant memories to stay with them longer than recent ones."

"Good."

"Joanna—"

She ignored Ethan's warning. "He doesn't have to tell us about today. He can help us if he tells us something about the past." She pulled up a stool and sat in front of Elmer's chair. "Do you know who I am?"

Thanks either to Elmer's incompetence or something more purposeful, the chain of evidence on her rape kit had been "compromised." The lack of admissible circumstantial evidence, combined with his recommendation that she was too distraught to make a reliable witness, had convinced the district attorney that there was no point in going forward with charges against Elmer's nephew.

Would he remember how his actions had changed her life? Would he remember the man he'd helped to escape justice once before?

For a moment, his dark eyes narrowed beneath bushy white brows. Then his wizened face creased into a smile that revealed yellowed teeth. Even without the dribble of tobacco juice staining his lips, it wasn't a pleasant smile. "You're the girl who was supposed to marry my nephew. Wound up with that no-good Ralph Kuchu, instead." He sat back in his chair, sneering. "Why are you pestering me, girl?"

Not the way she'd intended this to go. Bile burned at the back of her throat, but she could still make this work. "That was Naomi, my mother. I'm Joanna."

"I can see why you turned Sherman's head." The correction didn't register in his addled mind. His low opinion of her mother, however, was crystal clear. "So when are you and Ralph gonna pay back the money you owe my nephew, you lyin' tramp?"

"Ma'am," the orderly urged. "He can get pretty bitter."

Martinez politely tried to stop her. "Agent Rhodes—"

"Let her work." Ethan's deep voice quieted the room and washed over her misfiring nerves like a soothing hand.

Her nostrils flaring with a steadying breath, Joanna nodded, slipping into the character Elmer Watts could communicate with. "That's right. I'm Naomi. I'm looking for Sherman so I can pay back that money. Have you seen him?"

"You swindled my boy. Promised him things you

never delivered. Did you blow it all at the casino? He loves you, you know."

Sherman Watts's idea of love for her mother had cost Joanna dearly. Far more than the missing two grand that had brought him to her trailer after the funeral that afternoon. Joanna squeezed her hands into fists and continued. "I expect Sherman's pretty mad at me. Do you know where he might have gone? Where he'd go to get away when he's angry or worried?"

"You can leave the money with me."

"No, thanks." Joanna swallowed hard. "I'd like to pay him back personally. Apologize."

"He'd like that." Elmer nodded and shook his head in the same motion. Was his mind wandering away already? "Can't keep that boy at home. If you want to find him, try the Ute Mountains. That boy loves to go fishing."

Mountains. Pretty vague. Pretty vast. About sixty square miles of not enough information. "The Utes are a big place. Anywhere in particular he likes to go?" Joanna asked.

"Rising Sun Creek is his favorite spot."

Ethan whispered behind her, "That's up on Sleeping Ute Mountain." The mountain cluster's highest peak. "Even a fit climber couldn't get that far in five hours."

Joanna absorbed the information without taking her gaze from Elmer. "Where else does he like to fish?"

"McElmo Creek. Across from the bluffs along the Silverton River. It'll be flooded this time of year with the spring runoff pouring into it. He might find a spot on the bluff side, though. Fishing won't be too good with the current that strong, but—" the old man leaned forward, crooking a gnarled finger to invite her to come closer "—I expect fishing isn't what you have in mind." He pulled back, chuckling. "To hear Sherm tell it, the two of you never made it out of the tent the first time he took you up there."

His laughter grated against her ears and clawed its way through her self-defenses. Her mother had spent time with Sherman on the mountain? Willingly? Or had he forced Naomi the same way he'd forced her daughter? Was that why she'd suddenly dropped one man and turned to a big, lazy lug like Ralph Kuchu? Was that why Naomi had turned to alcohol? Why there'd always been such animosity between their families?

The familiar nightmare tried to sneak its way into her brain, but Joanna slammed the door on the painful memories. "So where will I find him this time of year, Elmer? Rising Sun Creek or the Silverton?"

But the conduit of lucid communication was already closing. "Sherm grew up on those mountains. Knows them better than his own room at home."

"You're sure he'd go up Sleeping Ute Mountain?" She could confirm that much, at least.

"Sometimes he'll disappear for days on end, and come back with more fish than his aunt can cook in a week. Then the rivers dry up to a trickle and he turns to hunting rabbit or deer."

Joanna reached out, needing a definitive answer. "Elmer—"

He slapped her hand. "When are you gonna pay what you owe, you whore? You ruined him, I tell ya. Ruined him. Get out of my house, you no-good Kuchu!"

If someone called her name, she didn't hear it. If she let professional protocol slide when she kicked over the stool and shoved her way past Patrick Martinez, she didn't care.

Joanna dashed out the door, hurried down the hallway and shoved open the front door. She didn't stop when the rain splashed in her face. She didn't stop when the cool air hit her lungs. She didn't stop when a bolt of lightning pierced the night and sent a wave of goose bumps pricking over her skin.

The answering thunder drummed along her pulse and kept her moving until the past finally overtook her.

"You owe me, Naomi." Sherman Watts's words slurred together as he backed Joanna against the counter in the kitchen. "I'm never gonna get the money Ralph owes me now. But we can work out some other kind of payment."

"I'm not my mother," Joanna pleaded, turning her face from his sour breath and desperately searching the small trailer for a way she could escape him. "I know I look like her, but I'm Joanna. Naomi's dead. You were at her funeral this afternoon. You've had too much to drink and you're not thinking straight. You're making a mistake."

"My only mistake was letting you get away from me in the first place. I miss you, baby."

And then his grubby fingers touched her hair.

Joanna groaned with the effort it took to block the rest of the memory before it played itself out. At some point she'd stopped running and was clutching a two-fisted grip around a wall of black steel—the tailgate of a black pickup truck in the parking lot. She blinked the rain from her eyes and stared hard at the red imprint of Elmer's hand on her skin.

"Get over it," she coached herself, squeezing her

roiling emotions out through her fingertips into the un-bending steel. "Do your job. Just do your job."

But the red mark stung. The rain trickled along her scalp, cooling her skin to match the chill within. Naomi Kuchu hadn't been a great mother, but Elmer Watts had no right to call her names. No right to strike—

"You okay?"

Joanna jumped at the deep voice behind her. Ethan. She jerked her head in a nod as he moved in beside her.

"The death grip on my truck makes me think…" His big hand covered both of hers, short-circuiting the chaos inside her. "Damn. You're ice-cold, *Nüa-rü*."

"Don't call me that." She pulled her hands from beneath his, swiped the rain from her eyes and retreated from the broad chest and moving arms and concern. "I'm fine."

"I've known you to be headstrong and independent. But you never were a liar."

"I'm not…" His dark brown jacket swirled around her shoulders, interrupting her protest. She immediately tried to shrug it off, but Ethan pulled the collar together at her neck. She shoved at the placket. "Please. I don't need—"

"Stop. Just stop." His knuckles brushed the underside of her chin as his grip on the jacket easily outmuscled hers. As soft as the caress of his voice, the action stilled her.

Joanna tilted her chin and looked up into his eyes. The pools of midnight-brown said he knew where Elmer's words had taken her. The weight of secrets heaved inside her chest and eased out on a long sigh.

She was soaked to the skin, but she was warm.

She was blind with pain and anger and fear, but she could see a light of hope, a shelter to move toward, inside those irises of pure dark brown. "Ethan, I shouldn't—"

"Shh." He stroked his fingers lightly beneath her chin again. Nerve endings awakened, remembered, beneath the comforting touch.

A woman could lose herself in the depth of those eyes. When she was eighteen years old, she'd found understanding there. Caring. A faith in her that she'd longed for, but in the end, couldn't believe.

There were lines etched beside those eyes now, a few as deep and craggy as the rugged landscape he loved so well. There were secrets hidden there, too—secrets the young Ethan had never kept. The Ethan standing before her now, taming her with his gentle touch and deep, hushed voice, was a seasoned, more potent version of the young man she'd loved. He was a bigger mystery to her now than he had ever been. The years had taken the faith from his expression, but the caring was still there.

It was a caring she didn't deserve. And yet... A yearning for something lost, something new to be discovered, sprouted like a tiny seed inside her, waiting to be nourished. Infused with his scent and warmth, Ethan's jacket reminded her of what it was like to be sheltered and claimed by this man. She inhaled a deep, stuttering breath and pushed her hand through the front opening so that she could reach up and touch the sharp angle of his cheekbone.

He wore his Ute heritage beautifully, proudly. Far better than she or her parents ever had.

"You're getting wet." She brushed the rain from the smooth leather of his skin, savoring the friction beneath her fingertips.

"So are you." The corner of his mouth crooked into a smile, luring her touch to the spot.

A slow breath warmed her fingers as his lips parted. A different warmth, deeper inside, unfurled as he pressed a kiss to a lucky fingertip. She remembered his mouth, maddeningly patient, excruciatingly thorough, pressed against her own as he'd taught her what passion between a man and woman could be—should be.

Lightning flashed in the sky overhead, reflecting heat in the night of his eyes, sparking the desire to bring the best part of her past to life again. Her own lips parted as she stroked her finger across the firm male line that ended with a tiny scar at the opposite corner. Like the closely cropped style of his raven's-wing hair, the scar was new.

There was a lot to admire in the changes she was discovering in the mature man. Plenty of ridges and hollows of muscle being revealed as the rain plastered his white dress shirt to his skin. Plenty of raw, masculine energy in the sheer size of him. Parts of her body strained to move closer to his earthy scent and heat. Even the physical battery and scars of her rape hadn't dimmed the memory of how intoxicating a kiss from Ethan could be. Though she'd dated a few men in recent years, she'd struggled with intimacy. Even before the rape, it had been hard to trust or depend on anyone besides herself. Her parents had always depended on her, not the other way around. After their deaths, after the rape and the debacle of justice that followed, it had just been easier, safer, to concentrate on her career because it required an emotional detachment that kept her sane, kept her functioning—allowed her to succeed. But her choices also kept her lonely.

Could Ethan sense the attraction he rekindled inside her? Could he also sense the reluctance to act on the need that simmered in her veins?

Of course he could. What few details Ethan's eyes missed he seemed to intuit with that sixth sense of his. Joanna curled her fingers into her palm and offered a rueful laugh. "Seems I don't have my act together any better than I did fifteen years ago, does it?"

"You've got nothing to apologize for." He tucked his fingers beneath the collar of his jacket, closing it more securely around across her chest. "All those years you took care of your parents, putting them first. And now it seems as though you put your job first. When are you going to start taking care of yourself?"

"I am. I just…" She wound her fingers around the nubby tweed of his lapels, denying the urge to reach out to the man himself. "I didn't expect Elmer to say things that would take me back to that day. It felt as though, after all this time—after all the work and therapy I've done—that nothing had changed. The Watts family always said I'd asked for what happened to me. I wasn't prepared for that."

Ethan's hands slipped to her shoulders, instilling his warmth with a gentle massage up and down her arms. "Did you want the old bastard to show remorse? Elmer doesn't even remember who you are."

"I know." Joanna shook her head. "I can't let him get to me. Every day I put together profiles on murderers, kidnappers, drug dealers and more. This shouldn't be any different. I talk to people. I get inside their heads. It's what I do. I can't let it be personal."

"It's already personal. You barely survived once—"

"You don't think I can survive this place again?" Joanna tugged the jacket from her shoulders and pushed it into the middle of his chest, forcing him to take hold of it—forcing her fingers to let go and pull away. She didn't need his warmth. She didn't need his caring. She didn't need him to make her feel weak or vulnerable or dependent on anyone again. "I'm not a girl anymore, Ethan. I'm not a victim. I'm going to prove that I can do this."

Her eyes filled with rain, and she had to blink away the moisture before he finally spoke.

"Walk away from this assignment, Jo. Walk away before you can't outrun the demons anymore."

"What do you know about demons? I know you mean well, but you can't possibly understand what I've been through—what I need in order to make my life whole again."

"Demons come in many forms." The deadness in his tone was more unsettling than the words themselves. "Trust me, I know exactly how hard they are to shake."

"What does that mean?" Was there something in that comment that explained the harder edges and protective obsession of this older, more cryptic Ethan Bia? Did he think what had happened to her fifteen years ago was somehow his fault? That the challenges she faced now could be solved by anyone besides herself? He pulled his keys from his pocket and circled around her to the cab of his truck. She turned and followed. "Ethan? Don't speak to me in riddles. Talk to me."

"Agent Rhodes?" Patrick Martinez's voice called from the nursing home's front door.

Joanna huffed at the untimely interruption, and glanced over her shoulder to see the sheriff approaching them across the parking lot. She quickly caught up to Ethan, stopped him by laying a hand at the center of his back. "This is my battle, Ethan. I'll be okay." Her issues were her own to deal with.

"It should have been *our* battle." He spun around, leaning in close enough that his chest pushed against her hand before she could snatch it away. "Is it because I didn't protect you from Sherman Watts?"

What? "You couldn't know—"

"Is that why you didn't give me a chance to help you afterward? You didn't believe I'd be there for you?"

"I had to find my own strength. I couldn't do that here. And you couldn't leave. You belong here. I wasn't about to turn your life upside down in an effort to save mine."

"You never even asked. We could have talked about it."

"I was eighteen and damaged and scared out of my mind. I didn't know how."

That fathomless gaze captured Joanna for a moment, reached down to her, found its way beneath her defensive armor, conveying emotions as deep and turbulent as her own. Then, as abruptly as he'd breached her personal space, he retreated. "You have to tell Patrick."

"Tell me what?"

Ethan was hurting. He was angry. She seemed to have a bad habit of bringing out those negative feelings in him. Guilt warred with the feminine instinct to wrap him in her arms and get him to share his secrets. To listen and comfort the way he had with her just a moment ago. She owed him so much more than the few minutes she could give him before climbing onto a plane and leaving Kenner County again as soon as her interview with Watts was completed.

Because that was how this reunion was destined to play

out. She hadn't come back to resurrect a relationship with Ethan. She would never drag him into her world again. She'd never allow her world to hurt him again.

So she pasted on a smile and turned to face Patrick. "I guess we're climbing a mountain."

"*I'm* climbing the mountain," Ethan corrected, casting a shadow like Sleeping Ute itself as he stepped up beside her. "You can do the talking once I bring Watts in."

"Good work in there," Martinez complimented her. "Sorry it got ugly, but that intel definitely narrows our search." Patrick pulled his hat forward to shield his eyes as he looked up into the storm clouds overhead. "Provided we can get anywhere tonight. The chopper will be useless until this clears. As long as there's lightning, I won't allow a search team to take it up."

An expressionless mask slid into place on Ethan's face before Joanna could get a clear read on what he was thinking. "We can catch him on foot. I know the paths he'd most likely take, and have a couple more ideas on fishing holes he might go to. But we'll need daylight. The rocks will be treacherous enough with all this rain. Elmer was right about the rivers and creeks topping their banks. And washouts on the trails are pretty common since the rest of the year is so dry."

Patrick shifted his gaze to Joanna. "I suppose the FBI will want to take over the pursuit?"

Ethan shook his head, denying her the chance to answer. "It's too dangerous for inexperienced climbers to tackle the ascent under these conditions."

"I'm not an inexperienced climber," she argued. "I grew up with those same mountains."

"The terrain can change a lot in fifteen years."

"You'll need as many eyes as you can get to help with the search."

"Whoa. Am I missing something?" Patrick raised his hands, signaling a time-out as Ethan's will to take care of her warred with Joanna's need to take care of herself.

Joanna curled her lip between her teeth. Arguing in front of the ranking local officer wouldn't earn her any cooperation, or a good review for her boss back in D.C. "No, sir. Ethan and I just…see the way to proceed differently."

There was no mistaking where Martinez chose to put his trust. "Ethan's been running search and rescue for Kenner County for the past three years. When it comes to finding someone on those mountains, it's his call."

Ethan's call was equally clear. "I'll take in a small team who know what they're doing. If the FBI is joining the search, they'll be under my command."

"I'll tell them," Patrick agreed. "Safety first."

"I'll round up a couple more guides—men who've worked S and R with me know the area. We'll assemble at the north trailhead of Sleeping Ute Mountain at daybreak. We can each take a destination and pray the weather hasn't washed away every trace of Watts's path. If we travel light and move fast, we should be able to close ground on him." Ethan's tone held none of the warmth he'd shown Joanna a few moments earlier. "I don't want anyone on that mountain who doesn't know what he's doing. My best men will be tied up with the search. Communication may be spotty, and if I have to spare them for a rescue, we could lose Watts."

The sheriff gave a wry laugh. "You have any *good* news for me?"

"Watts is dealing with the same weather and hazards. That should slow him down. He won't make it to Rising Sun Creek tonight. He'll have to make camp somewhere along the way. Even if he moves on in the morning, finding his camp will put us on a clear trail."

"Get your men lined up," Patrick ordered. "I'll get on the horn to Ben and Dylan. I expect Tom Ryan will want to be part of the search, too." He grumbled as he pulled his phone from his belt. "I hate calling a man in from his honeymoon. Agent Rhodes, can I give you a lift to your hotel?"

She wanted to stay with Ethan and find out what miracle he had up his sleeve to track down Watts. She wanted to be on that hike tomorrow morning and be a part of bringing Watts in herself. As difficult as it would be to face her rapist across an interview table, it would be impossible to find closure and move on with her life if Watts disappeared into the wilderness and she never even got the chance to nail him for his more recent crimes.

She had to make Ethan understand that.

But he was already climbing into his truck. The conversation was over.

"Yes, Sheriff, thanks. I'll be right there." Joanna hurried to the truck cab and caught the door before Ethan could close it. "Ethan?"

He peered through the windshield, straight ahead into the night.

But Joanna had made a career out of getting people to talk. And sometimes, that meant she was the one who had to open up first. Inhaling a steadying breath, she stepped into the Vee formed by the truck frame and door. "I'm sorry I hurt you. That was never my intention. You were the best part of my life here."

"Yeah. Things were so good between us, you had to leave." Sarcasm was a new twist to Ethan's personality. But he was talking.

"I had to survive." Tears burned in the corner of her eyes, but she blinked them away. She had to keep the emotion out of her voice and say exactly what she needed to. "I would have gone nuts if I'd stayed here. People on the rez and in Kenner City already talked about me—talked down to me—because of Mom and Dad. They were either going to pity me or laugh at me because I was stupid enough, helpless enough, naive enough—whatever—to let the Watts men take advantage of me. I couldn't handle all that and heal. My problems would have destroyed us. I would have brought you down with me. You couldn't fix me or the situation. No one could. I had to get away. I'm a stronger woman now. Like you said before, it was the first time I ever put myself first. I left because that's what *I* needed. I'm just sorry you had to pay the price."

Apparently, her explanation was fifteen years too late. For the longest time, he just sat there, staring into the rain, saying nothing.

"Ethan?"

"So facing the worst part of your past—entirely on your own—and beating it, is the ultimate therapy for you?"

"Something like that." Lightning flashed overhead, and the answering thunder urged Joanna a step closer. She lightly brushed his pant leg, asking him to listen a little bit longer. "Can you really find Watts after a night like this?"

Not entirely on her own.

Ethan glanced down at her hand, then turned in his

seat, slowly assessing, then accepting her unspoken request. "I'll bring him in if that's what you need from me."

She summoned a shaky smile. "That's what I need."

He reached out, palmed the back of her head and pulled her up onto her toes as he bent his head to cover her mouth in a deep, hard kiss. Joanna's fingers dug into his corded thigh. Her lips parted in surprise, then welcome. His tongue snuck inside to dance with hers and she moaned at the raspy caress that tasted of earthiness and man. She braced a hand against the damp wall of his chest, leaned in. Kissed him back.

Ethan's hand found its way to the curve of her hip and her feet left the ground entirely as he lifted her into the heat and hardness of his upper body. The rain splashed a cool warning against her cheeks, but Joanna ignored it. She wound an arm around his neck, found an erotic stubble of short hair at his nape to rub her palm against instead of the silky, shoulder-length strands where she'd once tunneled her fingers.

It was a kiss of rediscovery—of years gone by and apologies accepted. It hinted at life lived and changes made and opportunities missed. This kiss was more seasoned and sure than the ones she remembered. There was no youthful exuberance, no hesitant testing the waters. It was a grown man's kiss of passion. A kiss of promise.

Joanna was breathless and hot by the time he pulled away.

She sank back onto her heels, her fingers still hanging on to his wet shirtfront, his hands still clamped possessively at her neck and hip. She'd felt no fear of Ethan when he kissed her. But Joanna feared what his kiss made her feel. "I—"

"Don't say anything." Ethan's dark eyes glowed like obsidian glass in the light from his truck. "I've missed you so much, *Nüa-rü*. I've needed you. I remember when you were all sunshine and curiosity and a strong, forgiving heart. I needed that."

She frowned with confusion, ached with compassion, at the sorrow heard in his voice. "Ethan—"

"Shh." He pressed a finger to her lips. "I'll do this for you. I may not understand it, but I'll do whatever it takes to get the spirit Watts stole from you back." His uneven breath fanned warmly across her cheek as he rested his forehead against hers and made her a promise. "Watts may know those mountains. But I know them better."

Chapter Five

"Love to love ya, baby…"

Sherman Watts sang a familiar melody, his eyes closed, his hand stroking his thigh from crotch to knee, remembering better times up here on the mountain. The air crackled with electricity from the storm. His clothes were wet and sticking to his skin. But ghostly memories blended with reality. He didn't care about any discomfort he should be feeling.

The chilling mist that dotted his face blended with visions of long black hair, sweetly perfumed, caressing him. The thunder added percussion to the music playing in his head. He pursed his lips around the mouth of his Jack Daniel's bottle and tipped it back, letting the whiskey ignite a fire all the way down to his belly.

He licked the rim of the bottle, stroked his thigh and pretended he wasn't alone. "I need your—"

The shrill chirp of a cell phone startled him from his hazy fantasy. Sitting bolt upright, he knocked the bottle from his lap. "Son of a bitch."

A pool of amber liquid sank into the dust. Cursing at the waste, and his ungainly movements that couldn't right the bottle faster, he stopped to pound the cork into the bottle before he reached into his pack to grab the phone. He leaned back against the back wall of the shallow cave where he'd taken shelter and flipped open the phone. There was only one caller who ever contacted him on this line.

"What do you want?"

"Boyd Perkins is looking for you."

Sherman wasn't so far gone with lust or drink that his head couldn't clear fast. He braced his hand against the gritty sandstone wall and staggered to his feet. For a moment the rustle of static in his ear made him wonder if he'd heard right. "Boyd Perkins?"

"Yeah. He's got a job for you."

"Now?" He turned his mouth to the phone, raising his voice over the noise of the thunderstorm that was draining the sky. "You told me to disappear. That's what I've done."

"The sheriff and that hotshot agent from D.C. talked to your uncle this evening." His caller paused. "They plan to launch a search up in the mountains tomorrow morning."

That news deserved a curse. Or two. But he'd discovered places in these mountains that his dear old uncle never knew about. "Thanks for the heads-up."

But he wasn't that worried. The feds would still be chasing shadows long after he made his way down the far side of the range and was miles away from Kenner City. It was his plans for surviving *after* he left the mountains that needed a little fine-tuning, especially when he hoped his work for Perkins would give him an inside track on getting some jobs in Vegas. Failing to be at Perkins's beck and call now could mess up his plans for later.

He hated that he was even tempted to ask, "What exactly does Perkins want?"

Was that laughter he heard through the static? "They just pay me to be the messenger. You'll have to work the details out with him."

"How am I supposed to do that? I can hardly meet him at my place. You know the cops are watching it." The measly fire he'd built was giving off more smoke than heat because everything around here was so freaking wet. Including him. He looked past the smoky embers into the darkness beyond the lip of the cave. He needed to be sharp to make sense of the shadows and night surrounding his perch here on the bluffs of the Silverton River. If he couldn't distinguish a rock or a tree from a man, he could end up caught.

Or dead.

Storm or distance or both garbled his contact's reply. "All he said was…family loyalty… The feds have a decent lead on your whereabouts, and Perkins insisted…can use you. And then he'll help you get out of the country."

Sherman's attention shifted as he slipped and kicked a rock into the smoky fire. The hiss of damp wood tumbling closer to the heat was an uncomfortable reminder of the danger of his situation.

Wait a minute, Sherm. Think.

"You son of a bitch." That's what this phone call was really about. His contact thought he could outsmart ol' Sherman.

No. Way.

"Am *I* the job? What did you say to him? He knows I'll keep my mouth shut. Nobody's gotten a word out of me for six months. Did Perkins put you up to this?" The cell phone might hold a secure number, but anyone who knew it could put the code into the system if he had access to the technology required to locate pings on cell towers. And this guy had access, he was certain of it. Though he didn't have a name—his instructions had always come over the phone or through Perkins himself—his contact knew too much about the KCCU and the FBI's investigation to be anything but an inside man.

"Don't get your shorts in a knot. He said…lead on Del Gardo's money. If you distract the agents and deputies looking for you while he…meet up…Vegas and then get you out of the country."

"What?" he shouted through the static.

"Perkins…your help…pay well." More static.

"Are you tracing this call? Reporting my location to him?" Why would a cold-blooded hit man bother with pulling him out of hiding for one more job? Why would he go to the effort of sneaking him out of the country when he could lure him to a meeting with the promise of money, then silence him permanently with a bullet or a garrote? A job right now didn't make sense.

This bozo didn't make sense. "Sherman—"

"To hell with you. And to hell with the money."

He disconnected the call. Turned off the phone. He went to the cliff's edge and hurled his last link to civilization into the chasm below.

He swatted the water off the brim of his hat and plunked it on top of his head. So much for his trip down memory lane and a few hours of sleep. He kicked the biggest logs from the fire, scattering them out into the rain to douse the flames and smoke. Hell. Why not just send up a signal flare? Come morning, even a tenderfoot could spot where his fire had been. The roar and splash of the swollen river crashing over the rocks below him gave him an idea.

Kneeling beside his pack, he pulled on the work gloves he'd bought and picked up the glowing logs. Following the sounds of the river, he inched his way to the edge of the bluff and tossed the remains of his fire into the water. He never heard, much less saw the evidence of his camp get swallowed up by the depth and fury of the river racing through the darkness below.

Sherman had lived without money before.

He could *live* without it again.

With the rain promising to pour down around him throughout the night, he opened his pack and pulled out a small shovel and went to work. He could spare thirty minutes or so to ensure that anyone who *was* lucky enough to spot this location—be it cop or hit man—would be slowed down and hopefully thrown off course.

Then he turned up the mountain, making a path of his own and erasing it behind him as he disappeared into the night.

RED AND ROSE AND orange chased away the gray gloom of the rainy night as dawn colored the rugged landscape.

Joanna tilted her face to the eastern horizon, trying to soak in those first rays of sunlight amid the efficient bustle and clipped conversations of setting up a command post at the base of the Ute Mountains. *"I remember when you were all sunshine and curiosity and a strong, forgiving heart."* Ethan's words after that emotional armor-dissolving kiss last night had hinted at new wounds inside him, something he needed that her absence—her abandonment—had denied him. Had she changed so much? Held her heart in rigid stasis for so long that she no longer had the power to give to someone she cared about?

And she did care about Ethan. She'd allowed the love she once felt to grow dormant. But they'd been through too much together—reservation gossip about that poor, disreputable Kuchu girl dating the tribal elder's son, escaping the demands and embarrassment of her parents, losing them—for Ethan not to hold a special, honored place in her life.

She missed feeling passion for something more than her job. She missed how normal it felt to be held in a man's arms and want him desperately. He'd given her a taste of both last night. She hadn't seen the full sun in almost thirty-six hours and wanted to embrace its heat. She wanted to be able to embrace life—and relationships, as well—the way she once had.

But she was going back to Washington, D.C. when this case was over. Getting involved with Ethan and leaving him was a cruelty she didn't intend to inflict on him twice. The whole idea of hurting that good man again made her shiver. In spite of her turtleneck and an insulated down vest over her jeans and boots, the sun couldn't warm her on the outside, and her good intentions didn't offer much warmth from the inside, either.

"Look at it while you can." She startled as the young man who'd introduced himself as Bart Flemming reached past her into the back of the SUV where she stood. "We're supposed to have another storm by later today. All this rain makes it damn hard to work on my tan."

Though he'd misread her introspective shiver and her

fascination with the sunrise, Joanna laughed as she was meant to. But Bart's joke made it easier to switch her focus back to the investigation. In the back of her mind, she tried to calculate just how many hours of daylight and clear sky they'd have before the next wave of severe weather forced them to turn back from their search for Watts. "You think it'll hold off until this evening?"

"It better." Bart picked up a portable generator for the tent where the crime unit, FBI and sheriff's department were setting up their base camp at the edge of the gravel parking lot. "You want to grab those cords and my laptop?"

"Sure. Is that everything?"

"Yeah. Go ahead and close it up." Bart, whose spiky brown hair stuck out in a half dozen directions, was the self-described techno wizard of the KCCU lab. According to his animated conversation all the way from downtown Kenner City, his job this morning was to rig up a complex system of radio, satellite and online communications at the remote location. Since he'd been kind enough to swing by the hotel to pick her up, she'd volunteered to help him unload his field equipment from the SUV.

Joanna looped the strap of the duffel bag filled with power cords over one shoulder, then picked up the computer case with her free hand. She nudged the SUV shut with her hip and followed him to the open-sided tent.

"Dump the laptop at my station." Bart directed her to one table before disappearing beneath another one. "Then bring the cords over here. I have to get us hooked up to the lab so that Miguel can have them run some prints through AFIS."

She followed the direction of Bart's finger over to the

far side of the lot where Miguel Acevedo from the crime lab was processing a beige-and-rust Chevy pickup cordoned off by official yellow tape. Though Elmer Watts's information had led them to this area, confirming that the fingerprints on the abandoned truck belonged to Sherman would make everybody on the scene feel a lot more confident that they were closing in on his trail. Switching vehicles was not uncommon for a man on the run, but thus far Watts's newer truck hadn't been found. Evidence they could retrieve from this old junker might allow them to retrace Sherman's actions over the past twenty-four hours, including pinpointing any accomplices or even verifying whether or not Boyd Perkins was back in the area.

Knowing where Sherman had gone and who he'd been talking to would benefit her interrogation, as well. Reason enough to quit thinking and start moving.

Hefting the heavy bag higher onto her hip, Joanna wove her way around equipment and personnel, swinging her gaze over to the group of men gathering at the back of Ethan's pickup truck and sharing an animated conversation. He didn't have to stand taller than the others for her to notice him. Ethan Bia wore an air of calm serenity about him that commanded attention. It might be the military training Elizabeth Reddawn had mentioned. Or it might simply be that Ethan Bia was as at home in the rugged outdoors as Bart was in his computer lab.

Ethan's dark gaze slipped across the parking lot to find her staring. He held her eyes for the longest of moments. Then he gave her a slight nod, sharp as a salute yet intimate as a caress, before turning away to answer a question from the man beside him.

Oh, Lord. She was finally feeling that burst of warmth that had eluded her earlier. She pressed her knuckles to her cheek. Definitely blushing.

"Smooth one, Joanna," she chided herself on a whisper. *Real professional.* She wasn't wearing a gun at her hip so that she could reminisce about late-night kisses and racing pulses and promises made between former lovers. She was here to conduct business.

With a flare of her nostrils, she inhaled deeply. As she exhaled, she set aside the purely female thoughts that had snuck into her brain and forced herself to think like an agent. Observe. Assess. Decide. Act.

Besides Sheriff Martinez and the FBI agents she'd met yesterday—Ben Parrish and Dylan Acevedo—she vaguely recognized the two other Native Americans with Ethan. Men from the reservation about her own age, maybe former schoolmates grown up. They probably knew the Four Corners area as well as Ethan. Working with an all-business precision, the Ute men were suiting up with multipocketed hiking vests and light backpacks. The two agents wore similar backpacks, but instead of strapping on ropes and pitons and water bags, they were checking magazine clips on their guns and adjusting holsters beneath the Kevlar vests they wore.

The bag she carried weighed heavily on Joanna's shoulder. She should be suiting up and joining those men. Instead, she'd been relegated to pack-mule duty. Not that she didn't understand or appreciate the importance of prepping and manning a cohesive command center to coordinate search efforts across such a vast area of wilderness. But Sherman Watts was *her* suspect, *her* responsibility. Ending his career as a criminal and finding them a new lead on the Julie Grainger murder was her professional mission.

Ending his career as a free man was her personal mission.

Despite Ethan's vehement vow to track down the bastard for her, Joanna's feet shifted with the need to control her own destiny. To be mistress of her own success.

Or failure.

Her gaze dropped to the scrub trees and new grass greening beyond the edge of the tent. No. Failure wasn't an option for her. She couldn't allow herself to even consider the possibility. Losing Watts, or breaking down when she faced him across that interview table, would mean that the past fifteen years of rebuilding her life had been for nothing.

Sherman Watts had taken her trust in men, her confidence in herself and her faith in the world that afternoon in her parents' trailer. She wouldn't let him take anything else from her.

The idea sprouting at the back of her mind needed a few minutes to grow into a workable plan. She needed to figure out a way to take a more active part in bringing in Watts. In the meantime, she'd do the job assigned to her—haul equipment. Adjusting the cord bag higher on her shoulder, she swung around.

And nearly mowed down a fellow agent.

"Easy." Tom Ryan—the newlywed agent Sheriff Martinez had introduced her to when she first arrived that morning—grabbed her by the shoulders and absorbed the brunt of the collision. "Need a hand?"

"I've got it, thanks." Joanna retreated a step and looked up into his stern countenance. An idea was definitely growing. "Congratulations on your marriage, Agent Ryan."

"Thanks." The hint of a smile appeared. "I think I did all right."

Better than all right, judging by the way Bart Flemming had spoken in such glowing terms of Dr. Callie MacBride-Ryan, the crime lab's chief forensic scientist.

"You could have stayed with your wife, you know." Joanna fixed an appropriately considerate smile on her mouth and made him an offer. "I'd be happy to take your place on the search. I grew up in the area, so I know the mountains fairly well. And nobody around here knows Sherman Watts better than I do."

Let him assume her knowledge of Watts and his behavior all came from research files.

Agent Ryan slipped his backpack over his shoulders. He seemed friendly enough, though his expression remained stern, making it difficult to tell whether his next sentence was a compliment or criticism. "Ben and Dylan said you were a go-getter. I appreciate the offer. But I've been on this case from the beginning, and Julie Grainger was a friend of mine. Callie understands my need to see this thing through to the end. Besides, I believe Watts helped the man who tried to murder my wife escape capture. That makes this assignment personal."

He had no idea how well she understood that remark.

"Allegedly helped, you mean. Do you have any proof that Watts is an accessory to attempted murder?"

He checked the clip of bullets on his Glock 9 mm, and

tucked a pair of spare magazines into the side zip of his pack. "You ever been on a manhunt detail, Rhodes?"

"I've worked on several criminal cases."

"Meeting a perp in a closed room isn't the same as tracking him across open territory. Out here, he has the advantage. The unexpected can happen and he can turn at any moment. Suddenly, *you're* the prey and he's the hunter. You stick to your interview room. I promise not to shoot him until you've had the chance to ask him a few questions."

"Shoot…?" Of course he was kidding. Wasn't he? But he was already past her, striding toward Ethan's truck to meet the rest of the search party.

She hadn't considered that there were others working with the crime unit who might have a personal grudge against Watts because of his dealings with Boyd Perkins and the Wayne crime family. She had to believe that they'd all behave in a strictly professional manner, but what if Watts resisted capture? What if he threatened one of the trackers or agents, and they were forced to fire their weapons? They were all trained to stop an attacker. Stopping sometimes meant killing.

Could she ever put the past behind her if she was denied the chance to stand face-to-face with her rapist?

She had to be a part of the search.

"Yo, Rhodes. You coming with those power cords or not?" Bart's summons from beneath the next table prompted Joanna to move. But even as she crawled beneath the table and helped him link the equipment to the field generators, she never stopped thinking about the best way to get on that mountain.

TEN MINUTES LATER, the sun had cleared the horizon and the entire team on-site—searchers and base personnel alike—had converged at the trail head. Patrick Martinez was finishing up his don't-take-unnecessary-risks-out-there speech. "I'm keeping the choppers grounded unless we have a good fix on Watts's location. I don't want to give him any more of a heads-up as to how close we are than he might already have. That means stealth and speed are key. Watch your backs out there—we know Watts took a gun and ammo from his trailer. We have every reason to believe he's armed and dangerous. Miguel?"

The crime-scene investigator stepped forward with a nod. "The truck in the parking lot was reported stolen last night from the casino in Towaoc. The prints on the wheel are definitely Watts's, so we can add that to the list of crimes we suspect him of. I found smudges on the outside of the vehicle, as well, from someone who was probably wearing gloves. The kicker is I found traces of explosives in the bed of the truck. Now, the truck's owner works for a construction company, so it's entirely possible the trace is related to his job."

Patrick nodded. "But don't discount the fact Watts may have done a little shopping himself. He's proven to be a jack-of-all-trades over the years. Wouldn't surprise me if he knows a thing or two about working with C-4. Wouldn't surprise me if those smudges belong to whoever leaked the info to Watts that we were after him in the first place. Eyes open, men. As badly as we want our suspect, I want all of you back here in one piece by sundown." He ended his speech and turned the briefing over to Ethan. "This is your game now, big guy. I know you'll keep it short and sweet."

Though Joanna stood at the back of the gathering, wedged between Bart Flemming and her guilty conscience, Ethan's eyes sought her out. She didn't need her ability to read people's expressions to know he was sending her a message, silently telling her he'd accomplish this mission for her.

Joanna blinked and looked down at the ground, pretending a rapt interest in a small tuft of grass, fighting for life in the gravelly muck at her feet. She rationalized that it was a smart rather than cowardly maneuver, to keep Ethan's intuitive perception from reading her intentions. The pause in his briefing might indicate that he suspected something, but time and the priorities of the moment didn't allow him the chance to probe for more information.

"Since the Ute Mountains are sacred ground, completely encompassed by the reservation, the land has restricted access. That means there are few roads or trails, so traversing them can be difficult." Joanna peeked up to see that his attention had shifted to the sky. "Overnight temperatures will have turned the rain and dew to frost or even ice at higher elevations, so watch your footing. Even dry lightning can be a danger to climbers, but if another storm hits, you'll need to worry about washouts, mud slides and flash flooding, as well. If you get wet, be on guard against hypothermia."

And those were just the natural hazards they'd have to deal with.

"Check your radios. Cell reception out here is unreliable." He shifted his gaze over to Bart Flemming.

"Bart, I need you to coordinate and triangulate our positions here at the command post. I want hourly check-ins. You don't hear from somebody, I want to know about it ASAP."

"Yes, sir."

"And keep an eye on the Doppler radar. I want to know in advance when we're getting a repeat of last night's storm." He looked to Ben Parrish, who was buckling his radio onto his vest. "Ben, you're with me. We'll follow Cottonwood Wash up to Rising Sun Creek on Ute Peak. Joseph, you and Tom circle around Marble Mountain to Whispering Falls. And, Garan, you take Acevedo here through the pass between Horse Peak and Black Mountain. See if you can get as far as McElmo Creek. Good hunting, men."

The group dispersed, with the majority of them moving back to the command post tent. Tom Ryan and his guide headed south into the scrub pine forest at the base of the mountains, while Dylan Acevedo and his guide headed north toward the Canyons of the Ancients National Monument.

"Give me a sec," Ethan said, telling Ben Parrish to start on without him. With a nod, Ben dropped down into an arroyo and moved toward the slope on the opposite side.

Ethan and Joanna were left alone for a few precious moments. He moved silently over the gravel and mud as he walked off the distance between them. "Will you be okay waiting here?" he asked.

In lieu of lying, Joanna chose not to answer. Instead, she reached out and flicked her finger across the handle of the long hunting knife he'd strapped to his waist. "You're not taking a gun?"

"I had my fill of guns in Afghanistan. I don't like to carry one anymore." In a deceptively casual gesture that conveyed something more, he brushed the callused tip of his index finger across her forehead and tucked a loose strand of hair behind her ear. "You worried about me?"

His tone was tender, his touch even more so.

"Yes." She was quick to catch herself and shake her head. "No." *Not for the reason you think.* "I'm sure you'll be just fine. I mean, the wind or the rocks or that sixth sense of yours will tell you the bad guy's coming before he gets there, right?"

"Hope so."

She drummed up a smile. "You'll know. I never have doubted your skills as a tracker."

"Then what's bugging you?"

Joanna's gaze sank to the zipper on his vest. He'd handcuff her to his truck if he knew what she was planning. "Watts getting away. Losing my chance to confront him."

Could he hear the truth in her voice? Could he sense what she *wasn't* saying?

That same finger tapped her beneath the chin and asked her to look up into those beautiful onyx eyes. "He won't get away."

Joanna nodded. Believed. Longed to trust in those words. But ultimately, she knew it was up to Joanna Rhodes to take care of what Joanna Rhodes needed. She peeked around him to nod toward Agent Parrish's disappearing figure. "You'd better get going."

"Stay put. Stay safe."

Joanna's breathing hitched at the dark husk of Ethan's voice. Protocol wouldn't allow a goodbye kiss, and she suspected that the next time they met in private, he'd be more likely to lecture her than to share any affection. Nonetheless, Joanna craved some kind of personal contact with him, something kinder than the tears and running away that had ended their relationship fifteen years ago.

So she pulled his hand from her chin, wrapped her fingers around his and squeezed.

He turned his big hand to engulf hers and squeezed back.

Hidden from the view of any colleagues who might happen to glance their way, Joanna slid her palm along Ethan's. Sensitive nerves awoke. Her skin warmed. Her pulse raced.

"You're a hard man to get over, Ethan Bia."

He leaned forward, ever so slightly. But he came close enough that she could feel the warmth emanating from his body. So much strength. So much heat. Every cell in Joanna's body leaped with the desire to burrow into that warmth. Her lips parted. Her breasts tingled at the tips.

"You were impossible," he whispered.

And then he pulled away. Backed away. Left her standing there with her mouth agape, her insides quaking with a riot of emotions. After all this time, after all she'd done, did he think he still loved her? She didn't deserve that. She couldn't handle it. She couldn't handle hurting him again.

"I'll come back to you, *Nüa-rü.*"

He turned and climbed over the lip of the arroyo, his long legs quickly eating up the ground as he caught up to Ben Parrish.

When he was finally out of earshot, when she could finally squeeze the inevitable truth past the lump in her throat, she answered him.

"No, you won't."

Chapter Six

"Here." Ethan plucked out of the mud the reedy stalk that had been snapped in two. He handed the sign up to Ben and unsheathed his knife to poke aside the tall grass wedged in the triangle between two granite boulders, so as not to disturb the ground. "And here. He came this way. He's trying to keep to the harder surfaces of the rocks to mask his trail." He brushed his hand across the shady underside of the rock and came away with dewy fingers. "But the rocks were probably slick until the sun hit them, and he slipped every now and then."

"You're sure it's Watts and not some big cat or coyote?" Ben Parrish asked.

"The cat's not going to slip." Pushing to his feet, Ethan pointed to the depression captured in the grass at the foot of a granite boulder. "And the coyotes around here don't wear boots."

"Point taken."

Ethan wiped the dampness of his knife blade off on his pant leg and fastened it back in its leather sheath. He pulled the tube from his water pack free and sucked down a couple of good swallows. He reminded Ben to

do the same. Drinking water became even more important as the air thinned at the higher elevation. Nasty
headaches or muscle cramps could force them to call off
the search before they had their man in custody.

Ben pulled off his slim, wraparound sunglasses and
shed his pack to retrieve a bottle of water. "Are we sure
this is a legitimate trail? At our last check-in, Bart said
Dylan and Garan had followed a dummy trail for almost
a mile before it doubled back on them."

Ethan nodded. "Watts had a busy day yesterday. But
that print was made last night. A lot later in the day than
what Garan reported. From what I know about the man,
we're on the most likely path. If he truly wants to disappear, this is the way to reach the most rugged, inac-
cessible part of the mountains."

"My money's on you, big guy." After taking a drink,
Ben climbed out onto a granite outcropping to study the
steep grade below them. "How high up are we?"

Climbing straight up instead of zigzagging back and
forth would have been a shorter, more direct route to the
summit, but with the potentially deadly combination of too
much water and typically dry soil, Ethan had opted for the
longer, safer route. The chance to reach Rising Sun Creek
before Watts had been negated by the danger of landslides
or a simple misstep with nowhere to fall but way down.

"Considering the base altitude was sixty-two hundred feet above sea level, and we've been climbing for
almost four hours, I'd say we're—"

"Pretty damn high." Ben pulled his cell phone off his
belt and punched a few numbers. With a shake of his
head, he clipped it back onto his belt and rejoined Ethan.
"We're out of range."

"No surprise there." The sun was warm on his back through the layers of thermal and flannel shirts he wore, but the air was cool for a spring day—a sure indicator of the next round of storms heading their way by nightfall. Knowing the roughest part of their trek still lay ahead of them, Ethan breathed in deeply, taking stock of his body. He felt no sense of being winded or fatigued—not that he was prepared to rest until he had Watts in his hands. But he'd been hiking the mountains for decades. Ben here was a city boy, certainly fit, but he couldn't afford to be slowed down by a partner who suddenly passed out from exhaustion. "You need a break?"

"Do you?"

Closing his eyes and turning his face toward the sky, Ethan tried to get a sense of company in the area, how much daylight was left, and how willing he was to return to camp to face Joanna without Watts. He might not understand her plan to get rid of Watts's influence over her life by going one-on-one with him in that interview room, but he understood demons. He understood how badly it could gnaw at a person if salvation from those demons was denied.

Ethan still carried that most awful day of the war with him. The day the carnage was too much. The day his team couldn't recover one living soul. The day his buddy, Sam, had cracked on the battlefield and put his own gun to his head.

He slowly opened his eyes, slowly relaxed the white-knuckled grip of his fists at his sides.

Like Joanna, Ethan had come back home to heal.

But unlike Joanna, he'd always believed that reclaiming the best in his life—her, them—was the only way to truly defeat those demons. Joanna believed she had to embrace the worst.

Maybe there was no way they could both have what they wanted. But Ethan would never let her down again. He'd have to die on this mountain before he'd come back without Sherman Watts.

"Ethan?"

He'd been too quiet for too long. But his decision was made and he damn well wasn't going to try to explain just how certain he was that he was doing the right thing to a man—to a world—that needed facts and science to believe anything.

Pulling the radio from his vest, Ethan turned to face his partner. "I'm going to send Joseph and Tom back to base camp with Dylan and Garan."

Ben's eyes narrowed skeptically. "You're calling off the search?"

"I figure we've got three hours before the rain starts up again, maybe an hour of daylight after that."

"Screw the rain. If we give Watts two nights of a head start, we'll never catch him."

Ethan spelled it out in black-and-white. "I'm not turning back. Either I locate Watts or I make camp for the night and find him tomorrow. We're the only ones who have any chance of reaching him at this point. But if we stay, we'll be trapped up here when the storm hits."

"I'm game."

"It'll be a tough night," Ethan warned him.

"You're that certain we're on Watts's trail?"

"Yes."

Ben put on his sunglasses and grinned. "That's good enough for me."

"You want Watts as badly as I do, don't you?"

Ben nodded without offering a reason why. "Call it in. We're not leaving this mountain."

"WHAT AM I SUPPOSED to do?" Joanna's dark eyes were red and puffy with tears. Her skin was pale, making the fist-size bruises on her cheek and jaw stand out in angry relief.

When Ethan had knocked on her trailer door that night and gotten no response, even though a light was on and her car was parked outside, he'd let himself in to check on her. He'd never seen such devastation of property—or woman—in his life. For a few minutes, he'd been in a bit of shock himself. But then the anger had kicked in, clearing his head.

He'd gotten Joanna dressed. Found a clean towel to stanch the bleeding from the wound across the top of her left breast. He'd wrapped his denim jacket around her shoulders to keep her warm.

And now, after buckling her up inside his truck, he handed her the ice pack for her lip, ran around to climb in behind the wheel and start the engine. The police would meet them at the emergency room in Kenner City.

"Nüa-rü, you gotta talk to me. Who did this to you?"

Silence. Hell. His insides were shriveling up with anger and hurt and helplessness. "Do you know who attacked you?"

Finally, a nod.

Double hell. "Who? After the hospital, we have to talk to the cops."

"They won't listen to me. I'm a Kuchu. They've seen me too many times to believe—"

"You were bailing out your parents! You were taking care of them!" Too loud. Too harsh. Ah, hell. Somebody punch him for making her shrink against the passenger door like that. "I'm sorry. You weren't the one in trouble with the law. They'll listen."

For the longest time, he thought his outburst had silenced her. He was too big a man to be yelling at a woman like that, even if it was out of frustration, or indignation on her behalf. "Talk to me, Joanna. Tell me what happened. I'll listen."

His knuckles turned white around the steering wheel as she whispered bits and pieces of her nightmarish attack into the darkness of the truck cab.

"He hit me when I fought back. He found a knife in the kitchen drawer and cut me. He held it to my throat while he... And then he..." Her soft sob clawed its way straight into his heart.

Ethan had been raised to be a peaceful man. Had made a point of keeping things gentle and patient with Joanna so he didn't scare her off. But he sensed he could murder a man right about now. "Who—?"

"He thought I was my mother. He called me Naomi— kept saying he needed her. Said Mother owed him. He was making her pay."

Just a few hours after burying her mother? What kind of sick bastard would go after a woman while her grief was still so fresh? Who would be cruel enough to use that grief against her?

"Who was it, Joanna? Tell me, and I'll pound the son of a bitch."

For a moment, she roused herself from her shock. "Your father wouldn't approve of that."

"My father wouldn't approve of what happened to you, either."

"You can't get in trouble with the law. Not for me. I'm not worth you losing your father's respect and jeopardizing your future."

"Don't say that." He reached across the seat to squeeze her hand, but she jerked it into her lap almost as soon as his fingers brushed against hers. Curling his fingers into a fist, he pulled away. Of course, she wouldn't appreciate a man's touch right now. He pressed a little harder on the accelerator to get her to the hospital sooner. She needed someone to take care of her tonight. Even if it couldn't be him. *"I love you."*

"I know."

"Joanna..." What was he supposed to say? How could he make her believe he would always be here for her? *"This doesn't change the way I feel about you."*

She drew her legs up into the seat and curled her body into a ball. *"It changes how I feel."*

"About us?"

"About everything."

"Who the hell did this to you, baby?" Her soft, voiceless sobs triggered a gritty dampness behind his own eyelids. She was so hurt. How could he have allowed the woman he loved to get hurt like this? *"Who raped you?"*

They raced another mile through the night before she spoke again.

"He was drunk."

He quickly narrowed a short list down to one. The SOB had been drinking at the funeral. He had history with her late parents. *"Sherman Watts?"*

Ah, hell. As he hit the outskirts of Kenner City, Ethan took a silent vow.

That bastard would never hurt Joanna again.

"Up or down? Ethan!" The sharp, authoritative voice cut into Ethan's thoughts. For a split second, he was on recovery recon in the mountains of Afghanistan, and his lieutenant, Sam Keller, was warning him to start talking about where their unit's point man was taking them. "Up or down?"

Ethan had trudged along for an hour, guided by instinct, haunted by the past. But Ben Parrish's urgent voice dragged him back to the present.

"You okay, man?"

Shutting down those old feelings and snapping his gaze into focus, Ethan made a quick survey of the area. Ben was right to demand guidance. Their steady climb was about to get tricky as he eyed the washout on the trail ahead of them. "I'm okay. Take a breather while I check things out."

They'd reached the Silverton River gorge. The roar of the river slamming through the narrow canyon three stories below them drowned out the ominous cadence of thunder that rumbled in the sky overhead. With the charged ions of dropping barometric pressure pricking the short hair at his nape to attention, Ethan was certain he hadn't miscalculated the time of the storm. But anything in the sky sounded closer and more threatening at this altitude.

He hoisted himself up onto one of the scrub pines that had been tipped at a dangerous angle over their path, testing the strength of the exposed roots clinging to the steep incline to their left. After one good bounce, the roots began to lose their grip on the soil and the tree made a deep, yawning sound as it bent closer to the drop-off on their right. Ethan jumped back to the ground, shaking his head.

"Soil's too wet. We can't count on them to hold our weight if you miss a step."

"So I won't miss a step." Ben's sunglasses were long gone, but the keen, assessing eyes remained. "Can you pick up Watts's trail again once we get past this mess?"

Ethan splayed his hands at his waist, opening up his chest to take in a deep, fortifying breath, giving Ben a chance to do the same. So far, their solitary hike up Ute Mountain had been an endurance trek that burned through the muscles in his legs. But from what he could see, the real climb was about to begin. Automatically checking the gear strapped to his vest, belt and pack, he swept his gaze back and forth, up and down, familiarizing himself with the changes in the landscape.

"I think so." He nodded toward the split in the rocks about forty yards ahead where the softer sandstone on either side of the gray granite outcropping had eroded away to form a natural fork in the trail. Going up and over the granite would lead them to Rising Sun Creek and the summit beyond, while climbing down would take them into the gorge and onto the narrow or possibly nonexistent riverbank.

Unfortunately, between their location and the fork in the rocks lay forty yards of do-not-try-this-at-home terrain. Gravelly soil and a few larger boulders had tumbled down with the trees, obscuring the path worn by wild animals, a few intrepid hunters and hikers—and most likely—one whiskey-steeped, resourceful fugitive on the run.

"You don't say much, do you, Bia?" Ben teased. "Don't tell me we're turning back."

"Wouldn't think of it." Ethan unhooked a rope and a clip of carabiners and tossed them to the FBI agent. "But we are going to tie ourselves off before we cross here." He glanced over the broken treetops below them. "That's a mighty long way to fall if you do miss that step."

Ethan secured a rope around his waist and looped his climbing hammer around his wrist before moving through the fallen trees and crawling up the steep, crumbling incline to find solid rock where he could anchor a series of pitons and run a guide rope through. He rode the miniature slide of loose gravel his descent created back down to Agent Parrish and secured his rope to the mountain face, as well.

"Ready? We're going up and over the slide. Remember to sit back on the line and walk up the slope. Step where I do."

Ben pulled his rope taut. "Lead on, MacDuff."

Twenty-five painstaking minutes later, they'd reached the fork in the rock. Ethan had broken out into a sweat and Ben was visibly breathing harder. He ordered the agent to take another drink while he secured their lines.

"You think Watts got caught in this mess?" Ben asked, sucking his water bottle dry.

"No way to know until I scout up ahead." Ethan inspected the diverging paths, running his hands and eyes along the crags and lichens of the bluff wall, and stooping down to search the scrub vegetation that clung to the rock face leading down to the river, looking for signs left by man, not nature. "I haven't seen any evidence of scavengers, or vultures overhead. They'd find a dead or wounded man before we would."

"You're a laugh a minute, big guy. You want me to radio in our progress? What the hell…?"

Ethan felt the first cold drop on his cheek even before he glanced back to see Ben's upturned hand.

"Rain?"

"Rain." Ethan took note of the slightly pale cast to Ben Parrish's skin. Tough was tough, but even *he* was beginning to feel the exertion of their ascent. Sherman Watts had taken two days to climb the ground they were covering in one. Rather than push Ben so far that he wound up collapsing from exhaustion, Ethan ordered a longer break. "Call it in. Tell Bart that we've reached Cougar Fork. Martinez will know where we are." A line of thick clouds rolled over the sun overhead, casting the late afternoon into twilight and darkening the shadows among the trees. "Tell them we're staying the night. Unless we find Watts and need the helicopter to fly us out, we'll resume contact at first light."

"Will do. Ute Base—this is Scout One. Ute Base, come in." Static crackled over the radio in response. "Damn. Have we lost the frequency?"

"The weather must be interfering. Try another channel."

Ben nodded, turning the volume down, adjusting the reception through a series of piercing pitches, trying to find a working band. "I'll ask if Bart can soup up the power at his end so we don't lose contact."

Ethan took a few steps along the lower path. There was plenty of mud and enough foliage in the crevasse to mark the tracks of a group of foxes—probably a mother and her kits. But nothing human. As he suspected, Watts's trail meant they had more mountain to climb.

Ben tinkered with controls until the shrill tones narrowed into silence. "Bingo." He raised the two-way radio to his mouth again. "Ute Base—this is Scout One. Do you read?"

"Scout One—this is Ute Base." Bart Flemming's voice sounded small and distant. "You sound like you're all the way down in New Mexico. What…your position?"

"Cougar Fork." Ben raised his voice to be heard. "Hey, Bart. Can you work some of your magic from that end? You're breaking up. Could be the atmosphere with this storm. How hard is it going to hit us?"

"The Weather Bureau…" While Bart and Ben exchanged and repeated pertinent information, Ethan explored a few yards ahead.

Lightning streaked across the sky, and for the next half a moment, reception completely cut out. In that one beat of silence, Ethan heard it.

The crunch of gravel beneath a foot.

Thunder rumbled. Static answered, masking the sound. Another man might think he'd imagined it.

"Be apprised, Agent…arrived." Then more static.

"Sounds like Tom and Dylan and your men are back at camp." Ben stood as he relayed the message to Ethan and signed off. "Ute Base—this is Scout One. Out."

The radio crackled. The sky rumbled. Ethan braced his feet and closed his eyes and listened to the world, sorting through the sounds around him.

"I hate to say it, big guy, but we may be incommunicado until after this storm—"

Ethan raised a fist beside his ear and Ben instantly

fell silent. He turned to meet the agent's eyes. Good. *Their* communication was clear.

Man approaching.

In one smooth, noiseless movement, Ben set the radio on the ground beside his pack and pulled his gun.

Ethan pointed down the path to the gorge, indicating the direction from which the footstep had sounded. He could hear them clearly now. The steps were soft, steady, slow to approach.

Their unsuspecting quarry was coming to them.

He wasn't on a battlefield, and Ben wasn't a soldier under his command, but the two of them instantly reacted as though they'd suddenly found themselves in enemy territory.

After exchanging a few cryptic hand signals, Ben retreated behind a stand of scrub pines while Ethan hoisted himself up onto the rocky ledge overhanging the path. Drawing his knife and turning it in his fist, he crouched low and waited for their man to appear.

Come on, Watts, he urged silently. *Let's get this damn mission over with and get you back to Joanna.*

Lightning split the sky overhead, charging every nerve, flashing in his retinas. The answering thunder ripped through the air, loud and fierce, right on top of them.

The footsteps neared. Slowed. Retreated.

Damn. Watts must have heard a sound or—hell, Ben's gear was right there in the middle of the path. Watts must have seen it.

Ethan didn't wait to find out if that click and whisper of sound was a gun being drawn.

He jumped.

Springing like a mountain lion from his perch, Ethan

tackled the tall figure that crept beneath him. With a startled "oof," their visitor went down. They hit the ground hard, rolled, smacked into the rocks.

Watts wasn't about to make this easy. With a growl, he twisted beneath Ethan, a sharp elbow catching him in the gut. Something harder clipped him in the chin. The blow rang through Ethan's skull. And in the moment it took to blink the dots of light from his eyes, Watts grabbed his wrist and shoved the knife away.

Ben charged their position, gun drawn. "FBI! Drop your weapon!"

"Oh, my God… E—"

Enough! Watts was fast for an older man. Scrappy. Tough. But Ethan was stronger. And that hellish night Joanna had been raped was still so fresh on his mind…

"Ethan! Bia!" Ben Parrish was shouting at *him*. "Back it off!"

Ethan flicked the knife into the brush and shifted his grip to pin his opponent's wrist. He captured the other wrist and knocked it against the ground. Once. Twice, dislodging the gun Watts had clobbered him with. He pinned that wrist.

"Ethan?"

His opponent had gone slack in his grip, giving him an easy advantage. He kicked the perp's legs apart, pinned the left leg. Pinned the right.

"Ethan," his slender attacker wheezed. "Please!"

The haze of adrenaline cleared his system enough to recognize that precious voice. It took another second to focus in on the man spread-eagled beneath him.

Not a man.

Breasts—small, pert, proud—thrust up to meet every

deep breath of his chest, again and again as his captive breathed in deeply, trying to catch *her* breath.

Hell. Oh, hell.

Ethan looked down into deep brown eyes and a swath of midnight-colored hair, tangled with pine needles, mud and gravel.

He'd attacked the very thing he'd so fiercely wanted to protect.

Joanna.

"Did I hurt you?" Joanna asked, brushing the muck and gravel off her jeans as she bent to retrieve her weapon. Just as quickly as Ethan had leaped from the heavens and tackled her, he'd rolled off her and put a good ten feet of space between them.

"I'm sorry, *Nüa-rü*. I'm sorry. I had that knife… What you must have thought…" His black-eyed gaze swung over to Ben Parrish and Ethan fell silent.

She could well imagine where Ethan's thoughts had gone. For a split second, she'd gone back to that night, too. But for only a split second. She'd had fifteen years of self-defense training to make the instinct to fight back second nature. Yes, a man had forced her down. Had held a knife to her throat. Had even trapped her in that completely vulnerable position beneath the heavier weight of his body. She hadn't allowed herself the time to think of the rape, to compare, to fear. She'd simply fought for her freedom.

Now she was fighting to reassure the one man who might give a damn that he'd reminded her of that most painful chapter of her life.

"I'm okay, Ethan. Are you?" Did he understand that

she meant more than physical pain? Ignoring the twinge in her wrist from having it pummeled against the ground, she holstered her Glock and tried to read beneath the stoic mask of Ethan's face. "You jumped me from behind. For all I knew, you could have been Watts. I had to defend myself."

He scraped his palm over his jaw, wiping the moisture from his face. Yep. The spot where she'd clocked him with her gun was going to leave a mark on his tanned skin. "What part of 'stay put' don't you understand?"

Okay. Anger.

She curbed the impulse to snap back with a *What part of "you're not the boss of me" don't* you *understand?* His anger was justified, and not unexpected. Knowing that she seemed to be the only one who could elicit that particular emotion in the normally gentle giant added another brick onto the weight of guilt she carried where Ethan was concerned.

Verbally duking it out in front of an audience wouldn't have been her first choice, but at least Agent Parrish had the decency to look utterly focused on radioing in her location to Bart Flemming down at the base camp. She was safe. All search party members had been accounted for.

Joanna had been exhausted by her climb, but wrestling with Ethan had fired enough adrenaline through her system to give her renewed energy. She blinked the rain from her eyelashes and took a step toward him, but halted when his chiseled jaw clenched and he turned away. Fine, she'd give her explanation from here. "When Dylan Acevedo and his guide returned to base camp without any success, I knew I couldn't sit there or in my hotel room, waiting for someone to call and tell me Watts had slipped through your manhunt. It sounds as though Agent Ryan and Garan Coons are back at camp now, too."

"I sent them back for their own safety."

Right on cue, lightning sparked on and off like a strobe in the sky. Joanna jumped as the clap of thunder, amplified by the altitude, followed just a couple of seconds later. She understood that if the lightning came much closer, exposed on the mountainside like this, they'd make prime targets for a strike.

Did the man think he was invincible? That he was so one with nature that the storm would somehow spare him? She ignored the invisible fortress of solitude he'd erected around himself and crossed right up to him. "You're in danger up here, too. How is it okay for you to worry about the rest of us, but I can't worry about you?"

And she had been worried. But that wasn't what this discussion was about, apparently.

"Parrish and I have Watts's trail. He'll be forced to take shelter on the mountain tonight, too." With a sigh that sounded almost as if he was disgusted that he couldn't keep himself from touching her, Ethan plucked a twig from her hair and tossed it to the ground. "There's no reason for anyone else to risk their lives when we're this close to catching up to him."

"You can't leave me behind. This case is too important to me." Would he welcome *her* touch if she reached up and brushed away the debris that clung to the nappy collar of his green-and-tan flannel shirt? The instinct was there, but she fought off giving in to the temptation.

Instead, she busied her hands by unhooking her fraying ponytail and smoothing all the damp, wayward strands around her face. She bound them back into place at the back of her head. "There's nothing for me to do down at base camp. Flemming is monitoring all the communications and coordinating with the crime unit. I told Martinez I was familiar with the area and wanted to do some exploring on my own and he okayed it."

"He let you come up here without a survival pack or radio?"

She wasn't a fool. "I took my pack off and left it on the trail up to the fork when I heard a man's voice up here. I wanted to be able to defend myself if I needed to. Looks like I did."

"Does he know how far you were planning on going? How dangerous it is to hike along the river with it cresting like it is? Night's falling. The storm's almost here. You could have been injured or kidnapped, or just have gotten lost, and no one would have known it."

"I'm not going to sit down there and twiddle my thumbs when I can be doing something useful up here."

"You don't think I can do my job?"

"I'm not implying that."

"The hell you aren't, Superwoman. You can't give up control of one damn thing, can you? You can't trust anyone to do you a favor or help with your job or… protect you." He hunched down to bring his face eye level with hers, dropping his voice to a low-pitched whisper. "Accepting help is not a sign of weakness. It doesn't mean you're going to fall apart or fail or be hurt if you can't control every last detail of your life."

Joanna frowned. "Is that really how you see me?"

"Am I wrong?" He straightened to his full height, forcing her to tilt her chin to read every nuance of his next taunt. "Tell me exactly who you trust, Joanna. Give me a list of names of people you rely on without question."

The wind picked up, splashing cold raindrops across her upturned face. But Joanna couldn't look away. She was too stunned to realize how much she hated—how much it hurt—that he was right.

"I didn't think so." He spun around, spotted his knife at the roots of a gnarled pine bush and strode over to reclaim his weapon.

She followed on his heels, forgetting for a moment that they had an audience. "Who the hell was I ever going to count on, Ethan? My parents? The family friend who raped me? The sheriff who let him get away with it?"

But Ethan hadn't forgotten the other agent who was with them. "Ben. Pack your gear and climb on up to that next ledge. There are some caves up there where we can take shelter for the night. Make sure there aren't any visitors before you go in. The snakes and smaller predators will be looking for a warm, dry place, too."

"Got it. You two, um, take your time."

From the corner of her eye, she saw Ben gear up and disappear above the granite overhang. But her gaze was glued to Ethan, as she waited for an answer, waited for understanding.

When he faced her again, the anger was gone. Something ancient and hard and cynical had replaced it. "How about the man who loves you? You ever think about giving him a chance? Trusting him?"

"Don't say that."

"What? Don't throw my pride to the wind and beg

you to let me back into your life? Or don't…?" He shook his head, uttered a sound that was not quite a laugh. "Hell. Haven't you figured it out? I never got over Joanna Kuchu. Once the big guy fell, it stuck."

"No."

But it was there, clearly stamped on his honest, care-worn features. It was the love they'd once shared—twisted and neglected and beaten down into something far different than the innocent hope and endless desire they'd found in each other at eighteen and twenty-one.

A shiver—of guilt and sorrow and the love she missed trying to break through—rippled down her spine. "I'm sorry, Ethan. I'm just not that girl anymore."

"You don't want to feel a thing, do you? You're the uncompromising lady FBI agent. All business. All the time. You even changed your name to erase a past that didn't fit in with this newer, tougher version of you." He gentled his tone, but the truth of his words was still hard to stomach. "You don't want to let another person in because you're afraid Joanna Kuchu will get hurt again."

She pressed her lips together in a thin, taut line, afraid of what might come out if she tried to answer.

"That's real strength, *Nüa-rü*. To love. To trust. To allow yourself to need someone." He stuffed that long, wicked knife back inside its sheath and tied it off with the leather cord at the top. As her emotions were surfacing, his appeared to be shutting down. "Someday, I hope you find that again. I hope you find friends. And someone who's more than a friend. Your life's going to be empty until you do. And that…truly breaks my heart."

The sky opened up and the rain beat down like the relentless chill in her heart. His words had broken down

some indefinable barrier, fracturing her carefully struc-
tured world. But she tried to piece together what she
could. "What do you want me to say? That I loved you
once? I did. Maybe a part of me still does because
it…hurts…to know how badly I hurt you." She swiped
the rain from her face, taking with it the tears she didn't
want to cry. "But I have to be the way I am. That's how
I handled my parents and rape and recovery. That's how
I got through Quantico. That's how I'll get up this
mountain and do my job and get back to my life in D.C."

"I'm sure Joanna Rhodes will handle it all just fine."
He nodded toward the rock face that Agent Parrish had
climbed. "Go on. You're next." He picked up his backpack and waited for her at the base of the wall. "Watch
your step. It'll be slick."

"That's it?" End of discussion? Climb the wall?
"You're not sending me back to base camp?"

He tested a couple of handholds, and tugged at one
protrusion about a foot above his head. "Grab on here.
This one's solid." When she didn't immediately move
to obey, he circled behind her, planted his hands at her
waist and lifted her onto the wall in front of him. "I don't
like the idea of you being alone in the same room with
Watts when armed guards and hidden cameras are
watching his every move. I sure as hell don't want you
running into him out here in the wild where he has the
advantage."

Joanna automatically tightened her grip and secured
her feet. When she shook the rain from her eyes and
pulled herself up to the next handhold, he released her.
The warmth of his hands and his unreadable mood
remained. "I'm not here to be a burden, Ethan. I would

think another set of eyes and another gun up here would be welcome. I never asked you to protect me from Watts."

"Get your ass up that mountain. And don't you leave my sight."

While Joanna Rhodes resisted the order, some little part of her that was still Joanna Kuchu warmed at the growly declaration that she was now part of the team. And that Ethan Bia, in some skewed way, still cared.

She tested the next grip, found a pool of slimy mud and hunted for the next hole or protrusion where she could grab on. The next one wasn't deep enough. "I don't see where…"

Ethan was on the climb beside her now. He reached for her hand and pulled it closer. "Here."

He cupped her fingers over a knob of granite. Following his example, Joanna shifted her weight and pulled herself up another foot. But she stopped abruptly. "I forgot my pack down—"

Boom!

A deafening noise exploded overhead. With her breath startled from her lungs, Joanna instinctively hugged the rock face. "Was that thunder?"

Only if lightning had struck the bluff above them.

Maybe it had. A low hum, like the distant reverberation of running hooves, rumbled overhead. The spatter of raindrops became the clacking of tiny gravel sprinkling down over the face of the rock. Joanna tipped her face up as the hoofbeats crescendoed into a stampede of a thousand buffalo charging straight toward them. The granite itself shook beneath her hands.

"Ethan?"

"Move!" Ethan snaked his arm around Joanna's waist and leaped.

The first pebble thunked off her scalp as Ethan shoved her beneath the overhang and sandwiched her against the granite wall, shielding her with his body. Joanna grabbed two fistfuls of his vest and shirts and buried her face against his chest as the mountain came down on top of them.

Chapter Seven

"Joanna."

The voice against her ear was as soothing as the solid thump of the heartbeat beneath her hand. She felt drowsy and warm and content.

"Joanna." The voice was slightly more urgent this time, rousing her to the bruising rocks poking into her back and bottom. She tried to squirm away from the discomfort.

"*Nüa-rü.* You okay?" Hard hands, running along her body from shoulders to hips and up into her hair, probing for injury, chased away the last of her shocked stupor. The rock slide. They'd survived.

"Ethan?" She lifted her head and inhaled a deep breath, but wound up with a noseful of dust that triggered a coughing spasm.

"Easy." The rough pads of Ethan's thumbs stroked across her eyes and nose and lips. Moist, tender kisses followed every touch—to an eyelid, the corner of her mouth, the tip of her nose—offering comfort and stirring memories after wiping away the dirt and debris that seemed to cover every part of them. When the coughing passed and her airways had cleared, he framed her jaw between his hands and inspected her with his eyes. "Better?"

Even with the shadows of rocks and rain and the encroaching night, his eyes seemed to pierce the darkness with a light from within. It was a light she could cling to when the world was literally falling down around her. It was a light that could guide her to safety. If she let it.

"I'm okay." She released her death grip on the front of his vest and reached up to brush small chunks of rock off his shoulders. His face needed a wipe of her hands, too. She ran her thumbs along the creases from sun and laughter beside his eyes, and cleared the dirt from the stern line of his mouth. "Are you hurt?"

"Some bruises, maybe. Nothing serious."

"Same here." The rain beyond Ethan's back was already tamping down the rising dust as the last few bits of rolling rock settled into their new resting places. "Looks like I *did* need you. You saved my life. Thank you."

"Anytime. See? That wasn't so hard, was it?"

She shook her head. Allowing herself to need him, just this once, hadn't been hard at all.

His striking black hair had been coated with a mix of ruddy red and gray debris. Even as she combed her fingertips through the short, damp silk, she was imagining a picture of what he might look like forty years from now—or after a can of paint had spilled on his head. The thought of an elegantly aged Ethan, or one who might be klutzy enough to make mistakes like she did, curved her lips into a smile. Her smile seemed to please him, relax him. The hands that had framed her face were suddenly sliding around her waist, pulling her closer. He bent his head, his lips hovering over hers.

"That would have crushed us. Sent us over the edge of the mountain. I could have lost you again."

The almost moment of shared tenderness vanished in unison. How long had they been standing there? Seconds? Minutes?

Joanna said it first. "Agent Parrish."

"Ben!"

Ethan was already moving, hauling himself out of the recess where they'd taken shelter, onto the new incline of rubble that had completely wiped away the path to Cougar Fork. As Joanna dug herself a toehold in the crumbled rock, Ethan reached down and clamped his hand around her wrist, pulling her right along with him as he climbed.

"Ahh!" She winced at the dull ache that throbbed in her arm.

He set her on her feet beside him and immediately released her. "You *are* hurt."

She brushed aside the hands that probed the scrapes and red marks encircling her wrist and wiggled all her fingers, showing him it was just sore, nothing broken. "It's from our wrestling match earlier."

"I'm sorry. I should have waited to see—"

"Go." She tried to turn him, urge him on up the slope ahead of her. "Find Ben. I'll get there."

"*We'll* get there." Moving and making promises all at once, he switched his grip to her other hand. The ground beneath them shifted like a giant pile of sand beneath every step, but he helped her reach the wide ledge of the bluff far more quickly than she could have managed on her own. But once they reached the relatively flat surface high above the river, he released her and went into search mode. "Ben! Can you hear me?"

"Ben!" she echoed.

There was less debris here, but still enough loose boulders and larger rock to pick through. Ethan jogged ahead, checking the entrance to one shallow cave and then the next.

Joanna's feet followed her gaze to the edge of the bluff where dusty treetops and other plant life sprouted from the jagged wall that dropped down to the Silverton River. She peered over the rim and visually skimmed small ledges and roots and tree trunks where a strong man might still be clinging to life.

"Ben!" Though she could hear the river roaring past below her, the rain and darkness prevented her from seeing all the way down to the water. She glanced over her shoulder, following the pyramid of rubble to the next rise above them where the slide had started. Nothing but dark clouds and flashes of lightning and more rock. Could he have gotten up there before the mountain gave way and swept him over the edge into the gorge? A sinking feeling gnawed in her stomach as she looked back to the chasm below her. "You don't think he…?"

"Over here!"

Clinging to a renewed surge of hope, Joanna hurried over to a depression in the bluff wall where Ethan was lifting softball-size rocks and tossing them aside. She joined him in his excavation efforts, scraping aside armloads of mud and gravel until the entire pile of rubble bowed out and sank back in, as if the mountain itself were breathing.

"Ben?" She called to the man she could hear cursing and grunting and clearing rock from the opposite side.

Two more rocks. A little more gravel. Then a gritty

hand poked through. An arm followed. And then Ethan was pulling her back as the remaining pile collapsed and Ben Parrish emerged from the cave where he'd been buried alive.

"Oh, man." On apparently steady legs, he climbed out of his hidey-hole and swatted the dirt from his jeans and fatigue sweater. The white *FBI* letters on the Kevlar he wore had been dusted a dull, brownish gray. "That was exciting," he drawled.

Like Ethan, Joanna checked his light brown eyes for clarity and scanned him from head to toe for any signs of injury beyond the nicks and scrapes on his hands. If she could believe appearances, her fellow agent had survived in one piece. "Good thing you had that cave you could take cover in. Were you injured?"

Ethan had already completed that assessment and had a very different sort of question for him. "Could you pinpoint the source of the blast?"

Blast? Joanna's eyes widened. "You mean that rock slide was man-made?"

Ben nodded and apologized at the same time. "Almost straight above us. I'm going out on a limb and confirming that Watts stole some C-4 along with that truck." He summoned them both to follow him back over the pile of rubble into the cave that turned out to be about the size of her apartment's bedroom back in D.C. "This is a lot deeper than the others, thought I'd found a dry place for the night. I was heading inside when I hit a damn trip wire buried in the dirt across the opening." The two men squatted beside what was left of a filament that had been partially covered by the slide. "Looks like we don't just have the weather to contend with anymore. Watts has booby-trapped his trail."

Meanwhile, Joanna had pulled out her flashlight and was staring at the roof of the cave. The granite was gray, with bits of quartz and other sediment impurities sparkling with the reflection of her light. But there was one spot that was grayer, duller, than the rest of the cave. Joanna indicated the spot with her light. "Could this have been Watts's camp last night? There's evidence of smoke from a fire. I don't know how to tell if it's recent, though."

"It's recent," Ethan stated unequivocally. Joanna turned her light to the spot where he was digging in the dirt. He held up a palmful of dark, gravelly mud for her and Ben to inspect. "This ground has been freshly turned. Ashes from a wood fire have been mixed in." He squeezed the mud into a clump and tossed it at his feet as he stood. "I'd say Watts is covering his tracks in more ways than one."

Her pulse quickened with a jolt of anticipation. "So we're closing in on him?"

Ben reminded them that they weren't the only ones interested in capturing Sherman Watts. "I'll radio it in. Looks like we may need backup after all."

The rain seemed to wash away the dust that coated Ben almost as soon as he pulled the two-way from his pack and stepped outside. "Ute Base—this is Scout One. Ute Base, come in—do you read?" Static crackled. "I need to move farther away from the rocks to see if they can pick me up. "Ute Base—this is Scout One."

Joanna turned her attention back to Ethan, and waited for an answer. "Can you still find him? Or has this explosion obliterated any trace of him?"

His dark eyes didn't offer the immediate assurance she was used to seeing. "I don't know. I need to think this through. Maybe in the daylight—"

A distinctive pop of sound jerked through Joanna's body. She didn't have to hear the second shot, or the one after that, to pull her weapon and dive for cover.

Gunfire.

And they were the targets.

"DAMN IT, ETHAN, let go!"

Ethan had ducked behind the pile of rubble with Joanna, tugging on the back of her belt to hold her down beside him as she crawled to the top to try to pin down the shooter's position. "The shots are coming from above us."

"Exactly. We're sitting ducks down here."

She wiggled out of his protective grasp. "Then let me do my job." She spotted Agent Parrish first, running toward the edge of the bluff, firing blindly behind him. "Ben?"

"Under fire. Repeat, we are under fire!" His body jerked and he cursed. The radio smashed to the ground.

He was an open target.

When Joanna saw the circle of red blooming on the sleeve of his sweater, she knew she had to help him. "He's hit!"

Joanna scrambled down the other side of the rock pile and raised her gun to the flatland above the caves. From this angle, she couldn't make out the shooter, but that didn't matter. She could back him away from the edge. Keep him from getting close enough to shoot in this direction. She could protect Ben.

Steady. Breathe out. Squeeze the trigger.

Squinting against the rain assaulting her vision, she

fired off round after round, emptying her gun into the abyss above them, hopefully laying enough cover fire for Ben to drop down to a ledge or duck behind a boulder for safety. When her clip was spent, she fell back against the rocks and ejected her magazine.

But when she reached for the spare clip on her belt, Ethan's hands were already there, pushing the fresh ammo into her hand. "What are you doing? You're unarmed. Stay put."

"Like that command ever worked with you. Ben took one in the chest."

Joanna's heart sank. "No."

"It hit him in the Kevlar, but he went over the edge."

"Unless he caught a ledge or tree, that's at least thirty feet to the ground."

"Or the river." To her horror, Ethan wrapped her fingers around the magazine of bullets and squeezed her hand. He pointed out the silence overhead. "He's reloading. Cover me."

"Ethan!"

As quick as a coiled snake, he bolted behind a nearby boulder, then zigzagged out to a smaller one. The shots overhead started again, changed direction, zeroed in on Ethan's position. There was nothing more between him and the other side of that ledge big enough to hide behind. *Oh, hell.*

"Do it, girl." Joanna urged herself into action, locking the clip into place and sliding the first bullet into the chamber. "Now!"

Between the thunder and her gun and the shooter above, it was the loudest thirty seconds of Joanna's life.

"Ethan?" She wasn't the only one who'd stopped

firing when her clip was spent, but when she looked out across the outcropping of granite, she saw she was alone. She raised her voice. "Ethan? Where are you? Are you all right?"

He must have gone over the edge, as well. But on purpose, or… "Don't go there."

What she wouldn't give for clear skies and daylight. But she couldn't even risk shining her flashlight out there and giving their attacker—Watts, she presumed— a clear target.

"Don't be dead," she mouthed. "Please, God, don't be dead."

Huddled against the rocks at the base of the cliff, she squeezed her eyes shut and tried to listen to the world the way Ethan did, the way he'd taught her to all those years ago. She heard thunder, wild and deafening, up in the sky and rattling through the air around her. She heard her own crazy heartbeat, hammering in her ears. The wind whooshed past her. The rain pummeled the ground.

Or were those footsteps? The rustling of movement in the trees beyond the ledge? Or…it was no good. Her ears were still ringing from all the noise of the shoot-out. She couldn't even tell if the movement was real or imaginary, much less whether or not it came from above or below her.

"Think this through, Joanna." She climbed back over the top of the rubble and rolled down the other side into the cave, keeping a low profile until she was certain the danger had passed.

Her gun was empty; she had no more ammo. Ben was wounded, Ethan was missing and she was alone. That was the way she liked it, right? Alone? She'd built up her strength by learning to think and do for herself. Self-reliance was the only way to keep the Sherman Wattses of the world from having any power over her again.

But Ethan's share-your-strength-to-build-your-strength philosophy had gotten into her head and she couldn't seem to make clear choices and know her own mind the way she did back in D.C. Away from this place. Away from Watts.

Away from Ethan.

A purely emotional reaction, gut deep and as true as anything she'd ever known, chased away her logic. She had to go out there. She had to see if Ethan was all right. Ben, too.

But first, she had to secure the scene. Fears aside, she had to protect both men. To do that, she needed a weapon. Using her gun as a steel club again wouldn't be her first choice, but…

Ben Parrish.

She flipped on her light and searched the cave for Ben's backpack. "Yes."

She grabbed the pack and unclipped the top, turning it over to dump out the contents. He carried a bureau-issue Glock like her own. If he wasn't wearing it when he'd gone over the cliff, he'd have a spare magazine she could use. After she pulled out a reflective hypothermia blanket, water bottles and energy bars, other survival gear tumbled out—along with an entire box of 9 mm bullets. "That'll do."

As she sat down to restock both magazines, clip one onto her belt and load the other into her gun, she wondered just what kind of confrontation Ben had been expecting with Watts—or if the wisecracking agent was one of those macho men who simply hated to travel light. Either way, his excess was to her advantage, and she was on her way up and over the rubble that masked the cave opening.

Tucking her gun into the back of her belt for instant access, Joanna slid along the cliff wall until she reached the unaltered rock beyond the blast area above the cave. Then she turned and began to climb, searching for the holes and bumps and recesses in the granite where she could find a grip or place a toe. Her muscles were feeling the strain of the arduous day, and her bruised wrist ached each time she pulled her weight with her right arm.

Soon after she crested the top and crept over to inspect the area above the caves, Joanna realized that their attacker had abandoned his position. She recognized the path that could lead her on up to Rising Sun Creek, which was where Watts had most likely run off to hide. Instead of maintaining the pursuit on her own, she followed her nose in the opposite direction, to the source of the sulfuric odor of gunpowder lingering in the air. In addition to dozens of metal casings scattered across the rocks, an empty bottle of generic-label whiskey marked the dip where he must have lain. He would have been almost completely protected from every direction but the sky, and had a clear view of the outer ledge below.

Odd. "I thought Jack Daniel's was your brand."

She supposed a fugitive with little money in his pocket couldn't afford to be choosy. But then, she wouldn't have suspected that Sherman Watts would position himself like a sniper and take potshots at federal agents, either. Blowing up a mountain to cover his tracks so he could hide out like the weasel he was, accepting whatever collateral damage occurred, she could believe. But intentionally firing a kill shot at Ben Parrish?

Quit profiling. Help Ethan.

Joanna pocketed three of the casings for comparison later, but left the bottle. She wasn't up here to collect evidence. If Watts was gone, the scene was secure. Time to find Ethan and Ben. She climbed back down as quickly as slippery grips and sticky, rain-soaked clothes would allow.

"Ethan?" she shouted once more into the darkness, but the storm swallowed up the uneasy concern of her voice. "Where the hell are you, big guy?" she whispered.

"Is it clear?" Though it sounded as though it had come from miles away, Joanna swung her flashlight around, instantly drawn to the deep pitch of his voice. She saw a pair of big hands gripping the edge of the outcropping where Ben Parrish had fallen.

"We're clear!"

If that was a sniffle of relief, she ignored it. She was too busy running. "Ethan!"

A long, muscular leg appeared, hooking itself over the granite lip, and he pulled himself up onto the ledge.

Joanna was on her knees, dragging him back from the edge of the precipice, looking for anything more than the tear in his shirtsleeve or the scrape on his elbow to indicate he'd been hurt. When he pushed up onto his hands, Joanna tugged on his gear vest to help him sit up. She wound her arms around his neck and hugged him tight, his chest heaving in and out against her stomach as he struggled to catch his breath. His hands settled at

her hips. The strength of his grip indicated he was tired,
but he was holding on. He felt strong and solid and safe.

She kissed his temple. Kissed the chiseled angle of
his cheek. She pulled back just far enough to press a
hard kiss to his mouth. His fingers found a renewed
strength, turning to stretch down to the curve of her
bottom, to squeeze, to claim, to lift her to his mouth for
another kiss.

"Lord, woman. You'd think I'd been gone fifteen
years instead of fifteen minutes."

"Don't be sarcastic. That's not you, Ethan. I was
scared you'd been shot."

"Shh. I'm in one piece."

She hugged him again, needing the reassurance that
his body was whole and unharmed by feeling its warmth
and vitality with her own. "I found the shooter's position,
but I don't know. Something's not right. I don't want to
think that…" The stillness that engulfed him finally registered. He was breathing deeply and evenly; his heart
had steadied into a healthy rhythm. But the line of his
mouth was grim as she pulled back. "What's wrong?"

He rested one hand on her thigh. With the other, he
pulled a wet strand of hair from her cheek and smoothed
it all the way back to the band of her ponytail. "I know
I promised to find him for you, but we have to let Watts
go tonight."

Don't say it.

"I climbed all the way down to the rocks by the river.
I can't find Ben. Not even a body."

Joanna touched his face, cupped his jaw the way she
once had every time she greeted him or said goodbye.
He seemed to need her reassurance, her forgiveness,

even. She nodded her understanding. "I'll help you look for him. You said the second shot hit him in the vest. The first hit was an arm wound. Neither is fatal. If he didn't land on his head, he could have survived the fall."

"He could have been swept away by the river."

"And he could just be lost in the dark. We'll find him."

After a long silent moment, Ethan turned his lips into her palm and pressed a kiss there. "Look at you having hope." He nodded, approving, maybe even finding a little hope of his own to cling to. "Okay." The vacuum of energy surrounding him dissipated and he rolled to his feet, catching Joanna's hand and pulling her up beside him. "I'll scrounge up what gear I can. There's no way down to the river from this side except over the bluff now."

"Watts can wait." She found herself agreeing, and meaning it. "I'll call it in. We'll get helicopters and lights out here as soon as the storm has passed. We'll get all the help we need."

Her search for Ben's radio ended quickly.

They weren't getting any help after all.

The radio had been shot to pieces.

Chapter Eight

"It's definitely blood."

Ethan held his fingers out to the spray coming off the river that raced just below his feet and let it wash the sticky red goo from his fingers. He might be trailing a wounded animal as easily as a wounded man—if all he had to go on were the fading drops he'd found on the lee side of this cone-shaped boulder. But he'd never known any animal up on Ute Mountain to leave its blood trail in the shape of a partial handprint wrapped around the trunk of a small tree.

With a pair of flashlights to light the bluff on his second trip down, Ethan had been able to see where the roots of a small pine had ripped from the shallow, waterlogged soil. Ben Parrish must have grabbed on to it as he fell. The weakened tree couldn't catch him, but it must have held tight long enough to slow his descent and break his fall at the bottom.

Now, ten yards away, Ethan had found the second bloodstain. Ben must have stumbled straight into the river.

"With his injury, he might not have been able to make the climb back up." Joanna had to shout to be heard over the thunder of the water. "Or maybe with the shooting still going on, he swam across and went to get help."

Ethan threw out his arm like a crossing guard when Joanna slipped on the bank's muddy slope. She caught herself, ignored his arm and squatted down to shine her light on the blood. She was perfectly fine without his help. But the need to protect her was more powerful than ever. The worry that he might not be strong enough or smart enough or aware enough to provide that protection when she needed him most was just as troublesome.

Because it was just the two of them now. Just the two of them alone on the mountain like those long, balmy summer nights they'd shared when they were younger and more innocent. Like the night when he'd spread a blanket on a flowery knoll and they'd made love for the first time, under the stars.

Only this wasn't summer. The weather sucked. And there was nothing innocent about fugitives and explosions and missing, wounded FBI agents.

Though she probably didn't need his help getting up, either, Ethan still slipped his hand beneath her arm when she started to rise. He kept it there to turn her back up the slope.

But she planted her feet and tilted her chin. "Aren't we going across to see if we can pick up his trail on the other side?"

"No." He nudged. She balked.

"We're both strong swimmers. And it's not that wide."

"It's not the distance. It's the speed of the current and the rocks hidden below that worry me. We're not swimming in that death trap, period." That little dimple of a frown appeared on her forehead, and he could see the urge to argue the point with him flashing in her eyes. Surprise, surprise. But this was a small battle in the grand scheme of *discussions* they'd shared since her arrival some thirty-six hours ago. Why fight it? "There's a natural bridge about a mile down where we can cross."

The frown disappeared. "And then we can come back this far on the opposite bank to see if there's any sign that Ben climbed out on the other side."

She headed on out before he even reached the top of the bank. In a wave of sheer orneriness, fueled by a growing fatigue that was wearing down his keep-it-patient-and-polite filters, Ethan raised the beam of his light to the sweet sway of her tush. Now, *that* was the one piece of scenery he'd missed since coming back to Colorado. Yeah, that was a view he could follow all night long.

And judging by the pace Joanna set on the narrow but relatively flat strip of land, he just might have to. But he wasn't about to be outtracked by some wannabe city girl from Washington, D.C.

Night had fallen. Lightning flickered in the clouds overhead as the storm moved on and left a soft, steady rain in its wake. Ethan lengthened his stride and quickly caught up to Joanna. "You know, we could wait until dawn to continue the search. Or at least until the rain ends and we get some moonlight to guide us."

"If *I* was the one who fell over that cliff, would you wait for moonlight?" *She* was the one he was trying to look out for. If he was this tired, she must be running on fumes. "Besides, the land here runs through your veins. I bet you could track someone blindfolded if you had to."

He grunted a laugh. "I'm good. But I'm not that good."

"Don't be so modest, big guy. I think that's why you feel so at home here on the reservation and around the Four Corners area. You feel the earth and its secrets and power in your blood." Yet she never had, despite her curiosity to learn everything he had to teach. He'd always felt so settled, so strong here, whereas she'd been determined—destined, even—to move on. That's why he'd nicknamed her "the wind." *Nüa-rü* inhaled a deep breath before tilting a shy smile up to him. "That was one of the things that fascinated me about you when we first met. I remember when your brother, Kyle, bragged that you knew every rock and stalk of grass on Ute Mountain. I thought he was exaggerating, of course. I remember that first Saturday—Mother and Dad had chewed me out for not coming up with the money to bail them out of jail the night before. Where was I going to get four hundred dollars? They were lucky I could find enough money to put gas in the car so I could get to Towaoc and drive them home. And then they passed out on the couch. I don't think I ever really understood what kind of sickness their alcoholism was until that morning. That was the day I finally accepted that neither one of them was ever going to be the parent in our family. I was so mad. I had to get out of there."

Fifteen years and her matter-of-fact retelling of her sad, challenging childhood didn't change how hard it was to hear the things she'd grown up with. The best thing he could do for her then was just to listen.

He was still listening.

"I called Kyle to see if he wanted to hang out or shoot some hoops, and he said he and his big brother had made plans to go hiking, but that I was welcome to join you guys."

"I remember that day. You were, what, seventeen?"

Joanna nodded. "My first thought was 'boring,' but Kyle dared me to go. He said that if I didn't find the day interesting, then he'd buy my lunch for a week. And since I'd just spent my lunch money on gas, it sounded like a decent deal."

"Stinker. He should have bought you lunch, anyway."

She laughed. "I think he took pity on me and did."

"As I recall, you kept challenging me that day. You pointed to everything and said, 'What's this?' 'Where does that path lead?' I believe you were trying to stump me."

"I was," she admitted. "Of course, if you'd given me the wrong answer, I wouldn't have known it. I was so ignorant about nature back then. But even by the end of that first day…" Their pace finally slowed as she allowed herself to reminisce. "I knew you were someone unique, someone special. You had a bond to something so strong that it was almost supernatural to me. You understand the land in a way I never even understood my own family. I wanted to learn your secrets. I wanted to be like you. I wanted a connection like that."

Other than the rhythmic *swish-swish* of their sodden jeans rubbing together with every step, they walked the last few yards to the land bridge in silence. When they reached the rock arch that had been carved out by eons of the Silverton River pouring through its base, Ethan stopped and turned.

He reached for Joanna, even if she didn't need his help to make the step up. "*We* had a connection like that."

She seemed unsure of what to do with the outstretched hand. She was thinking again. Good thoughts? Regrets? But then she slid her palm into his and held on as he pulled her up beside him. "I know. But I destroyed it."

"Sherman Watts destroyed it." Ethan's grip flinched as the old guilt surged through him. "I should have kept you safe."

"I never blamed you. Not once."

"I know that. But you were mine to protect. My responsibility. And I failed you."

"*I* was the failure, Ethan. I didn't know how to fight for what I wanted." She laughed, but it was a sad sound. "I was so messed up, I didn't even know *what* I wanted." She tried to pull her hand away and bow her head, but Ethan wanted to hear this. Hear all of it, finally. No matter how painful it might be, he had to know why she'd left. After tucking his flashlight into his belt, he stroked his fingers across the cool dampness of her cheek and urged her to continue. "All I knew was that I wasn't happy. So, in my eighteen-year-old brain, that meant happiness must be somewhere else. I kind of came up with my own twelve-step plan. Go to college and get a career so I could earn some respect, make some money so I wouldn't be broke every day of my life. Turn myself into somebody who was strong enough to stand up to Sherman and Elmer Watts and others like them. It was too late to do it for myself here on the rez, but I could do it for others. That'd be a bit of payback, and maybe no one else would have to go through what I did."

"So you reinvented yourself as Joanna Rhodes, a smarter, tougher version of the girl I knew. Bound and determined to save her own day."

A wry smile crooked the corner of her lush, pale lips. "I thought I was just surviving. But that does sound like I'm trying to be Superwoman, doesn't it?"

"Sounds like a different story to me. Come on." He urged her ahead of him onto the almost stairlike path of rock worn between the grasses and moss that covered the top of the bridge. With his hand enjoying the delightful assignment of resting on her backside to steady her along the steepest part of the path, he asked, "Did I ever tell you the legend of Sleeping Ute Mountain?"

"I know that if you look at the Ute Mountains from about twenty miles away, their profile looks like a giant Indian lying down on his back. One slope creates his knees, the highest peak forms arms crossed over his chest. There are toes that stick up, a headdress that tapers down to the town of Towaoc."

She'd paid attention in social studies class. With the rain making the mossy stones extra slick, he had her sit to shimmy safely down the opposite side. "You're talking about the shape of the rocks. I'm talking about the ancient story behind them."

He heard her laughing above the spray from the river hitting the rocks below them. "Tell me the story, oh wise one. I'm sure there's a lesson to be learned here."

"The discount version is that in the very old days, the Sleeping Ute Mountain was a Great Warrior God. He came to fight against the Evil Ones in the land. Their battle created the mountains and valleys in the Four Corners area."

"And the blood from the battle created the creeks and rivers?"

"You always were a quick student."

"Fourth in my class at Yale. First in my class with you." She held his hand to pull herself to her feet, then eyed the distance between the rocks and the grassy field beyond and leaped across the muddy bank. "Just how does this legend pertain to me?

Ethan followed her over the mud and continued. "The Great Warrior God defeated the Evil Ones, but he was so wounded that he lay down to rest and fell into a deep sleep. Our ancestors believed that when he is needed, the Great Warrior God will rise again to help them in the fight against their enemies."

"So, the men who murder FBI agents, and rape teenage girls—they're the Evil Ones. And since you're such a part of the land here, you're the Warrior God fighting our modern battle."

"No." He gripped the straps of his pack in front of his chest and looked down at her. She was tall and bed-raggled and muddy and gorgeous as she watched him with those dark, expectant eyes. "You are."

Joanna's gaze dropped to the center of his chest. "Nice story." When she looked at him again, he could see she didn't believe. "I don't belong here. I've spent fifteen years making a point of *not* belonging."

"You were born of this place, Joanna. You spent a year with me on this mountain. Yes, you went to Yale, went to Quantico, went to D.C. But you came back when we needed…when your people needed you." He touched the corners of her mouth, nudging it into a smile again. "And the warrior name fits. As I recall, you were the one doing the ass-kicking up at the caves above Cougar Fork."

That earned him a genuine laugh. "That's only because you don't like guns."

"That's because you're fighting for something—the safety of the people on this mission. Justice. Truth. You're a warrior goddess who has returned to help us fight our enemies again."

Her smile didn't need one dot of makeup to turn his head. "Warrior goddess. I like that a lot better than Superwoman."

"It fits." Ethan dipped his head, and when her gaze locked on to his and she didn't pull away, he pressed a kiss to that smile. Joanna's lips were wet and cool with the rain. But after that first tentative contact, they softened and warmed, and parted to welcome him.

He'd have thought a shared conversation, a long walk and a gentle kiss would take him back in time to when he and Joanna first became lovers. But as her fingers curled up beneath his collar and latched on to his neck, as his hands found her hips and pulled her trim curves into the harder lines of his body, as her husky moan matched a similarly needy sound in his throat, Ethan discovered he was firmly rooted in *this* moment. With this particular woman. The old memories were there, yes, but he was making new ones tonight. He tasted the heat inside Joanna's mouth. Their wet clothes sparked a delicious friction and left little to the imagination as she rubbed against him, stretching up on tiptoe to alter and deepen the angle of the kiss.

And Ethan obliged the unspoken request. He was a mature man now, one who'd seen the miracles of life and the worst of death and whose character had been shaped by both. The hunger he felt for this woman went far deeper than the lustful innocence of his youth. His blood surged, his heart opened. He *needed* this connection to be whole again. He found solace in her acceptance, healing in her desire for him. He widened his stance and pulled her into the throbbing response of his body. He cupped the nape of her neck, cradling her head as he plunged his tongue inside her mouth, mimicking all the sweet, sensual things he wanted to do with the rest of her strong, beautiful body.

Ethan wasn't recapturing a sweet moment from the past. He was laying claim to everything he wanted for his future.

If only the woman was willing.

If only she could see a future with him.

A guilty conscience made one hell of a chaperone. He had promises to keep. One, he'd made to Joanna a long time ago—the other, just last night. And neither of them involved throwing her down in a muddy field and making love to her.

"Joanna." He skimmed his lips along her jaw and nuzzled the soft skin beneath her ear. He needed to pull back, to curb the eager wants of his body, to guard his heart before he screwed up the rest of his life by falling in love all over again with a woman determined to leave him. "We need to stop."

"We should." But her lips brushed against his neck, sending a shiver of desire straight down to his groin. His fingers tightened their grip in her hair. "It's been so long since I've wanted…anyone. I'm not afraid when you touch me. I…want…you to touch me."

Ah, sweet mercy. He was fighting to be a good guy here. He nuzzled the wet silk of her hair. She smelled of earth and rain and everything he'd ever wanted.

But he needed to pull it back. They had a job to do. People were counting on them. *She* was counting on him to help her accomplish this crazy-ass mission to bring in Sherman Watts and square off against him in an interview room.

That was what she'd asked of him.

And that was what he'd give her.

"I can't, baby. Not right now. I shouldn't." Reaching down beneath the soles of his boots, Ethan called on a will more powerful than his own to unwind her arms from his neck and pull his lips from the smooth caramel cream of her skin. He cupped her shoulders and put a good six inches of space between them. The rain would cool their clothes and the sensitized skin beneath soon enough. Until the wet and chill and discomfort could steal the moment back, Ethan rested his forehead against hers, savoring the warm breeze of her ragged breaths caressing his cheek, closing his eyes to imprint this precious, tentative connection to Joanna in his mind forever.

"You're right. Bad timing. Job to do." Too sarcastic. Too tough. That was Agent Rhodes talking.

"Listen to me, *Nüa-rü.*" He opened his eyes to absorb the natural beauty of her long dark lashes resting against her cheeks. His own pulse beat like a war drum in his ears, drowning out his brain's attempts to send a message of control to his hormones. "I want to be with you the way the earth wants to see some sunshine tomorrow. But I have to make sure we're in a safe place for the night." A vague notion of the wind shifting or the barometric pressure dropping—of some change in the world outside this cooling embrace crept across his senses.

"And I want to look for Ben a little longer tonight. I—"

Her eyes popped open and looked straight up into his. She heard it, too. "Is that the river?"

"Is that thunder?" they asked in unison.

They separated, turned, searched.

The percussive noise was steady, mechanical—and growing louder by the second.

"Ethan, helicopter!" Joanna pointed to the blinking lights in the northern sky, coming in across the meadow and picking up altitude to clear the bluffs across the river. She waved her arms and shouted. "Hey! Down here!" She turned and gave him a smile. "They must be looking for us. Where's my flashlight?" She ran toward the oncoming bird, fumbling to get her light switched on while she was moving. "Base camp must have gotten at least some of Ben's last radio call and sent it in to pick us up. Get your light. Hurry!"

"Joanna, wait." Ethan jogged after her, feeling less sure about a rescue. Martinez had been adamant about grounding the official helicopter until it was safe enough to fly. "Joanna!"

"Hey! Come back!"

But it whipped past overhead without any indication that the pilot or passengers had seen them.

She was breathing hard from her run by the time he caught up to her. "So much for a rescue. Maybe it was one of those tourist helicopters that flies guests around to show them the scenery. Do they still do that here?"

"Yeah. But not at night. I don't think they were looking for us or the scenery."

Joanna turned, letting him read the thought processes on her face. She'd figured it out, too. "He was flying at night without using a spotlight. He wasn't looking for anything."

Ethan braced his hands on his hips and nodded agreement. "That's something else we'll have to report when we reach base camp. Somebody violated the sheriff's no-fly order. If Watts saw that, too, he'll go even deeper into hiding."

"Unless Watts has a friend with a helicopter who'd give him a ride out of the country?"

"I doubt it."

"Me, too. Although the trace I found at the shooter's position on top of the cave bluff…"

"What?"

"It made me think that Watts wasn't the man shooting at us. That someone else is on the mountain."

"Like who?"

"Maybe that shoe print Miguel Acevedo found *does* belong to Boyd Perkins."

A hit man on the mountain with them? Ethan scanned the limited horizon, automatically sizing up the places where a man could hide—or where a couple could safely escape for the night. That was a dangerous complication this already messed-up search didn't need. They needed to get moving. "Did you see a similar print up top?"

Joanna shook her head. "It was all rock. It's just that what I saw there wasn't what I would have expected from Watts. But then maybe he's trying to throw us off his trail again. Besides, if Boyd Perkins was here, he'd be going after Watts to keep him from talking, not shooting at us, right?"

Ethan wrapped his hand around Joanna's elbow and pulled her into step beside him to get them off the open field and back to the relative safety of the trees and rocks. "I suppose that makes logical sense."

All of a sudden, Joanna planted her feet and twisted her arm from Ethan's grasp. "Wait a minute. The helicopter—you don't think…?"

"What? That Perkins flew in, found where Watts was hiding and killed him?" He started walking again. "I doubt it. Watts thinks like a rat. My guess is he's holed up somewhere nice and tight for the night."

She hurried to catch him. "So what's our next step? Keep looking for Ben?"

"I say we wait and give one last look for him in the morning. The storm will have passed by then, and we'll have the light so we can move quickly and efficiently. Maybe allow ourselves an hour to search. Then we'll need to head on down to base camp to make our report—at least get close enough so we can use a cell phone to call in his disappearance."

"And Watts?"

Ethan stopped, faced her, pinched her chin between his thumb and forefinger. "I said I'd find him for you. It may be delayed a day or so, but I intend to keep that promise. I'll be back out here tomorrow after we handle Ben's disappearance. I'll pick up Watts's trail again."

She closed her fingers around his wrist and pulled it from her chin. But instead of releasing him, she laced her fingers with his, letting him know that she was in this hunt with him for just as long as it took. "So we wait until daylight to resume our search. What are we going to do tonight?"

Ethan tugged on her hand and headed back toward the natural bridge. He already had a plan. "We told HQ we'd be staying on the mountain tonight. I know a dry place where we can warm up and get some sleep."

"Can you find it at night?"

"I could find it blindfolded if I had to."

SHERMAN WATTS STRAINED with the effort it took to keep the sapling bent at an angle while he tied it off. He pushed harder with his legs, tried to make his cold fingers work faster. One. More.

There. He held his breath as he backed away. *Nice work, Sherm. You always were good with your hands.*

"You know it." The voice in his head was female. Familiar. Though strangely out of place. He shook his head to clear the phantoms from his mind, and wound up shaking the ball bearings back and forth inside his skull. "Son of a bitch."

Clutching the brim of his hat, he pulled it down on either side of his head, as though he could keep the raging headache from leaking out of his ears. He plopped down on his backside in the brush and closed his eyes, waiting for the world to stop spinning.

He was in serious need of a drink and racing toward dehydration. He might have laughed at the ironic thought if his stomach wasn't crawling with hunger and he could catch a decent breath.

Where had he gone wrong? What mistake had he made that ended up with him hiking back down toward Marble Mountain and Towaoc? No way could he get back to his borrowed truck and Mesa Ridge or his uncle. The cops would have watches posted around anything remotely connected to him. He couldn't even call his anonymous "friend" at the crime unit and beg a favor. Of course, he shouldn't have needed to. His plan should have worked.

He'd made it all the way up to Rising Sun Creek and had erected a lean-to. He was set to stay up there right until the first snows began to fall again. When he'd heard the blast and rock slide behind him, he knew he'd just cut off any easy access to his remote location. In fact, he'd been feeling so damn fine sure of himself that he'd opened his pack and pulled out his fishing tackle. He'd had to chunk up some of the ice near the bank to get water to drink, but in the deeper pools, he'd be able to find something small and tasty and fresh to grill over a fire.

As far as he was concerned, life didn't get any better than that. The law could just go hang their sorry selves if they thought they were going to mess up *this* gig for him. A man didn't need thousands of dollars and the pressure of answering to any boss, or anyone, period, in order to be happy.

Yeah, he'd toss a line in…

Paradise had ended abruptly when the shooting started.

Sherman dropped his pole, cursed as he watched the current catch it and take it downstream to get jammed in the ice and snapped in two. He'd scrambled back to the lean-to for his pack, had to dig all the way to the bottom of it to find his gun—broke his last new bottle of whiskey in the process.

He'd thrown himself to the ground, crawled on his belly like a snake to the edge of his lookout position. But by the time he'd reached any kind of vantage point, the gunfire had stopped. "What the hell is goin' on?"

Must have been kids from the rez playing with their daddies' guns—kids he'd like to take a stick to for messin' up his… But then the shooting started again. Did the cops think they'd found something? Had they somehow gotten past the caves and picked up his trail again? Did they think they were going to corner him up here like a pack of huntin' dogs surrounding their quarry?

Sherman had lain there in the rain and the muck for a good forty-five minutes before he realized the cops weren't coming. He'd laughed at his success, craved a drink to celebrate it.

He sat up with the sobering thought that if the cops hadn't been shooting at him, then he'd been royally screwed. What were the chances of someone else hiding out on Ute Mountain? Someone armed and dangerous and reckless enough to exchange gunfire with those pesky federal agents?

He hadn't wasted any time pondering about who else might be on the mountain, or what his purpose might be. He wasn't running from just the cops now.

He was running from Boyd Perkins.

Smart money would have bet on him to stick to the high ground because it was so much harder to reach. The chopper he'd heard flying overhead confirmed that as it headed toward the summit of Ute Mountain. That's why he'd chosen this spot down in the gully at the base of Marble Mountain. Perkins wouldn't think to look down here. The trees would warn him if anyone got too close. He could catch some shut-eye now before he made the long trek into Towaoc tomorrow. Once there, he could borrow some wheels and drive down to Mexico.

Then the cops couldn't harass him, Perkins couldn't kill him, and he'd live happily ever after. Maybe he'd change his drink to tequila and live another fifty-eight years just fishing off the end of a boat. Nah. The money here in Kenner County had been good while it lasted, but he didn't need it. It was a good plan.

I don't know anybody more resourceful than you, Sherm. The woman's voice praised him, comforted him. The voice in his head probably should have freaked him out because that sweet, loving woman had abandoned him a long time ago.

But he was tired. He was wet. He was cold.

Lying down, he pulled his pack beneath his head, turning his nose to the tangy scent of sour mash that permeated the damp canvas. With his fingers resting on the gun tucked at the front of his belt, he curled up on the ground with his traps, his headache, his memories of Naomi Kuchu to keep him warm and fell asleep.

Chapter Nine

"I found some more dry fuel in the underbrush. Should be enough to keep the fire going through the night." Ethan announced himself, tossing up an armload of dead tree branches he'd harvested before hoisting himself up and entering the cave again. The last time he'd climbed up without a word, a startled Joanna had whirled around, her Glock poised to blow a hole right in the middle of his chest.

Several apologies and assurances later, he'd gotten a small fire started near the mouth of the raised cave. They'd shared an intimate dinner of energy bars and bottled water by the firelight, and then he'd excused himself to make one more check on the security of their camp farther downstream on the bluff side of the Silverton River.

"The rain's keeping everything quiet," he said, pulling himself in and shoving the wood against the granite wall. "I think we should be able to sleep for a good—"

This time, Ethan was the startled one. He turned around and froze in his tracks.

"I asked you to wait. Didn't you hear?"

How was a healthy man supposed to hear anything when every drop of blood in him was swimming straight south of his belt buckle?

"Ethan?" Joanna stood beside a boulder where she'd laid out her vest and blouse and turtleneck to dry in front of the fire. The wet jeans she'd hurriedly tried to pull on were stuck between her knees and calves and slowly sliding back down toward her feet as she modestly crossed one arm over her breasts and the other over the plain white panties she wore. "You're staring."

"It's still the prettiest view on the whole mountain." She might have blushed, but his gaze hadn't made it up that far yet.

Suddenly, his own soggy clothes felt sticky and hot. She'd spread out their hypothermia blankets on the dirt floor, and though he was sure there was nothing more to it than creating a place to sleep, his body read it as a blatant invitation. And his pulse was tapping out a definite RSVP.

There was a lot to be said for the sexiness of basic underwear, especially when there were so many miles of taut golden skin stretched out in between. The firelight dappled her long, lean curves with a rosy warmth, and he was inspecting every inch of it, from the dimples beside her knees to her hollow little belly button and the nip of her waist to…

"Do you mind turning around?"

"Yeah." He grinned like a schoolboy, ached like a man who'd been too long without the one woman who haunted his dreams.

She muttered something and turned her back to him to battle with the wet denim again. Though, to his way of thinking, this view was just as enticing. "I remember when you used to be a gentleman about things like this."

And he remembered when she'd come flying apart in his arms, all breathless and wide-eyed with wonder, and had asked him when they could do it again.

"I've missed you," he whispered on a ragged breath.

The jeans had made it up to her thighs before she hugged her arms around herself and glanced back over her shoulder. "What am I supposed to say to that?"

"Nothing. I'm turning." Summoning a strength he didn't know he possessed, he managed to turn and study the layers of strata in the wall without really seeing them. "There were so many nights I needed…I needed what we had. I needed you. After that day, did you ever once need…me?"

He breathed in deeply, tried to steady his pulse, tried to look away. But the movement of her hopping on one leg to slide into those uncooperative wet pants drew his attention. The gentle bounce of her breasts, hidden by nothing more than a strip of lace and her long, dark hair, kept it.

"Forget the jeans. We both need to dry off so we can stay warm tonight. Here." He unzipped his vest and draped it over another rock, then went to work on the buttons of his shirt.

"What are you doing?"

"Practical survival. Come on. Lose the pants. I promise to be a gentleman if you promise to avoid hypothermia."

"You're going to strip down to your undies and expect me to think that nothing's going to happen between us tonight?"

He forced himself to turn away and peel off his shirt and the insulated Henley he wore underneath. That was the hell of loving a woman, he supposed. His own body could simmer away unfulfilled, and he wouldn't complain so long as she was taken care of. That was true with this one, especially, who'd already been victimized by men she should have been able to trust.

Ah, hell. A familiar fist punched him in the gut as he imagined just what Sherman Watts and his uncle had said and done to her. Ethan had to say something to lighten his mood, or he'd wind up scaring her further with his own anger. "Well, I prefer to call them boxers or shorts, but I promise, nothing's going to happen tonight unless you ask me."

"But you…" Instead of finishing that argument, she pointed to the unmistakable bulge pushing at the front of his unzipped jeans.

He was sitting on the rock, untying his boots, but he quickly pushed to his feet. "Would you feel more comfortable if I slept outside?"

She seemed to consider it for a moment. But then she shook her head. "You'll freeze."

"Joanna…" He turned away from those big, dark doe eyes and stretched the shirt back over his head. He'd endured worse than arousal on a cold night. "No way in hell do I ever want to say or do anything that reminds you of that bastard."

"Hey." When her fingers brushed the middle of his bare back, he jerked. "Whoa."

With a shared startle like that, he would have expected her to withdraw her touch. But not the Warrior Goddess with the strength to conquer demons. Instead of pulling away, she flattened her hand against his skin, burning him straight down to his bones. But he supposed what he was feeling inside didn't necessarily broadcast through the rest of his body.

"You're chilled already." He looked down over the jut of his shoulder to see the concern stamped on her courageous features. "We're mature enough to handle this. We both need to be strong for tomorrow. And we'll move faster if our clothes have a chance to dry. Confined space, small fire, shared body heat—that's the only way we'll stay warm tonight." She even had the strength to stand there gloriously half-dressed, and smile. "So, you and your boxer shorts are welcome to stay with me."

God, he wanted her. But he wanted—he needed— something else from her even more. He tossed the shirt back over the rock and faced her. "Just to sleep."

"Unless I ask."

"You trust me to do that?"

Those beautiful earth-colored eyes locked on to his for the longest time before she nodded. "I trust you."

Her words were a true gift. One that erased fifteen years of guilt.

By the time Ethan had finished stripping down to his socks and Skivvies, Joanna was sitting on the hypothermia blankets she'd spread on the relatively flat cave floor. "Go ahead and lie down closer to the fire, otherwise I'll block the heat." He untied his knife from his belt and carried it to the far side of their makeshift bed. "Will it bother you if I sleep with this?"

She reached beneath the blankets and pulled out her gun. "Will it bother you if I sleep with this?"

He laughed and lay down beside her, flat on his back with his fingers lightly clasped over his chest. "I'm definitely keeping my hands to myself unless you okay it."

"It's not for you."

He dismissed her apologetic look with a smile and patted the blanket beside him. "I know. Come on over here. Body heat doesn't work unless we're closer."

At first she lay down on her left side, facing the fire. Ethan matched her position, scooting up behind her and pulling the top blanket over them. He had his left arm curled beneath his head for a pillow, but his right arm couldn't seem to find a comfortable—impersonal— place to settle. Stretching it out along the length of his body put a hitch in his shoulder. He tried resting it on Joanna's hip, but even as he recognized a possessive sense of rightness by claiming the curve, she squirmed. So he moved it a little higher to let it curve over her waist. But she twisted again, hunching her shoulders and moving away from him.

"Joanna." He pulled his arm away and rolled onto his back with a sigh. With a granite mattress beneath them, it was no surprise to feel her still wriggling to find a comfy position. But he suspected this was something more. "Are you sure you don't want me to sleep outside? I take up a lot of room. Maybe more than you might be comfortable with."

"No. It's just…" She rolled onto her back and turned her face to his. "I don't want you behind me. I thought it wouldn't matter, but…I haven't actually *slept* with a man since…" She squeezed her eyes shut, working past a tough moment, before opening them again and boldly meeting his gaze. "That's how Watts—"

Ah, hell. Ethan didn't need to hear the rest of that ex-planation. He shifted onto his side and pulled Joanna into his arms, lying with her face-to-face, settling her cheek on the pillow of his shoulder. Their legs tangled together and he hugged her tight. She didn't have to say another word as she curled her arms between them and settled against him with a sigh.

He brushed her hair off her face and let it fall down her back. "Better?"

She closed her eyes and he felt the tension leave her body. "Much."

Much better. He smiled over her head, watching the light from the fire dance across the walls of the cave. His body was a little worse for wear, his bed was hard, but Ethan felt as though he was settling in for the best sleep of his life. He pressed a kiss to Joanna's temple. "Good night, *Nüa-rü*."

"Good night, Ethan."

An hour or so later, the storm had eased into a light patter of rain and Ethan was dozing in a pool of languid heat. He had Joanna in his arms. They were hidden and safe. He'd just added some more wood to the fire to at least keep the embers glowing until dawn.

But something wasn't right. There was a low, almost moaning sound filtering into his dreams. Then he became aware of something lightly tapping against his chest and he roused himself to take clear stock of his surroundings.

The touches became the unintended caress of Joanna's fingers bumping against him as she twisted and worked her fingers in that nervous habit of hers. The moan became a whisper of words. "Just say it. He'll never hurt you. You can do this."

"Hey."

Joanna fell silent as soon as she realized he was awake.

"Who are you talking to?" He wrapped one hand around both of hers, stilling their fretting movements. She held herself so still, so stiffly, that Ethan grew immediately concerned. He brushed her hair off her face to read the clarity of her eyes. "You weren't having a nightmare, were you?"

She shook her head. "I was psyching myself up."

"For what?"

"You don't have any protection, do you?"

Ethan reached for his knife and sat up, instantly on alert. "Did you hear something?"

"No." She pushed his hand and his knife back to the ground, sitting up beside him. "Not that kind of protection."

If this was a dream, Ethan had no intention of waking up.

"I want you. I want to try."

JOANNA FELT AS THOUGH it were her first time all over again when Ethan returned to the blankets and pulled her on top of him. "I think you should know that I…" With one forearm propped atop his chest, she traced the column of his neck and the strong line of his shoulder with her finger. It was a shy, girlish thing to do, but she didn't want to spook him or herself by moving things along as quickly as her feverish body seemed to want. "I'm not any more experienced at this kind of stuff than I was before the rape."

His dark eyes reflected the firelight and seemed to glow from within. The tiny muscle that pulsed along his jaw revealed anger on her behalf that she'd been forced that way, but those beautiful onyx eyes showed her nothing but patience and desire. "Anything you want, *Nüa-rü*. Anything you don't want. You tell me. I want this to be right for you."

He was all heat and muscle, coppery-skinned and supple right down to the waistband of his black shorts. He was such a big, broad specimen of masculinity that even with her tall, athletic frame, Joanna felt feminine and delicate, by comparison. "Can we just start slow and see where it goes? Is that asking too much?"

When she drew her finger across the tension in his jaw, he turned and caught the tip of her finger with his lips and gave it a delicate suckle that seemed pull a taut response from deep inside her. "Anything," he reminded her.

And for now, that *anything* meant taking their time reacquainting themselves with each other's body. Moving in no more of a hurry than the gentle rain falling outside, they touched with their hands and toes, their lips and bodies.

As Joanna tasted the smooth line of his jaw, she curled her toes against the rougher texture of his leg. Ethan settled his palm over the curve of her bottom, warming her skin through the thin layer of cotton between them. If she wasn't kissing his mouth, then his lips were busy exploring her eyelids, her cheek, the newly discovered bundle of nerves beneath her right ear.

She nuzzled his skin at the juncture where his neck and shoulder met and breathed in the invigorating smells of rain and the outdoors. She touched her lips to the point of his chin, gently nipping at the salty tang of his skin there. He lifted the weight of her hair and drew lazy circles that tickled the skin of her nape, making her muscles bunch and quiver, again and again, creating a growing friction between their stomachs and chests with each helpless shimmy.

Her legs parted and caught his thick, muscular thigh in between. When he bent his knee, pressing against the warmest, neediest part of her, a knot of molten heat ignited at her core.

Joanna buried her face against his neck and moaned at the pressure building inside her. Her skin was extra sensitive to every touch, her lips extra needy to every kiss. The warmth inside grew fluid and flowed through her blood like a river rising, growing with speed and power. Every sensation felt new, unfamiliar, as if her body had forgotten what it felt like to be sexual. To want. To catch fire and need a thing the way she needed Ethan.

"You keep making sweet sounds like that, babe, and I don't know how much longer I can handle slow and easy." His voice vibrated against her skin like a drowsy caress.

"Touch me, Ethan. So I can really feel it. Touch me."

He stroked his big hands—callused and firm enough to arouse, gentle enough to soothe and reassure—up and down her back. Each pass of his hands was slightly different. He reached between them to skim his thumbs over the tips of her breasts, to flick, to tease. He reached a little lower the next time to slip inside her panties to squeeze her bottom, to move her hips over the heavy evidence of his arousal.

"More," she begged, catching his bottom lip between her teeth and giving him a gentle nip.

He laughed deep in his throat and gave her lip the same little nip.

"More."

"You're sure?"

"I'm sure."

The next pass of his hands unhooked her bra. In another move, the bra was gone and he was lifting her, dragging her up to claim her breast with his mouth. He swirled his tongue around the hard button at the tip, then pulled on it. Gently, harder. Gentle again. Then more demanding, until Joanna was writhing on top of him, wanting more, wanting everything.

"Ethan…" she gasped. "Ethan."

He sat up, spilling her onto his lap, dipping his head to catch the other, neglected breast in his mouth and torment her with his tongue. She raked her fingers across his scalp and held him against her. "Tell me what you want, babe."

"I want you. Now," she demanded.

He raised his head and smiled against her mouth before he claimed it in a deep, drugging kiss. In a matter of seconds, her panties were gone, his shorts were off and she was back in his lap with his sheathed, throbbing desire nudging against her.

He brushed her hair off her face and smoothed its length down the line of her back. In a moment of calm before the certain storm, he rested his forehead against hers, looking deep into her eyes, deep inside her. "This is what you want?"

Would he really stop now? Yes. If she asked it of him. Because he was Ethan—her teacher, her lover, her protector and friend. He was the earth that gave an anchor to her wind.

"I want this," she assured him, winding her arms around his neck and lifting herself against the wall of his chest, feeling herself primed and ready to become a sexual woman again. "As long as I can see your face. I want to know it's you."

He pulled her legs out on either side of him, his hands guiding her into position in his lap. He'd decided not to crush her with his weight. Whether it was consideration for the hardness of the floor or the trauma of her past, it was a beautiful thing to do. With two fingers he pointed to his eyes. "You look right here, *Nüa-rü*. Right here."

She held her breath as he entered her. She didn't blink or look away as her body adjusted to the size and feel of him inside her.

"You okay?" he asked. She could see it in his face, in the stretch of muscles across his chest, what it was costing him to be so patient with her.

She nodded, smiled, loved him for it. "I think I'm going to be better than okay. I can do this. With you, I can do this."

And then, with a kiss, with his arms wrapped tightly around her, he began to move inside her. He showed her what it was to want a man, to trust a man, to be with a man again.

Had she ever felt this alive? This whole? This desired? Her entire world was this man, this moment. There was no past. There was no tomorrow. There were no fears. No doubts. No fifteen years apart. There was just her. And Ethan.

She tipped her head back, her cries of joy echoing inside the cave as he brought her to the peak of pleasure and they tumbled down the other side, together.

ETHAN WOKE AGAIN, some time later, with a naked woman sprawled like the best kind of blanket across his chest. The relative silence of the cave told him the rain had finally stopped and the fire was dying. He felt warm, rejuvenated, content. His arms and heart were full, his world in perfect alignment. With Joanna in his arms, he was at peace.

"I'd forgotten how hard you sleep…right after. Don't worry. I kept an eye on things while you were out."

"*You* were watching over *me?*"

"Warrior Goddess and all that, remember?"

He smiled at the voice that didn't know whether to be shy or seductive. Joanna had always managed to be an intriguing mixture of both. He opened his eyes to find her serene smile just in reach of his lips, and he lifted his head to gently claim them. "You okay?"

"I'm better than I thought I'd be. No regrets."

Words of healing to a once-broken heart. "Me, either."

When he rested his head back on the blanket, she settled in on top of him. "I think one of us wound up with the more comfortable bed last night. How are you doing?"

He propped one hand beneath his head and with the other, played with the midnight silk of her hair, smoothing the tangles, crumbling a tiny clump of dried mud and brushing it away. "I've had worse nights, believe me."

"So. When can we do it again?"

Ethan laughed. "I guess some things never change, do they?" Catching her around her waist, he rolled them onto their sides facing each other. Her long hair tumbled over her face and he loved catching it and combing his fingers through it all the way to the ends as he pulled it back and took in his fill of her classic Native American features and long, lithe body.

But then, some things did change. His eyes and fingers were drawn to the small white scar that marked the golden tan at the top of her left breast. "Is this what he did to you?"

She batted away his hand and quickly covered the spot with her own. "Does that turn you off?"

"No. Hell no." He dipped his head and kissed the mark. Then he caught her mouth and gave her a hard kiss, telling her in no uncertain terms just how beautiful she was to him. "It's a badge of honor. Of all you've been through. Of how you survived. But when I'm reminded of how much you were hurt, I just…" His fingers clenched convulsively at her waist.

"You want to hurt *him?*" Were his coarser, unenlightened instincts that obvious? She pried his hand from her waist and laced her fingers together with his. "Get in line. My therapist said those kinds of feelings are healthy and normal. Unless you get obsessive about it, of course. It's okay to feel anger. To feel rage. Some days you don't, as time goes on. More days than not. And sometimes it hits you so hard you want to scream or punch something. That's normal, too."

"But I'm not the one who was hurt."

"You were collateral damage, Ethan. And I'm sorry for the part I played in that."

"Leaving me wasn't your fault."

"It wasn't my fault I got raped, either. It still hurts, though, doesn't it?" No argument there. Her dark eyes showed an understanding he was just now beginning to accept. "It changes how you deal with people, how you live your life."

And there the understanding stopped. The connection he and Joanna had resurrected during their time here on the mountain was destined to end.

Joanna dealt with life by committing herself to a career because it was safer than committing herself to a relationship. He'd made love to Joanna Kuchu last night. But FBI agent Joanna Rhodes was leaving come Monday, or as soon as they found Watts and her interview was finished.

Then he and Joanna would be finished.

Again.

The predawn chill filled the cave. Their fire must have died.

Ethan pressed one last kiss to her lips and sat up, bracing his elbows against his knees, steeling himself for the day ahead. Trying desperately to steel his heart against loving her, as well. "Looks like the sun will be up soon. We'd better get dressed."

She sat up beside him, pulling the crinkly blanket up over her breasts and laying a gentle hand on his arm. "Do we need to talk about this?"

No. Talking wouldn't make the inevitable any easier to take. Ethan pushed to his feet and walked buck naked over to the fire pit to stir the embers and add the last of the fuel. "I'll get us some fresh water we can heat up. I've got a couple of coffee packs in my bag."

Joanna squinched up her face, accepting the abrupt change in topic, if not necessarily approving the avoidance tactic. "Not that nasty stuff you used to bring on camping trips? Why don't you just boil some tree bark?"

"Hey. It survives anything and it's hot." He pulled on

his shorts and jeans and checked the dryness of his boots. "You want to crimp your taste buds, try eating MREs for a month."

"That's right. Elizabeth said you served a stint in the army. That you went to Afghanistan. That explains the haircut."

He let the boots sit for a few minutes longer and picked up his shirts. "Six years as an army ranger. I specialized in casualty recovery."

"Casualty...?" The crinkle of stiff material told him Joanna had risen. She wrapped the material around her as she began to dress. "You brought back the dead?"

"Or wounded. Or lost."

"Search and rescue. Why doesn't that surprise me? You've done that your whole life, haven't you—finding souls and saving them?"

"No." He thought of that night in his truck when Joanna had left him. He thought of Sam Keller putting a gun to his head in the middle of a battlefield because he'd seen too much blood and death. Saving souls? Ethan hadn't saved the ones who counted the most. "Sometimes, I lose them."

She wasn't a fool to miss the hidden meaning in that remark. But he was done with this conversation.

"Gear up. If we don't find any trace of Ben in an hour, we're heading back down to base camp."

Chapter Ten

"Nothing." Ethan sounded frustrated, grim.

Joanna came up beside him as he pushed to his feet. "But you're sure the helicopter landed here?"

Though the storm and wind had beaten down much of the strawlike grass and wildflowers just beginning to bud out on the high meadow across the Silverton River, even Joanna could now see that something heavy had crushed the vegetation here. An exploration along the lee side of the river in the sunlight had turned up nothing new on Agent Parrish's disappearance—no shred of clothing, no shoe prints, no body. But after their allotted hour of futile searching, Ethan and Joanna had reluctantly started their trek back to the command post where they hoped that by some miracle, Ben and the rest of the KCCU had somehow found each other.

It was a miracle that Ethan, with his keen eye and that sixth sense that was tied to the land, had noticed the differences in the flattened plants at the far edge of the meadow. But the discovery of anything useful stopped there.

"*A* helicopter landed." He tossed aside a stalk of

scrub grass he'd been inspecting. "If there was any trace of blood left behind, it's been washed away. There's no way of knowing if Ben made it this far and got picked up by a rescue team or a good Samaritan, or even if the chopper we saw is the same one that set down here."

He walked to the edge of the grass, where wind and water erosion had worn away the soil and root system that held it in place, shearing it down to bare rock. Ethan jumped down to the gravelly incline below the cut and reached up for Joanna's hand. He held on firmly, giving her the balance she needed to make the same five-foot jump and land gracefully on her feet.

But just as soon as she nodded her thanks, he released her and headed for the first hairpin turn that would take them back and forth at a modest rate of descent into the forested gully about thirteen hundred feet below. The plan was to find Elk Thunder Creek at the bottom and follow it on out to the trail head where the KCCU had set up their temporary camp.

So that was how it was going to be this morning, hmm? Back to the taciturn Indian who refused to say a lot because he didn't want to waste words. And he said that *she* was two people.

She missed the Ethan she'd walked with and talked with last night. He'd reminded her of a time when she'd been open to new experiences, hopeful that there was something better for her out there in the world—if she could learn enough, and be tenacious enough to go after it.

She missed the Ethan who'd been so patient with her last night. The man who'd kissed her so thoroughly, had loved her so well. In the quiet seclusion of that cave, they'd formed a bond that felt deeper, richer, more precious than the love they'd shared before the rape. Last night, Ethan had listened to her fears, adjusted to her needs—he'd made her feel like a whole, normal woman again instead of the unemotional shell who normally walked through every day of her life.

But somewhere between giving him her trust and the dawn of a new day, their fragile new bond had been buried inside that cave, altered the way yesterday's rock slide had changed the shape of Ute Mountain. For them, there could only be the present. The reality of their missing partner's uncertain future, and the omnipresent shadow of her tragic past, demanded their attention this morning.

He wanted to protect her. She needed to be independent.

He talked about lost souls and relentless demons, of letting them go before they consumed her. She wanted to hunt hers down and look him in the eye.

He was a man of the earth. She was the restless wind.

He belonged in Kenner County. Her career was in Washington, D.C.

How could they ever make the magic of their time on the mountain the reality of their everyday lives?

Today, there were no easy conversations, not even arguments, no lessons to be taught. There was just walking and silence—and an uncertain wish that somehow her world and his could meet and meld and survive for more than one night.

ELK THUNDER CREEK was much narrower and more shallow than the Silverton River. But with snowmelt and the heavy rains feeding it, the water tumbling below Joanna's feet was just as noisy.

"It's no use." She shut off her cell phone to save the

battery, and tucked it back into her pack. She raised her voice to tear Ethan's focus from the small pines that blanketed the short, steep drop to the creek. "We're still too far out to get reception."

He nodded, indicating he'd heard. "We'll try again after another mile."

When he didn't face her, or give any indication of climbing back up to the path where she stood, Joanna grabbed on to one small tree after another to join him at the creek bed. "What is it? Do you see something?"

Though relationship discussions were apparently taboo this morning, he hadn't hesitated to share information about a danger in their path or any possible clue that might lead them to Ben Parrish or Sherman Watts. He hunched down to bring his shoulders level with hers, and pointed to a stand of young trees across the creek. "Look at those pine saplings. The trunks have all been broken near the roots."

"Could it be from flooding?" she suggested, eyeing the line where mud met drier soil just beyond her feet. "Looks like the water level is already going down. If this was moving even half as fast as the Silverton, it'd mow down pretty much anything that size or smaller."

"I don't think that's it. Look." With one long stride, he stepped across the creek and pointed to the watermark about halfway up one trunk. "Here's where the creek crested. They were standing tall when that happened."

Joanna needed to take a short run at it, but she, too, crossed the creek to investigate more closely. She touched one of the thigh-high boulders at the edge of the water. "It looks as though something made a nest here. With the rocks to provide a windbreak, bending the trees over creates a small shelter."

Ethan was down on one knee, sifting through a spongy bed of wet leaves and pine needles. "*Things* that build nests don't use wires to hold them together." He pulled a strand of copper wire from the stacked-up leaves.

Bracing her hand on his knee, Joanna knelt beside him and began to imagine the size and shape of a grown man curled up beneath the canopy of saplings. A surge of adrenaline kicked up the beat of her pulse. "Do you think Ben spent the night here?" She was already scanning the slopes on both sides of the creek, looking for footprints in or out of the deep V of the landscape besides their own. "Why wouldn't he come back to us if he survived that fall and the river? Could a disoriented man make it this far?"

"Easy, Sherlock." Ethan caught her chin between the gentle pinch of his fingers and directed her gaze to the evidence at hand. The skin cells beneath his touch instantly leaped to attention. *She* came to attention when his hand settled over hers at his knee, as if he was reaching out to her one more time, holding on to something he knew he was about to lose.

What did he know that she didn't? "What is it?"

His expression hardened.

"You have to look at all the information." He twirled the wire in front of her eyes. She looked closer. Finally recognized it. Understood.

Sherman Watts.

Her awareness of Ethan's shifting mood turned into a very different kind of awareness. "Watts was here last night."

He nodded, made no effort to reclaim her hand as she stood and surveyed more carefully each way in or out of the gully. He zipped the wire into a vest pocket and pushed to his feet. "This matches the filament we found at the blast site. Something is making Watts head back toward civilization instead of sticking to the high country."

"The helicopter?"

"Who knows? But he's moving south, southwest— on about the same course we are. And…"

"And?"

An internal debate darkened Ethan's eyes and lined his expression. Her breathing quickened, deepened with anticipation before he finally made his decision to speak. "The leaves at the bottom of that shelter still hold a little warmth. He's not that far ahead of us."

Ethan's reluctance to share that bit of news was probably in direct proportion to her eagerness to act on it.

They had one more chance to catch Sherman Watts. She had one more chance to bring in her rapist and face him across an interview table—today. Now. She had one more chance to break him in every legal way possible. The key to solving Julie Grainger's murder could be lurking in this very stretch of woodland.

"We have to go after him." Joanna circled the rocks, looking for one of those hidden signs that Ethan rarely missed. "Can you tell what side of the creek he's on now? Is he on the path? Cutting through the trees?"

"Give me a minute."

She came back to him, tugged at his sleeve. "I understand the need to get word to the others about Ben. But if something happened to him, and Watts gets away…Ben's sacrifice will have been for nothing." She pleaded with him to understand. "Sherman Watts can't get away from us again, Ethan. I need to face him."

"Don't worry, you'll get the chance to do your job. I promised I'd find him for you, and I will. But the bastard's armed and more than a little bit desperate if he had to change his escape route. We need to be cautious."

Joanna pulled away as soon as he touched her, tried to protect her from the challenge that was hers to face. "I need to do this before I get it in my head that I can't."

"He'll be drunk or detoxing, either of which makes his behavior unpredictable. The man already blew up half a mountainside trying to throw us off his trail—I don't think we can be too careful about dealing with him." He checked his watch and scanned the horizon. "We could make it to base camp in another two hours, an hour and a half if we book it. We'll return with backup, surround him."

She didn't have two hours, not even an hour and a half before she'd lose the mental advantage they had right now over Watts.

Joanna knelt down and picked up a stick to poke it through the bottom of the man-made nest, looking for a clue that would point an arrow toward the man they were after. Maybe some of the wet leaves would stick to his boots and leave a trail. She dropped the stick and began to search the surrounding ground, looking for remnants of leaves that matched the bedding in size and shape and color. These were too light a green. Those too long and narrow. "How long do you think he's been gone?" She looked up when he didn't immediately answer. "Ethan, how long?"

He knew. She could see it in the hard glint of his onyx

eyes. That damn mystical sixth sense of his knew which way Sherman Watts had gone. He knew where to find him. "Probably a matter of minutes."

She rolled back on her heels and stood. She wrapped her hand around a small tree to help pull herself up the steep incline. "Then we can catch him. Don't tell me to wait for backup when we're this close. I've already waited fifteen years."

"Joanna—"

"Look." A muddy boot print. A dark green leaf like the ones in the shelter. She followed them up the hill. "Tracks. Right here. Right through here." Topping the gully, she found another print, embedded with the same leaves, and a flatter path. "They go up right beside that broken sapling. Come on."

"Joanna—wait!"

She was vaguely aware of Ethan charging up the slope behind her. She turned, stepped.

Snap.

She felt the telltale give of tension beneath her foot. The milliseconds of each reaction passed by like watching a movie one still frame at a time.

Not a broken tree.

Ethan shouting her name.

Copper trip wire beneath her foot.

A sleek brown missile hurtling toward her.

With another blink, real time returned and she couldn't move fast enough. Joanna jumped, braced for the certain impact of the pine tree whipping toward her. But in a blur of motion, Ethan slammed his arms around her and spun, taking the brunt of the collision.

Like a spring-loaded catapult, the tree hit hard

enough to lift them off their feet and launch them into the gully. *Oof.* "Hell."

They hit the ground hard and rolled, toppling end over end until the cold splash of water at the bottom stopped them.

Joanna lay on her stomach for a moment—stunned, dizzy, feeling damn lucky she hadn't broken her neck. The creek water streamed over her dangling hand, its biting chill rousing her as effectively as a dose of smelling salts. She pulled her hand from the water and rose onto her bruised knees. "Ethan?"

She'd been snug in his arms. Safe, as always. But now she was alone. Where was he? That sapling must have hit him like the front grill of a speeding car. She staggered to her feet. Turned. "Ethan!"

Wading ankle-deep into the creek, Joanna grabbed his big, still form as he floated into the current, and tugged him to the bank. With a groan of effort, she dug in her heels and fisted her hands in his clothes, dragging him several feet up the slope before laying him down and falling to her knees beside him.

How badly was he hurt?

Why wasn't he moving?

Why the hell was she crying now, when she needed to see what she was doing?

"Ethan?" She checked his pulse and thankfully found a strong one beating beneath the cold skin of his neck. After a quick, loving caress to the sculpt of his cheek, she checked his head, his neck. Cuts. Scrapes. Bumps. Nothing as serious as she'd expected. "Come on, big guy. I need you to talk to me. I need you."

She unzipped his vest and laid her ear to his chest,

listening to make sure he was breathing. All at once, his lungs expanded with a deep, agonizing groan and he tried to sit up. "Ah, hell."

"Ethan!" Joanna eased him back to the ground. She pressed a quick kiss to his lips and squeezed his hand, studying his hooded eyes all the while to make sure their focus was clear. "Don't move. Relax. For a minute there, I thought I'd lost you."

The hand she held down at his side tightened around hers with the subtly reassuring grip she recognized. "Now you know how I felt when you left me," he whispered, letting his eyes close again.

"So this is some cosmic lesson you're trying to teach me? I don't like it. Nobody's dying on me today. Get it?"

A tight smile flickered between the white lines of pain bracketing his mouth. "I'm sorry, baby. I'm not dying." He breathed in, groaned. "It just hurts like the blazes."

She smoothed her hand across his cheek again, brushing away the chilly moisture from the creek. "Did you hit your head? Where does it hurt?"

"Just had the wind knocked out of me."

"I'm sorry. This is the second time you've saved my life. I should have looked more carefully, but I was so anxious to get Watts. I didn't mean for you to get hurt. Ever."

"Shh." He raised his hand to brush the tears off her cheek. "Don't you cry for me, *Nüa-rü.* I'm a tough old army ranger. I've survived worse." Though that taut muscle in his jaw pulsed, his breathing seemed to be evening out. "Are you injured?"

"Nothing to worry about. Just lie still."

"I always worry."

"I know." Finally moving far enough past the fear to

think like an FBI agent and not a woman who'd nearly lost her man, Joanna swiped away any lingering tears and shrugged out of her backpack to find a first aid kit. "Does it feel like anything's broken?"

"I'll be fine."

A blot of crimson seeping through his clothes at the left side of his waist drew her attention. "Don't tell me you're fine. You're bleeding."

As she unzipped his gear vest and pulled it open, Ethan leaned onto an elbow and tried to push himself upright. "Watts could still be in the area. Forget me and—"

"I am not forgetting you. I could never forget you. Now lie still until I check every inch of you." She stepped over his legs and knelt to check the wound. "You must have a pretty deep laceration. Wait. I said to lie down."

Ethan groaned a mighty curse as he fought off her attempt to ease him back to the ground. "If he rigged up one tree, then there'll be other traps out here. Who knows what other sick tricks he's prepared for us? We can't stay here in the open."

"Fine." She peeled aside his vest. "Then let me get you wrapped up enough so you can move." When she caught sight of raw flesh, Joanna's own muscles clenched at the pain he must be feeling. "Oh, my God."

The sapling Sherman Watts had tied to the ground had whipped Ethan as effectively as a cat-o'-nine-tails. The force of the blow had cut right through his clothing and left bleeding red welts along his left flank.

"I need to borrow this." With her hand at his belt, she untied his hunting knife and pulled it from its leather sheath. She unpacked gauze and sterile salve from the first-aid kit and set to work slicing his shirts and vest open and cleaning the wounds.

Any disorientation he'd felt earlier had cleared. His grip was firm as he pulled her hands from their work, and his mood was turning grumpier by the minute. "I said we can't stay here. Watts is close. I sense it. I know it."

"We're not going anywhere until I'm sure you can be moved. If one of those ribs is broken, it could puncture a lung." She twisted her hand free and gently probed his side. A wince and a curse were enough to confirm her suspicions. "They could just be bruised or cracked, but I'm definitely wrapping these."

"Fine. But not here." He bent his knees, trying to get his legs under him. "Help me up. Take me back to camp. You're right. I need medical attention. We can't stay here."

"Damn it, Ethan. I wear a badge and gun. I can take care of myself. I've been taking care of myself my whole life. I can damn well take care of you, too."

The discussion ended abruptly at the tiniest of sounds from the woods above them.

A single step.

Moments later, a handful of pebbles cascaded down the steep slope and rolled beneath the surface of the water.

Joanna's hands stilled over the gauze she'd taped to Ethan's wounds. He'd heard it, too.

Everything inside her tensed. Waited. Listened.

"No." He tried to grab her wrist, but she moved more quickly than the stiffness of his injuries allowed. She crawled a few feet up the slope, pinpointing the direction of the sound. "Joanna," Ethan growled through gritted teeth.

"Stay put."

Stretching out onto her belly to keep her profile as low as possible, Joanna pulled her gun and shimmied up to the top of the slope to see what kind of company they had.

But she already knew.

Creeping through the underbrush like the cockroach he was, she saw him. Thin black hair, hanging in long oily tendrils across his shoulders. Dark, squinty eyes.

Sherman Watts.

"Don't you—" This time, Ethan couldn't stop her. He rolled onto his hands and knees, tried to stand. "Joanna, no! Not on your own!"

The hunt on Ute Mountain had all come down to this. She sprang from her position and gave chase.

Her blood simmered, speeding the pace of her heart. Her chest expanded, giving her the oxygen she needed to race across the flats. Her vision was razor sharp, taking in roots, dips, rocks and other obstacles in her path while she closed the distance between them. A hundred yards. Sixty. Forty.

Had he actually come out of hiding to see what kind of damage he'd done to them? To gloat? To finish the job? Had he seen the long black hair and realized just who it was pursuing him?

You can do this, girl. Look who has the power now, you SOB.

He scurried away from the creek, over the next slope and down the other side, his wide-brimmed black hat quickly disappearing beyond her line of sight.

Joanna slowed her pace and quieted her footsteps, listening to the sounds of a pudgy fifty-eight-year-old knocking his way through the trees and brushes. Sliding.

Falling. Cursing. She used that moment to top the hill without being seen.

And plummeted down the same washout that Watts had stumbled upon. Joanna slid a good twenty feet through the mud and gravel on her bottom before her feet hit solid ground and stuck. Ah, but fifteen years of intense physical training versus a lifetime of drinking too much and avoiding honest work paid off in spades. She was closing in before Watts could even get on his feet again.

"Sherman Watts! I'm a federal agent. Stop where you are!" She paused long enough to point her gun into the sky and fire off a warning shot. Birds screeched and cawed and took flight from the trees. Her lungs burned, but she dug down a little deeper and shouted a fair warning. "Come peacefully and it will go easier for you!"

His response was to turn with his gun drawn and fire wide of her position.

Joanna dove for cover. "Don't make me shoot you!"

She didn't want him dead. She wanted him to answer for all he had done.

But he was zigzagging away through the trees, huffing back up the incline. Joanna breathed in deeply, in through her nose, out through her mouth. She pushed herself to her feet and ran after him.

Twenty yards. Ten.

Close enough to hear the ragged rales of his breathing. Close enough to see the sweat staining the back of his denim jacket. "Drop your weapon and get on the ground!"

"Get away from me, bitch!" he rasped, and turned, raised his gun.

Joanna never broke stride, never hesitated. She barreled into his gut full force and knocked him flat on his ass.

His gun went flying. They rolled over her bruised wrist and she yelped at the pain, losing her grip on her own weapon.

Armed, unarmed—didn't matter. She was a different woman than the last time they'd exchanged violent blows. She wasn't going to lose this fight.

When his fist came at her, she locked her arm and deflected the blow. She rammed her fist against his throat. He slapped wildly at her, gurgled with the pain she caused him. When he spotted a gun and lunged for it, she caught his knees with her feet and knocked him to the ground, quickly stretching, diving to retrieve the weapon herself.

But one thing about the disgusting cockroaches of the world—they had an innate knack for survival.

As Joanna's fingertips touched the grip of her Glock, she heard the ominous ratchet and click of a bullet sliding into the firing chamber of a gun. Joanna froze.

"Get your hand…away…from that gun, you bitch." As halting and gaspy as the threat was, she believed it.

For one awful moment, her stomach heaved, her body clenched with an instinctive fear. But in the next breath, she found an inner calm—from her FBI training or her lessons with Ethan, she didn't know. He'd once held a knife to her throat. Today it was a gun to the back of her head. She wasn't going to be his victim anymore.

"Put the gun down," she suggested calmly. "Threatening a federal agent is not a good idea."

"I don't care what you think. I ain't goin' nowhere with anybody. I'm disappearing into the world. Understand? I've got nothing to say to you."

"Well, I've got a thing or two to say to you."

Rolling onto her back despite his huff of protest, Joanna looked up into the blotchy red face of her rapist. Other than a few more pounds and a nose that was purple and swollen from years of alcohol abuse, her squinty-eyed nightmare looked pretty much the same as she remembered. "I'm arresting you on suspicion of—"

"Naomi?" His face spasmed with shock. The gun wavered.

Joanna pushed up onto her elbows. "I'm Agent Joanna Rhodes of the FBI."

"Shut up! You're dead." He raised the gun, steadied it enough to aim at her chest. "Or you will be."

Watts's body jerked and Joanna's entire body jolted in response. Her fingers dug into the mud beside her as she instinctively clutched her chest.

"Get away from her, you son of a bitch."

The threat, as fierce and low and wonderful as any sound she'd ever heard, flowed through her like the spirit of the mountain rising from the ground itself. There was no bullet hole, no pain. She hadn't been shot.

Watts, on the other hand, began to tremble. His fingers popped open and his gun fell to the ground. Joanna wisely scrambled after it and picked it up before he collapsed to his knees. He turned to the voice behind him and she saw a long, wicked-edged hunting knife protruding from the back of his shoulder.

"You stabbed me," he whined, dropping to his knees.

Joanna looked up at the warriorlike intensity of Ethan's eyes. He stood tall, erect—but tattered and pale—clutching his left arm to his side, with blood already seeping through the bandages she'd wrapped around his ribs.

How could she not love him?

"Does it hurt?" Ethan's nostrils flared with every deep, painful breath.

"Hell yes."

"Good." Ethan pulled the knife from Watts's shoulder, ignoring his yelp of pain. He wiped the blade on his pant leg and wandered off a few feet, where he lowered himself to the ground and endured his own pain in noble silence. "Don't worry. You're not going to die from that wound. It's not any worse than what you did to me."

Watts tried to reach the wound over his shoulder, and cursed at the blood that stained his fingertips. "What the hell kind of cop are you?"

"He's not a cop." Joanna was on her feet. "But I am." She picked up his gun and stuck it in the waist of her filthy, muddy jeans. She holstered her own weapon and pulled out the handcuffs attached to her belt. Kicking his feet apart to put him flat on the ground, Joanna knelt beside Watts and pulled his wrists behind his back, ignoring his plea to spare him pain. "Sherman Watts, you're under arrest for assaulting a federal officer—maybe two or three of us—grand theft auto, resisting arrest, accessory to murder—"

"What?"

"And whatever else I can think of once I catch my breath." She quickly read him his rights. "Do you understand?"

"Yeah."

"Good. Now lie there and shut up until I'm ready to talk to you."

"And you?" She went to Ethan, gently checked for further injuries, then clasped her palm around the back of his neck and kissed him very, very thoroughly. By the time she pulled away, he'd returned the favor. His hand lingered at the back of her neck, massaging her nape as she ripped off the placket of his flannel shirt and used it to secure one of the gauze bandages over his ribs back into place. "You're really wreaking havoc on my quest for independence, you know that? That's the third time you've saved my life."

"I said I wasn't going to let you face that bastard alone." He gingerly inhaled a deep breath and leaned in to rest his forehead against hers. "Get used to it."

THE KCCU BASE CAMP was a hive of activity. Calls were being made. Machinery was being dismantled and packed away. Sherman Watts was handcuffed in one ambulance, getting stitched up by a paramedic and treated for dehydration. While two other medics tended to his injuries, Ethan sat at the back of a different ambulance, debriefing Sheriff Martinez, Tom Ryan and Dylan Acevedo on the status of their friend and fellow agent, Ben Parrish.

An extra helicopter was being called in. Search teams were being formed. Dr. Callie MacBride-Ryan and Miguel Acevedo from the crime lab had their heads bent over the shell casings and copper wire Joanna and Ethan had brought back from the crime scenes on the mountain.

Joanna sat in the middle of the chaos, wrapped in a blanket and sipping a cup of hot, bitter coffee. Up on the mountain, she and Ethan had worked—and loved—like partners who understood and complemented each other the way the earth and the wind, the fire and water created a balance of all that was needed to survive. But here, she was an element out of sync with the world around her.

Yes, she'd given her preliminary report to Martinez. She'd personally thanked Bart Flemming for rigging up whatever kind of super cell he had that finally enabled her to call for a chopper to evac her, her patient and her prisoner safely and quickly down to the command center. And she'd already given herself three separate pep talks to keep her calm and focused and ready to interrogate Watts as soon as the medics cleared him and he was transported back to the station house.

Her gaze slid over to Ethan across the parking lot. Even in the middle of a tense, animated conversation, he sensed her and looked over Agent Acevedo's head to meet her gaze. *I love you,* she whispered on a thought. If there was any way she could find a place in his world where she was so out of sync, if he could break his ties with the land and become a part of hers...

His dark eyes narrowed, questioned, as the medics lifted his gurney into the back of the ambulance. Joanna blinked and looked away, hating the pitiful signals she must sending. The man was going to the hospital for X-rays and a deep debriefing of his wounds. He didn't need to worry about her when he should be taking care of himself.

"Agent Rhodes?"

Joanna pulled herself from her thoughts and turned to meet Elizabeth Reddawn's polite smile. The older woman had brought her the coffee earlier. Now she was opening a plastic container of wrapped sandwiches. "I imagine you haven't had much solid food the past couple of days and it's almost dinnertime. These are from the Morning Ray Café. Personally, I like the pimento cheese on sourdough. But you can't go wrong with a turkey and swiss on rye, either."

Though she had no appetite, Joanna knew she'd need every bit of her strength to face Watts. She picked the first sandwich sitting on top. "Thank you."

"Ham and cheese kind of girl, eh? Enjoy." Elizabeth snapped the lid back into place and moved on, heading for the communications table where Bart was, once again, underneath the table connecting or disconnecting some cord.

Connect. Disconnect.

A lightbulb went off inside her head. It couldn't really be that easy, could it? Just plug herself in somewhere? Make herself a place where she belonged? When had she ever *not* had to fight for anything she wanted in this world?

Joanna threw off her blanket and hurried after the sandwich lady. "Elizabeth?" The petite Indian woman stopped and turned, smiling expectantly as she approached. *You can do this, Joanna. You can do it.* "I know I wasn't as friendly as I should have been when I first arrived, and I wanted to apologize for my rudeness."

Elizabeth tutted, waving aside the apology. "You weren't rude, honey."

"I was."

"I expect certain memories make it hard for you to be here."

Joanna nodded. She wasn't used to doing this, but over the past two days, she'd proven to herself that she was strong enough to do anything. "I need to ask you a favor."

"Sure."

"I have to go to the sheriff's office to write my report and—" she thumbed over her shoulder toward the ambulance where Watts was being treated "—and take care of some business. Would you ride with Ethan to the hospital? Make sure he lets the doctors take a look at him and, and…"

Elizabeth took her hand and winked as she leaned in to whisper. "And call you to let you know how he's doing? Of course I will. I care about Ethan, too."

"Thank you." Elizabeth smiled and turned to finish her deliveries and get her things, but on impulse, Joanna kept hold of her hand and pulled her attention back to her. Elizabeth turned with a question on her face.

Joanna squeezed the older woman's hand and declared herself a friend. "And you call me Joanna."

That earned her an even bigger smile. Elizabeth patted her hand and promised, "I'll call you as soon as I know anything. Joanna."

Joanna nodded, feeling something warm and hopeful—and maybe just as strong as her rigid independence.

She'd made her first connection.

Chapter Eleven

Joanna rose from her chair, adjusting the hem of her suit jacket and buttoning it as she strolled around the interview room's gray metal table.

"Being drunk isn't a defense." Her voice was articulate, clear, unemotional save for the scoffing note of pity she had in reply for Sherman Watts's last statement regarding his motive for his crimes. "They don't serve whiskey in prison, you know."

"That's a shame. I'd have gone long ago."

The creep thought she'd find his lowlife sense of humor amusing? She'd already gotten him to sign a statement about his activities on Ute Mountain. Threatening her with a gun, planting explosives, rigging the tree that had cracked three of Ethan's ribs and earned him twenty stitches. Though he adamantly claimed he'd never shot at any human being in his life, she had him dead to rights on enough charges to keep him in prison for a very long time.

Yes, he'd stolen a truck. Yes, he'd *borrowed* the explosives he'd found in the back of it. Yes, he'd set several traps on the mountain, including a couple he proudly announced she and Ethan hadn't been smart enough to find—she'd already alerted the forensic team that Ethan's friend Garan Coons was leading up the mountain tomorrow to be on the lookout for the hidden dangers.

But he claimed to have done all that because he was guarding the exact whereabouts of his favorite fishing hole and had wanted to ensure himself a little privacy.

The one thing she hadn't gotten him to talk about was Boyd Perkins, and his association with the hit man and Julie Grainger's murder.

Logic hadn't worked. Nice talk certainly hadn't.

But the man's fingers were drumming almost uncontrollably against the side of the table where he was handcuffed. He was detoxing, probably feeling a nasty headache and some stomach gripes. The knife wound on his shoulder hadn't injured anything vital, and would probably leave an attractive scar to make him look a little tougher to his comrades behind bars. But without allowing him anything more than a couple of aspirins to dull the pain, he was probably aching pretty good right about now. His efforts to remain cavalier and play stupid to those questions were beginning to cost him.

Time to push him a little further over that nervous edge.

She knew she had an audience taking down every word on the other side of that two-way mirror and on the camera recording Bart Flemming was making in the observation room. But this show she was gearing up for was for Sherman Watts alone. *Do it, Joanna. No matter what he says, no matter how he reacts, get in his face and do it.*

You are stronger than this bastard ever imagined.

Joanna turned, coming in right beside him, brushing

her arm against his as she braced her hands on the table. "Here's what's going to happen to you, Sherm. You're going down for Agent Grainger's murder. With DNA from that leather necklace of yours, we can put you at the site where her body was found. That's not a life sentence, that's a death penalty."

"I didn't kill no FBI agent."

"Yeah?" She leaned in, getting right in his face. "She was a woman, wasn't she? Women are nothing to you. They're trash you use up and throw away, just like those bottles you suck dry every day of your life. If she got in your way, if she didn't do what you wanted, you'd take care of her. You'd put her in her place. You like beating up on women, don't you, Sherm?"

"That woman wasn't beaten!"

Joanna straightened. Walked around to her side of the table and softened her voice to a more reasonable timbre. "Now, how do you know that?"

His head shot up. His dark eyes glared. He dropped his gaze when she didn't so much as blink. "Okay. I was there. I helped throw her body into the river, but she was already dead, I swear."

"Who hired you to dispose of the body? Who's been paying you ten thousand dollars a month for the past six months?" She smacked the tabletop, startling him when he didn't immediately answer. "Who hired you?"

Bam. She'd hit the trigger.

His chair toppled backward and crashed to the floor as he rose to face off against her. "Look, bitch—I don't owe you anything. There are scarier people in the world to be afraid of than you, with your mouth and your gun and your hair—thinking you're all that.

Thinking you can use me to get what you want. That ain't right!"

Joanna dodged to the side as he shoved the heavy metal table at her, and sent it screeching into the wall behind her. She put her hand in the air, waving off the cadre of agents and deputies no doubt running to that door to rescue her right now. She kept her eyes on Watts's sad, sour, superior expression as he dragged the table behind him, advancing on her. "You think you've got something on me. You think you're smarter. I can handle you."

When he lunged at her, she twisted his arm behind him and put him down, face-first, on the table. "Yeah. You did that real well. Who *can't* you handle, Sherm? Who are you afraid of if you're not afraid of me?"

Trapped in the ignominious position, shaking as the rage and whiskey and fear worked through his system, Sherman Watts suddenly seemed like a scraggly, pathetic little man—not the nightmare who had turned her teenage world upside down.

She had the advantage. She didn't even have to talk tough anymore. "Now we're going to walk back here and have a seat. You and I are going to have a nice little chat." Once he'd pulled the table back into place and righted his chair, Joanna sat back down across from him. She asked the fifty-million-dollar question. "Did Boyd Perkins kill Agent Grainger? Is he the man who hired you to help cover up the crime? To help him hide out on the reservation so he could continue looking for a crime family's missing money?"

"He'll kill me if he knows I talked to you. I think he tried to kill me already when I was up on Ute Mountain. Can you give me some kind of protection?"

"I'll see what I can do."

At last, he nodded. "Then I want a lawyer. I'll tell you what I know."

"All right. Let me get someone to take your statement." Feeling less victorious over an enemy than she felt the satisfaction of knowing she'd done her job well, Joanna got up and headed for the door.

"Agent Rhodes?"

She turned.

"I know something else. If I tell you, you'll make that death penalty thing go away, right?"

"It depends on what you tell me."

"I don't have a name but…Perkins and me, well… he's got a man on the inside. Somebody who works with you. He's got our numbers and he…well, he called me and told me you all were lookin' for me. I know he calls Boyd Perkins, too."

Sheriff Martinez's suspected leak. So there was a traitor in their midst. Joanna slid her gaze to the window, knowing each of them was hearing this, too. But Watts was more interested in how the information was going to affect him.

"So, even without a name, you're gonna take murder one off the table, aren't you?"

"That's for the courts to decide. But if you're lucky, you'll get out of prison for one last drink before you die of old age."

"What kind of crack is that?" For one fleeting moment, his eyes narrowed, and she thought she detected a glimmer of recognition—not that she was Naomi Kuchu's daughter, but something else, something much, much more personal. But if any recollection of the day he'd violently used her body to repay an emotional and monetary debt had passed through his mind, he must have dismissed it as some kind of drunken hallucination. "You speak to me with respect, girl. This is a legal situation. You don't want me suing you for harassment. You owe me that much."

Joanna would never be able to simply dismiss the crime, but now she could move past it. She could heal. She could put Sherman Watts behind her. Forever.

She opened the door. "Mr. Watts, I don't *owe* you a damn thing."

WHEN JOANNA CLOSED that interview room door behind her and walked into the beginning of a brand-new life, the first thing she walked into was the solid wall of Ethan Bia's chest.

Literally. She instantly pulled back from his deep-pitched groan, taking in the green hospital shirt and the thick ridges of bandages wrapping his chest underneath. His skin color was good, coppery and warm, his eyes glinted like finely polished onyx.

And while Joanna stood there in an openmouthed stupor in the KCCU hallway, he wedged a finger beneath her chin to close her mouth before leaning down to press the lightest of kisses to her lips.

"You okay?" he asked.

"Ethan." She clutched her fingers into fists, then uncurled them. She wanted to touch him. But she might hurt him, and what was he doing here, anyway? "You're supposed to be in the hospital. Elizabeth told me they were keeping you overnight."

He caught her fingers in one big hand and stilled

their nervous flexing. "Were you not just in that room alone with Sherman Watts?"

"You know I was."

"Did I not promise that I would never let you face that man alone again?"

"You did."

"Don't you trust me to keep my word to you?"

One heartbeat passed. And then another. And then Joanna was stretching up on her toes and winding her arms around his neck. "I do."

She supposed this PDA wasn't the most professional behavior Martinez could list in his recommendation letter to her supervisor in D.C. She was marginally aware of people passing back and forth in the hallway, discreetly looking away or covering up a laugh as Ethan held her lightly against his chest and she willingly, eagerly—not wanting to aggravate his injuries, of course—kissed him back.

It was when the hallway had quieted and she was simply leaning close, her head tucked beneath Ethan's chin, that a different conversation did catch her attention. The tones were hushed, urgent and probably meant to be private.

"I can't shake it, Miguel," a young woman said, trying to hide the fear in her voice. "It was definitely Boyd Perkins I saw in my vision. I sense his presence close by, creeping around in the shadows where we can't see him—and he's looking for something. Do you believe me?"

Miguel Acevedo's voice she recognized. Though the tender tone was a new twist from his usual sarcastic humor. "Well, after what I just heard from Sherman

Watts, I'm not going to say I disbelieve. Come on, I think we ought to talk to Sheriff Martinez about it."

"I know you're a skeptic, but I felt this one particularly strongly. Thank you for listening."

"I'll always listen, sweetheart. Always." When they rounded the corner, Joanna pulled away, concerned by the distress she'd heard in the woman's voice. Miguel had his arm around the brunette's shoulders, pressing a kiss to her temple, when he realized they had company in the hallway. The woman with him seemed a little shy, but judging by the way she clung to Miguel's waist, it was very clear that they were a couple. "Hey, big guy," Miguel greeted them. "You're looking a little worse for wear, there. Ethan, you remember my wife, Emma."

"Of course." He smiled as he kissed Emma's cheek. "I heard you two eloped to Vegas. Congratulations."

"Thanks." He turned to his new wife and completed the introductions. "Emma, this is Agent Joanna Rhodes. She's the newest member of our team. She played Watts like a Steinway in the interview room."

The *team* appellation felt good. It felt like she might have earned a little respect, and maybe a friend or two more here in Kenner County.

"Pleased to meet you, Agent Rhodes." Emma Acevedo smiled warmly and extended her hand.

"It's Joanna Kuchu, actually." Yeah. It felt right, shaking Emma's hand and saying those words. "Kuchu is my Ute name. It means 'buffalo.'"

It meant a lot more to Ethan.

At least, once he pulled her into the empty interview room and stopped kissing her long enough, he seemed impressed that she had used her given name.

Joanna stood between his legs as he sat on the table, looking at her with those mysterious eyes and lightly brushing that wayward strand of hair off her face. "Has Joanna Kuchu really come home?"

She reached up to stroke her finger over the proud contours of his cheek and jaw. "I want to stay. I've been doing a little research."

She felt the muscle bunch along his jaw, heard him breathe in deeply to force himself to relax. "When did you have time for that?"

"On the ride into town from Sleeping Ute Mountain. Bart let me use his laptop."

"Sounds like you work too much." His second deep breath echoed her own. "So tell me about this research. What does it have to do with staying in Kenner City?"

All right. She'd thought this through. She knew the details. She had a plan. "I found out there's no trained profiler or interrogation specialist in the Durango FBI office. I could be the first one in the area—consult with the crime unit here in Kenner City and serve the entire Four Corners area. Maybe one day I could select and train my own team."

"Sounds ambitious. But then you always did dream big." His hand settled at the nape of her neck, the skin-to-skin contact warming her straight down to her toes. "I'd like to point out that Durango is a hell of a lot closer to Kenner City and the reservation than Washington, D.C. But it's a lot smaller, too. You might see a lot less action in this part of the country."

Joanna smiled—nothing fake, nothing forced. It was a genuine, unburdened smile. "I don't care about that. Seems like I've seen plenty of action here these past few days." She tiptoed her fingers around his neck and tried to look as deep into his soul as he'd found his way into hers. "I never considered dreaming dreams about this place. I always thought a better life for me was out there somewhere. The only dream I ever had about the reservation was making a life with you."

"Joanna," he growled on a dark husk of emotion.

She pressed her fingers to his lips to silence him. "No. Let me say this. That was the dream I had before everything changed—the rape, Sheriff Watts, feeling so suffocated by the shame and rage and helplessness I felt in this place. Now I understand the healing powers of coming home. That is the most important lesson you've ever taught me, Ethan."

He moved his hands down to her hips and pulled her close enough to rest his forehead against hers. "Tell me more about that dream about a life with me."

"I want to make things work for us if it's not too late." She looked straight up into his beautiful eyes. "I love you, Ethan. Maybe I forgot how to for a little while. But I feel it inside me, burning stronger than ever. I know what that kind of love means now—how much I need to treasure it." She took a deep breath and then laid her heart in his hands. "I know I have some issues…but maybe if we work on them together… Do you think you could have that kind of patience with me?"

The perpetual spring rain might have started falling once again outside. But when Ethan smiled down at her, she felt sunshine. She felt hope.

"Hell, woman. I waited fifteen years for you. I think I know how to be patient."

He palmed her bottom and pulled her up against his

chest, holding her tight, kissing her and kissing her and kissing her, groaning with a mix of pain and delight. When they finally found the courage to ease some space between them, knowing that the connection between them would never be broken again, Joanna smiled against his mouth. "All right. I just spilled my guts. It's your turn to say something now."

Ever a man to choose his words carefully, Ethan had only three for her now. "I love you."

Joanna was finally where she was supposed to be. With Ethan.

Epilogue

"Over here!" Ethan shouted over the rumble of thunder and unceasing drumbeat of rain. "I found a shoe print. Too big to be the kid's, though."

He dropped his flashlight beside him and gritted his teeth against the aching stiffness in his rib cage so that he could pull off his KCCU jacket and lay it over the vanishing evidence.

The Griffin Vaughn estate was a huge expanse of house and land and hidden tunnels underneath, where crime boss Vincent Del Gardo had once lived and died. And now someone had used those same tunnels to get inside the millionaire's high-tech mansion and kidnap his three-year-old son, Luke.

Ethan hadn't even gotten Joanna back to her hotel room or asked her out on a proper date when the call had come in. All available agents, deputies, CSIs and support staff had been called in to search the grounds for any trace of the boy and what might have happened to him. While Sheriff Martinez interviewed Vaughn and his new wife, Sophie, a forensic team was dusting the interior for any prints or other trace evidence. Meanwhile, Ethan was leading a team over the grounds before this damn storm washed away anything helpful out here.

"Miguel!" he shouted again. He'd found a print outside one of the tunnel entrances that reminded him of the fancy-soled hiking boot they'd found at Sherman Watts's trailer just three nights ago. But the rain and runoff from the tunnel's domed entrance was quickly washing it away. He needed to get up, make his voice heard over the storm. "Miguel! You coming?"

Before Ethan could push to his feet, Joanna was there, grabbing his flashlight and bracing herself against his uninjured side to help him stand. Miguel ran up seconds later. He lifted Ethan's jacket and shook his head. "Would've, should've, could've. That print is too far gone to make a comparison."

Lightning flashed in the sky, illuminating the worry on their faces. Joanna voiced what they were all feeling. "How's a three-year-old boy ever going to survive a night like this?"

After a crackle of static, an announcement came over all three of their radios at the same time. It was Callie MacBride-Ryan, one of the forensic specialists working inside the house. "It's a match. The fingerprint I found on the basement stair rail belongs to Boyd Perkins. He took the boy. I repeat. It's Boyd Perkins. He's back in town. He took the boy."

Miguel swore. "I hate it when Emma's visions are right. The damn thing is, they're always right. I'd better get in the house to see if I can help out."

Once Ethan and Joanna were alone again, she shook off the water from his jacket and draped it over his shoulders. "Now will you let me take you to the hospital?"

"It doesn't fit Perkins's profile to want to hurt the boy. Odds are, he's using him for leverage—to get money, or information. Still…" He didn't need to feel her fingers tucking and smoothing his wet clothes into place to know how worried she was—about him, about little Luke Vaughn—about changing her plans for the future to include him, to include *them.*

Ethan tucked his finger beneath her chin and let her see the conviction he felt. "He's Kenner County stock, *Nüa-rü.* That means he's strong. You survived when you had to. The boy will survive, too."

Ethan felt Joanna's fingers lacing with his down at his side. They squeezed each other's hands, sharing their strength, sharing their unique connection to the Four Corners area and to each other.

Together, Ethan and Joanna, Martinez, the crime lab, Agents Ryan and Acevedo and all their support staff formed a formidable team.

The bad guys didn't stand a chance.

* * * * *

Mills & Boon® Intrigue
brings you a sneak preview of …

Cassie Miles's Bodyguard Under the Mistletoe

Young widow Fiona only had one thing on her
Christmas list: keeping her daughter safe. So when a
body was discovered on her property, Fiona jumped
at bodyguard Jesse's offer to stay for the holidays.
He had a stoic face, but honest, caring eyes. And no
matter how she ached to feel his toned and chiseled
arms around her, she needed the protection that
only a man like Jesse could provide.

Don't miss this thrilling new story available
next month from Mills & Boon® Intrigue.

He wasn't dead yet.

The darkness behind his eyelids thinned. Sensation prickled the hairs on his arm. Inside his head, he heard the beat of his heart—as loud and steady as the Ghost Dance drum. That sacred rhythm called him back to life.

His ears picked up other sounds. The *beep-beep-beep* of a monitor. The shuffle of quiet footsteps. The creaking of a chair. A cough. Someone else was in the room with him.

The drumming accelerated.

His eyelids opened—just a slit. Sunlight through the window blinds reflected off the white sheet that covered his prone body. Hospital equipment surrounded the bed. Oxygen. An IV drip on a metal pole. A heart monitor that beeped. Faster. Faster. Faster.

"Jesse?" A deep voice called to him. "Jesse, are you awake?"

Jesse Longbridge tried to move, tried to respond. Pain radiated from his left shoulder. He remembered being shot, falling from his saddle to the cold earth and lying there, helpless. He remembered a gush of blood. He remembered…

"Come on, Jesse. Open your eyes."

He recognized the voice of Bill Wentworth. A friend. A coworker. *Good old Wentworth.* He'd been a paramedic in Iraq, but that wasn't the main reason Jesse had hired him. This lean, mean former marine—like Jesse himself— always got the job done.

They had a mission, he and Wentworth. No time to waste. They needed to get into the field, needed to protect...

Jesse bolted upright on the bed and gripped Wentworth's arm. "Is she safe?"

"You're awake." Wentworth grinned without showing his teeth. "It's about time."

One of the monitor wires detached, and the beeping became a high-pitched whine. "Is Nicole safe?"

"She's all right. Arrests have been made."

Wentworth was one of Jesse's best employees—a credit to Longbridge Security, an outstanding bodyguard. But he wasn't much of a liar.

The pain in his shoulder spiked again, threatening to drag Jesse back into peaceful unconsciousness. He licked his lips. His mouth was parched. He needed water. More than that, he needed the truth. He knew that Nicole had been kidnapped. He'd seen it happen. He'd been shot trying to protect her.

He tightened his grip on Wentworth's arm. "Has Nicole Carlisle been safely returned to her husband?"

"No."

Dylan Carlisle had hired Longbridge Security to protect his family and to keep his cattle ranch safe. If his wife was missing, they'd failed. Jesse had failed.

He released Wentworth. Using his right hand, he detached the nasal cannula that had been feeding oxygen to his lungs. Rubbing the bridge of his nose, he felt the bump where it had been broken a long time ago in a school-yard fight. He hadn't given up then. Wouldn't give up now. "I'm out of here."

Two nurses rushed into the room. While one of them turned off the screeching monitor, the other shoved Wentworth aside and stood by the bed. "You're wide-awake. That's wonderful."

"Ready to leave," Jesse said.

"Oh, I don't think so. You've been pretty much unconscious for three days and—"

"What's the date?"

"It's Tuesday morning. December ninth," she said.

Nicole had been kidnapped on the prior Friday, near dusk. "Was I in a coma?"

"After surgery, your brain activity stabilized. You've been consistently responsive to external stimuli."

"I'll say," Wentworth muttered. "When a lab tech tried to draw blood, you woke up long enough to grab him by the throat and shove him down on his butt."

"I didn't hurt him, did I?"

"He's fine," the nurse said, "but you're not his favorite patient."

He didn't belong in a hospital. Three days was long enough for recuperation. "I want my clothes."

The nurse scowled. "I know you're in pain."

Nothing he couldn't handle. "Are you going to take these needles out of my arms or should I pull them myself?"

She glanced toward Wentworth. "Is he always this difficult?"

"Always."

FIONA GRANT PLACED a polished, rectangular oak box on her kitchen table and lifted the lid. Inside, nestled in red velvet, was a pearl-handled, antique Colt .45 revolver.

In her husband's will, he'd left this heirloom to Jesse Longbridge, and Fiona didn't begrudge his legacy. She'd tried to arrange a meeting with Jesse to present this gift, but their schedules had gotten in the way. After her husband's death, she hadn't been efficient in handling the myriad details, and she hoped Jesse would understand. She was eternally grateful to the bodyguard who had saved her husband's life. Because of Jesse's quick actions, she'd gained a few more precious years with her darling Wyatt before he died from a heart attack at age forty-eight.

People always said she was too young to be a widow. Not even thirty when Wyatt died. Now thirty-two. Too young? As if there was an acceptable age for widowhood? As if her daughter—now four years old—would have been better off losing her dad when she was ten? Or fifteen? Or twenty?

Age made no difference. Fiona hadn't been bothered by the age disparity between Wyatt and herself when they married. All she knew was that she had loved her husband with all her heart. And so she was thankful to Jesse Longbridge. She fully intended to hand over the gun to him when he got out of the hospital. In the meantime, she didn't think he'd mind if she used it.

Her fingertips tentatively touched the cold metal barrel and recoiled. She didn't like guns, but owning one was prudent—almost mandatory for ranchers in western Colorado. Not that Fiona considered herself a rancher. Her hundred-acre property was tiny compared to the neighboring Carlisle empire that had over two thousand head of Black Angus. She had no livestock, even though her daughter, Abby, kept telling her that she really, really, really wanted a pony.

Fiona frowned at the gun. *Who am I kidding? I'm not someone who can handle a Colt .45.* She turned, paced and paused. Stared through the window above the sink. The view of distant snow-covered peaks, pine forests and the faded yellow grasses of winter pastures failed to calm her jangled nerves.

For the past three days, a terrible kidnapping drama had been playing out at the Carlisle Ranch. Their usually pastoral valley had been invaded by posses, FBI agents, search helicopters and bloodhounds that sniffed their way right up to her front doorstep.

Last night, people were taken into custody. The danger should have been over. But just after two o'clock last night, Fiona had heard voices outside her house. She hadn't been able to tell how close they were and hadn't seen the men. But they were loud and angry, then suddenly silent.

The quiet that followed their argument had frightened her more than the shouts. What if they came to her door? Could she stop them if they tried to break in? The sheriff was twenty miles away. If she'd called the Carlisle Ranch, someone would come running. But would they arrive in time?

The truth had dawned with awful clarity. She and Abby had no one to protect them. Their safety was her responsibility.

Hence, the gun.

Returning to the kitchen table, she stared at it. She never expected to be alone, never expected to be living in this rustic log house on a full-time basis. This was a vacation home—a place where she and Abby and Wyatt spent time in the summer so her husband could unwind from his high-stress job as Denver's district attorney.

Water under the bridge. She was here now. This was her home, and she needed to be able to defend it.

INTRIGUE...

2-IN-1 ANTHOLOGY

SHE'S POSITIVE
by Delores Fossen

FBI agent Colin and his ex, Danielle, put their differences aside to rescue a young hostage. But they can't ignore the chemistry that's still burning between them.

UNEXPECTED CLUE
by Elle James

Wanted for a murder he didn't commit and being chased by dangerous criminals, Ben needs to clear his name if he wants to protect his pregnant wife, Ava...

•••

2-IN-1 ANTHOLOGY

CAPTIVE OF THE DESERT KING
by Donna Young

Jarek was unimpressed when journalist Sarah arrived at his castle. But during a terrifying chase across the desert he realised she was a temptation he couldn't resist.

THE UNEXPECTED HERO
by Rachel Lee

Troubled Kristin is horrified when a killer begins to strike at her hospital. Worse: she's a suspect! Can gorgeous David clear her name and heal her heart?

On sale from 15th October 2010
Don't miss out!

Available at WHSmith, Tesco, ASDA, Eason
and all good bookshops

1010/46a

www.millsandboon.co.uk

INTRIGUE...

2-IN-1 ANTHOLOGY

BODYGUARD UNDER THE MISTLETOE
by Cassie Miles

When Jesse became worried for Fiona's safety following a dramatic kidnapping, he moved in with her. Yet as he searches for the culprits, he starts to fall in love…

CAVANAUGH JUDGEMENT
by Marie Ferrarella

Judge Blake doesn't need a bodyguard after being threatened, especially not a young, attractive woman! But he can't deny Greer's bravery or the chemistry between them.

•••

SINGLE TITLE

BIG SKY DYNASTY
by BJ Daniels

Dalton thought his past was dead and forgotten. But it's back and threatening Georgia, the woman he's falling in love with. Can he save her from his past mistakes?

On sale from 5th November 2010
Don't miss out!

2 FREE BOOKS
AND A SURPRISE GIFT

We would like to take this opportunity to thank you for reading this Mills & Boon® book by offering you the chance to take TWO more specially selected books from the Intrigue series absolutely FREE! We're also making this offer to introduce you to the benefits of the Mills & Boon® Book Club™—

- **FREE home delivery**
- **FREE gifts and competitions**
- **FREE monthly Newsletter**
- **Exclusive Mills & Boon Book Club offers**
- **Books available before they're in the shops**

Accepting these FREE books and gift places you under no obligation to buy, you may cancel at any time, even after receiving your free books. Simply complete your details below and return the entire page to the address below. You don't even need a stamp!

YES Please send me 2 free Intrigue books and a surprise gift. I understand that unless you hear from me, I will receive 5 superb new stories every month, including two 2-in-1 books priced at £5.30 each and a single book priced at £3.30, postage and packing free. I am under no obligation to purchase any books and may cancel my subscription at any time. The free books and gift will be mine to keep in any case.

Ms/Mrs/Miss/Mr _____ Initials _____

Surname _____

Address _____

_____ Postcode _____

E-mail _____

Send this whole page to: Mills & Boon Book Club, Free Book Offer, FREEPOST NAT 10298, Richmond, TW9 1BR